MICHAEL DOBBS

THE LORDS' DAY

Also by Michael Dobbs and published by Headline

Churchill's Triumph
First Lady

Other novels by Michael Dobbs

Winston Churchill Series
Winston's War
Never Surrender
Churchill's Hour

Tom Goodfellowe series
Goodfellowe MP
The Buddha of Brewer Street
Whispers of Betrayal

Francis Urquhart series
House of Cards
To Play The King
The Final Cut

Other Titles
Wall Games
Last Man to Die
The Touch of Innocents

MICHAEL DOBBS

THE LORDS' DAY

headline

First published in 2007
by HEADLINE PUBLISHING GROUP

1

Cataloguing in Publication Data is available from the British Library

ISBN 978 0 7553 2686 0 (Hardback)
ISBN 978 0 7553 2687 7 (Trade paperback)

Typeset in Hoefler by Avon DataSet Ltd,
Bidford on Avon, Warwickshire

Printed and bound in Great Britain by
Clays Ltd, St Ives plc

Headline's policy is to use papers that are natural, renewable and
recyclable products and made from wood grown in sustainable forests.
The logging and manufacturing processes are expected to conform
to the environmental regulations of the country of origin.

HEADLINE PUBLISHING GROUP
An Hachette Livre UK Company
338 Euston Road
London NW1 3BH

www.headline.co.uk
www.hodderheadline.com

To Rob.
A charming godson and an inspiring young man.

It was generally accepted as being unthinkable, a proposition to which no one dared give a name.

Until the day it happened.

Prelude

HE KNEW HE HAD BEEN wounded, but he felt no pain. He had answered a knock on his door and when he had opened it, unsuspecting, two men had forced their way in.

He had put up a stern fight. He had once been a top-class athlete, even though confined to a wheelchair, and he had warded off their first blows. His attackers were small in stature, youthful, wiry, and he had been able to hurl one of them back into the other, causing them to stumble while he retreated down the hallway. But after that there was no place to hide. You can't hide, not on wheels.

Perhaps they had come to rob him, but he wasn't worth much, that should have been obvious, living in a dump like this. There were his cups and medals, yet what were they worth? They weren't real gold or silver, only sentimental value, like the photograph of him shaking hands with the Princess Royal just a couple of years earlier. There was nothing in here for them; they had made a mistake and, as soon as they realised this, they would go.

Yet they had pursued him – not run, but followed him inexorably, silently, not in anger but with unflinching intent, into his living room.

'Why, why?' he had screamed when they had produced the knife, 'we are of the same skin.' He could tell that their fathers, at very least their grandfathers, must be some sort of cousins to his own, children of the same region with sun and dry dust in their boots; perhaps this was simply a case of mistaken identity, but they wouldn't listen. And they wouldn't talk. They stalked him, held him. Then they cut him.

He hadn't been able to speak after that, something in his throat wasn't working properly. And they didn't ransack the place but stood watching, their dark eyes troubled, almost sorrowful. Everything was so very strange, he thought. Nothing was making much sense any more.

It was only when he looked down and saw his chest covered in rich, fresh blood, his blood, that he realised his throat had been cut and that he was dying. Like a sheep, slaughtered at festival in the old country, as his father had described to him in a childhood tale. He had always wondered if they felt pain as they bled. Now he knew.

One

Before dawn. The 5th of November.

THE LORDS' DAY. It was to be a day of atonement, a day of anguish, of terrors that would squeeze the country so tight it came close to expiring, but Harry Jones had no way of foreseeing that. For the moment he was having difficulty seeing anything. He struggled to focus, only gradually becoming aware that the object he was staring at, from very close quarters, was a nipple. Hell, what an evening.

As a pale, reluctant light seeped through the window and started to unwrap itself in front of his eyes, Harry began taking stock of the damage. The bedroom was a mess, clothes strewn haphazardly in a trail that led like a paperchase across the floor and away beyond the partially opened door, while the duvet was knotted uncompromisingly round his lower limbs, binding him tight. He was sweating; too much alcohol, a bottle of twenty-year-old Islay full of peat and feathers that now lay abandoned somewhere on the other side of the door, near where he'd left his self-respect.

Beside him, Melanie stirred in her sleep, turning away from him and curling herself up like a hibernating mouse. Harry cursed once again and stretched, as far as the bonds of the duvet would allow, but she didn't stir, still out of it. Oh, what a night it had been, one to look back on in years to come with a touch of awe. It wasn't every evening

3

your estranged wife invited you out to dinner then ended up ripping your clothes from you.

He looked round the bedroom – *his* bedroom, as had been, until three months ago – and began to spot little changes, the marks of where his presence was gradually being erased. The photograph of him in the jungle of Belize that had once adorned the dresser was gone, and his dressing gown with its frayed cord and gentle memories was no longer on the back of the chair. The table on his side of the bed that he couldn't remember without its tottering pile of books was now uncomfortably bare, and he searched with growing alarm for his copies of Robert Louis Stevenson. They were the original Cassell's editions, 1880s. Gone. Damn, he hadn't taken them; did she realise what she was throwing out? Of course not, any more than she'd done when she threw him out. Not that she had referred to it like that. A trial separation, she had suggested, to get her mind clear. Well, whatever was cluttering up Melanie's mind, it certainly wasn't good literature. Yet in spite of it all she had invited him, allowed him back. What did it mean? A knot of curiosity began to grow inside him, competing for elbowroom alongside the part of his brain that was trying to tunnel its way to freedom through the thicker part of his skull. Had she changed her mind? Back into her bed, and back into her life? He couldn't tell, had always been rubbish at reading her, and now she was stirring, her eyelids fluttering innocently.

As she saw him, a look of bewilderment crossed her face. It took several moments to fade. 'Oh, shit,' she sighed. Then she threw back the duvet and made for the bathroom.

Didn't sound much like someone who wanted him back, yet he knew she wasn't good on her own, she needed a man around. So . . . so who? Had someone else been in his bed, between his sheets and with his wife? It was supposed to be a trial separation, no one else involved, but he began to wonder if she might have been finding it rather less of a trial than he had. No wonder the photo was missing.

Beads of suspicion began to prickle on his forehead and his eyes wandered round the room looking for clues, tell-tale signs of someone who didn't belong there. But Melanie wouldn't be that stupid. He lay back on his pillow, realising with surprise that what he was feeling was jealousy. He wanted her back, very much. He hadn't realised that, not until this moment. So much anger and frustration had spilled over between them, but there were still feelings. Last night had daubed his grey life with colour once again and he was surprised how much he missed it all. And her. The laugh, the lilting irreverence, that body. They'd been married more than three years yet still it was like getting laid for the first time, never knowing quite what to expect. Full of surprises was Melanie, that was part of her appeal and he missed it much more than he had realised. But what was she missing?

From the bathroom came the sound of water splashing as she washed the traces of him away. Curious, and jealous, Harry disentangled himself from his winding sheet and began rummaging through the drawers of the bedside table, but he found nothing, not on his side. No one had yet laid claim to his space, not even Melanie, it seemed, and suddenly he was filled with remorse that he could have suspected her. They'd both agreed that their separation was intended to be a means of refreshing their relationship, to remind themselves all over again how much the other meant – Melanie had emphasised that point to him. So as he ransacked the drawers he chastised himself for his suspicions, but that didn't stop him, even when he discovered the drawers on her side of the bed were overflowing with little more than tissues and trinkets and . . .

A one-page leaflet. A flyer, an ordinary handout. He didn't know it just yet, but it was to be a moment when Harry's life changed. In the trembling of a single breath his suspicion was smothered by pride, a sense of fulfilment that for an instant grew to unbridled joy before he realised he was being a fool. And it wasn't often that anyone made a fool of Harry Jones. In another breath he had slipped into the darkness of a very rare anger, the sort of rage that on the last occasion had been put aside only when he'd killed a man, for as he searched through Melanie's drawer he found himself clutching a pamphlet from the Marie Stopes clinic. The people who dealt with sexual health. Unwanted pregnancy. Abortion. It was also the moment he heard his wife throwing up in the bathroom.

The house was small, part of a run-down terrace in the middle of Southall, and typical of so many rented properties in western London, ill-painted, unremarkable, shrouded in anonymity. The curtains were tightly drawn to ward off prying eyes, and the windows were closed, too, shutting out the noise. In the back of the house, the bedrooms were stifling.

'Are you awake, Mukhtar?'

'How can a man sleep?'

'It's time, anyway.'

For a moment they grew quiet as their eyes adjusted to the first light and they contemplated what lay ahead of them.

'It's so airless and hot in this place,' Mukhtar complained. 'It's like lying on the doorstep of Hell. How I miss our home.'

'Remember, it is for our homeland that we came here.'

Mukhtar sighed, a sound of deep sadness. 'I would like to have seen it – one last time.'

'Don't weaken, don't you dare weaken. Not today!' Masood's voice grew sharp, betraying his own inner tension. 'Remember what they have done to us. Remember, Mukhtar, that day when you held your mother's broken body.'

'I shall have her name on my lips when I die.'

'And hate her killers more with every breath.' Masood stirred. 'It is time to wake the others.'

'They will not need it,' Mukhtar replied, and from elsewhere within the small house they could hear the sounds of movement.

'Remember our pledge, Mukhtar, to go on to the end. To fight them not only in the caves and mountains of our home, but to fight them in their own land, with ever greater courage, no matter what the cost may be. To make war on them, father and son, just as they have done to us, and never give in.'

'You make fine speeches.'

'The words are not mine. I borrowed them, or words like them, from one of their own leaders. It is time for them to feel their own pain.'

'May it rain on them like the winter snows, but –' Mukhtar hesitated.

'I'm listening, my friend.'

'It is what we did last night, to those men.'

'Does it trouble you?'

'A little.'

'That is good, Mukhtar. To care, to have compassion, is good. It sets us apart from our enemies.'

'But, Masood, there is something else you should know.'

'What is that?'

'I think I am scared. Very scared.'

She came through the bathroom door, still naked, dabbing at her mouth. 'What the bloody hell's this?' Harry demanded, the voice low but filled with menace as he waved the pamphlet.

'You've got a nerve, Harry, going through my drawers.'

'They're my drawers, remember. I paid for them.'

'Yes, you did. And now they are my drawers,' she replied primly, 'so keep the hell out of them.' She snatched at the piece of paper but he was too quick for her.

'What are you hiding, Mel?'

'Nothing!'

He began quoting from the leaflet. '*Marie Stopes. The country's leading reproductive healthcare charity. The first choice for those seeking expert help and advice*. Help and advice in what, Mel? Well, I don't see you offering yourself for sterilisation and you scarcely qualify for a vasectomy. So what is it?'

'Harry, I've got to say you look ridiculous, sitting there shaking with indignation when you're stark naked. Even a man with your physique can't quite get away with it.' Her voice was light, teasing, attempting humour, and also avoiding his question.

'You're pregnant,' he whispered.

She didn't answer immediately but reached for her robe, wrapping it carefully around her before sitting down on the end of the bed, keeping her distance. 'It's why I invited you last night. One of the things I wanted to tell you.'

'That you're pregnant. And going to have an abortion.'

He made it sound like the summing up of a prosecuting lawyer and she blushed, while Harry's world began to spin slowly out of control, taking him back to a different place. He remembered the last time he'd been told his wife was pregnant – not Melanie, but Julia, his first wife. It had been so clinical, in a side room of a Swiss hospital, just below the mountain where that early spring morning they'd gone skiing off-piste. His choice, his passion, one in which Julia had tried to follow him, as she had always done. Except they hadn't made it. Too much fresh, unstable snow. And then he was lying with a drip in his arm and a broken leg and porridge for brains, trying to shake off the effects of a bad concussion as a doctor with a dark brow and exquisitely starched white coat broke the news to him. That Julia had been a couple of months pregnant and in all probability hadn't even known it.

'You did not know, either? I am so sorry, Herr Jones, we did all we could,' the doctor had said in his over-precise manner. 'If it is of any consolation, it is my view that your wife would not have suffered in any way.'

'Suffered?'

'It was instantaneous, you see.'

'What was instantaneous?'

A look of despair had crossed the doctor's brow. 'No one has told you?' Or had the delayed effects of the concussion wiped it all from his mind? 'The fall, Herr Jones. It broke her neck. And, of course, the baby . . . My profound regrets.'

Beautiful, loving, two-months pregnant Julia. After which Harry's life had never been quite the same, never reached its old heights. It couldn't, not when he was drenched in so much guilt and with the accusations of Julia's distraught father ringing in his ears. Yes, it had been his fault, and after fifteen years carving out a career in the British Army, Sandhurst, Life Guards, Pathfinders, MoD, the lot, he was used to taking his share of the responsibility, but not like this. Something had switched off inside Harry, and not all the years his country had invested in teaching him to be one of its most effective killing machines had been able to keep him from suffering more hurt than he ever thought was possible. Until Melanie came along. 'Time to put Humpty back together again,' she'd said, covering everything with laughter. She was what he had needed, never took anything too seriously, except her body, of course, and that was worth taking very seriously indeed. Got him back on his feet until he was able to walk again. Yet Harry was never content simply to walk; he was the type of man who always wanted to do things his way, and at a pace that left most in his wake. It wasn't that Melanie couldn't keep up; what had begun to hurt was the realisation that she never truly tried. He'd been blinded by pain, too eager to find something and someone to hold on to once more, and it was another thing he'd got wrong. She didn't want to follow; while Harry rushed off in search of dragons, she was content to sit elegantly beside the large pot of gold that had been left to Harry through his inheritance. Different routes, different destinations, and now different lives.

'I'm sorry, Harry,' he heard her saying. Just like the Swiss doctor. Everybody was always fucking sorry. So why didn't it make a difference?

'You were going to talk about it with me, weren't you? And we are going to discuss it, aren't we?' His tone was untrusting, full of accusation. She hated it when he grew angry. There was, perhaps, something in her that feared Harry, even when he was naked, when his body reminded her of what Harry in his anger could do. The scars, the bullet wound in his back.

'Harry, there's something else I wanted to talk to you about.'

'What could be more important than our baby?'

'Harry, I want a divorce.'

The spare, balding man looked out from his high window and stared down the Mall. From the street below he would have seemed a small, insignificant figure in such a grand building, and at times like this he felt it. His eyes wandered past the ceremonial flags hanging limply from their gibbets towards the outline of the palace that was beginning to emerge in the grey, oily light. He stood for a considerable time, motionless, the only sign of his inner turmoil being the relentless twisting of the crested cufflink on his left wrist. He would be on duty today, just as he had been, and would continue to be, every day of his life.

He turned from the window. A mahogany clotheshorse stood next to the dressing table. From it hung the uniform of the Welsh Guards. He'd first been fitted for that uniform more than thirty years before, yet it had remained unaltered, like so much else in his life. Duty, obligation, the sense of being owned by others, hadn't faded with the years, unlike the hairline and his patience – particularly his patience. Later that morning he would climb into the uniform and once again do his duty, even though he wasn't Welsh and had guarded nothing more than his reputation these past years, and that often poorly. He was commanded to attend upon the State Opening of Parliament, an annual ritual stuffed to the studded collar with symbolism yet without the slightest trace of any substance. Just like his wretched life. He had been ordered to take part – ordered, him, a man of sixty! Yet in spite of all his years he was in no position to refuse. So he would damn them and do what was required of him, as he so often did, with reluctance.

No, not reluctance. Stupid word! He didn't feel reluctance, instead he felt a burning, blinding resentment. How dare they? It would be kinder to send the bloody clotheshorse, yet kindness didn't come into it; there wasn't even a sub-clause in the constitution for compassion. With a low curse he started tugging once more at his cufflink.

He'd wriggled out of the occasion for years, but this year was different. His father was ill, too wobbly even to climb into his boots, so in his place they demanded the son. England expects! They commanded his presence, yet they were unwilling to pay even the simple price he asked. And what could be simpler, more dignified, more appropriate, more just, than to permit him to walk with his wife? A woman who had done none ill, a lady who gave none harm, who had brought only joy and gentleness to his life. Yet they wouldn't let her be. She'd been the reason for the divorce so they treated her like an outcast. They deemed his wife's appearance . . . inappropriate.

Inappropriate. That was the word they'd used, those cowards and courtiers, as they shuffled round the issue like three-legged spaniels. It was no explanation at all. So she had taken herself out of London to avoid causing him any embarrassment while he was left on his own to—

Bugger! The cufflink, tired with its mistreatment, shot from its post and disappeared somewhere in a dark corner. He cried out, first for assistance and then in an outpouring of unremitting despair. He was the grandest man in the land, yet also the most powerless and pathetic. From the other side of the window the outlines of the palace seemed to be mocking; it was so close, yet in some respects so very far away from him. It was from near this point, several hundred years before, that they had taken one of his ancestors, walked him across the park dressed in a double layer of clothing to prevent him shivering, and when they had reached Whitehall they had chopped off his head. Right now, that seemed the very best part of the deal.

Charles Philip Arthur George, heir apparent to all he surveyed yet master of not even a humble cufflink, let forth a howl of frustration and sent a footstool crashing into a corner. It was going to be one of those lousy, screwed-up days.

Masood was their leader, although not the eldest of the men gathered at the table. Ghulam, the bomb maker, made up their simple breakfast of paratha flatbreads fried in butter, with which they ate the remnants of the lamb pulao that had gone unfinished the night before. Mukhtar sat quietly soaking his bread in the dark, bitter-sweet tea, and chewing thoughtfully. No one spoke much.

A portable television flickered mutely in the corner of the kitchen; the breakfast news showed scenes of preparation for the State Opening and warned of traffic disruption in Central London. All was as it should be.

When they had finished their food, they prayed, for the last time, in the formal manner. 'We shall not pray like this again,' Masood announced. 'It will only persuade them that we are what they call fundamentalists or fanatics. Then their hatred for us will burn all the more. No, we must show them that we are simple men, who wish nothing more than to show them justice.'

'Until they choke on it,' Jehanzeb, the eldest, added.

They were dressed in different clothing; some in suits, some in workmen's garb. Masood made one final inspection. Then it was time. They left the house without cleaning up after their breakfast. There was no point. None of them would be returning.

6.40 a.m.

It would be a long morning. This was, after all, the most significant state occasion of the year. The State Opening of Parliament is more than merely the beginning of a new parliamentary session, it is an occasion snatched from the furnace of British history. The ceremony is held in the House of Lords because the Monarch has been denied access to the House of Commons ever since her ancestor, the hapless – and soon to be headless – Charles kicked down its door while trying to arrest several of its members. Faced with the inhospitality and not infrequent hostility of the Commons, the Monarch retaliates by summoning a member of the Government to the palace and holding him hostage for the duration, just in case. Uneasy sits the crown.

There was also the lesson of Guy Fawkes, of course, when he and other Catholic conspirators stocked the cellars with gunpowder and attempted during the State Opening to blow up not only the King but also the entire government, lock, stock and explosive barrel, yet that was more than four hundred years ago. Affairs had settled on a gentler keel since then. Even the royal hostage is treated gently and to a glass of something suitably old.

As the skies above London yielded to the first rays of a sickly sun, the Household Cavalry was well into its preparations. Reveille had long since been sounded and the members of the Sovereign's Escort were mucking out the stables at Knightsbridge Barracks, surrounded by spit and polish and the pungent smell of horse piss. On the roads around Westminster, access routes were being blocked. Metal crowd barriers already lined the Mall and large concrete barriers were being hauled around in the jaws of forklift trucks to divert the traffic away from the processional route. Nothing would be allowed through, unless it was waving the right pass or arriving in a gilded coach.

Inside the ornate Gothic gingerbread Palace of Westminster, the members of the Works Department were making last-minute adjustments to the chamber of the House of Lords, where the red leather benches had been rearranged to permit the largest possible number of peers and guests to be seated. Behind the chamber, in the Robing Room that the Monarch would use as her private chambers, the Head Housemaid was making one last sweep while the Staff Commander himself gave the dainty toilet with its ancient blue-porcelain bowl one final discreet check. Flowers bloomed on all sides. Elsewhere, employees from the tailor Ede and Ravenscroft, the oldest tailoring firm in London, stood by to assist peers into their erminc robes, while seamstresses were at hand to help those in need. No stitch would be left unsewn, no corner left undusted or unsecured.

The ceremonial was as old as time itself, but all was not as it once had been. Standards were changing, and some would say slipping. What had once been a close-knit, almost family affair had been slowly squeezed dry in the vice of equal opportunities and Exchequer meanness. Posts were opened up to all comers, even part-timers. The magnificent doorkeepers who kept order throughout the place had once been drawn exclusively from the ranks of the military and conducted themselves as though still on parade, yet now they found their jobs offered to all and sundry, even women. Black Rod himself, the Lords' most senior official, was always a knight and, typically, at least a Lieutenant-General or Air Vice-Marshal, yet even his job was advertised in the pages of the *Evening Standard*. New times, new manners. Traditions came and went, and so did the cleaners, ever since the contract had been put out to tender. Lowest cost, and often lowest common denominator. Some cleaners had been busy inside the palace since five that morning, and many more arrived in the ensuing hours. Three of them came through the underpass that led from Westminster tube station. It wasn't an entrance open to the public, only those who were authorised, and they came forward, small bags in their hands, their photo IDs strung round their necks. As he stood before the revolving glass security door and passed his swipe card through the electronic reader, one of the men smiled faint-heartedly at the policeman on duty. The constable barely acknowledged the greeting.

'What's in the bag, sunshine?'

'Only lunch,' the man replied in a thick accent, as the other man also passed through. Although they had not been asked, the three competed in their eagerness to open their cheap hold-alls for inspection, revealing little more than sandwiches, a couple of chocolate bars and several cans of Coca-Cola each. 'We hold a little party with other cleaners. After Her Majesty has left. When our work is done,' the first explained.

'Coca-Cola, eh? The dear old Queen Mum'll be rolling in her grave just to hear of it.'

His little joke was met with the blankest of expressions; the policeman sighed and nodded them through. He nudged his colleague as they passed.

'And where d'you think those little teetotallers crawled in from, then?'

'Dunno,' the other replied. 'Could be Pakis. There again, might be African, Sudanese, Ethiopian. Bleedin' Iranian, for all I know.' He sighed, the deep, distracted sigh of an unreconstructed Englishman. 'So many asylum seekers clogging up the works these past years.'

'Yet you don't dare say it.'

'But it's true. They do,' the other man insisted.

'Can't argue the point.'

'Extraordinary, ain't it?'

'How they all look the ruddy same.'

'Makes you feel nostalgic for the Irish.'

Their attention was soon diverted by a parliamentary secretary who had struggled through the security door with an armful of papers, only to spill them on the pavement and reveal a quite unnecessary length of thigh as she bent to retrieve them. The dark skinned cleaners walked on. One, Mukhtar, had beads of sweat gathering below his hairline; he wiped his brow with his palm, Jehanzeb gripped his arm in reproof. Their eyes met, exchanging a private prayer. Mukhtar's fingers searched for the *tehwiz* at his neck, a small square of fabric into which was sewn a verse from the Quran. *Inshallah*. Already he felt better. It was remarkable how nervous a man could grow, even when he had volunteered to die.

7.30 a.m.

Robert Treat Paine, the US Ambassador to what is formally known as the Court of St James's, had also risen early that day; indeed, he had been awake since four and had barely slept. It had become something of an uncomfortable habit with the tall, angular Bostonian ever since his wife had died suddenly two years earlier from a brain haemorrhage. She might have been saved, had they not been miles from help on a walking holiday in the Lake District where mobile phones don't work and passing shepherds were nowadays as scarce as undiseased elms. 'She died in one of the most beautiful spots on earth,' he told her memorial service, 'and facing up to God.' Their only son, also named Robert T, hadn't attended; he had been away serving with the Marine Corps in Afghanistan. He was never to come home. A roadside bomb. And there were no saccharined words of comfort that could soothe that particular death. It hadn't been a good year for the ambassador.

Slowly he climbed from the bed that he now shared only with his red setter and stood at the window of his cavernous bedroom. Winfield House, the US ambassador's official residence, looked out over Regent's Park and the ambassador spent some time watching a young urban fox stalk the grounds looking for breakfast, scratching at roots, sniffing at the fungi that had sprouted beneath the birch trees. Strange, and sad, the ambassador thought, that this garden would probably be as close as the animal ever made it to real countryside. Everything in this turbulent world seemed to have been snatched from its proper place. His eyes, as so often, were drawn towards the photograph on his dresser. It showed his son in his Marine captain's uniform, a young man so full of confidence, brimming with ambition, yet . . . he was gone, another thing taken from its rightful place. And now the name of Robert Treat Paine would be no more. That noble line had come to its end, a story closed.

Oh, but what a magnificent story it had been! The first Robt.

Treat Paine had been one of the signatories of the Declaration of Independence, signing it with a bold flourish that would forever mark his name in history. Now he lay buried beside the likes of Sam Adams and Paul Revere in the Granary Burial Ground in Boston, a hallowed place, a spot reserved for American heroes. Old Robt. had left a clear trail and the ambassador had followed in his ancestor's footsteps, through Harvard and law school before embarking on a sparkling career that had left successive presidents in his debt. The Paine family had always played its part, but now the wheel of family life had turned full circle. The youngest and brightest of all the Robert T. Paines had gone off to war and got himself killed. The wheel had stopped.

For the father, there were few consolations. He buried himself in his work and was excellent at his job, everyone said that, including the President when she had called him after his son's death to tell him that the post was his as long as he wanted it. She understood the ties of blood, being the third member of her own family to have won the White House. And he should have been happy with this posting in a country that had given him his Old English roots, yet there was something missing in this New Britain. They knew what they used to be, but couldn't decide what they had become. They'd allowed their culture, and with it their self-confidence, to slip through their fingers, leaving them clutching at little but empty air. It was a modern sickness, and Paine had come to the conclusion that they would never find a cure. Sometimes, it seemed to him, he cared more for their customs than they did.

He reached for the phone and pressed the button. His steward answered it.

'Breakfast in half an hour, I think, O'Malley.' He stretched his vowels in the slow, New England manner.

'The usual, Ambassador Paine?' That would be easy. Fresh grapefruit, muesli and sweet black coffee. Paine did little more than peck when he had to eat on his own.

'No, this is a special day, O'Malley.'

'You mean Guy Fawkes and all the bonfires.'

'You really are a totally unrepentant Irish rebel, aren't you?'

'I hope so, sir.'

'I'm talking about the State Opening of Parliament. I'm going to rub shoulders with the Queen.'

'I'm sure you'll be having a wonderful time, sir,' the steward responded, his voice hoarse with irony and nicotine.

'It'll be a long day, O'Malley, and we'll need more than prune juice to get through it. I think we'll celebrate the occasion with something a little more substantial. The Full English.'

'The Full Irish, it'll be, sir.'

Paine replaced the phone. He tolerated O'Malley, was even amused by him. At least the fellow knew who he was.

Yet in a bedroom in a different part of town, matters were progressing less smoothly with another of the actors who would play a significant part in the events that were to mark this day. It was by no means such an expansive bedroom as that in Winfield House, but Tricia Willcocks had done pretty well for herself by any measure. It had taken three marriages and a fair bit of swallowing of male smugness during her earlier years in government circles, but she had ended up as Home Secretary. At times, even she had to pinch herself. Not bad for a woman who had been forced to struggle mightily through these meritocratic times to live down her expensive convent-based education. Girls from St Trinian's had long been out of fashion. Yet still it wasn't enough for Tricia. She'd built her career on an adroit mixture of tokenism and toe sucking, and it had left her with a disagreeable taste in her mouth. She knew men, knew their ample shortcomings, and also knew she was as able as most, yet, in spite of these qualities, she was forced to live off their finances and upon their favours. That made her irritable, while age had made her a little menopausal, and the combination was not always a happy one.

She had spent the last hour in bed going through the papers in her ministerial box. Normally she liked to finish off her boxes at night but she had been out late at an official dinner and her schedule had been kicked out of kilter. Now, reading by lamplight, she was getting a headache – oh, God, not one of those migraines, she prayed. And her husband was proving more than normally useless.

'Colin, what do you call this?' she demanded as she looked at the tray he had placed beside her on the bed.

'Breakfast,' he shouted back from the bathroom.

'You run a hugely successful commercial law practice, yet somehow can't even manage to boil an egg properly.'

'What's wrong with it?'

'It's raw.'

'Like your humour, my darling.'

'Colin, I've got a million things on today . . .'

'And, as you say, I've got a law practice to run,' he said, emerging from the bathroom fully groomed and suited. 'So I'm off. Put the dishwasher on before you go, will you? And have a wonderful day, dear.' He didn't even glance at her as he left.

She pushed aside the tray in exasperation and returned to the paper. It was a complex, closely argued brief about the legal implications of putting on trial Daud Gul. He was but one wretched man, yet he had managed to leave the combined legal minds of Whitehall twisting like wind chimes. It had been such a glorious coup when the British had hauled him out of his mountain hidey-hole along the Afghan-Pakistan border, like something out of an old black and white film with Cary Grant in the lead; half the American Army had been trying to find the bugger for ten years while a ten-man SAS team had done the job in little more than forty minutes. He was now settled, hopefully uncomfortably, in a cell on Diego Garcia. They'd snatched him because Daud Gul led one of the most notorious terrorist organisations in the region, responsible for untold numbers of outrages against Western interests in that part of the world. At least, that was his reputation. Yet as they had begun to build the detail of the case against him, large flakes kept falling off it. Sure, he hated the Americans and the British, the Russians too, come to that, any one of the many white-faced tribes that had set their imperious feet upon his land over the last two-hundred years, but that wasn't enough to convict him. Disliking Americans wasn't of itself a crime, not since George Bush had left the White House. There was certainly much wickedness for which Daud Gul was blamed, yet acts that had been done in his name were not, perhaps, done by him, or so the lawyers were arguing. Put him on trial for most of the outrages of which he'd been accused and they'd have trouble finding a single scrap of incriminating paper to prove his involvement, and he'd left no fingerprints on the bombs – 'it would be like charging Christ with responsibility for the Inquisition,' one of her senior civil servants had said. Idiot. They were all the same, those lawyers, like a wicker fence with a broken back, flopping first one way, then the other, as the wind blew. Willcocks knew what they had to do, they had to hang Daud Gul out to dry, but how? They couldn't simply lock him up and beat the crap out of him; Guantanamo had given those devices such a bad name, and handing him over to local warlords would be like throwing a side of beef to a pack of starving dogs. So there was no other option, they had to put him on trial, but how – and where? Those pathetic ridiculous lawyers had been shuffling back and forth about it for months.

Then she cried out. It *was* a migraine. Her legs had turned to ice, her head was beginning to feel as though it was being operated on without anaesthetic. And it was the State Opening, all those television lights and military barking. She knew she'd never get through it. She'd faint or do something foolish, get all flushed up and show some feminine weakness, and they'd never allow her to forget it. She couldn't let that happen. They'd barely miss her in the crowd, her private secretary could compose some suitable excuse. As the pain began to take hold of her, Tricia Willcocks made up her mind; she wouldn't go, couldn't go.

It was a decision that was to save her life.

7.50 a.m.

The three cleaners had made their way to their changing room in the basement. It was a dingy affair, containing mean, narrow lockers and grimy plastic chairs, far inferior to the other changing rooms that were reserved for the housemaids – the female cleaners who were responsible for the chamber of the House of Lords. Tradition decreed that the male cleaners were confined to the public places such as the stairways and toilets, economics decreed that they need not even be British.

Without a word the men moved to their lockers, opening them to reveal a dozen more cans of Coca-Cola. A vacuum cleaner was brought over and the top taken off; they bent over it, like witches around a cauldron, filling the inside of the cleaner with the cans, treating them with unusual respect, their eyes dashing nervously between each other. So intent were they on their task that they entirely failed to notice the young policeman who wandered in from his security beat.

'Hello, there, having trouble?'

The policeman was young, optimistic about life, even a little idealistic, with a wife and baby back home. He was one of those who had time for others, always keen to help, not that the cleaners had asked him for any.

'My Lord, what's this, then?' he muttered in puzzlement as he leaned over the cleaner.

He was still trying to do his duty, reach for his radio, struggling to cry out a warning, even after they had put a knife through his neck and blood was streaming from his throat.

Two

Harry – or Henry Marmaduke Maltravers-Jones, which was the name on his passport – was, as that passport implied, more than the man who initially met the eye, although that in itself was impressive enough. He was in his early forties but looked younger, and fitter; a lean frame with broad shoulders hidden beneath a traditional Jermyn Street suit and an easy, measured stride that suggested something very purposeful about him. The effect was underlined by the eyes, which were exceptionally bright and moved slowly, like an animal studying its prey from a distance.

Harry had money, too, handed down from a father whose own inheritance had been blown away by the misguidance and complacency of the grandfather. What hadn't been lost in the Great Depression had been siphoned off by death duties, so Harry's father had gone out and rebuilt the whole shooting match again from scratch, taking particular pleasure in doing unto others in the City what had been done to his own father. It had left him with an unreasoning fear of the gene pool, that his own father's weaknesses might be handed down to his son. From his earliest days, therefore, Harry had been pushed – through an English prep school, followed by an international elysee in Switzerland and interspersed with any number of exotic escapades in the company of his father's international business colleagues and occasional mistresses. Before the age of sixteen he had surfed at Malibu, sailed off Dubai, learned to scuba in Borneo and lost his virginity to a considerably older woman in Hong Kong – and owed it all to his father's arrangements. Yet it was entirely through his own efforts that he got a place at Cambridge. But the day Harry ripped open his acceptance letter, his father announced he was stopping his allowance; Harry would stand on his own feet, or not at all. Brutal. It was the father's own theory of natural selection. Lucky, then, that Harry had won himself a scholarship, and made up the rest by sneaking off to do double shifts at weekends at McDonald's. He had bumped into Julia one brilliant summer's day, on the riverbank, nearly sending her flying and catching her only in the nick of time. After that, she had rarely left his arms.

Harry always made waves, wherever he went. It was in the nature of the beast. But he never knew when to pick his battles. Perhaps this was the reason he had gone into the Army – that, and the fact that Julia was an Army brat. Yet he had a habit of making his superiors uncomfortable. He would fight his commanding officers with as much tenacity as he set about the Iraqi Republican Guard, so they kept moving him on, while his talent kept moving him up. Life Guards, the Airborne Brigade, and eventually the SAS where they turned Harry into one of the most effective killing machines anywhere in the Army. The consummate warrior. That was why they sent him behind the lines during the first Gulf War, into a conflict where radios didn't work, rifles didn't fire, resupply rendezvous were missed and patrols inevitably got lost. It came close to being a fiasco. Some men came out of the desert and wrote books about their experiences; Harry went straight to his CO and had another blazing row. After that, his days were numbered. He was farmed out to the Staff College at Camberley and eventually sentenced to a spell at the Ministry of Defence, but word had got round. Harry was his own man. In military language, that meant he was disloyal. Not one of us.

Shortly after, Harry's life had taken a decisive turn when his father died. His heart had stopped while he was riding a mistress forty years his junior. He'd been warned by his doctor that such distractions could lead to unwholesome consequences but, like Harry, he was his own man. 'Who the hell wants to die with his boots and breeches on?' he was alleged to have replied. And the father who had cast out Harry at eighteen without a penny left him the lot, a thoroughly immodest fortune that gave him an independence of action matching that of his mind. It made Harry totally unfit for further duty in the army, a conclusion shared by his superiors, so he quit and went into politics, became a Member of Parliament. At first Harry had flourished, made his mark, climbed through the ranks until he had made it all the way to the Home Office as Minister of State. He had become a man who in some observers' eyes was most likely to succeed, yet because of that, in the eyes of others he was a threat, and the combination of mind and money proved to be a highly combustible mixture in the underachieving world of Westminster. He was a man who insisted on seeing the big picture in a system that rarely looked further than tomorrow's headlines. Another brilliant career blighted by envy and the doubts of his superiors.

So Harry had returned to the backbenches – it was never clear whether he had jumped or been pushed – and instead of being driven in a ministerial car he now walked – or, as this morning, ran. He ran to pump adrenalin through his befuddled mind and to put as much distance as possible between him and his blazing row with Melanie. They had sat for the best part of two hours in his old kitchen in Mayfair, hurling accusations at each other. She had planned it all, he claimed – the separation, the divorce, next would come the settlement, everything calculated, like a shopping list. And she retorted that it was just that harsh, uncompromising view of the world that had forced her away from him. She said she was heartbroken, had struggled to make things work yet had met in return only indifference and emotional cruelty. Already she was practising for the lawyers.

Yet it was their discussion about the baby that had turned anger to outrage. Pregnancy was the one thing she hadn't planned, joining the club just as she was about to become an independent operator. So they had sat and flung clichés at each other, about a woman's right to choose, a father's right to be consulted, a child's right to life, her right to control her own body.

'So many fucking rights, Mel, where does it all end? You'd think no one ever did any wrong in this world.'

'Climb down from your pulpit, Harry. Save the moral righteousness for the press releases.'

'What has that poor unborn child done to deserve this?'

'We don't get what we deserve in life, aren't you always telling me that?'

'Mel, I want the baby.'

'What, you'll apply for visiting rights?'

'I'll fight you.'

'Don't threaten me, Harry. You want a fight – I'll give you one that'll crawl over every front page in the country. Can you stand that?'

Somewhere inside his head an alarm bell was ringing, warning him to back off. She wasn't the Republican Guard; he needed her. 'Please, Mel. Think about this. Even if you want the bloody divorce, let us have the baby.'

'I didn't think you believed in one-parent families,' she mocked.

'Don't, Mel. Please.'

'Too late, Harry.'

'It's never too late,' he whispered, meaning it, no matter how trite it sounded.

'Will be by Friday afternoon,' she spat back.

Friday. Two days. What was so special about Friday?

She realised she'd gone too far, and tried to dissemble. 'That's when you'll be getting the lawyer's papers.'

But he knew she was covering up. Friday afternoon. Marie Stopes. The day after tomorrow. That was when she was having the abortion.

'You want me to beg?'

'I'd love you to beg, Harry. It would be the first time I'd ever seen it, might even make me believe in miracles. But it won't do any good.'

'I'll never forgive you,' he said, and they both knew that was true. How could he forgive her, when he hadn't begun to forgive himself? And for the first time in his life, Harry had to run.

8.43 a.m.

Baroness Blessing arrived early at the entrance to the House of Lords, as was her habit for the State Opening. On a day such as this, some of the most senior peers were assigned specific places, but for the rest of the pack it was a matter of first come and first seated. The baroness was a diehard romantic and loved the lavish colours and costumes that the occasion provided, so for nearly ten years she had defied the onset of arthritis and increasing age to be the first in line. She was a forthright figure whose old hips made her rock to and fro like an old barn door and she smelled vaguely of horses, and she was deeply affronted when she discovered that she had been beaten to the post. Her resentment grew as she recognised the culprit. Ahead of her, leaning on his walking stick by the ornate fireplace near the entrance to the chamber, was Archie Wakefield.

They went back a long and, at times, deeply wounding way. Theirs was a clash not only of parties but also of personalities. When she had been a tough-minded and notoriously sceptical Foreign Secretary, he had described her mind as being like a laundry basket, where the dirty linen took up so much more room than the fresh. He also claimed that her politics were easily understood once you had read *Mein Kampf* in the original. He, on the other hand, was an unrefined former sailor in the merchant marine who had come up through the ranks of the working class, in the days when there was still a working class, and had difficulty understanding why she took his gentle humour so seriously. None of his colleagues took him seriously; he was a token son of toil in a party that had long since forsaken its

27

working-class roots, while she had progressed partly through her sharp intellect and finely whetted tongue in a party that didn't understand women and had tried to bury her energies in responsibility. In making her Foreign Secretary they had hoped that she would travel but, as they soon discovered, she didn't much care for abroad, or for foreigners.

She was now seventy-three, he was a couple of years younger, and while she had developed a face like orange peel after spending too long in the sun, he had recently come to fat with a swollen, very pink face and was totally bald. It gave him the appearance of a baby in a bathing cap. She disliked self-indulgence and thoroughly detested Archie Wakefield; she thought of turning on her heel and tottering off, but that would only hand him the victory. She had never been known to duck a fight and this moment, with this man, was scarcely the excuse to start.

'Morning, duchess,' he greeted in an accent that fell one side of the Pennines or the other, she couldn't be sure which. And she wasn't a duchess, merely a common or garden variety of peer, like him.

'I always thought royal sports too rich for your appetite, Archie.'

'Try anything once. Twice, even, if there are no cameras about.'

'Ah, I'd forgotten you were sensitive to cameras. What was her name, that diary secretary of yours who enjoyed being photographed so much? Sonya, wasn't it?' She remembered Sonya all too well, and the photographs – well, anyone in the country who was older than thirty did. The resulting scandal had required Archie to resign from the Cabinet but it had made him a household name, and since the headlines he created had smothered media interest in a financial crisis, it had seemed only fair that he should be kicked upstairs to the Lords.

'You ever get tempted, duchess?'

'Not by you.'

'Thank God. For a moment I thought you were pursuing me.

Being seen with you at this time in the morning is just a little more than my reputation can take.'

'You're welcome to leave. I won't be hurt.'

'Then I'll stay.'

'You are the most studiously offensive man I have ever met.'

'You're wrong there, duchess. Never studied it. Never studied much at all, as you well know. My type of people didn't get the chance to go to posh universities like your lot.'

'Oh, spare me the working-class chip on both shoulders.'

'If I have, it's given me a balanced outlook. Which is more than anyone's ever said about you.'

'Dammit, man, why have you come? You hate the Royal Family, you hate the House of Lords, you're always mocking us. You've never been anything other than a professional complainer, so what the devil are you doing here anyway?'

'Curiosity, I suppose,' he replied. 'Never done it before. Thought I'd try it, while I've the chance.' And he turned his back on her, not intending to be rude, but to hide the sudden stab of pain that ran like quicksilver across his face.

9.00 a.m.

The first major deadline in the official schedule had been reached, and a cordon was thrown round the Palace of Westminster. The last of the concrete barriers were hauled into position across the approach roads, and all checkpoints were manned by a small army of police in bullet-proof vests, many of them armed with Heckler & Koch semi-automatic carbines. In Wellington Barracks the Sovereign's Escort was tacking up, while at the Palace of Westminster the first party of the Queen's Bodyguard was assembling to prepare for her arrival.

A short walk away, the doors to the House of Lords we swung open to allow peers to begin taking their seats. Archie Wakefield and Celia Blessing were both relieved not to have to continue their sulk of silence outside the doors, but unlike most days, when they would have sat on opposite sides, they were forced by the restrictions of the day to take seats close to each other. They both wanted the best view; the baroness sat in the third row of the benches to the left of the throne, while he took the seat immediately behind her, muttering to himself that he was getting her best profile.

It was at this time that the final security meeting of the day took place. In a small office near the chamber, an inspector from the Metropolitan Police who was responsible for security outside of the palace sat down with members of Black Rod's office who were responsible for matters inside – an overlapping web of security that was supposed to provide multiple layers of protection, although some thought it top heavy and unfocused. Why wasn't just one man in charge, one man whose neck was on the line? But this was the way it had been handled for many years and it had worked pretty well since . . . well, since Guy Fawkes.

While the men talked, police sniffer dogs ran one final check through the chamber and in the surrounding rooms and corridors, but the cleaners' room in the basement always retained a powerful smell of cleaning fluids and polish, which made it difficult territory for the dogs. They failed to detect the body of the young policeman which had been bent double and locked inside a cupboard alongside several open bottles of bleach. More bleach had been used to wipe away any trace of his blood, and no one had yet noticed he was missing.

Neither did the dogs detect what was hidden in Coca-Cola cans which had been placed carefully inside the vacuum cleaner, and which Mukhtar had hauled to a corridor close by the chamber. One dog did approach, but Mukhtar switched on the apparatus and the noise and odour of stale dust that it threw out were enough to distract the animal. Even as the security forces carried out their carefully laid plans to secure the building and a large chunk of Westminster around it, no one realised that the killers had already beaten their trap.

9.11 a.m.

Harry came out of the shower and dripped over the carpet of the bedroom. He had stayed a long time beneath the cascade of water, hoping it might wash the pain away, but it hadn't. Through the open door of the bedroom he could see into the rest of the service apartment he had taken on Curzon Street, a few hundred yards from his home. The accommodation was antiseptic and utterly anonymous. He had been able to ignore it when he assumed this was merely a temporary lodging, somewhere to squat before he moved back home, but now he realised that wasn't going to happen. He had no home any more. This squalid little place was his life, until he changed it, a life of shirts wrapped in impersonal cellophane, a fridge full of afterthoughts, and a few boxes of books and papers piled in a corner.

He towelled himself roughly until his back felt raw and sat on the bed, his laptop beside him. Beyond the grimy, metal-framed windows the street was cast in coppered sunlight yet it did nothing for his humour. He logged into the Marie Stopes website, and his mind grew still darker. *Before 12 weeks pregnancy* ... That would be about it. Melanie wouldn't have left it any longer, she wasn't one for harbouring doubts. *At this stage gentle suction is used to remove the pregnancy from the uterus.* 'The pregnancy'? Didn't they mean the baby, *his* baby? *This is a very quick and simple procedure, taking less than five minutes to perform.* It made it seem like an ingrown toenail or treatment for a head cold; the moral equivalent of sweeping out a blocked gutter. The clinic offered lavish promises about the physical treatment and mental welfare of the mother, yet there wasn't a word about the father. *It is completely your decision who you tell about your treatment* ... Didn't the father have rights? Couldn't he feel pain, too? He had obligations aplenty, the law laid them down in meticulous detail and all costed to the last penny, but there wasn't a sniff of what those obligations bought.

Friday afternoon, she had told him. Little more than fifty hours, and then . . . He had to change her mind. Harry felt sick, as if an animal was tearing at him inside. It shocked him, how passionately he felt about it. He couldn't remember if he had ever been as distressed in his life, or as powerless. He threw his towel into a corner and lay back on his pillow, his wet hair sending trickles of dampness down his cheeks. His cheeks were still damp, long after the hair had dried.

9.30 a.m.

As the peal of bells alongside Big Ben struck the half-hour, the security net tightened. Not all the preparations went smoothly. A peer came bowling along Parliament Street on his bicycle, anxious that he was a little late, only to run into a roadblock. Although he had his red-and-white Lords' pass he was denied access. 'Can't take the bike in, m'lud,' a policeman told him. 'You don't have the right pass for it. And you can't leave it here, neither. Otherwise we'll have to take it away and blow it up.' The peer retired hurt.

Two of the earliest arrivals, clutching proper passes, were in wheelchairs. Their passes were little more than a piece of printed pale green card with a number and a name written on it, and the two men were required to provide some additional form of photographic identity to match the names on the cards. They both produced well-worn British passports. With the courtesy and smooth efficiency that characterised the occasion, they were then conducted to a spot reserved for them in the Royal Gallery, a special place for wheelchairs where they would be directly beside the processional route and only a few feet away from Her Majesty as she passed. The two men expressed their thanks and, somewhat to the relief of the over-stretched attendants, declined the use of the disabled toilet facilities.

On another part of the processional route, the Norman Porch, where the Queen would mount its steps, a BBC technician was reprimanded for failing to display his pass clearly. 'If you don't mind, sir,' a doorkeeper remarked, 'we need our medals on parade.' They couldn't take anything for granted, least of all the BBC. Some standards had to be maintained. Sadly, there were many other miscreants. Peers frequently forgot to wear their passes, and many Members of the House of Commons simply refused; they liked to assume everyone knew who they were, even if they hadn't made it all the way to the front page of the *News of the World*.

In the nearby Moses Room, Ede and Ravenscroft were dispensing the robes of scarlet wool trimmed in ermine that their Lordships were required to wear, yet even here, standards were slipping. In some cases, at the insistence of the peer, the ermine was in fact rabbit, and, in one or two cases, artificial fur. The robes covered many sins. Beneath their robes the peers were instructed to wear full dress uniform, morning dress or lounge suit, but Archie Wakefield had no right to wear uniform and refused the class-ridden pretensions of morning dress, so he made do with a suit, one of only two he owned. It may have taken pride of place in his wardrobe but it had clearly travelled many a mile. The trousers seemed to be fashioned from material reclaimed from a worn-out concertina while the jacket succeeded in both stretching and sagging at the same time.

This was also the moment for one of the most celebrated traditions of the day. Ten members of the Yeoman of the Guard, the oldest military corps in the country, were given the order to start their ceremonial search in a colourful re-enactment of the moment that their predecessors had discovered Guy Fawkes's stash of gunpowder. Four centuries later, no chances were being taken. With lamps in one hand and ceremonial four-inch axes in the other, dressed in uniforms of brilliant scarlet with knee-breeches and ruffs that stretched back to Tudor times, they marched in step to their duty, through the chamber and down a staircase into the cellars. Once they had finished they would be taken to the Terrace overlooking the river for a glass of port. It was, of course, merely ritual. After all, the cellars had already been searched by sniffer dogs and police with metal detectors. No surprises, that was the order of the day. Everything had to move like clockwork, to the minute.

It was a day that, in the words of the police inspector, had been planned to death. But others had their plans, too. By this time, there were already seven assassins inside the building. One more to go and they would have a full set.

9.37 a.m.

A blue armoured BMW with two-inch thick windows and a suspension that seemed to sag just a little lower than most pulled slowly into Downing Street. It was Robert Paine's car and was followed by a British Special Branch unit, but the Stars and Stripes weren't flying from the bonnet. This wasn't an official call.

The door of Number Ten opened for him as he approached and he walked straight through into the black-and-white-tiled hallway. He was a regular visitor, felt comfortable here, was on first-name terms with the doorman, but even he was surprised when a football suddenly bounced his way.

'Sorry, Mr Paine,' an American voice called out, laughing.

'Can we have our ball back, mister?' another voice added in a plaintive mock-Cockney accent.

'You turning Downing Street into a soccer pitch?'

'My father would call it the maximum utilisation of public resources,' the Englishman replied.

'And Mom'd say we were only getting our own back on the British for burning down the White House,' the other chimed in.

The two young men smiled as they strode forward to take the ambassador's hand. 'Thanks for offering the lift today, Mr Paine,' the American said. 'We could have walked, you know, wouldn't take above ten minutes.'

'Your mother asked me to take care of you,' Paine replied. 'I think she meant I should make sure you got there on time and didn't upstage the Queen.'

'Aw, mothers.'

'Not to mention fathers!' added the other.

They both laughed. They were in their early twenties and clearly good companions. By any stretch theirs was a remarkable friendship, forged at Oxford, where they were both studying. It wasn't often that the sons of a British Prime Minister and an American President had the opportunity to make mischief together and grow close.

Magnus Eaton, the Englishman, was a slight, wiry, copper-haired individual with an irreverent smile who was making his own way in the world, despite his parentage. He had insisted on being sent to state school rather than some fee-paying establishment, much to the private relief and public credit of his father, and had rarely had his photograph published except for the family Christmas card. Despite the inevitable accusations of nepotism when he had gained his place at Oxford he had proved himself to be a highly talented young man, adept not only at his mathematical studies but also an excellent musician and a tenacious cross-country runner. He had kept a clean slate, apart from the time he had got himself arrested in The Broad for being drunk in charge of a bicycle. The charge was later dropped when it was shown that even in the hands of the entirely sober and upright station sergeant, it simply wasn't possible to persuade the rusted bike to travel in a straight line.

Magnus's life had been led largely in the shadows at the edge of the public arena. By contrast, William-Henry Harrison Edwards was never going to get away so lightly, not when his mother was the first female President in US history and the third in the family to make it to the White House. Great things were expected of William-Henry, and he had delivered. A Harvard history undergraduate, *summa cum laude*, currently a Rhodes Scholar in Oxford and predicted to become a rowing blue. Life had been a chest crammed with many treasures, most of which he had deserved, yet it had caused his mother much soul searching before she'd agreed to let him continue his education abroad. After all, the sons of America weren't exactly welcome in many parts of the modern world, but Britain, she had eventually been persuaded, was different. 'Mom, it's the Special Relationship. Harry

Potter, Prince William, motherhood and organic apple pie, all that sort of gentle stuff,' her son had declared. 'And you cannot – you simply *can not* – send tens of thousands of other American sons halfway round the world to fight our wars while you keep me wrapped up at home. Heaven's sakes, Mom, Oxford's not like Afghanistan.' So, reluctantly, she had let him go.

'By the way, Mr Paine, Dad sends regards. And his thanks and apologies,' Magnus was saying, ticking off his fingers. 'I'm quoting here. Regards, because you're the best ambassador he's ever had dealings with. Thanks, for taking me off his hands this morning. And apologies, because he's tied up in some stuffy meeting and can't give you all this guff himself. Something about Daud Gul, I think. Trying to decide if they can stuff and mount him in order to put him on public display.'

'I understand his difficulties. Hooking the fish is one thing, landing him is another, I guess. But I fear we have no time for high politics. We must leave. It wouldn't do to keep Her Majesty waiting.'

'We haven't even had breakfast,' the younger American complained, searching for his jacket. 'Hell, I wonder what Daud Gul will get for his last breakfast. You know, as and when—'

'Revenge, perhaps,' the ambassdor offered. 'These matters have a history of producing the most unexpected results.'

'I hope when he drops he falls all the way to hell. Don't you agree, Mr Paine?'

'As a diplomat I'm supposed neither to agree nor disagree. And I think you'll find that the British no longer hold with retribution and all those Old Testament edicts. Such beliefs are becoming a uniquely American preserve.'

'Pity. We should Saddam the bastard.'

'And as for the long road to hell, I've often found that it doesn't lie as far away as most of us think,' the ambassador continued, leading them out of the door towards his car.

'Say, do they do croissants and coffee at this State Opening thing?' William-Henry enquired.

'When grown men start dressing in silk stockings and wigs, there's no way of being sure what to expect,' the ambassador replied.

9.42 a.m.

The day really wasn't working out for Harry. A state of near-paralysis was spreading through the arteries that led from the Palace of Westminster until it had choked much of Central London. Harry tried to call a taxi, but nothing was moving, forcing him to go by foot. Not that this was unusual. In his early days as an officer in the Household Cavalry he had once taken his troop on an unscheduled six-hundred-mile route march down the spine of Norway, much to the delight of his men and the consternation of his CO, who just hated surprises. Harry had an extraordinary knack of pissing off his superiors. His last outing with the Special Air Service had proved to be one hell of a yomp, too. He'd loved the SAS, not so much for what it was but because, after Julia's death, he had been able to lose himself within its monkish company of warriors. He had shown himself to be utterly fearless, some said reckless, but only with his own life. Others did their damage with little more than a pen. No sooner had his squadron proved its mettle in counter-terrorist operations throughout Northern Ireland and many other parts of the world than an order was signed placing them on role rotation. They were intensely honed experts in urban warfare; now with little more than a few weeks' training behind them, they were sent to fight in the desert. It was the inexorable Law of Sod. They found themselves thrust into something called Gulf War One. The equipment had been crap – some of it literally melted – the intelligence had more holes than a whore's knickers and they'd been dropped in a location that was supposed to have been empty for miles around but turned out to be within spitting distance of a major deployment of the Republican Guard. After a disastrous firefight

Harry had been forced to walk more than two hundred miles to safety with a bullet in his back and a wounded colleague slung over his shoulder, and only two litres of water between them. Yes, Harry knew how to walk.

Now, as he hurried through the park at the back of Downing Street, he wondered if he was still able to do it, to take all that pain. He knew he'd changed, perhaps gone soft. He was used to controlling his feelings, not letting the anger show, so why was this baby thing getting to him? Christ, he'd even voted for the abortion bill, but now . . . He strode on, trying to work off his frustration. Soon he was cutting through St Margaret's churchyard where, in the lee of the abbey, the lawns had been planted with a spreading tide of tiny wooden crosses bearing poppies. Remembrance Day was less than a week away. He slowed his pace. Small family groups were gathered, pointing to crosses, planting their own, talking in low voices washed with pride about those they had lost. Harry came to a halt for a few moments, struggling with his own memories.

As he stood in this field of poppies, much of his immediate anger passed from him. He had to regroup, get back in control of the situation. He couldn't leave things where they were with Mel, buried in lurid recrimination. Whatever he thought about her, he needed her, had to find some way of changing her mind. He tried her mobile but she wasn't answering, not to him, at least. He left a mumbled half-meant apology and asked to meet up to talk things over – perhaps over dinner again? Tonight? The suggestion might promote a few happier memories; after all, less than nine hours ago they'd been having sex in the communal lift.

A few strides later and he had reached the crowd barrier manned by armed police at the edge of the security cordon.

'Have you got your pass, sir?' one of the constables, a woman, asked. Harry took in the brightly manicured fingers hooked around a Heckler and Koch MP5, and still couldn't persuade himself that such things were right. He began scrabbling inside a pocket for his green-

and-white barred security pass when the other policemen, without waiting, drew back the barrier.

'Morning, Mr Jones, no need for that.' The bobby saluted.

'I'm sorry, do we know each other?'

'You won't remember but we met, briefly, after you gave a speech at the Hendon police academy. Fine speech you made that day; not heard a better one since. Pity you left the Home Office, that's what many of us thought.'

'Yeah. I thought that, too.'

And he was through, past the security cordon, crossing the empty street. Instead of the usual barriers of concrete and steel that protected the parliament building, now there was nothing but wide, open space. The forecourt of the House of Lords had been cleared of all the regular security checks and devices, and where armed policemen normally patrolled, today Harry found nothing but a troop of young adventure scouts, boys and girls, standing in the sun. Here, everything seemed peaceful and was assumed to be safe. In fact, by this time the policemen who usually patrolled the corridors within the parliament building were being withdrawn as their presence was deemed to be not fitting with the pomp and splendour of the occasion. To Harry, this seemed to miss the point. Hadn't almost all serious threats to the lives of monarchs come from within this building, not from without, from the likes of Guy Fawkes and Cromwell and the rest? For a moment, it struck Harry that all the forces of security he had passed that morning were looking the wrong way, but life was often absurd. Then his mind strayed back to the field of poppies outside the church, and the small gatherings of loved ones who had come to remember. A disturbing thought suddenly grabbed hold of him and began to shake him. If he died, right now, today, who would be there to mourn? Who would bother to remember him? Who would come to plant a poppy in his name? Lacking any answer he found acceptable, Harry hurried on.

10.25 a.m.

It was almost time. The senior judges were en route from the Royal Courts of Justice in a convoy of cars. The adventure scouts listened to their final instruction. The men and women from the BBC ran one final test. Yet not everything was running smoothly. The Vice-Chamberlain of the Household, the government minister who was to be held hostage at Buckingham Palace for the duration of the ceremony, was descending into a state of panic. A fly button on the grey-striped trousers of his morning suit was hanging by the slenderest of threads and would never last the morning. This was his first time; he was nervous, and all but screamed with frustration. His secretary, as always, came to the rescue with a soothing word and a needle and thread, trying not to laugh at the sight of his dangling double cuffs and pale pastry knees.

The benches in the chamber were beginning to fill. The first bishop had already taken his place, and behind him ambassadors and envoys were gathering. The first to arrive was the High Commissioner of the Islamic Republic of Pakistan, a portly man dressed in a bright gold and highly decorated *achkan*, a long coat that ended at the shins. He leaned heavily on a walking stick, and at his special request had been placed at the end of the leather bench rather than being forced to squeeze between many others. The high commissioner had only recently arrived in London, following the turmoil and revolution that had left his country with a second change of government in less than a year. Robert Paine sat nearby, but they exchanged nothing more than the briefest greeting; the weight of his country's troubles seemed to weigh heavily on the Pakistani's shoulders. Paine looked up and offered a private smile to Magnus and William-Henry who had taken their places in the gallery. It was a narrow and desperately uncomfortable perch, designed for women of a delicate Victorian stature, but the two friends hadn't a care, leaning forward to spy on the scene below. They found a sight that was staggering and, to their young eyes, even faintly comical. Television lights danced upon a brimming sea of tiaras, medals, brooches, silks, jewels, decorations and dog collars. Their programme told them they were looking down on Pursuivants Ordinary and Extraordinary, heralds and high men, barons, bodyguards and bishops, earls and ushers, and they thought they could see Pooh Bah and Uncle Tom Cobley mixed in there, too.

'Straight out of Gilbert and Sullivan,' Magnus muttered in awe.

'Like one of those fifties films with the colour control on full blast,' William-Henry replied.

'Designed to impress the masses, of course.'

'The cradle of democracy.'

'Not quite,' Magnus responded. 'Technically, this is a royal palace. Funny place. You know, that makes it almost impossible to die here. To have a death certificate record your place of departure as the Palace of Westminster, it's got to be signed by a royal surgeon. Buggers are never around when you need them. So if you stop breathing, you're put in an ambulance and carted off across the river to St Thomas's. Dead on arrival. Somehow takes the splendour out of it all, don't you think?'

'Magnus, you are a fount of the most useless information imaginable.'

'Just wanted to make you feel at home.'

'Then get me some breakfast! Hey, that one's a waiter, isn't he?' William-Henry said, pointing to a black-clad figure below.

'I think you'll find that's the Gentleman Usher of the Black Rod. Good for a brandy but not bacon and eggs.'

'Then I'm going to die of hunger, no matter what you say.'

The truth was, no one was supposed to die in the Palace of Westminster. It was against regulations. It was yet another of those rules that, in the next few hours, was going to be torn up.

10.30 a.m.

Even as the young men gently mocked their elders, the main gates to the Sovereign's Entrance were being opened in preparation to receive Her Majesty. At the same time, her hostage was being driven up the Mall to Buckingham Palace, his trousers now intact. He held his top hat on his lap in one hand and his wand of office in the other, and fidgeted nervously.

Heading in the other direction down the Mall, in its own coach, came the Imperial State Crown. It was the finest piece of jewellery in the world. Its sapphire had been taken from the ring of Edward the Confessor, its diamond was the third largest in the world, and the egg-sized ruby had once belonged to the Black Prince, making it one of the oldest known jewels known to man. To add a little sparkle there were more than three thousand other diamonds, pearls and precious stones embedded in it. The Crown was heavy, it could not be otherwise, and too heavy for comfort on most heads. Wearing it required both patience and a little practice. Palace footmen reported seeing Elizabeth wearing the Crown over breakfast, with her newspapers, in preparation.

Along with the Crown came the Sword of State and the Cap of Maintenance, a crimson velvet affair carried on a stick and whose origins lay so far back in the shadows of the past that no one could remember what it was for, although it was still treated in much the same way as if it had been the bones of St Peter. Except that, for some reason no one was entirely clear about, it seemed to have spent the last year tucked away in a drawer of Prince Philip's desk. No one had been unwise enough to ask the Prince why; he was sick, and in any event probably wouldn't have a clue how it had ended up there, but he'd be sure to throw one of his castle-cracking fits if he thought they'd been raking through his desk drawers. No telling what might turn up in them.

At 10.52 precisely the coach carrying the royal regalia arrived at the Sovereign's Entrance. Here the Crown was passed to the Royal

Bargemaster before being taken under guard to the Robing Room, where were waiting the other necessary props required for the occasion. These necessaries included the Queen's robe, six yards of it, four page-boys to carry it, and a bottle of sherry which had been brought from the palace by one of the Ladies-in-Waiting. Elizabeth was partial to sherry on such occasions, for medicinal purposes. Great care would be taken to ensure that what remained of the sherry was taken back to the palace afterwards. It wouldn't do to have a half-empty bottle of *oloroso royale* popping up on eBay.

Back at Buckingham Palace, Her Majesty was being seen off from the inner courtyard by a group of officials, in the midst of whom stood her ministerial hostage. He bowed his head low. The day was unusually clement for November, the palace basked in the sun like a contented walrus. The Irish State Coach was drawn by four white horses, their hooves echoing back from the walls of the inner archway as, with her son beside her, the Queen set out for that other palace of illusions that lay on the far side of the park. A squadron of the Household Cavalry led the way.

As the noise of the hooves died away, the Lord Chamberlain touched the elbow of his parliamentary guest. 'You are now my prisoner, young man. Come with me.' The junior minister was escorted up to the Lord Chamberlain's offices, walled with bookcases and equipped with several fine cracked-leather armchairs and a television. A bottle of old champagne was standing on a low side table.

'Now that the Boss has gone, we can get down to business. Will you pour or shall I?' the Lord Chamberlain enquired.

'You know, I think I might learn to enjoy being a hostage,' the young politician replied, at last relaxing.

The Lord Chamberlain offered a modest smile. 'The House of Windsor does its best.'

As they made themselves comfortable in the armchairs, on the other side of the park, in the heart of parliament, the last of the assassins, who now numbered eight, was taking his own seat.

11.02 a.m.

The Royal Gallery that adjoins the chamber itself is not so much a gallery as a vast chamber, larger even than that in which the peers sit. It is sumptuous, and dominated by two extraordinarily long tableaux that commemorate the British victories over the French at Waterloo and Trafalgar. The paintings are vivid and bloody, with bodies and broken bits scattered everywhere, most of them French. This is where guests who are unable to be in the Chamber itself are seated, and through which, with pomp and circumstance and just a touch of carnival, the Queen and her royal entourage pass. A tremor of excitement ran through the guests waiting here, for it was their day, too. There were sikhs, sultans, saris, rabbis and minor foreign royalty, commoners black, white, yellow and brown, Nepalese and Nigerians and a couple from Nottingham. The wife wore a creation of plumes and plucked feathers that on a different day would have done as dusters. The hat was also as broad as a London bus, lacking only the advertisement stuck on its rear end.

Without any apparent signal, the Royal Gallery grew still. Expectant. The Yeomen of the Guard stamped their way through to take up their positions. Then sounds of the Arrival began to drift through: much banging of ancient axes, crashing of boots, the shouting of commands that had echoed through these chambers for generations, except, of course, for the instruction to switch off mobile phones. From somewhere outside came the strains of the National Anthem. On the tower above the Sovereign's Entrance, the Union Flag was struck and replaced by the Royal Standard. She was here.

Then, at 11.27 precisely, the doors to the Robing Room were opened and the Queen, on the hand of her eldest son, advanced into the Royal Gallery, followed by four serious-faced and over-stepping page-boys who carried the train of the royal robe. It was a moment dripping with solemnity, when the English reached back deep into their history and touched their ancestors' souls.

Oh, but the atmosphere was so rich that Ethel, the lady from Nottingham, almost swooned as the play was performed only feet in front of her; so many actors, so many wonderful costumes. Ladies-in-Waiting walked with a Gold-Stick-in-Waiting, a Clarenceux King of Arms marched in time with a Garter King, while an Earl Marshal rubbed shoulders with a Master of the Horse. It was a Queen's cornucopia.

'She's so lovely, bless her,' Ethel whispered, nudging Arthur, her husband, as she rose from her curtsey. 'And so close. I swear I could've touched her, if only I'd stretched a little. But look at the Prince, hasn't the poor dear aged so?'

'Men over sixty do, you silly girl,' he muttered back from the corner of his mouth. 'He's older than Cousin Mavis, and we buried her a year ago. Now shuddup!'

And in a mere heave of Ethel's bosom, the procession was gone, through to the House of Lords itself. A few moments before the Queen arrived the two large television screens set at height on either side of the throne went blank. Nothing was meant to distract from her entrance, not even her own image. Before the screen in his royal cell, the ministerial hostage raised his glass and offered an extravagant toast of loyalty. He was already a little squiffy. The Lord Chamberlain eyed his guest and quietly wrote him off. No, this one wasn't for the top, not the very top. Insufficient stamina.

And on the packed benches in the House of Lords, as the screens turned black, Celia Blessing sensed more than heard some form of disturbance behind her, a feeling that was like being shrouded in a mist of pain. She turned and saw that Archie Wakefield's ruddy cheeks were floating in a sea of ash.

'Everything OK, Archie?'

'Never better,' he lied, struggling.

She looked at him with an expression that was typically sharp but filled more with concern than distrust. 'Silly man. You shouldn't be here. Why *did* you come?'

11.30 a.m.

She walked slowly up the steps to her throne as behind her the page-boys nervously laid out her train upon the carpet. 'My Lords, pray be seated,' she commanded as soon as she was settled. The voice sounded a little cracked and tired; she was, after all, well into her eighties and she had been fighting a cold. Beside her, on her left, sat the Prince of Wales, but on a throne an inch lower; no one, not even he, allowed to sit as high. As the rustling died away and the room was returned to stillness, she gazed through her glasses at a scene that stretched back through more than fifty years of her life, to the time when she was a young woman. This was not what she had wanted or least of all expected. It wasn't meant to be, not for her, not until Uncle David – Edward, the Seventh and Most Wanton of that name – had just . . . given up! Abdicated! Thrown away the love of an entire Empire for the dubious affections of a pinched-face American divorcee who had, according to some reports, honed her feminine wiles in a Shanghai whorehouse. Her uncle's desertion had cast her beloved father into a task he hadn't wanted and for which he was ill-prepared, woefully, but which he had taken to his heart and fulfilled to his last breath, a dedication that had, year by year and speech by stuttering speech, worn him down until it eventually killed him. How different things might have been, not just for him, but for her, too. What opportunities she might have had, in another life, the life she had been born to. A chance to breed horses, or to fish the streams, to watch the flowers blossom. Simple pleasures. But it was never meant to be, not after bloody Uncle David.

She raised her eyes. Around the walls at the distant end of the chamber stood eighteen sombre statues of the barons and bishops who had forced King John to sign the Magna Carta, a reminder of how vulnerable is any throne. Even today she was required to make this speech – the Queen's Speech as it was called, yet not a single word of it would be hers, all written down to the last comma and little conceit by politicians. Her life was spun round in many golden threads, and so tightly that they formed the most confining of cages.

She nodded, almost imperceptibly, that she was ready. It was the signal for Black Rod to summon the Commons. Dressed in black tailcoat, breeches and stockings with his sword at his side, he set out on his task, striding towards the House of Commons, only for the great oak doors to be slammed in his face in the traditional act of defiance to the monarch. He raised his black rod, struck three times upon the door, and slowly it opened to allow him entrance.

The House was crowded, in gentle humour. A voice was raised. 'Oi, look, here comes the Black Magic man,' and the Members dissolved into laughter that had Black Rod himself struggling to keep a straight face. He bowed, and advanced.

'Mr Speaker, the Queen commands this honourable House' – a polite nod in the direction of both sides – 'to attend Her Majesty immediately in the House of Peers.'

And so they came, filing through, side by side, the Prime Minister and Leader of the Opposition, the Chancellor of the Exchequer, all the most powerful men and women in the land – all, that is, except Tricia Willcocks, who was lying down in her darkened bedroom, hiding behind eyeshades. Many other Members of the Commons came for the trip, for while in the Lords the occasion is treated as high ceremony, in the lower house it's not much more than a bit of a show. Light entertainment. A morning off.

The Bar of the House of Lords is a barrier erected just inside its entrance that is designed to prevent visitors progressing any further into the chamber. For the State Opening the Bar had been moved forward to allow as many members of the Commons as possible to have a sight of the proceedings and they crowded in, spreading out and standing like spectators at a football match. It was uncomfortable, but it wouldn't be for long. Apart from the Cabinet, only around a hundred MPs bothered; there was no point standing outside like naughty schoolboys, but for those who succeeded in getting a view, it was magnificent. At the far end of the chamber the Throne and its glittering gold canopy stood like a temple that had been snatched from the timeless world of Shangri-la. No one did this better than the British. At Elizabeth's left hand sat the heir, and on either side stood the four page-boys and her ladies-in-waiting, while at the foot of the steps that lead to the Throne were gathered her closest advisers and courtiers. Before her stretched the sea of scarlet that were her barons, viscounts, earls, marquises, even a couple of dukes. And those who would be her assassins.

11.36 a.m.

Harry had filed along with the crowd. He was passing through the Central Lobby, that echoing Gothic crossroads that stands between the two houses of parliament, when he saw an old friend, one of the doorkeepers, nodding in his direction.

'Morning, boss,' the doorkeeper mouthed.

'Hello, Brains,' Harry responded. 'Brains' Benjamin had been one of Harry's NCOs in the Life Guards, a former Corporal Major and one of the finest horsemen in the regiment, so good, he was said to have his brains in his backside. It was a characteristic of Harry's life in the army that for every senior officer he had exasperated beyond endurance, he had made a hundred loyal friends among the troops he led. Brains Benjamin had been one of them. 'Good to see you,' Harry called out as he passed. 'We must have a jar; it's been too long.'

'As long as it's not north of the Arctic Circle again, you're on, Boss.'

Harry managed a smile – the first time the warmth of human contact had begun to melt the morning's ice – and was about to reply when he felt his mobile phone vibrating. He'd left it on for Melanie, just in case. He stepped to one side in order to answer it. He caught his breath; it was Melanie. A text: *If u insist. 8 pm The Ivy.*

He stared at the cold, formal response – so different from just twelve hours ago in the lift. It was clear that her heart wasn't in it. She was playing a game, and forcing him to play along, too, at least until Friday morning.

He began punching buttons. 'Looking forward to it,' he began, then hesitated before adding: 'Sorry about this morning.' He didn't mean it, of course, but his training screamed for caution. He knew his anger, if left raw and unrestrained, would play into her hands, all the way up the steps of the divorce court, so buck up, Harry, fight the battle on your ground, not hers, if you can. And yet it was a battle he didn't want and couldn't win. It seemed such a waste, a marriage over in a morning. One bastard of a day.

And as he looked up, he saw that he had lost the moment. The entrance to the Lords with its exquisite, one-and-a-half-ton brass doors designed by Pugin was now awash with MPs trying to peer over the shoulders of those in front. No more room at the inn. Bollocks. Still, it just couldn't get any worse. Not unless the Ivy was fully booked. He decided he'd better call the restaurant and see if he could claim at least one small victory.

11.38 a.m.

From the back of the Chamber a doorkeeper lifted his head to indicate that the MPs behind the Bar had settled. This signal was picked up by the Earl Marshal, who in turn nodded to the Lord Chancellor. In dark black cloak and wig he stepped slowly forward and began mounting the steps to the Throne. He was a portly figure, not as agile as once he was, and he trod with considerable caution. Not the moment to stumble. In his right hand he held an embroidered purse that held the speech, and with suitable humility, he withdrew it and handed it to his sovereign. She offered a barely perceptible nod.

She gazed at the booklet she had been handed. The Queen's Speech, yet not a word of it her own. She prepared herself, but first turned to her son, sitting beside her. This was a deliberate gesture, full of symbolism. She wanted to remind them that soon, in God's time, he would be here, in her place, and he had waited so long already, almost longer than any other heir in British history. It was why she had brought him here today, kept him at her side so that people could grow accustomed to the idea. Charles. On the throne. Perhaps they would never grow to love him, but they might yet learn to accept him, and he to be at ease with them.

It was time. She looked over her glasses, and every one of the three hundred-and-sixty-two souls crowded into this one room returned her gaze.

'My Lords and members of the House of Commons. My Government will—' She hesitated. Her eye was being dragged away from the letters on the page. A little to her right, close at hand, she became aware that there was some form of disturbance . . .

Three

I T WASN'T THE FIRST TIME that Elizabeth had felt threatened. When she was a young girl there'd been all those bloody Luftwaffe bombers, dropping incendiaries and high explosives on the palace. Made a mess of the swimming pool. And she'd been shot at six times in the Mall while riding her horse towards the Trooping of the Colour. She'd ducked, patted her horse, and ridden on, unaware that the shots were blanks. Then had come the bizarre moment when she had woken to find a strange young man sitting on her bed. He said his name was Michael Fagan and he asked for a cigarette. She had pressed the alarm button, but no one answered; apparently the bell couldn't be heard above the noise of a vacuum cleaner. She'd made two telephone calls for help, but still no one came. So she had sat and chatted to the young schizophrenic until she was able to persuade him that she had no cigarettes and they should go into the corridor to search for some. It turned out that the young man had scaled the walls of the palace and simply begun walking around. He'd been seen, of course, but mistaken for a workman, even though he was in bare feet. Once inside the cordon of walls and wire, no one had asked. It seemed that everyone had jumped to the same conclusion: if you're inside the tent, they expect you to be pissing out, not over each other. The official report had described the security of the palace as diabolical – Prince Philip had used considerably more robust language – and surely all those lessons had been taken to heart and acted upon. Hadn't they?

Security is a state of mind, a sense of well-being, and all had been well in the Lords ever since they had dragged off Guy Fawkes and butchered him. So it was difficult to believe what was now taking place in front of them. The High Commissioner of Pakistan had risen to his feet and was waving what seemed, even to the untrained eye, something suspiciously like a small assault rifle, and which to those with more experience in these matters looked exactly like a Kalashnikov AK-102. With its side-folded butt it was less than two feet in length, had a magazine that held thirty rounds and could fire every single one of them off in three seconds. It was a most awesome weapon for use in confined spaces, and every inch of it easily concealed beneath the ambassador's colourful national dress. Much to the surprise of those around him who had seen him arrive as a frail, overweight envoy, he appeared to have been transformed into a noisy and even agile demonstrator who was leaping from his place on the diplomatic benches, only feet from the Throne. And it was that measure of surprise that gave him the advantage. The only people between him and the Queen were elderly officials who had their back to him; with a shove he sent them sprawling to the floor. There was a royal protection officer inside the chamber, but he was standing in the shadows at the other side of the chamber. He was as surprised as everyone else. It took only a moment for him to recover his wits, but in that single moment the Pakistani had already reached the steps before the throne and was standing upon the embroidered train that the page-boys had laid out so carefully, and which now pointed directly like an arrow towards Elizabeth.

To those who were witness, these happenings seemed to be taking place as though through a telescope trained on a distant world. They were gripped by unsteadiness and indecision, even as the High Commissioner raised his weapon, let forth a great cry and fired. Not until that point had arrived could anyone tell if this was a stunt or an outburst of insanity, yet now there was no doubt. Splinters of gold-painted frieze fell from the canopy above the Throne and spattered about the Queen. From all corners there came screams; people buried their heads, or were frozen in disbelief. Page-boys fell to their knees and cowered. A lady-in-waiting fainted. As others screamed and ducked for cover, Elizabeth alone seemed unmoved.

Charles was the first to respond. He began to rise from his throne to place himself between the gunman and his mother, but she took his arm, held him back. If the gunman had intended to kill her he would already have done so, and there was no point in senseless sacrifice.

The same thought had come to her protection officer. The gunman was in a much better position than he; if a firefight began in such crowded conditions the damage could be terrible and would in all probability involve the Queen herself. Better to wait, bide his time, seek some advantage, perhaps even some surprise. He left his weapon in its holster.

But the world did not stand still. The doorkeepers who manned the two exits behind the throne instinctively began to push them open to let those who could do so escape, but as the doors were drawn back, they allowed others in. As the first sound of gunfire echoed throughout the building, the apparently disabled pair who had been sitting in wheelchairs only a few yards away in the Royal Gallery suddenly underwent a miraculous cure, springing to their feet and racing towards the action. They, too, had weapons in their hands and for some reason were dragging the cushions of their wheelchairs with them.

From the distant end of the Chamber, where the Prime Minister and members of the Commons were gathered, came the sound of another burst of gunfire. The three cleaners had been hiding in a nearby washroom; now they had emerged and were waving more weapons, and shooting them. Bullets riddled the woodwork above the heads of those gathered at the entrance to the Lords. Most of the

MPs began to run for cover, back the way they had come, but this was precisely what the attackers had intended for it eased the pressure of bodies around the doors. Those who tried to stand their ground, like the principal doorkeeper and the police inspector, found themselves staring directly down the muzzle of a Kalashnikov and you couldn't argue with those things. As the tide of humanity turned into a flood, emptying the doorway, two of the cleaners began to haul at Pugin's great brass doors. Within seconds they were closed and padlocked.

On the other side of these doors, by the Bar of the House, confusion had turned to consternation amongst those around the Prime Minister, but none of his protection officers were within yards; this was, after all, deep inside the security cordon. Who was going to threaten the Prime Minister here, apart from his Chancellor? Yet in this part of the Chamber there were two additional exits. These doors led to corridors that were used as voting lobbies, and MPs began to swarm through them. But those who reached these exits first were only the minnows, the big fish of the Cabinet were still pressed in by the weight of bodies all around, and long before any of them had the chance to escape they found the cleaners standing outside these side doors, pointing their guns. Even so the attackers were permitting some to pass, hurrying them on with their barrels. Only when the first member of the Cabinet drew near, with the Prime Minister at his shoulder, that one of the gunmen stopped the flow and fired once more into the ceiling above his head, forcing them back. Much the same was happening on the other side of the Chamber.

And above, in the narrow, mean galleries that ran on every side of the Chamber, guests were fleeing – all, that is, except Magnus and William-Henry. As they rushed to the door that led to the staircase and freedom, they found themselves staring at weapons in the hands of two men who, moments beforehand, had been seated in the press gallery. Stechkin APS machine pistols, and small enough to have been hidden by the cleaners two days earlier in the cisterns of the washrooms.

'Want to know something, old buddy?' Magnus said.

'What?' his friend demanded through clenched teeth.

'We're deep in shit.'

'Where are those Beefeaters when you need them?'

Below them, amongst the scarlet cloaks and tiaras, the self-possession of many was beginning to slip. No outright panic, no screaming, not yet, all terribly British, for the moment, but terror wasn't far from the surface. Elizabeth sat motionless. She could see that the attackers now controlled every door leading from the floor of the Chamber. Others could see it, too; on all sides people were swimming in fear, and some were about to drown in it. If that happened, they would drag many, many others with them. Then a woman cracked, howled, began to wail in dread and to fight her way through the crowd, creating waves of alarm all around her. A gunman raised his weapon. They were a moment away from disaster. The gunman took aim.

That was when the Queen rose to her feet.

Might it have been like that on the *Titanic*? In the face of tragedy, had someone taken control, brought calm to bind the wounds of chaos? Probably not. After all, they had no queen, had no Elizabeth, for as she rose, all eyes were drawn to her, even the attackers, and they grew still. Her voice was not loud, yet it carried to all corners.

'Be calm,' she said. 'Do as they say.'

And they obeyed. As Elizabeth took her seat once more, the mini-exodus continued beneath the menacing eyes of the guns. Royal officials, the page-boys, the ladies-in-waiting, all those with long titles but little power, were allowed to leave. One of her ladies-in-waiting tried to approach the Queen but was warned off with a stare; slowly, in tears, she left her mistress behind.

But not the judges, who sat directly in front of the Throne, nor the ambassadors, nor the bishops, not anyone of consequence. The same was happening at the other end of the Chamber. Only the minor players were allowed to leave the stage.

Nothing could resist the control of the attackers. There was no immediate security around the Chamber. On a day like this, it was supposed to be the safest spot in the kingdom, buried deep within the cordon that had been thrown wide around the parliament building. Most of the armed police who in normal times guard the entrances to the parliament building had been withdrawn for decorative reasons. Inside the Chamber there was little but a single royal protection officer and a couple of toothless retired generals with ceremonial swords. Most of the doorkeepers had backgrounds in either the military or the police, but they were unarmed and were long past being fleet of foot. The Queen's official bodyguard, the Gentlemen at Arms and the Yeomen of the Guard, were stationed in the Prince's Chamber and Royal Gallery. They were dressed magnificently in their plumes and garters, but their average age was in the sixties, and their weapons of Tudor origin. They would have had difficulty cutting their way through a bowl of syrup.

As the galleries above their heads were emptied, one of the gunmen scurried around attaching what appeared to be cans of Coca-Cola to the locks of the doors with pieces of wire – clearly grenades of some sort. On the floor of the Chamber, the two wheelchair attackers were fiddling with the cushions they had carried with them. Not only had these pads been used to conceal weapons, but also, it soon became clear, their contents were not foam rubber but high explosive. What had begun the day as cushions were soon transformed into a primitive explosive jacket like those worn by suicide bombers in the Middle East. One of the gunmen slipped it over his shoulders and went to stand directly behind the Queen. Westminster was rapidly beginning to resemble the West Bank.

11.45 a.m.

One of the first to react was Daniel, the BBC producer for the occasion, seated in an Outside Broadcast van in Black Rod's Garden just a short walk away. He was trained to believe what his screens told him, but even he required a few seconds for understanding to seep through the disbelief. He jumped up from his seat and stared, then he began to sweat, before swearing most violently. This was history in the making and the most exciting moment of his professional life, yet he knew that what he had to do was to take the safe option. These scenes were fascinating, but terrifying. His bosses wouldn't forgive him for putting out images that would have thousands screaming their way through therapy for years to come. He might even have to join them. He'd never watched anyone die before. The scenes gripped him, not out of any sense of ghoulishness but because he knew he might live to be a hundred and never be part of a moment like this again, a moment he knew would be talked about for as long as men had memories. It was with immense reluctance that he instructed his vision mixer to cut away from the action and cast the viewers back to the studio. Yet he kept recording everything his cameras saw. He would still be part of this.

The police inspector who had been chased away by the guns of the attackers was now standing in Central Lobby amidst a swirling sea of uncertainty. On all sides people were shouting and scattering. The chaos infected him, too. He had escaped with his life, but he knew his career was gone; there was no way he could survive this one. It was more than forty years since John Kennedy had been shot, yet still they talked about it, and this was heading in the same direction. Mechanically he began shouting orders, clearing the area of stray bodies, summoning the armed response units. He was a dead man walking, professionally, but he could still save others. All around Westminster, other links in the security chain were snapping taut.

And in the Chamber itself, curious things were happening. The mini-exodus that had been permitted had been entirely purposeful on the part of the attackers. About a hundred of the three hundred and sixty or so who had crammed into the chamber had already gone, considerably relieving the pressure and enabling the attackers to claim good positions and clear lines of fire. One of them stood in the gallery above, guarding Magnus and William-Henry while watching everything that moved below. Another stood on the steps of the throne, and in excellent if slightly accented English began demanding that they pay him attention. At first he had a little difficulty making himself heard since his voice was soft and there was still much commotion on all sides, but he backed up his instruction by firing several rounds into the embossed oak ceiling. The silence that followed was profound. Masood had their full attention.

He was a young man, not yet thirty, with a fresh olive skin and dark, lustrous eyes – handsome in anybody's book. He also had a gentle smile that, combined with his soft and courteous voice (he even thanked them for their attention) – rekindled hope in many who sat there. This impression was reinforced by his next instruction.

'Listen carefully. Very carefully. Your lives will depend upon it. We will let most of you leave,' he declared.

The announcement was met with a universal rustle of relief.

'But not all of you,' Masood added. 'Some of you, I regret, will be staying behind.'

11.47 a.m.

It was barely five minutes into the siege and already its consequences were beginning to flood across the landscape. Crisis has its own mechanics. Newsrooms across London were thrown into bedlam. It had often been claimed that the people who sat in such places had difficulty telling the difference between a bicycle accident and the end of civilisation; now, for once, they might be forgiven their eruptions.

It took no longer for a similar wind of hysteria to blow around those who sat in front of screens in the financial markets. The traders had no idea what was going on but, in the world of money, uncertainty is seen as the greatest threat of all. They began to squirm in their seats and to mark things down. Trading screens dripped red.

Calls began to flood out from the headquarters of the

Metropolitan Police at Scotland Yard to all those who had a role in dealing with emergencies. The fire brigade and ambulance services were put on alert, along with the utility companies in case gas, electricity, water or telephones needed to be cut off. London Underground was ordered to close Westminister and St James's stations. Buses were diverted. Various arms of the health authorities were alerted to deal with the possibility of wholesale casualties. The accident and emergency department at St Thomas's, directly across the river, was closed to the public, while scientists at Porton Down, the government's chemical and biological research centre out in Wiltshire, began their own disaster preparations. They couldn't take chances; there might be a dirty bomb in there.

A few hundred yards further along the Thames from where the siege was taking place, MI5's Deputy Director of Counter-Terrorism rushed into his superior's sanctuary. He found him staring at a blank television screen. It took some time for the director to respond to the intrusion; his face came round slowly, like a rusted crane, in tiny jerks.

'Are they Bin-Men?' he whispered. It was a reflex reaction. Anything that moved these past few years with a complexion darker than a suntan was assumed to be a follower of bin Laden.

'We're trying to match the faces with what we've got on the computers. It'll take a while.'

'But one of them is the sodding High Commissioner! What do we know about him?'

'Pakistani. A tribesman from the mountains. Name of Zaman Khan. Only been here a few weeks. Reputation as a bit of a hard man, apparently. But then, they all are, in their new government.'

The director began searching his pockets for a nicotine stick; he'd sell his daughter for the real thing right now. 'What did he shout, when he jumped up?'

'Sounded like *Azadi*. It means freedom.'

'And?'

'And . . . nothing. That's all. So far.'

'I hope to God they're Bin-Men,' the director said, sucking furiously on his stick, gathering his wits. 'Make sure they are, whatever you do. Don't let any of them be home grown, not domestics, not a single one.'

'We'll do our best.'

The director sighed and began punching buttons on his phone. 'And then, perhaps, we can blame this entire catastrophe on those delinquents across the river at Six . . .'

11.53 a.m.

As he stood on the steps to the throne, Masood sounded like a schoolmaster. *Some will have to stay behind* . . . He made it sound as if he were handing out detentions.

'All members of the Cabinet,' he announced, 'along with the ambassadors, the judges, the bishops – you will remain seated. And, of course, we must ask those members of the Royal Family who are here to stay with us.' He even turned to offer the Queen a little bow – a nod of deference? 'But I must remind you,' he said, returning to his audience, 'we know who you are. We know your faces. Those people I have mentioned – please, do as you are told. Don't try to sneak out.' He paused, his youthful face composed, his eyes casting slowly around him. 'Otherwise, I very much regret that we will kill you.'

He was clearing out those who were not essential to his plans, making room, giving him and his colleagues killing space.

'We will use those doors on either side of the throne,' he declared. 'Now, please move.' He shot a burst of gunfire into the ceiling to get them on their way. They began, mostly calmly, trying to be British about the whole thing, moving forward slowly, as if they were queuing for lifeboats.

From her seat which had given her such a perfect view of events, Celia Blessing rose and tried to pretend she wasn't shaking. Behind her, Archie Wakefield remained in his place.

'Come on, Archie. Get yourself moving.'

'Think I'll stay.'

'What?'

'I'm staying,' he repeated.

'What in the devil's name for?'

He paused, and ground his teeth. 'I might be useful.'

'You?'

He let out a deep, slow breath, which seemed to deflate and crumple his whole body. 'I'm dying, Celia. Got no more than six months. Nothing to lose. Not like most of the people here.'

'But you—' She began to protest, to argue, as had always been her way with him, but as she looked into his eyes she saw something she hadn't noticed before. Behind the pupils, buried deep, was a milky paleness that was beginning to take over inside and drain it of its proper colour. She knew what he had told her was the truth and his logic, at least on this occasion, was impeccable. 'Damn you!' she spat.

'What . . . ?'

'If you're staying, then I'm staying, too.'

'Why?'

She was scared, she didn't have any great yearning to risk her life, but she was of an age when she knew she didn't want to live for ever. Anyway, if he stayed and she left, he'd lord it over her for the rest of eternity, even if eternity in his case stretched to only six months. And she, too, wanted – how had he expressed it? – to be useful. To do her bit. It was what had always brought her to this place, this House of Lords, to turn out for her team even on those occasions when she knew they had no chance of winning. And she was a long-time widow, lonely; it was a pain that had shown itself all too often through her politics, making unnecessary enemies, like Archie Wakefield – and suddenly she was beginning to see him in a different light.

'Why?' he demanded once more.

'I'm writing my memoirs. Need a stronger closing chapter. Think this might do it, don't you, Archie?'

'Ridiculous woman,' he muttered, while she retook her seat.

11.55 a.m.

Amongst the confusion created by the exodus from the chamber there was also an arrival. Magnus and William-Henry, sons of most powerful parents, were to play a central part in this game, although entirely unwillingly. They were hustled down from the gallery at gunpoint and forced to join the throng of hostages. Their faces were flushed with reluctance and anger; they'd both thought about taking their chances and trying to jump the gunman who was prodding the muzzle of his gun into their backs but, even as they considered it, the moment had passed, and with every fresh, hesitant step their youthful optimism turned slowly to fear. They began to feel as though they were walking through water, having to force their way, as if their limbs weren't fully under their control. They stumbled through the door and on to the floor of the chamber, catching the eye of Robert Paine, whose face creased with concern.

Nearby, the Queen's protection officer made his own move, taking advantage of the inevitable measure of disorder to slide his way on to the bench where the ambassadors were seated. He was dressed in morning coat, as were many of them, and he disappeared easily amongst their ranks.

It was a young member of the House of Commons, imprisoned at the far end of the chamber when the Pugin doors had been closed, who showed least composure. He clambered over the Bar and began pushing, tugging at sleeves, even using his shoulder to force a path in his desperation to get away, until a peeress old enough to be his mother turned, eyes blazing, and slapped his face. He withered on the spot. Yet it was the minor members of the Cabinet who were in deepest turmoil. They had been instructed to stay behind on pain of death. Every one of them was left wondering whether the young attacker was telling the truth in saying that their faces were known; every one of them went through minutes of agonised soul-searching about whether they should take the risk and try to sneak out. In the end, they all reached the same conclusion. Even if they survived the threat inside the chamber, they'd find themselves torn to pieces outside for deserting their Queen and leaving her in jeopardy. Anyway, these were men and women who cuddled calves, drove dustcarts, served tea in hospital wards, kissed smelly old pensioners, did anything they could to escape the clutches of anonymity. They'd spent their lives wanting to be recognised, insisting on it. So, when it came to the point of decision, none of them took the risk.

Harry Jones was there, too, not inside the chamber, but close by. When the siege had started he had been only yards away, on the phone to the restaurant. His booking had just been confirmed when frightened politicians began running past, their eyes bulging in fear, their footsteps rattling across the mosaic floor. He didn't join them. Harry, as he had done all his life, went instinctively in the opposite direction. Perhaps it was arrogance, a desire never to be part of the herd, or simply a natural curiosity, but whatever it was had helped make him one of the best fighting men the British Army had ever had, and once again his instinct kicked in. Even as others fled past, Harry moved towards the sound of gunfire. He watched the three cleaners grappling with the heavy Pugin doors, forcing them closed and locking them before splitting up to stand guard on the doors at the side of the chamber. Harry followed one of them, still fighting against the tide of fleeing MPs, until he was standing within touching distance of the gunman. The cleaner didn't notice him; his concentration was fixed on those in front, not on Harry behind. That made him vulnerable and a dark, ugly emotion gripped Harry, urging him to take the bastard out; it wouldn't take much, a forearm round the throat that would lift him off his feet, the gun up in the air, a simple wrench of his neck. It would be a quick, noiseless killing, just as Harry had been trained to do, and had done before. But Harry couldn't win, not on his own, so instead he studied the man for as long as he could, his dress, his weapon, his body language, his face, even his hairstyle. Know your enemy, down to the last button. Then Harry moved on.

Three minutes later, as the doors beside the throne were opened to allow the non-essential players to leave, Harry was there, hiding in the mêlée, watching those who stood guard on the doors, measuring them up. He took in all he could, at close quarters, until, without warning and with people still trying to flood through them, the doors were slammed shut.

12.00 noon.

Not even the deep tolling of Big Ben could drown the cries of desolation that rose from those still trying to leave. They thought they'd been promised safety, passage to freedom, but the word of a terrorist was not to be trusted.

And, as the great clock struck the hour, another voice was raised in despair. The Prime Minister, John Eaton, saw the one thing he feared the most, and let forth a pitiful groan.

Eaton was in his early sixties, almost elderly by the standards of an age that worshipped youthfulness, but the silver highlights at his temple suited him and there could be no doubting his experience. He knew where most of his colleagues had buried the bodies from their murky pasts, and precisely when to resurrect them. He controlled the political machine with a combination of many favours and a few judicial threats, being generally content to let his younger colleagues fight out the details of government policy amongst themselves while he gave the impression of rising above it all.

Yet, like many before him, John Eaton had been driven to seek public office by private shame. It was a way of covering up, of burying disgrace, and where better to bury the past than from behind the desk in Downing Street? It was a surprisingly common practice; Winston Churchill had been driven by the failure of his father, Harold Macmillan by the fact that he was a long-time cuckold, not even certain about the paternity of children he claimed as his own, while Tony Blair – well, historians were still arguing whether there was any private shame of his that might match the shame that had been heaped on him in public since his departure.

Eaton's sense of humiliation was not a grand one by the standards of his predecessors. It was a sordid little thing, intensely private, nothing he should have felt guilty about, but when you are raised in a household with an abusive father who beats his wife when he gets drunk and then beats her again in order to sober himself up, it's the children who tend to blame themselves, for being the cause of it, for not being able to make it stop. Eaton had spent a childhood squirming beneath the sheets, trying to stuff his ears and drown out the sounds of violence, and he'd resolved that when he grew up he'd never be so powerless again. He had run away from home at sixteen, and hadn't stopped running until he'd reached Downing Street.

His lack of commitment to the higher reaches of political philosophy wasn't necessarily a weakness; it meant that he leaned heavily on his skills of presentation, honed early as a child in order to avoid the beatings dished out to his mother, and his well-groomed age gave him an appearance of maturity that he could use to intense and occasionally even comic effect, playing everyone's uncle, the father of the nation. If a fact or figure slipped through his fingers at the Despatch Box, he sometimes blamed it on the fading memory of a man who had done so much more than he remembered, at the same time always making sure to remember so much more than he had actually done. It made his opponents seem juvenile and petty. And if John Eaton liked a drink, he wasn't the first. Thatcher loved her whisky, while Churchill claimed to have drunk half a bottle of champagne for lunch every day of his adult life, declaring that he took more out of alcohol than alcohol ever took out of him. Yet, with the cases of both Winston Churchill and John Eaton, on occasions the race against alcohol was a damned close-run thing. Something of the Eaton father had been passed down to the son no matter how hard he tried to escape.

Another thing Eaton shared with Churchill was the fact that he had only one son. Wanted more, but it wasn't to be, so Magnus wasn't joined by Minimus or Minima or any other offspring. The result was that Eaton poured all his frustrated affection on to his son, loved him ferociously, intent on building for the boy the sort of life that had been denied to him. He did everything to protect the boy, sometimes went too far, to the intense annoyance of Magnus, but, if it were a fault, he told himself it was so very much better than being a drunken failure of a father.

Yet now, as Eaton made his way under gunpoint from the Bar to the other end of the chamber, he found his darkest fears come to life. He saw his son. As the implications hit him, he began to lose control. His knees would no longer carry him, for a moment he buckled, needed the support of others, but he was a seasoned oak and quickly recovered his poise, at least on the outside. But this was unlike any other storm he had known, and it was growing still more ferocious. He quickly came to realise that his initial fears had merely scratched the surface. It wasn't only Magnus they had caught, as terrifying as that was; the attackers had also taken the son of the US President and the son of the Queen. They had their hands not only on the most powerful people in the country, but also on the children of three of the most significant people in the world. Why? What was their purpose? This surely couldn't be chance. As his tumbling thoughts began to fall into some sort of coherence, they started to form a picture of horror that grew more vivid and cruel with every moment that passed. He slumped into his seat before his knees betrayed him once more; inside, John Eaton was screaming with terror.

12.03 p.m.
There were now less than eighty hostages remaining in the chamber. Their captors arranged them so that they were seated at the southern end, near the throne, where they could be watched more easily. This crowding together of bodies would also ensure that any firefight would inflict the maximum number of casualties. The attacker wearing the suicide jacket was standing behind the throne, which

gave him excellent cover and kept him only inches away from the Queen. Yet still the attackers acted quietly, almost courteously, given the extraordinary circumstances.

An uneasy calm descended. There were those who still prayed it was some sort of hoax, or tried to convince themselves that they had been caught up in the mother of all security drills – the desire to survive is unquenchable and grasps at the thinnest of reeds. Then John Eaton rose in his seat. He didn't know if he was physically a brave man, the matter had never been put to the test, but he was ashamed of his earlier show of weakness and he knew what was expected of him. He had to test the mettle of the enemy, even while he was testing his own. He stared directly at the young attacker standing on the steps of the throne.

'Who are you? What do you want?'

'Ah, Mr Eaton,' the gunman began, smiling. 'I hope your knees have recovered.' It was a cruel jibe and Eaton wanted to throw it straight back at him, man to man, just as he was used to in Parliament, but he wasn't a fool. He bit his lip. The young attacker had already won their first round. 'My name is Masood,' he continued. 'And you ask me what I want. I want three things. First, very simply, the television coverage must be restored. I want what happens here to be witnessed in every part of the world. We have nothing to hide.'

'Sadly, I don't control the BBC,' Eaton responded, trying to cast a net of lightening humour. 'Even you must know that.'

'At this precise moment you control nothing at all, perhaps not even your bladder. But you see, Mr Eaton, I think I am more powerful than you, more powerful than even the Prime Minister of Great Britain. I can persuade the BBC. I feel sure they are listening to us. And if the cameras in this chamber aren't working in sixty seconds and the television coverage restored, something – how shall I put this? – something quite unpleasant will happen.' He pointed to the blank monitors set high in the chamber. 'I want these screens back in action and showing us what the rest of the world is seeing. In sixty seconds. Or else.'

'Or else what?'

'Or else you might die, Mr Eaton.' The young man laughed, but it hit a false note. He was nervous, too, yet his hand was steady as he raised his assault rifle and pointed it directly at the Prime Minister. He began examining his watch.

Twenty seconds had already passed before Daniel, cocooned in his OB van, realised that the world was waiting upon him. He was the last link in the BBC chain. He had cut off the broadcast; he was the only one who could reinstate it. And the digital clock was ticking. He shook himself out of his daze and began staring at his phone, waiting for it to ring with instructions from any of a huge number of more senior BBC executives who might take the weight of responsibility from his shoulders, but the bloody thing remained ominously silent. No one was willing to lift the burden from his shoulders. Another fifteen seconds passed, and the next five seconds were filled by the young attacker reminding him they were running out of time. 'What do I do?' Daniel demanded in despair of his colleagues; no one had an answer or would catch his eye, and he knew there was nothing in the BBC's Producer's Guidelines that would save his hide. His head began to throb, he thought he was getting another one of his nose-bleeds – pity's sake, not now! Blood. Pain. Confusion. Despair. The only thing Daniel could be certain of was that he was on his own. The decision was to be his.

With less than ten seconds to go, he gave the instruction. They began broadcasting once more.

As the large screens in the chamber flickered back into life, Masood smiled once more. He had won another victory. 'Excellent. You see, Prime Minister, it wasn't so difficult after all.'

'What else is it you want?' Eaton demanded impatiently, desperately trying to regain a little of the initiative.

'What else? Ah, yes. I want Mrs Willcocks.' He looked around the chamber. 'I would like Mrs Tricia Willcocks to step forward, please.'

12.07 p.m.

Until two years ago Harry had been the minister at the Home Office, one of the senior briefs in charge of police and security matters. It was a role only one step away from the Cabinet itself, until he had dared to disagree with his Secretary of State in public. The Secretary had made a particularly woolly speech embracing multiculturalism and the melting pot; the following day, in an unscripted and uncharacteristically unguarded moment, Harry had responded that the quickest way for a nation to lose its will to live was to lose its roots. Just like an army needed to know what it was fighting for, he said, so a nation needed to know what it stood for. He followed up by suggesting that you couldn't build paradise on platitudes. Harry was the sort of man who always followed up. Stripped of the coded language used in Westminster, it was like throwing a bucket of ice water over his boss. That was unwise. Nobody could accuse Harry of being unfit for purpose, but it was made clear to him that he was no longer wanted on voyage, so before they made it official and asked him to creep out the back door, Harry had stridden out of the front door and quit. Melanie had been upset; she enjoyed the glamour of being a Minister's wife, the invitations, the attention, the coverage she'd begun to get in the *Tatler*, and the annual trips to Davos. The *Mail on Sunday* had even asked if she'd like to write an occasional travel column. She'd been too busy at the time to accept, but it was flattering to be asked – except they didn't ask any more, not since Harry had jumped ship. Perhaps that was where it had started to go wrong, he sometimes thought. She did so love the spotlight, sought it out, like a moth, or an exotic dancer. Yet his ministerial experience had left Harry with many things – an understanding of how the system worked, and a list of names and telephone numbers that was still able to open many doors, friends who were still at the heart of things. Now he used that knowledge. Harry had to report what he had seen, and he knew just the man.

'The Ops Room,' he demanded when the switchboard at Scotland Yard answered. 'Give me Gold.' They hadn't wanted to put him through at first, until he had explained who he was, and where he was calling from.

The Operations Room at Scotland Yard is the heart of their security control system, and Gold is the officer who is its head. Gold, in the person of Commander Mike Tibbetts, a twenty-three-year veteran of the force, was at that moment in his office struggling to cover his dismay as he looked out over an open-plan Ops Room that was wallowing in bewilderment, like a dismasted ketch. They were barely a few hundred yards from the action in the Lords, but they might have been on the other side of the moon for all they knew of what was happening there.

'Harry, long time – too long,' the policeman muttered, dispensing with the niceties, his voice tight as a piano string. 'What the hell's going on?'

'I'm in a corridor. Just along from the chamber. There are eight of them, so far as I can tell.'

'Eight, you say? We've only just got television pictures back and we're still counting.'

'All male, mostly young and fit. These are trained men, Mike.'

'A diplomat amongst them, so it seems.'

'Sent abroad to die for his country. So what are we doing about it?'

There was a well-rehearsed procedure for any siege – isolate, contain, evacuate and negotiate, in the words of the manual – but no matter how well rehearsed it might be, somehow Tibbetts feared this situation might be stretching the jargon to its breaking point. 'SO-15's up and running, CO-19 stood to,' the policeman said, referring to the counter-terrorist command and the armed response unit of the Metropolitan Police. 'They're ready to go. We're pushing the security cordon further back, establishing a stronghold.' He sighed, one of those deep outpourings of frustration that sound like a death knell on a career. 'We're still checking the rest of the parliament building for stragglers and explosives. But mostly it's clear, people couldn't wait to get out. You must get out yourself.'

'In good time, Mike. What about the Boys? Are they in the mix?'

The Boys. The Special Air Service. The most finely honed unit in the British Army, based at Hereford, from where they were called upon to do the dirtiest jobs in the world. They had a reputation for ferocity, adaptability and, when necessary, brutal success. Who Dares Wins. It had been Harry's last active posting before they'd sent him to count paperclips.

'No, not yet,' the policeman responded, revealing his reluctance. So long as this was a police show, he was in charge; once the SAS boys got involved, things had a habit of growing messy. 'There's still a view here that these are guys who have just got lucky and might want little more than the publicity.'

'Mike, these bastards are well trained and extremely well tooled. Kalashnikov assault rifles. Machine pistols. Best there is. You can't buy that sort of thing on the Portobello Road. They're the full Monty. I beg you, don't underestimate them.'

'So who in God's name are they?' the policeman cried out softly in exasperation. 'Arabs? Islamists? Al Qaeda? What bloody hole have they crawled out from?'

Harry leaned his forehead against the deep wood panelling of the corridor trying to round up his drifting thoughts. 'Not so much a hole as a complex of caves, I suspect. Somewhere in the mountains of the North West Frontier. They'll be Pashtun, Baluchi, something like that, not the rag-tag mob of the Islamic international brigade – from what I've seen of these guys, close up, they're remarkably similar. Same physiognomy. I've seen something like that before . . .' He began rhythmically banging his forehead, like a drumbeat calling his struggling thoughts to order, but they shuffled along at their own pace for a while; memories of his briefings on active service in Iraq, fragments from his researches in the clandestine corridors of Oxford. Suddenly they had all lined up together. 'Mike, I think I may have got it! I know who these bastards are. And if I'm right, I can guess what they want.'

Yet from the end of the phone there was no sound of enthusiasm, not even of enquiry, only an exquisitely painful silence. It was a few moments before the other man spoke. The piano string in his voice seemed to have broken. 'Harry, get over here. Now. You're right, these guys mean business. And I think we're going to need you.' Then he cut the link. He didn't even give Harry the chance to tell him what he knew.

12.12 p.m.

Inside the chamber, Eaton had been confused by the attacker's request. 'She's not here. Tricia Willcocks isn't here,' the Prime Minister said.

'I find that difficult to believe,' the young terrorist responded, looking carefully round the chamber.

'She's indisposed. Ill.' At last he had one over the bloody man, although the consolation was small.

'Ah. A pity. She has quite a reputation. I was hoping to meet her. So which other members of the Cabinet are absent?'

'I have one in China on a trade mission, another is attending the funeral of her father.' Eaton cast around him. 'Other than that, I believe we are all here.'

'Then I would like another female member of the Cabinet to come forward, please . . .' He put his hand to his temple, reaching for his mental list, hesitating over the name. 'Mrs . . . Antrobus. The Education Secretary. Am I right?'

'Why do you want her?'

He spoke slowly, as though talking to a dullard. 'I want to put her on television. Make her famous. But I can't see her, where is she?' he demanded, his eyes probing along the benches. 'I want you to point her out.'

'I'll not hand anyone over to bloody men like—'

He was interrupted by a voice that came from a seat behind him. 'That's all right, Prime Minister.' Marjie Antrobus stood, a tall, willowy blonde who had Norwegian blood in her somewhere. 'No point in hiding.' And she was right. There were only five women in his Cabinet, one was at a crematorium and another still in bed. That left only three.

'Ah, Mrs Antrobus. Please come and join me here on the steps.'

Slowly, delicately, being careful to take her time, for she wasn't a woman to be rushed, Marjie Antrobus picked her way along the row in which she was seated and made her way forward. She was the youngest woman in the Cabinet, with three children of school age, one of them still at nursery. That had seemed to Eaton to be as good a claim as any for being appointed Education Secretary and she had justified his choice, proving both popular and resolute. Not often you could find a Minister who could catch the fantasies of male colleagues yet still do the mother thing. She stepped forward. Her blue eyes held more curiosity than fear as she stood beside the young man.

And that was where he shot her, right between her blue eyes, on the steps of the throne.

Four

Tricia Willcocks came back from a dark pool of oblivion to discover that her head was still throbbing like a drum. Only slowly did she realise that it wasn't as simple as a migraine; at the very limits of her consciousness, out beyond the pain, someone was pounding on her front door. She tried to ignore it, to burrow into her pillows and slip back into comforting oblivion, but the noise was insistent. Whoever it was had no intention of being denied. With curses tumbling from her lips, she pulled aside her bedclothes and slipped into her robe. Shouts came from the front door, calling her by name, demanding her presence. She didn't recognise the voice, male, aggressive, and very strident. She decided it would be prudent not to open the door but to speak to them from behind it and give them a piece of her bloody mind, and she was standing by the panic button and about to let forth when the door seemed to dissolve into splinters and come crashing from its hinges. Standing in the blinding sunlight on her doorstep were shadows that, through her pain, she slowly realised were men in visored helmets, boots and body armour with the most extraordinary array of weapons, every one of which was pointed at her.

'Oh, fuck,' she said. Then she fainted.

12.25 p.m.

Scotland Yard is a monument to the Sixties. The architectural fashion of the time had been for drab concrete mausoleums, and unsurprisingly the Operations Room within it was low-ceilinged and dreary, crammed with old-fashioned communications consoles on the desks and portable fans to push around the stale air. The Ops Room was supposed to be replaced by new hi-tech premises in Lambeth – it had been promised for several years – but still they were stuck here amidst dinginess that reminded Harry of the control room on one of those Soviet-era submarines that had been left rusting in Sebastopol harbour. He arrived from the Lords still a little breathless; he'd run all the way. He accepted a mug of the institutional coffee as he and Mike Tibbetts gazed at the large video wall, watching events relayed by a dozen cameras from vital points around Westminster.

'Now we see if your theories stand up,' the policeman muttered.

'You have any doubts – after that?' Harry pointed to one of the screens where the body of Marjie Antrobus lay draped across the steps in front of the throne.

Slowly, sorrowfully, the policeman shook his head.

There is a special quality to the silence that follows an outrage, when no breath is drawn and the world misses a beat. It's like a tear in the curtain of time, where incredulity smothers the first sparks of understanding. But it doesn't last long, particularly in the City of London. The market traders who sat at their desks couldn't hear the echo of the gunshot that killed the Education Secretary, but no sooner had it died away than a strange fever began to spread across the trading floors. These floors were often the size of football pitches on to which were packed hundreds of young, edgy men and women. A sound began somewhere – no one could tell from precisely what point – and suddenly heads were up, like meerkats sniffing for danger. The noise level began to grow and spread, suddenly the screens that dominated every desk began to flash with red alarms, the open lines that linked them directly to brokers began to scream in unison, and in a single breath it seemed as if everyone was on their feet shouting into several telephones at once, selling equities, derivatives, money market instruments, and sterling, trying to find shelter from the storm. This wasn't yet 9/11, but it might develop into that; indeed, there was already the suspicion that it might be something worse. Soon the markets were tumbling downhill like an avalanche, sweeping everyone before it.

In newsrooms, too, they weren't waiting. The press began a rush to speculation that would grow increasingly lurid with the hours. After all, what was the point in a newspaper reporting news when the BBC had already carried it live and in devastating colour? Almost immediately the speculation was mixed with condemnation, not just of the attackers but also of those who had made their assault possible. The police, the security services and, of course, the politicians. Particularly the politicians, except for Marjie Antrobus, of course, who was already well on her way to sainthood in the view of her obituarists.

Across the country, word spread like leaves scattered by an autumn wind. Housewives watching television called husbands, who spoke to secretaries, who telephoned boyfriends and mothers. Workers returned from the john or sandwich shop to spread the news around the shop floor. Television screens in supermarkets, high streets, pubs, front parlours, main railway stations, even betting shops, were tuned to one programme. Across the country, lunch engagements and business appointments were cancelled, hair-dressers were kept waiting, taxis failed to arrive, congestion in city centres began to grow as drivers missed lights or stopped to listen. It was like an eclipse of the sun. An entire nation stood still, in darkness, waiting.

12.28 p.m.

Masood, still standing over the body of his victim, waved his weapon above his head. 'I hope I have your attention. You will listen, very carefully.'

He looked directly at Eaton, who tried his best to return the stare but it wasn't easy. Inside him a million conflicting emotions were tumbling over each other; fear, shock, astonishment, cruel incomprehension, the overwhelming desire to crawl away and hide. Yet he, of all people, was supposed to rise above adversity and somehow find a resolution. The attention of those around him was fixed on the young gunmen yet, at the same time, the Prime Minister knew they were also looking at him, expectantly, demanding that he do something. Without even realising what he was doing, he rose in his seat.

'Why? Why?' he demanded, breathless with emotion, pointing at the body. 'She was nothing but an innocent woman.'

'This is a world of many martyrs, Prime Minister. The graveyards of my homeland are full of them. Put there by your bombers and your guns, at your instruction.'

'Which is your homeland? What are we talking about? Iraq? Afghanistan? Pakistan?'

'Yes, all those. And many others. Wherever the British government and their American allies have meddled and murdered, all such places we regard as our homeland.'

'But what had she got to do with any of this?'

'She was part of it. Part of your rotten system, your democracy' – he made it sound like a curse – 'that has spread terror throughout my people.'

'She was innocent,' the Prime Minister insisted, his voice bubbling with grief.

'Oh, come, Mr Eaton, let's not debate your warped sense of innocence, nor your ideas of freedom and liberation that have piled the bodies of my people higher than the surrounding hills.

Why waste time? You have only twenty-four hours left.'

'I . . . don't understand.'

In the Ops Room at New Scotland Yard, Harry stiffened. He knew what was coming.

'Daud Gul,' he heard the gunman say. 'Release him. Within twenty-four hours. By noon tomorrow.'

'So, you were right, Harry,' Tibbetts said softly. 'Hit it right on the bloody nail.'

'I so wish I wasn't,' Harry replied.

'You see, I am a reasonable man,' Masood was continuing. 'I make no impossible demand. I even give you time to make your arrangements. More time than your bombers gave my parents and brothers and sisters, Mr Eaton. I want to do a deal. You have my leader. And I have you. We can arrange a swap, a fair exchange. You release him within twenty-four hours.'

'Or?'

'Or? Isn't it clear? Release him, or the hostages here will start to die. Perhaps you, Mr Eaton. Or perhaps your Queen. Perhaps everyone here. We shall see. Inshallah.'

'We don't deal with terrorists!'

'But in my country, you are the terrorists.'

'Ridiculous!'

'Have you forgotten your own history? You sent in your troops to teach us to fight the Russians, then the Taliban, and after that you came looking for bin Laden. And after you arrived, your enemies sent in their killers, too. We asked for none of this, yet because of you, and all the others, we became targets. And when your plans to wipe out all your enemies didn't work, when you found it too hot on the ground, you sent us your bombers, you and your American friends. And in the sights of the bombers, every village became an al-Qaeda stronghold, every roof a Taliban hideout. And you devastated my land, Mr Eaton.'

'We have never deliberately attacked civilians, but in war, mistakes are sometimes made. It's a messy business.'

'And you are soon to find out just how messy it can be.'

'We only ever wanted to get rid of the Islamics and the fanatics; they are your real enemy.'

'We would have been content to deal with them by ourselves, in our own way, as we have always done. We know how to deal with invaders and intruders. But you sent in the bombers.'

They were American bombers, but Eaton didn't think he was in much of a position to draw semantic distinctions.

'Your bombers brought us death, Mr Eaton. They broke our women, our children, our villages. And when we crawled out from under the rubble to bury our dead, you sent the bombers back to strip the meagre plots of land that the mountains give us to grow crops. You tried to starve us into submission.'

'Not you – the Islamics!' Eaton protested.

'You see Mukhtar there?' Masood said, pointing to a colleague. 'Your bombers murdered his crippled mother in her bed. He had nursed her for three years, but did you stop for one moment to ask if she was a zealot?'

The Prime Minister blinked, unable to hold Masood's eye. 'Why are you here?' he muttered.

'Ghulam' – Masood indicated one of the others – 'he is here because in one of your raids you hit a home in which his father was having dinner with three of his brothers. After the smoke had cleared, they found only small bits of those who had been inside. The next day, his mother threw herself to her death in a ravine. And Jehanzeb over there, he is here because three of his brothers fell into the hands of the Taliban. They were tortured because it was thought they had co-operated with you, and the Taliban do not shrink from their task, Mr Eaton, I assure you. When at last two of them had their throats slit and their heads cut from their bodies, it was said they cried out with relief. That is what the third brother told us, when at last they let him go.'

'And you?' Eaton whispered.

Masood raised his palms; they were pale, much softer than the rest of him. His voice grew very quiet. 'I pulled my wife's body from beneath the rubble with my own hands. The bombs had hit her so cruelly that at first I couldn't recognise her. I only knew it was she when I found the body of my baby son beneath her. She had been trying to protect him.'

'I am sorry,' Eaton said in despair.

'I think you will be.'

'I wish—'

'Yes, I'm sure you do. So you will give us Daud Gul.'

'How can I do that? What do you expect while I am held prisoner? I can do nothing while I'm here.'

'Of course you can. Look!' Masood exclaimed, pointing at the screens. 'The entire country is watching, perhaps the whole world. All you have to do is to give the order and the matter is done.'

Eaton looked up and found himself staring at a picture of the scene given by a camera in the distant public gallery. He felt like a puppet on a stage, looking so small and insignificant. 'No one will listen to the word of a prisoner given under duress,' he insisted.

Masood's eyes grew darker. 'And all of a sudden you sound like a campaigner for human rights,' he mocked.

'But what you ask is impossible.'

'Then, because of you, in a little *less* than twenty-four hours now, someone will die.' He turned towards Magnus and William-Henry. 'No, not just someone. Allow me to bring the reality of occupation and terror home to you, Mr Eaton. If Daud Gul is not released, we will start with your son. This time tomorrow he will die. And alongside him, the son of the American President.' He laughed, a cold, dry sound as he stared into the eyes of Eaton and saw the volcanic rush of fear. 'Welcome to the occupation, Prime Minister.'

12.35 p.m.

Tibbetts stood frozen as he stared at the screen. 'You dream about things,' he whispered. 'Nightmares. When it's just you against the Devil and you have nowhere to hide. But I never thought it would come to this.'

'You're not alone, Mike,' Harry responded.

'It's my decision, and mine alone, whether we send armed units in there right now and get the siege over and done with.'

'I don't envy you, my friend.'

'What to do, Harry?' the policeman asked, tearing himself away from the screen.

'Me – I'd get some help. It's too big for you to go in there unprepared.'

'But if I delay, hesitate even for a few minutes, it might only get worse.'

Tibbetts was a man who typically didn't rush things; in his spare time he bred budgerigars, and like every part of nature the birds did things in their own time, nesting, mating, breeding, and dying, too. The police commander was used to being patient, but this situation screamed for Executive Action, sending in his armed officers to storm the place before anything worse happened. Yet if they did that, they would never know if there might have been a better, less bloody way.

'You think we should negotiate, Harry?'

'Sure. Talk as much as you want. But when the talking's all done with, get ready to blow Masood and his chums apart. And to do that, you'll need help.'

Tibbetts knew what Harry was suggesting: sending for the SAS. The stuff of heroics and blood, everything that went against his instincts. That wasn't why he had joined the force. 'Is there no peaceful way out?' he asked.

Harry shook his head.

'You seem quite certain about these men.'

'I am.'

'How so?'

'You ever seen what a two-thousand-pound thermobaric bomb can do?'

It was Tibbetts's turn to shake his head.

'It explodes, it burns, it sucks the oxygen out of the air. It leaves nothing behind, not even a sense of justice. That's what the Americans use on caves, Mike, and that's why I know these men. I know what they've been through. If I were them, I'd probably be doing the same thing myself.'

'What? The same as terrorists?' the policeman demanded, looking up sharply.

'Men we once called terrorists are now running the Northern Ireland parliament and sitting in almost every presidential palace in Africa growing fat on huge amounts of Western aid. So when does a terrorist stop being a terrorist?'

'When politicians forget.'

'You know, Mike, I suspect at the root of it all, these people simply wanted to be left alone in their caves to slit each other's throats and screw each other's sheep, but then the whole world and its wicked mothers spilled in looking for hiding places from the wars in Iraq and Afghanistan, only for the wars to follow them there. Their homeland became a battleground between different groups of foreign bloodletters that didn't leave many sharp distinctions between terrorists and the rest.'

'They're still terrorists in my book.'

'Of course, but what's in a name? Better to deal with the facts.'

'You'll at least grant that they are murderers,' Tibbetts said through gritted teeth.

'So, they believe, are we.'

'You sound as if you sympathise with them!'

'I understand them, that's different. They're highly motivated and exceedingly well armed. That's why I don't think there'll be a thing you can do to stop them, except to blow them away.'

'We could give them Daud Gul.'

'Not your choice. That's high politics. An even messier game.'

'So . . . ?'

'So, as you said, it's down to you.'

Tibbetts stiffened, delayed for a few seconds more, hoping they might last for ever, praying that some miracle would happen or that he might yet wake up from this hideous dream. His fingers went to the knot of his black tie, then strayed to the place above his heart, agitated, unsure. He was blinking rapidly, as though blinded by the sun.

'OK, Harry, you win,' he sighed eventually. 'I'll call in the Boys.'

12.43 p.m.

A transformation had taken hold of Tricia Willcocks. She had come round from her stupor to discover that the hooded attackers who had blasted their way into her house were officers of the Metropolitan Police. For a while she flapped around like a pigeon with a broken wing, unable to concentrate, not understanding. She hadn't seen the siege, knew nothing of it, and even when they told her she didn't believe it. Not until someone turned the television on.

'Don't you understand, Mrs Willcocks?' a policeman was shouting at her, trying to barge his way past the incomprehension. 'You're in charge.'

'Me?'

'Yes, you.'

'But why me?'

'Because you're the only one left.'

She sat on her sofa, head in hands, hair like a besom broom, her robe pulled tight for modesty. She seemed in another world.

'You know what this means?' a policeman turned to his colleague in despair.

He was answered with a dull shake of the head.

'Means we go for the first substitute. The Industry Minister. Little plonker.'

Then her head was up. 'Oh, no you don't! I'm in charge of this so you do as I tell you. Give me five minutes to put on some clothes. Then we start sorting out this mess of yours.' Already she was on her feet and running for the stairs, but halfway up she paused and turned. 'And while you're waiting, get someone to fix my bloody door. Idiots!'

Diego Garcia. A coral island stuck about as close to the middle of the Indian Ocean as one could care to get, more than a thousand miles from the nearest land mass. It's covered in tropical vegetation that goes largely untended since the inhabitants were forcibly moved out. Its average height is four feet and north to south it's only fifteen miles long, a good chunk of which is taken up by a runway that runs for more than two miles. This is a US runway, for although the island belongs to the British, in 1966 they leased the place to the Americans. Since then it has become one of the most important – and most remote – strategic military bases in the world. Its main non-human population are warrior crabs and coconut rats. And it rains a lot.

Diego Garcia is a temporary home to around two thousand US military personnel plus many more support staff. There are also usually forty Brits based there, too, mostly Royal Navy and Royal Marines, to fly the flag and remind the world that, despite all appearances, the place is technically British.

It's a little like St Helena, that other ocean island, where Napoleon had been sent into exile. A million miles from anywhere. Escape impossible.

And that is where they had sent Daud Gul.

1.25 p.m.

She had insisted on sitting in the Prime Minister's chair, the only one around the Cabinet table with arms. The private secretary had tried to dissuade her – 'it might not look seemly, Home Secretary' – but she'd asserted that it would be unseemly to sit anywhere else. After all, she was in charge and *they* needed to know it. Who *they* might be was left undefined, but the implication was that its definition ran far wider than simply the gunmen.

They began to assemble in the Cabinet Room like penguins sheltering from an Arctic gale, looking downtrodden, settling in corners, waiting quietly for the rest to arrive: the representatives from the security services, the armed forces, with appropriate deputies and secretaries in tow, and accompanying them the most senior Ministers left in post at Foreign & Commonwealth, Defence, Transport and Health, the latter in case of a chemical or biological attack. Some brought with them slim files, others merely their wits, and they sat around the coffin-shaped table muttering in low tones. Outside the sun was shining in a clear sky, a wonderful day for a walk in the park. If only.

The last to arrive was Tibbetts. Harry was with him.

'Good afternoon, Home Secretary.' Harry offered a wan smile. It was the first time they had spoken in two years, since Harry had carved her speech on multiculturalism to the bone.

'Who brought him in?'

'I did, Home Secretary,' Tibbetts began. 'Mr Jones has a wealth of experience that has already proved invaluable.'

She glowered, clearly unconvinced. She cast her eye around the table – all men, every one of them. Condescending bastards. All thinking they were superior, belittling her because she was a woman. Well, enough of that. There had been a time when she'd been forced to play their game, but that was in the past. She'd stood on the doorstep of ambition long enough, now it was time to joint the feast.

'I think we'd better start with a situation report,' she said.

Through the thickness of the reinforced window glass, Tibbetts could see a seagull soaring above the parade ground of Horse Guards, playing lazily in the cross winds, lifting, soaring free, and at that moment he would have swapped everything he had with that one bird. Perhaps in another life . . . He cleared his throat and began his tale, of how the parliament building had been evacuated, and how all those inside were now sequestered in the Queen Elizabeth II Conference Centre for debriefing and exclusion as suspects.

'I hear the BBC is screaming blue murder,' she interrupted. 'Apparently their entire presentation team was in the palace, and now you're holding them. They want them back.'

Tibbetts scratched his heads in irritation. 'I think even the BBC might realise that there are other priorities right now than television. They can wait their turn.'

'Really? Can you seriously think that wise, Commander? To antagonise the media right from the start? This is a battle for hearts and minds as much as anything else.'

'I thought it was a battle for the lives of the most important group of hostages the world has ever seen,' Tibbetts replied, a little too starchily.

'Precisely. History will be our judge. And for better or worse, history is usually written by the media. So I'm sure you'll consider releasing them. Very promptly.'

And she had won the first battle. It was a purely symbolic victory, for in truth she didn't give a stuff about any of the BBC crowd, but it was important that she show those around her how she liked to work. So Tibbetts sighed, and carried on with his report. Of how he had stood to the armed police units of CO-19 and put on stand-by the SAS, who were en route from their base at Credenhill, near Hereford, along with the Special Boat Service, who, within the hour, would be patrolling the Thames in the stretches beside the parliament buildings. Helicopter surveillance was already in the air, and they had pushed back the security cordon to establish a stronghold around the Palace of Westminster.

'A case of the horse having bolted, surely,' she muttered loudly to no one in particular. 'Or, rather, kicked his way in,' she added, muddling the metaphor.

It had started. The recriminations. The blame game. Tibbetts was going to need his broad shoulders to accommodate the collection of knives that were likely to be buried in him, up to the hilt.

'Anyway, who are these particular horses?' she asked.

'All of us around this table are digging to find out what we can about the High Commissioner, of course, but if you don't mind, Home Secretary, I'd like Mr Jones to take this one. I think he has some ideas that are well worth listening to.'

Her eyebrows arched; Harry took that as his invitation.

'There's a range of mountains on the border between Pakistan and Afghanistan that is home to some of the most ferocious warrior tribes in the world,' he began. 'It's where many of the al-Qaeda leaders have been hiding out for years, or so we think. The tribes in these mountains go by a host of different names – Pashtun, Baluchi and so on, all stuff out of the Kipling legends, tales of the North West Frontier and Shangri-la – but the bunch I think we're looking for are the Mehsuds – the most fearsome of the lot. They live in an area called Waziristan. It's never been conquered or controlled, not even by the Soviets when they tried, and least of all by the local authorities.'

'It must surely have been part of the British Empire,' she suggested.

'And when our first units went in to do battle with them in the eighteenth century, only one man came back alive.'

'So what makes you think they have decided to come down from the hills and invade Westminster? Why couldn't they be al Qaeda or some of the other Islamics?'

'I saw one of these men up very close, almost eye to eye. It's the way they present themselves. Long Semitic noses and hair that's surprisingly straight – not wavy, like many of the Pakistanis and some of the other tribes, for instance, certainly not crinkled like Arabs. They also traditionally part it down the middle.' They all stared for confirmation at the television screen, on mute, standing in the corner.

'The Leader of the Opposition parts his hair in the middle,' she said, but Harry ignored the political insight and continued.

'It's not just the one thing – I saw several little signs, perhaps insignificant in themselves. Like his teeth are green. They use a type of chewing tobacco – I think they call it *nasvar* or something like that' – the man from MI6 was nodding – 'that leaves deep stains.'

'You were close enough to see his teeth? And you didn't think to do something about him? I thought you had a particularly . . .' she stretched for the right words – 'complicated background in violence.'

'Even if I had succeeded in taking out one, that would still have left seven – and your guess is as good as mine about how they might have reacted. These people are remorseless, hold to Mosaic law.'

Her eyebrow levitated again.

'An eye for an eye,' he explained.

'You seem remarkably well informed.' Somehow it didn't sound like praise.

He didn't explain that he had written a thesis on Islamic terrorist networks for his MLitt at Oxford after he had walked out of the SAS. That had been another stroke of independence that had brassed off his superiors – they'd had plans to send him elsewhere. He could see he was having the same effect on the Home Secretary.

'And I suspect that if we dig into the background of Daud Gul, we will find a blood line leading straight back to the caves of Waziristan.'

The MI6 man was nodding again, more vigorously.

'An eye for an eye,' Harry repeated.

'Well, perhaps his ancestry might be of interest to academics, but for the moment we've rather more pressing matters on our hands.' And, as the portrait of Robert Walpole gazed down from above the fireplace, she led the conversation away from Harry. Soon the man from MI5 was suggesting that Masood must have studied in this country. His accent, his command of the language, was all too good to have come from some correspondence course, wasn't it? Computers located in the darkest places within the government system were already scrabbling to find a match for everything they knew and could see of him.

'So why, why' – Willcocks was stabbing her finger into the tablecloth – 'did he call for me? What have I done to merit that?'

Her inference was clear. It was because she was a player, a figure of significance in the global battle against the forces of darkness. Wasn't it?

The enquiry hung in the air, surrounded by silence. Then, eventually, Harry.

'It's because you're a woman.'

'What?'

'The murder of Marjie Antrobus was about as cold and calculated as you can get. Planned – but not personal. Someone was going to die, no matter what, and it was going to be a woman. I think they wanted to show us right from the start that they would kill a woman. Any woman.' He let the idea sit with them for a moment. 'Yes, perhaps even a queen.'

As the thought began to unhinge the confidence of everyone in the room, a side door to the Cabinet room opened and the private secretary's head appeared. 'The President of the United States wonders whether you would be free to take a call in five minutes, Home Secretary.'

She took a breath; it seemed to raise her height an inch or two, then she turned to the men at the table. 'I think we're finished here for the moment. You all know what you should be doing. Please make sure you do it – and rather more efficiently than seems to have been the case to date.'

'In the meantime, what is the answer about releasing Daud Gul?' the man from Five asked.

'We play for time.'

'And not agree to release him?'

'Of course not.'

Yet they all thought they caught the echo of doubt.

As the others filed out, she called to Tibbetts. 'A quick word, Commander.'

When the door was closed, he was left standing; she didn't invite him to sit.

'Get rid of Harry Jones.'

'I beg your pardon?'

'I don't want him here.'

'But—'

'He's not a team player.'

'I'm not sure I agree.'

'Doesn't desperately matter whether you're sure or not. You're scarcely in much of a position to argue the point.'

'I think—'

Her eyes lit up with passion. 'What you think, and did, and failed to do, Commander, will no doubt be listened to in considerable detail by the commission of inquiry once this fuck-up is over. But in the meantime, from this point, I would be grateful if you would do as I ask. Do I make myself clear?' She offered a smile as she said it, but it didn't reach quite as far as her eyes.

He walked out without replying.

2.05 p.m.

Lunchtime. And in the House of Peers, despite the extraordinary succession of shocks that had been delivered to their systems, the needs of normal life were beginning to reassert themselves. They were growing hungry, and thirsty, and, in the case of Celia Blessing, distinctly uncomfortable. It happens, to elderly ladies with bladders.

'What do we do, Archie?'

'We wait, and sit patiently.'

'But I can't. Don't you see, I simply can't.'

Masood and the others had been busy. A chair had been placed behind the throne, on which sat the gunman wearing the explosive jacket. It also became clear what sort of device this was, not one operated by remote control, by any signal that might be blocked, nor by a push-button that might not be reached, but by the simple means of a pull cord. It was rather like that on a parachute. The cord had a ring at its end, and that ring was always either around the wrist of the jacket's wearer or attached directly to the throne. This would ensure that if he were shot or taken by surprise his flailing arm would detonate the device. The same thing would happen if he were blown off his chair or if he were even to fall asleep. So simple. Killing a queen had never been easier.

The other gunmen split into two teams. While one team guarded the hostages, the others secured the entrances to the chamber on the ground floor so that they, like those in the gallery, were blocked with grenades. With the exception of the Pugin doors, these entrances would present no great obstacle to an attacker, but they couldn't be overcome quietly or without destroying the element of surprise, and therein lay disaster for those who wished to protect their monarch.

And, like a bag of discarded rubbish, the body of Marjie Antrobus was dragged to the far end of the chamber.

It was while these preparations were underway that Celia, who was growing increasingly restless, took her chance. She had taken off her robe of scarlet and ermine, which was hot and uncomfortable, and had retrieved her personality, which was formidable. Her grey hair was pinned in a bun behind her head and her cheeks painted in a vivid shade of crimson while, above the eyes, she had gone wild with a palette of green. It was her way, always over the top. She often reminded Archie of a woman in an abandoned geisha house who had been left behind when the twentieth century moved on. Eccentric, outrageous, opinionated, but she was formidable, this old bird, with a voice that might have blown Battersea power station to bits if it had been let loose.

'Give me a hand up, Archie,' she said. 'Old knees getting stiff.' And she hauled herself to her feet, just as Masood was passing by.

'Young man,' she barked.

He turned, eyes ablaze with suspicion, his weapon trained at her.

'What do you propose to do about the necessaries?'

'The necessaries?'

'You know, food. Water. And toilets. Goodness, don't tell me you've forgotten about all these things. If we're going to be here for twenty-four hours you're going to have to do something about it, otherwise we're not going to very much care whether we live or die.'

'Easy does it, old dear,' Archie whispered in alarm, but she was not to be restrained.

'Really, what you seem to know about hostage taking could be written in a tin of treacle!'

Masood stepped forward, wary, like a fox, one paw at a time, watching with bright, alert eyes. 'Sit down, old woman.'

'I'm not old, I'm ancient. Which means I don't give a damn for all your thundering and threats. And I want a bloody loo.'

'*Shut up.* We are busy.'

'I will not shut up. There was a time when I would have required no more than a horsewhip to deal with a man like you.'

'And I need no more than a single bullet to deal with you.'

'What, you'd shoot an old woman in front of an audience of – how many millions' – she wagged her finger at the television screens – 'simply for asking to go to the loo? What's that going to do for the revolution, then, Abdul, or whatever your name is?'

Embers of rage were glowing in his eyes. 'One more innocent victim – what does that matter if we can change the world?'

'Change the world? From here? Don't be stupid, this is the House of Lords!'

She was goading him, in a manner she had perfected over decades of parliamentary debate, deliberately testing him to see how much he would take. Yet it was clear he wouldn't take much more – perhaps she had already gone too far – and she decided the moment had arrived when she should sit down, bladder or no, yet before she could manoeuvre her old hips back into their seat another hostage stood up. It was Robert Paine, the American ambassador.

'Might I suggest to the good baroness that this is perhaps not the best way to achieve her ambitions?' He spoke in the third person, full of formality, deliberately pompous, to deflect the moment. With more than a trace of relief and not a little awkwardness, she regained her seat.

'Sir,' he said, turning to Masood, 'could we at least ask what your intentions are with regard to a little food and water? And the other matters the baroness referred to?'

In reply, the young man smacked the stock of his weapon into the ambassador's belly and sent him retching to the ground.

2.17 p.m.

'Brave man, the ambassador. Not sure I'd have the balls to do that,' Tibbetts remarked as he and Harry drove away from Downing Street. They were watching events on small screens built into the back of the seats in the policeman's official car.

'But look, he's won.'

Even as they spoke, Masood was gesticulating at the camera and making demands for food, water, yes, two chemical toilets and a secure field telephone. He probably had intended to do all this in any case, but it marked a new phase in the situation.

'Our chance. Now we can start talking!'

At the heart of every successfully resolved hostage scenario is the ability to negotiate. To talk. To discuss, to deceive, to compromise, to wear down, to come to an understanding. Yet without dialogue, there is little to deal with but despair. Already Tibbetts was on his phone, issuing instructions. When he had finished, Harry reached over and grabbed his arm.

'Mike, let me take the kit in.'

'Can't let you do that, Harry. You should know better than to ask. You're a civilian now – worse, a bloody politician.'

'You send in a young policeman or a soldier and they're likely not to be coming out again, Mike. We're already seen what Masood's like.'

'And you?'

'The advantage of a few grey hairs. I don't represent a threat.'

'The Home Secretary thinks you do. She's told me to get rid of you.'

'All the more reason to keep me in the loop.'

Tibbetts sat quietly for a moment, debating the matter with himself.

'Of course, Mike, you send me in and you'll probably lose your job,' Harry added. 'But the way I see it, most of the senior coppers in London'll be out on their arse after this, anyway.'

The policeman remained silent, his heart churning as they drove through the silent, emasculated streets of his beloved London. He didn't speak until they were on the ramp that led to the underground car park in the Yard.

'You got clean underpants, Harry?'

'Why?'

'It's just that Masood's no fool. I think he's going to require you to strip.'

2.20 p.m.

It was, for some, a remarkable thing to have chosen a woman to become the President of the United States; it wasn't the norm, some thought it a huge mistake, but America was going through one of those intermittent bouts of introspection when it stood back, confused as to what it stood for and where it was headed. The American paw had got itself burned by being thrust into the fire of too many foreign adventures and, little by little, hoping that no one would notice too much, it was withdrawing, in pain.

That's what had won her the election, the promise that there was a better way forward, that they should move on, for America to 'come back home', in the words of her election campaign. It had won the day and now, little by little, corps by corps, their boys were being brought back. America first! She'd also been helped by the fact that most had seen the race for the White House as a choice between a black, a woman and a half-screwed religious nut, so they had embraced the traditional virtues of middle-American motherhood in the person of Blythe Elizabeth Harrison Edwards. She had many advantages. She spoke Spanish, treated all foreign leaders to a splash of mint julep and suspicion, had never started a war and had never been caught indulging in extramural sex, all of which helped. As a baby she'd also been photographed bouncing on John Kennedy's knee, which gave her campaign the blessing of Camelot.

Not that she was an outsider. Her money was old money, which meant there was no ambitious prosecutor trying to lift her petticoats, and she didn't have to raise her voice to be heard. She was a soft-spoken, a girl born in California who had an accent that had been polished in many places along a route that stretched from the sororities of Vassar College to the slopes of Gstaad. Her pedigree included a lot of lawyers, a bit of Mormon and, from way back, William Henry Harrison. He was a Civil War hero and Indian fighter who had got himself elected president and went on to deliver an extraordinarily overblown inaugural address in the middle of a biting storm. It turned out to be the longest inaugural address in American history – and the shortest presidency. William Henry succumbed thirty days later to the pneumonia he had contracted on the steps of the White House. His grandson, Benjamin, also became president, and admitted more states to the Union than any president apart from George Washington, but otherwise his career was undistinguished and he wasn't re-elected. It had left a legacy of frustration within the Harrison family that the new president felt most keenly and was intent on putting behind her. She had named her only child after the first president, and hoped that in his time he might become the fourth. The wind of history had always ruffled the Harrison hair, but it had turned to a seething storm when she had been woken in the White House by a phone call to tell her that William-Henry had been taken hostage. She had dressed, summoned her security advisers, said a prayer and put a call in to Downing Street, all in less than three minutes, but it had taken the British almost an hour to find someone she could talk to, Tricia Willcocks, a woman she had never met and knew very little about. She had plenty of time to express her frustration and for her fears to grow before they put her through.

'Madam Home Secretary,' she began, very formally, 'may I firstly express my relief that you personally have escaped this terrible situation. Let's hope that God is smiling on us today.'

And His blessings came in most peculiar ways, Tricia thought. She hoped no one had let on that she was still in bed when the attackers had struck.

'You can imagine my distress,' the President continued. 'What is happening?'

'Let me assure you we are doing everything that it's possible to do, Madam President,' Tricia replied, a little breathless. Despite the circumstances she was feeling exhilarated, as though in talking to the most powerful person on the earth she had stepped through a door and found herself in a world reserved solely for gods and titans. She began to talk about armed police units and strongholds and the SAS, all the details that had been passed on to her by Tibbetts and the others. As she did so it began to grow on her that, given the situation, they were remarkably thin. The moments of silence on the end of the phone suggested that the President thought so, too.

'I have, of course, asked all my intelligence agencies to do everything they can to assist you, Madam Home Secretary. What else can we do for you? Hostage negotiators, electronic surveillance equipment, weapons, personnel. I can have anything you want there with you in hours. You have but to name it and it's yours.'

'That is kind of you, Madam President, but . . . I think for the moment we have the situation under control. No one can get in or out of the building.'

'The terrorists seem to have gotten in.'

Willcocks bit a fingernail, trying to pretend she didn't feel the full impact of the remark. 'No one could conceive they would try anything like this, any more than you could have predicted 9/11.'

'I want to press you a little, if you don't mind. I have a very fine relationship with your Prime Minister, I am such a great admirer of his, and I feel sure we would be of one mind . . .'

She was using muscle, trying to pull rank, patronising her, implying that Tricia didn't belong in this super-powered world of hers. The magic of the moment was fading for Tricia, turning everything sour. A shard of chewed fingernail fell helplessly to the baize tablecloth.

'We have to stand side by side,' the President was continuing. 'Help each other out here. I'd like there to be some American presence beside your men to show the world we are united on this.'

Was she trying to suggest the British weren't up to the job, that she didn't fully trust them, Willcocks wondered? 'I appreciate your concern, Madam President, and I fully understand how you must be feeling, but I think an active American presence at this stage would be a little premature. Could lead to confusion, even make things worse in the eyes of the terrorists.'

'How much worse can things get there, Madam Home Secretary?' the President retorted.

'This has to be a British operation – for the moment, at least. It's our queen, our parliament building that's been taken hostage.'

'My ambassador, too – and my son!' The voice was tight, close to breaking.

'I will of course keep you fully informed of everything we're doing.'

'I'm watching it all on television – right now.' There was a noticeable catch in her voice. It was time to end the call, for both their sakes.

'I wish we could have met in happier circumstances, Madam President.'

But the other woman was gone. To hide her tears, and perhaps her rage. Damn. That hadn't gone very well at all.

3.17 p.m.

'You go in and out, no tomfoolery, just do the job, you understand?' Tibbetts said.

'Of course.'

'We need information, not heroics.'

'Yessir. Sure thing.'

The policeman sighed. 'And I'm teaching one of the oldest and meanest street dogs in the business to suck eggs.'

'You carry on like that and you'll sound just like the Home Secretary.'

'Promise me one thing, Harry. Before that happens – shoot me.'

They were walking briskly to the parliament buildings from Scotland Yard, which lay just beyond the new stronghold zone. Tibbetts wanted to see the scene first hand, and chose to go by foot – it would take only minutes longer and would give him the opportunity to blow fresh air through his troubled mind, but still the commander's official car prowled along a little way behind, just in case.

As they approached the cordon that now blocked off Victoria Street where it entered Parliament Square, an armed policeman saw them coming, and saluted as he drew back the metal barrier.

'That's how they did it, Mike,' Harry muttered.

'Did what?'

'That's how the terrorists got in. Sloppy security. People taking identities for granted. You know, not even I had to show my pass this morning – and you know what a street dog I am.'

'Everybody inside that place had been vetted. They'd have had to show a pass.'

'Look, let's pull the pieces together. We know how the High Commissioner got in, but what about the others?' Harry's pace seemed to stretch out with his thoughts and the commander was forced to skip to keep up with him. 'We know some of them were masquerading as cleaners – or, more accurately, probably *were* cleaners. Employed by the private firm that's responsible for sweeping up round much of the Houses of Parliament. We Brits are too posh to do our own dirty work nowadays, so these cleaners can come from all over the world; some are political refugees, most of them on minimum wage, the meanest jobs in London. Be easy enough to slip three more into the system, wouldn't it, given time and a little planning? They wouldn't even need to speak decent English.'

'Mother of God.' The policeman groaned as the weight of understanding began to pile up on his shoulders. They were passing beneath the shadow of Westminster Abbey, now silent, its queues of tourists scattered, the blood-red remembrance poppies abandoned on the field.

'And the others –' Harry continued, pounding his forehead as he continued pouring out his thoughts, 'well, they probably stole someone else's pass. You know what a ludicrous system it is. They're only paper passes for the State Opening, cards with someone's name written on them. Lovely calligraphy, bloody useless security. You wave it around, show it to security, dig into your pocket or purse for a forged photo ID or passport with the same name on it – and how much would a false set of documents set you back, fifty quid from the local dealer? Hell, underage teenagers order them from the bloody Internet so they can go drinking or get into clubs. Don't you see, Mike? A bit of paper with a name on it and one forged ID. That's all it would take. Then you're guided by some trusting soul in a uniform all the way up to your reserved seat. And there's a whole commonwealth of colours in there, so a few extra dark faces would never stand out.'

Tibbetts was growing breathless; perhaps the walk hadn't been such a good idea. 'Slow down a bit, for Christ's sake. That's all very well, in theory. But what would happen when the real pass holder turns up?'

'They won't.'

The policeman came to an abrupt halt and closed his eyes in pain. 'Oh, God. More bodies.'

Five

3.23 p.m.

THERE WAS STILL MORE THAN half an hour to go before the London Stock Exchange was due to close, but this was like nothing they had ever experienced, worse than 9/11, far worse than Black Wednesday.

They had struggled hard to reach the end of play, to pretend that it was just another day, but it wasn't. The collapse was unstoppable, and those that tried to resist were simply crushed beneath it. Traders were slipping in the blood that was swilling about the floor. It was an abattoir.

So the Exchange was shut early. That had never happened before. Impossible, so it seemed, but no more incredible than what was going on in that other city down the road, in Westminster.

It was like the foundering of a great merchant ship off the shores of ancient Devon. Those who could, jumped for safety. Those who tried to swim against the tide disappeared and drowned. And as the ship sank, surrounded by the sounds of the storm and the cries of its victims, its precious cargo was washed overboard, to float on the stormy sea until it found its way to a safer shore, and into other hands. The hands of the wreckers.

3.39 p.m.

Tibbetts had been right; they made Harry strip to his underwear, singlet and shorts. He was floating on adrenalin, senses alert, just like the old times. The touch of the old tiled floor on his feet was exceptionally cold but that was nothing to a man who had been trained at immense public expense to withstand sub-Arctic conditions – although, as he admitted quietly to himself, that had been years ago. Yet the sight of a loaded muzzle held by an enemy and pointed directly at his heart still set him ablaze with expectation. Yes, *just* like old times. He pushed his way into the chamber through a door that had been disarmed, its can of Coca-Cola hanging seemingly innocently by a wire, to find himself confronted by two of the gunmen, their weapons raised. Their eyes didn't leave him, testing, molesting him. He didn't return the stare but kept his head lowered in submission, hoping he had enough flecks of grey in his hair to convince them that he didn't look like a soldier. His hairstyle was no longer short and militaristic but fashionably irreverent – he had Mel to thank for that. He prayed they wouldn't instruct him to strip off his singlet, since beneath it they would discover not hidden weapons but a lurid scar along his back and side where the Iraqi bullet had passed. That would give the game away. Normal people don't walk around with bullet holes in them, not north of the river.

Harry was pushing a large supermarket trolley loaded with assorted sandwiches, bottles of water and juice, and supplies of fruit. There was also a box of confectionery. The haul had been provided, in something of a hurry, by the nearby supermarket in Victoria Street, but not in so much of a hurry that the manager hadn't found time to secure his shop's logo prominently on the trolley's side. However, not being entirely tactless, he had refrained from throwing in any cans of Coca-Cola.

'Where do you want me to leave it?' Harry asked the men behind the guns. 'I've got to go back for another load.'

'Middle of the chamber,' one of them said, gesticulating. 'And no tricks.'

And the game was on. In a matter of seconds Harry had established that more than one of them spoke English, which might prove useful intelligence. As Harry and his trolley ventured further into the chamber, he discovered more. Two of the attackers were already resting, stretched out on the leather benches. So, six on, two off. They were rotating duties, ensuring they remained alert. Clever. They clearly expected this siege to last. And those on guard had taken up excellent firing positions. These men knew their business.

And they didn't touch the food or water, not for the moment, at least. They inspected the packages, making sure they contained only food, then threw them to their hostages. It would be a couple of hours before they would take any food themselves. They were being cautious, letting others try it out first, making sure it wasn't drugged.

Many of the hostages knew Harry, of course, and that recognition lit a little beam of hope in many faces, yet their dreams soon faded. They'd been expecting a regiment of heavily armed rescuers to come storming in, not one man in his underwear pushing a supermarket trolley.

As the food distribution continued, a voice raised itself in complaint.

'The loos. We need the loos,' Baroness Blessing demanded.

'Shut up!' barked a guard.

'Look, shoot me if you must, but if we don't get toilet facilities soon there'll be more mess around here than if you hit me with every bullet in your barrel.'

'They'll be here soon. Next trip,' Harry said, anxious to defuse the tension. 'Along with the communication gear,' he added, for the benefit of the guard. Even as he spoke, the finishing touches were being put to the installation of a mobile telephone exchange that had been wheeled into the tiny post office that stood to the side of the Central Lobby, little more than fifty yards away. It was manned by a telephonist and four heavily armed policemen. Elsewhere in the Palace of Westminster, armed policemen were taking up positions at all the major points, but none close enough to be seen or heard from within the Lords.

It was during the inevitable diversion of Harry's arrival that the Prime Minister used the opportunity to whisper urgently to his son, who was seated in the row of benches behind.

'Magnus, listen to me. When he comes back with the toilet gear, take your chance. Slip out, duck down behind the benches. I'll try to distract them.'

'But they'll shoot me, Dad.'

The father choked. What could he say? They both knew the situation. The gunmen were probably going to shoot the boy anyway.

'You have to try, Magnus! Make a run for it, while the door's disarmed and they're distracted.'

Magnus turned towards William-Henry but the father grabbed at him. 'On your own, son. It's the only way. You can't take anyone else, just can't. That'll only double the chance of you getting spotted.'

Magnus looked intently at his father. The older man appeared to have changed, in small but significant ways. The tie was crooked, the hair was uncharacteristically unkempt, and the eyes had the edge of an alarmed horse. As he took this all in, the son's own features seemed to harden. He shook his head in refusal.

'Magnus, you must!' the father pleaded.

'Dad – I can't.'

The father gripped his son's wrist in torment, desperate to persuade him. His words came haltingly. 'Magnus, I haven't been the best father, I know that. I've not always been there when you needed me. Too many distractions, too much pride – too many other people's troubles to take care of. Neglected you, my only son. My fault.' The grip on Magnus's arm grew tighter. 'But I'm here now and I have never meant anything more in my life when I say that I would willingly trade my life for yours. A happy exchange. I would die with a smile on my lips. You are twenty, for pity's sake, you've got your whole life waiting out there for you. You've got to fight for it. Run for it, if necessary.'

'Dad, if I go, they will shoot someone else.'

'But you are the only one who matters!'

'I couldn't live with that on my conscience. The rat that ran.'

'You'd be a live rat.'

'Dad, you send soldiers my age to risk their lives all the time.'

'They are not my sons.'

'I'm as good as they are.'

'So very much better.' He twisted in his seat, trying to draw closer. 'Oh, this is hell!'

'I'll take my chances here, Dad.'

'Run now, I beg you,' the father groaned.

'If I did, I couldn't respect myself. And you would grow not to respect me, either.'

'Magnus, don't torture me! I can't sit here and watch—' The thought choked itself off. The next words came in a gasp. 'I love you.'

Magnus sat still.

'I love you,' the father repeated, almost in a whisper.

The son appeared strangely unmoved by the outburst. 'I think that may be the first time you have ever said that,' he said.

'You've always known it.'

'A life spent talking to the whole world, but not to me.'

The father hung his head, his silence dressed in guilt.

'If you love me,' Magnus continued, 'for once in your life listen to me.'

'But—'

'Listen! Stop worrying about saving me. Do your job, save us all.'

'How?'

'Give them Daud Gul.'

3.56 p.m.

Harry returned. He had with him the field telephone and two pallets on which were carried loos that had been hurriedly wrenched out of a construction site's transportable toilet system. It was as he was installing them, with some difficulty, that matters began to stumble out of control. Perhaps it was the food that had given the hostages back a little confidence, or the sight of Harry letting them know they hadn't been forgotten, or simply the fact that so many of them were elderly, or brave, or slightly daft and didn't give much of a damn. Maybe it was force of habit, or simple terror that bent their judgement. Whatever its cause, the hostages began to argue absurdly amongst themselves. About, of all things, the toilets.

Set into the structure of the great gilded canopy that stands immediately behind the throne there are two compartments that are largely hidden. Those who are keen-eyed enough to notice the two doors assume they must be of considerable significance – a private exit from the chamber, perhaps, or a security tunnel that might whisk the Queen to safety, or carry in her rescuers. But that is not the case. The secret of the doors is known to a relative few, because it is so totally banal. Behind the doors that stand next to the throne lie neither tunnels nor stairs nor rescue apparatus, but two large closets, stout and deep, within which are hidden not state secrets but a cleaner's paradise of buckets, mops, brushes and brooms. It might have been a private joke played by Sir Charles Barry, the embittered architect who had designed the chamber. Ministers had left so many of his unpaid invoices drifting around the place that perhaps he viewed the servants cupboards so close to the Queen as suitable punishment for their miserliness. But whatever their origins, it was here inside these two cupboards, that the attackers instructed Harry to place the chemical toilets. It afforded a small measure of privacy. Even those who might be about to die had their modesty.

And yet as soon as they were installed, a furious quarrel broke out. From somewhere amongst those huddled on the red benches a voice was heard suggesting that one of these compartments should be reserved for the Royal family. The monarchy needed to maintain its mystique, so it was argued, and the House of Windsor needed its own closet, too.

'What? We're going to have discrimination in the toilets – in *here*?' another voice broke out.

'If we ignore what makes us British, we may just as well be like them.'

'God's teeth, we're fighting for our lives, not some ridiculous form of *droit de seigneur*.'

'Look, if it weren't for *droit de seigneur* you wouldn't be in the House of Lords in the first place.'

'Right now I rather wish I wasn't.'

'It's a matter of respect. It's what made this country great.'

'And got us into this mess. Frankly, I'd swap all your wretched social baloney for a sunny day in Sunderland.'

'Sod Sunderland!'

At least, that is what legend would later record as the final contribution to this debate, but this might have been apocryphal since, in truth, no one could have heard what the last words were, not above the sound of gunfire. While disagreement had been breaking out on all sides, the hostage takers scarcely knew what to do or in which direction to turn. Theirs was not a parliamentary way, they didn't understand its occasional silliness and eccentricities, and what was not understood was feared. They raised their weapons in alarm but the flow of argument didn't ebb, not for a second, not until their young leader Masood fired his weapon into the gallery above their heads.

It was at this juncture, as the smell of hot gun oil hung across the chamber, that an act of immense symbolism took place. As hostages ducked and cowered from the bark of flying bullets, Elizabeth, the woman at the centre of this unexpected storm, turned to whisper to her son. Then she rose to her feet. She was a small figure, almost overwhelmed by the Gothic indulgence that surrounded her, but the silence that followed her gesture was as complete as it was sudden. She stood for a while, staring at them all, her captors included, the gaze that could freeze from fifty paces. She unclipped her train, while her son gathered the yards of ermine-trimmed silk and began to fold them into a large cushion, which he placed on the carpeted floor between the two thrones. Then she reached up and took the crown from her head. She handed it to her son, who, with great reverence, lowered himself to his knees and placed the rough emblem on the cushion of silk. The meaning was clear. The crown hadn't been abandoned but it had, for the moment, been put aside. Death, the ultimate leveller, was casting its shadow across them all.

Elizabeth took her seat once more, and when she was settled, nodded in the direction of Celia Blessing. Without a word the blush-faced baroness hauled herself to her feet, curtsied before her queen and, as gracefully as she could in the circumstances, disappeared inside the closet.

4.10 p.m.

So the rules of the game were set. Masood announced that all mobiles, pagers and ceremonial swords were to be handed over. There was to be no communication with those outside the chamber except by himself, while those inside the chamber were to engage in no sudden movements, no surprises, no changing of places or even trips to the toilet without permission. Transgressions would result in retribution, and it had already been made clear what form that would take.

There were conditions for the authorities, too, once the field telephone had been connected to the exchange. Power cuts and disruptions of any sort or for any reason would be treated as the prelude to an attack. Any hint of gas being introduced to the chamber or drugs hidden in the food, anything that might be designed to knock the hostage takers out, would be handled in the same way.

And Masood insisted that the live broadcasting of events within the chamber must continue and be played out in real time. No delays, no breaks, nothing but constant coverage. This was not just a siege, it was a cultural humiliation and he intended that it should be seen by billions around the globe. There would be no hiding place for the authorities, no sudden tricks that could be played out in darkness or behind the scenes. The glare of publicity had always been the rebels' friend, and this the biggest show the world had ever seen.

4.43 p.m.

Tricia Willcocks had at times been likened to a spring tide. Her water levels were always high, forming an irresistible wall of emotion that was bound to create extreme turbulence whenever it encountered something, or someone, standing in her way.

When she reached Tibbetts, he was in the small post office. He had temporarily deserted the Ops Room in order to supervise the installation of the portable telephone exchange and give Harry his final briefing. He wanted to be on hand if anything went wrong, and not be left looking helplessly at a television screen. No sooner had the telephone system been installed and initial contact made with Masood than one of the receivers began to ring. It was the Home Secretary, determined to make her presence felt.

'Commander Tibbetts,' she began, in a breathless manner that shrieked of irritation, 'I thought we had agreed you would get rid of Harry Jones.'

'I apologise, Home Secretary, I thought you instructed me to ensure he stops bothering you.'

'He's bothering me now. I'm told he's right in there with the hostages.'

'Then I'm sorry for your discomfort.' He tried to hide the irony in his tone.

'He's unreliable. He shouldn't be there. No telling what damage he might do. Get rid of him. Is that clear enough for you?'

'Perfectly. But—'

'No "buts", Commander.'

'Then how can I put this, Home Secretary? I'm afraid we can't get rid of Harry Jones. It's too late for that. You see, whether we like it or not, he's now part of our dealings with the terrorists. They know his face, and the more they see it, the more they'll relax in his presence. Perhaps give themselves away. Reveal some little weakness or other. And that's what we desperately need, to find some chink in their armour. Anyway, I think a familiar face reassures the hostages.'

'Are you refusing to follow my instructions?'

He paused, to gather his temper. 'I'm suggesting they make little operational sense.'

'Perhaps we should try to find someone who thinks otherwise, Commander.'

Damn the woman. His tone grew tougher. 'As is your privilege, Home Secretary. But from your point of view, I don't think that would make much operational sense, either.'

'What the devil are you talking about?'

'You start demanding resignations and . . . well, how should I put this? The press are going to start wondering just how far up the ladder the blame game should go. And I think they'll discover you sitting at the top of that particular ladder, won't they?'

'Are you threatening me?'

'Home Secretary, I'm merely trying to point out some of the facts of life, facts that might prove far more uncomfortable to you than the presence of Harry Jones. I've got a job to do and I'd like to get on with it. You want heads on a platter, then I suggest you wait till this is finished. If it all goes pear-shaped you can throw me to the wolves and hope they won't come after you, too. Use me as cover. And if, by some minor miracle, we manage to find a way out of this little shambles . . . well, you're a politician. I'm sure you'll find some way of using it to your credit.'

'I don't like your attitude.'

'You want me to deal with terrorists or take time off for charm school?'

'What sort of bloody-minded policeman are you?'

'One with twenty-three years' experience and with the worst job of his life to do. So I'll do my best to stay out of your hair, Home Secretary, and—'

He faltered. Harry had suddenly appeared at the door of the post office room. He was sweating, bending a little under the weight of his large and unwieldy load.

'And I'll make sure Harry Jones doesn't pitch his tent on your front lawn either. Anyway, he's a little busy right now. Taking care of Mrs Antrobus.'

4.57 p.m.

Eaton was a man who was practised in the art of recovering from those moments of inner insecurity that beset all politicians. He was no philosopher king troubled by deep thoughts; instead, he had built his career on the basis of being a masterful presenter. In politics, he had found, there were always others to tell him and the rest of the world what should be done, but it took a man with the skills of stage management and media manipulation to make those things happen. His politics were, above all else, practical, always capable of compromise, and with a theatrical wave of his hand and a tremble in his voice he could put himself across as a man who cared, and cared enough to do whatever was necessary. It had saved him a dozen times when the ideologues would have preferred him to head straight for the cliff, and now those abilities were needed more than ever. He wanted to save his career, of course, but most of all he wanted to save his son. He knew what he had to do. He smoothed the wayward strands of hair at his temples and rose slowly in his seat.

'Enough. We must put an end to it. It's clear to me what we should do.' He turned to Masood. 'May I?' He indicated the field telephone, a solid military-style piece of apparatus the size of a house brick.

Masood considered, then nodded, but took close position as the Prime Minister raised the receiver.

'This is John Eaton,' he announced. 'Would you please put me through to the Home Secretary . . .' He waited for several seconds while the connection was made; his eyes strayed to his son, who gazed up at him in hope. Then he was through.

'Home Secretary,' he began – he used the title, not her name, he needed this to be formal – 'the situation here is untenable. There must be no more deaths, no more suffering.' He closed his eyes, a father at prayer. 'I am instructing you to make arrangements for the immediate release of Daud Gul. You will report back to me as soon as these arrangements have been made. And you will also make provision for transportation to take his followers here wherever they wish to go in the world. They will leave unharmed. Is that clear?'

Rustles of overwhelming relief began to snake their way along the benches around him; a peeress began to sob quietly with relief. Masood stiffened in expectation. Eaton lifted his head, as though addressing a vast arena, as indeed, beyond the walls, he was. Above him, the last of the evening light was catching on the stained glass in the windows, and seeming to dance in delight. Eaton knew he could put this all behind him, the people would understand. What was one life in exchange for so many, some miserable foreigner traded for the restoration of civilisation and order as the British had known it for a thousand years? God, he so desperately needed a drink, his hand was shaking even as it held the phone, but it wouldn't be long now. He ran his fingers through his hair once more, knowing the eyes of the country – perhaps the entire world, by this stage – were upon him. Some would carp at what he was doing, of course, narrow-minded fundamentalists, the English ayatollahs who would want to flay him for allowing one wild mountain man to run rings round the entire Establishment and damn him for being the officer on watch when it happened, but most would heave a sigh of relief and praise him for his common sense. He had given them back the day, and tomorrow would take care of itself. He glanced across at Magnus once more and allowed himself a smile. His son returned the smile, and nodded in appreciation.

Yet, as Eaton listened, a change came over him. Slowly his face began to melt, as wax does when it is held too near the flame. He didn't move, not a muscle, yet at the same time his entire body appeared to shrink.

Without a further word, he tried to replace the receiver, but couldn't, his hand was shaking too much. His young captor took it from him. Eaton stood staring at his son. His lips moved, but for a while he made no sound. When eventually the words came, they sounded raw, as though each one had been torn from his throat.

'She won't do it!'

'Why?' his son mouthed, bewildered.

'Because of the damned protocol . . .'

It had been thirty years since terrorists had hauled Aldo Moro from his car on the streets of Rome. He was one of the most significant men in Italy, a politician who had been Prime Minister five times and who could expect still more. And now he was a captive. What happened in the ensuing days and weeks rewrote many of the rules for dealing with terrorists, not simply in Rome but across Europe.

The terrorists were members of the notorious Red Brigades, a Marxist-Leninist revolutionary group who insisted they would release Moro only in return for their own leaders who were languishing in gaol. During the course of the next weeks, Moro made several public pleas for his life. He wrote letters to the government that not only begged them to meet the terrorists' terms but which also heaped vicious criticism on the government and its actions in combating terrorism. The government refused to listen. They said the letters were written under duress and didn't represent Moro's true views, that in any event the government were committed to the principle that they would never negotiate with terrorists, for to do so would be to open the doorways to hell. Even the Pope joined the argument, pleading for Moro's life and offering to take his place as a hostage. But it was to no avail. Fifty-five days after he was taken, Moro was found in the boot of a car. He had been shot in the head.

There was, inevitably, an outpouring of sympathy amongst the public across Europe for Moro and his family, but amongst many governments the reaction was starkly different. They had watched Moro trying to blackmail his government into denying their principles and ripping up their policy on how to deal with terrorism. To have succumbed to such demands would have been moral suicide, so they said; catch one minister and an entire country might be held to ransom. Where would it end?

It was a precedent that bothered many, and the British Government decided to launch a pre-emptive strike. Deep within Whitehall, a secret ordinance was drawn up that forbade governments to obey any messages or instructions from ministers held under threat. This self-denying ordinance was never put before parliament or made public but nevertheless it became a central part of the code of governance, and gave ministers not only the excuse but also the duty to take a firm stand. From that point on successive governments committed themselves to the policy that they would never – *must* never, as a matter of fundamental principle – negotiate with terrorists. It was like a blood oath. And it was called the Moro Protocol.

It had lain gathering dust in the drawer for a generation. And it was all that Tricia Willcocks needed to refuse her Prime Minister's instructions.

5.07 p.m.
Eaton was a manipulator of words, a man of mirrors who could reverse images as quickly as he could a car. It had kept him from

digging deep inside himself about most things – his beliefs, his emotions, those inescapable sticking points. He had found himself able to dance around most obstacles and, like a Pied Piper, lead the unsuspecting off in an entirely different direction, yet now it wasn't working. He could no longer skim over the surface of things, he was forced to dig deep within himself, and he found himself lacking. As he confronted himself, his entire being shook. He lost control of his muscles. He sank slowly to his knees, struggling for breath, as Masood towered above him.

'It is what I expected,' the young man said in a calm voice. 'It is what you would have done, I think, in the same circumstances.'

The Prime Minister shook his head, although whether in disagreement or despair wasn't clear.

'That is a pity,' the young man continued. 'It appears they have not learned the lesson – yet.'

'I'll . . . try again,' Eaton sobbed. His hands were shaking uncontrollably.

'But they have not listened to you.' As he uttered the words, Masood raised the barrel of his gun towards the back of Eaton's head. 'So what further use are you?' Masood said as the muzzle reached the nape of his victim's neck. 'None, I fear. Goodbye, Mr Eaton.'

In pain, Eaton twisted his head, looking towards Magnus. 'I'm sorry,' he whispered, 'so very sorry . . .'

5.10 p.m.

Britain had ground to a halt. Even though it was the middle of the rush hour it was later estimated that thirty-six million Britons were watching at that moment, and hundreds of millions in other countries. There was only one camera broadcasting images, situated on a high platform in the public gallery at the far end of the chamber from the throne. Its operator had long since fled along with everyone else who could, but the unmanned equipment gave fair coverage of the area now crowded with hostages, and Daniel wasn't about to upset either the gunmen or his bosses by switching to any other shot. Through the eye of this solitary camera, the world watched.

In the middle of Piccadilly Circus, beneath a huge screen carrying live coverage of the happenings, two Benedictine monks knelt on the cold pavement. Many others joined them; the rest of the crowd stood in silent awe. Trains out of main stations stood abandoned as passengers and crew refused to board, their attention fixed on the news screens. The editor of the *Sun*, seated at his desk at the end of a newsroom frozen in apprehension, began scribbling his morning's simple headline: 'Sacrificed'. A producer in the BBC newsroom bent close to the ear of a young researcher, whispering the name of Spencer Perceval, the last Prime Minister to be murdered. In Downing Street, Tricia Willcocks reached for her glass of water, and spilled much of it on the tablecloth. The London Stock Exchange was closed, of course, but exchanges around the world were still open, and everywhere they began selling sterling and every type of British holdings with ever increasing determination.

It was at this point that a figure rose from the rich leather benches of the House of Lords. 'I think there may be a better way,' his voice rang out. It was Robert Paine.

The young Mehsud looked up. 'The ambassador of the United States of America can have nothing to say that will interest me,' he spat. 'Perhaps you would like to join your friend.'

'I am in your hands,' Paine acknowledged. 'But your leader is in other hands, too. Surely there is room for some deal.'

'What – you believe you can do what the British Prime Minister cannot?'

Paine looked at the broken, trembling man on his knees before them. 'I think so,' he replied softly. 'We Americans allegedly have some influence in these matters.'

'What are you proposing?' Masood asked, curiosity oiling his words.

'I'm not a politician but I believe I have some position here. And some skills. I'm a diplomat. Allow me to do what I am trained for. Let me see if I can bring about a resolution.'

'You misunderstand us badly if you think you can romance us out of our demands.'

'Sir, I see no romance in a muzzle. I know your purpose. I have no reason to deny it.'

'Then what will you do?'

'Let me out of here to talk face to face with those who can give you what you want. Try to persuade them.'

'Let you out? But I have only just captured you, Mr Ambassador,' the young man mocked. 'Let you out to sing like a canary? Or to fly away like some fluttering pigeon? No, I think not.'

'I give you my word. I will return. By ten o'clock tomorrow.'

'The word of a diplomat!'

'You know I must return. You have the son of my President.'

'We do. Yes, so we do,' Masood agreed, nodding ruefully. 'Perhaps we should try your suggestion. But first' – he raised his gun once more – 'I think I will shoot the Prime Minister, just to encourage you in your efforts.'

'No! You shoot him and you show the whole of humanity your word cannot be trusted. You would give me nothing to negotiate with. Shoot him, and I can only assume you would shoot us all. I could not – would not – speak on your behalf.'

'You would barter with me?'

'Your leader in exchange for the lives of everyone here. Isn't that what we're about?'

Masood examined the other man, his eyes wrinkled in suspicion, as though inspecting a mountain ram he had been offered at too low a price by some passing Pathan. Eventually his eyes flickered away to the digital clock behind the ambassador's head.

'Then, Mr Ambassador, you'd better make a start. You don't have too much time left.'

5.44 p.m.

Many people were to play a role on that day. Maria Melo Almeida was one who was about to participate in a minor but, for her, a life-changing way. She was in her sixties but still working to keep her mildly incapacitated and chronically indolent husband in cigarettes and Sky subscriptions. Portuguese by birth, she lived near the flyover in Notting Hill and worked as a cleaner for several people during the week. This day had been spent at a local travel agent's dusting around catalogues and washing up several days' worth of coffee mugs, and after the office closed she decided to pop in on another of her clients whose apartment was on her way home. She bought some milk at the corner store in case he needed it, and a small bunch of flowers with which to brighten his utilitarian living room. He needed help like that, and she liked to add these little courtesies to her job, turning clients into friends. That way they kept her on and she could relax into a routine, otherwise she would end up spending her days sweeping around her wretched husband.

Maria had her own keys to the apartment, which she carried on a large ring along with many others. She let herself in and picked up the newspaper from the hallway floor. Strange, she thought, that he hadn't taken it himself. Perhaps he was having one of his off days, like people confined to wheelchairs sometimes do. She walked into the living room fumbling with milk, flowers, newspaper and the large bunch of keys, and at first didn't notice what was waiting for her. When she did, when she saw what had happened to her client, she let out a piteous scream that reached all the way to Downing Street and left her so emotionally broken it ensured she would never do another day's cleaning for the rest of her life.

6.10 p.m.

'Bob . . . how are you?'

Paine didn't care for the diminutive, usually insisting on the use of his full name, yet it was but one of many indignities he had endured in the last few hours. Anyway, who was he to argue with his President?

'I'm fine,' he said, into a secure phone, but his slight hesitation betrayed the strain.

'You poor man.'

He was sitting in the back of his ambassadorial BMW, near the Cenotaph in Parliament Street, just beyond its intersection with Downing Street. It was inside the security cordon and eerily quiet. A stray newspaper bowled along the gutter, pushed by a gentle breeze until it caught beneath the wheels of a parked coach, one of several that had transported the armed units of CO-19. A little further down the street stood a soup kitchen, emblazoned with the name Teapot One, serving drinks to a small group of snipers, yet the usual banter that marked such occasions was gone. Everyone seemed lost in his own world. Even as Paine watched, a column of unmarked white vans drew up and the doors flew open. Men began to scurry out. The SAS had arrived.

'Bob, give me your assessment.'

'I haven't yet had a chance to talk with the British authorities. I insisted on reporting to you first.'

'We don't have a great deal of time, Bob. Can they cope, the British? I need your gut feeling on this one.'

He rubbed his gut, still sore from the blow of the rifle butt. It told him all he needed to know. 'The terrorists are serious. It's going to be tough negotiating our way out.'

'So what's the alternative?'

'I'm a diplomat, Madam President. You're asking for a political judgement.' And a deeply personal one, he thought, with her son inside.

'What do you know of their Home Secretary, Tricia Willcocks? Is she up to this?'

He considered the question as yet another convoy of white vans pulled up and began unloading a small arsenal of weapons. 'She's ambitious, a little too obviously so for many. Has a reputation for taking advantage of every opportunity – and any man – that might be useful to her.'

'A tough cookie, then.'

'The sort of woman who insists on making her mark. Has a personalised number plate on her car, and in this country that's still considered brash.'

'Not a team player, then.'

'Her colleagues wouldn't think so.'

'I sense she has no overwhelming desire to climb into bed alongside me, either.'

'You asked me for a gut feeling, so I'll risk it. If she stays true to form, it's my judgement she'll play this for her own advantage.'

'Meaning?'

'Whatever else happens, she'll not give up Daud Gul unless she's forced to do so. And there's no one left around here to force her. She knows the British media will crucify her if she is seen to be weak – the woman that wobbled. Cracked up, just like John Eaton has. They'll compare her to Maggie Thatcher and conclude she has nothing but a cotton bud for a backbone. She won't allow that to happen. So she won't let Daud go.'

'Kind of narrows the options.'

'The trouble is, Madam President, that I don't think the terrorists are in a mood to accept anything less. We are – all of us – walking very close to the edge on this one.'

There was silence from the Oval Office; the President didn't seem to care for what she had heard.

'Madam President, I need your instructions.'

'Bob, tell me . . .' The words hobbled along in torment. 'How is my son? How's William-Henry bearing up?'

'Oh, you can be so proud of him, Madam President. A chip off the Harrison block, if you'll permit me to put it like that. He gave me a message. Simply asked me to tell you that he loves you very much.'

Silence screamed down the line. For a moment he thought the connection had been cut.

'I need to know what you'd like me to do,' he pressed.

'I can't order you back inside there, Bob. This is too personal. You've got to use your own judgement.'

'My judgement is very simple, Madam President. If I fail to go back, they will shoot your son. But if I do, I think they will shoot me.'

'Bob, if I could take your place, you know I would.'

'I don't doubt it for a second. But I also hope you know me well enough to trust that I'll do whatever is necessary.'

'I'm struggling to know what the right thing is here, Bob.'

'The Harrisons have always found it in the past.'

'The Harrisons and the Paines – I guess our families go back a long way, don't they?'

Yet only the Harrisons will go forward, he thought, but dared not say so. The memory of his son swam before his mind and he bit his lip until it bled. 'Yes, Madam President,' was all he could summon up as a response.

'I think I know what the first William-Henry would have done. He wouldn't have sat on his butt and waited to be told what to do by others.'

'I don't doubt it.'

'But what will Tricia Willcocks do? That's the question.'

'Sadly, Mrs Willcocks remains something of a mystery.'

'Then perhaps we should find some way of giving the lady a shove . . .'

6.33 p.m.

'They found them, Harry, just as you said they would,' Tibbetts said.

'What's that, Mike?'

'The missing guests. The ones in wheelchairs. Two of them, meant to attend as representatives of the Disabled People's Council. Instead they had their throats cut and were left to bleed to death.'

The policeman slapped the table in bitterness. 'Why the hell didn't they just shoot them, get it over and done with cleanly?'

'Makes no noise, slitting a throat.'

'I'll take your word for it.'

'Anyway, they're mountain people, Mike. Never been conquered or suppressed, not in all their history. Moghals, Sikhs, Russians, British, we've all tried it and none of us has succeeded,' he said, pouring out the contents of a thermos flask into two Styrofoam cups and handing one to the policeman. 'But then we got lucky and dragged their leader off in chains. Bound to end up messily.'

'They're terrorists! They created this mess.' The policeman spat the coffee back into the cup. 'And there's no bloody sugar.'

Harry tossed him a sachet of sweetener. The table they had commandeered in the small post office was already covered with coffee smears and crumbs. 'When the British first fought them and we got beaten, we took our reprisals by tying our prisoners across the barrels of loaded cannon. Now that's what I call a mess.'

'Right now I'd settle for that.' Tibbetts pinched the bridge of his nose, trying to squeeze life back into his battered brain.

'But there's something I really can't understand, Mike,' Harry continued.

'Ah, at last, something you don't understand either. Thank God. Frankly, I was getting rather brassed off being left behind by you all the time.'

'They're mountain people,' Harry said again, ignoring the sarcasm, 'from halfway round the world. They're street fighters – or whatever passes for streets in the villages of Waziristan. These people don't mount campaigns, they just descend upon you one evening to slice the balls off you, then it's back to chasing sheep. They don't plot and plan, they just do it.'

'And your problem?'

'So how come they end up here so well prepared?'

'The weapons, you mean?'

'Not just that. It's . . .' He kicked a wastepaper bin for inspiration. 'Look, they know what to do – and who to do it to. They've tied up the House of Lords tighter than a nun's knickers. Figured out the security, knew where to get the passes . . .'

'The Pakistani High Commissioner. Perhaps he did all that.'

'Come on, Mike, you've seen him in there, he's not the leader, he's not much more than a mule employed to carry the stuff in for them. Anyway, he's only been in the country a few weeks.' Absentmindedly he retrieved the battered bin, then placed it carefully on the table, suddenly regarding it with exceptional curiosity as if it had changed from a bit of tin to something of wondrous value. 'You know, it was the loos that did it for me.'

'Beg pardon?'

'The loos. The portable lavatories.'

'You must be very tired.'

'No, Mike. When I brought them in they told me where to put them, in those closets. I didn't know about those closets. Been around this place ten years or more, never knew they were there. I doubt most people have the slightest idea they exist; they're not part of the usual tourist trail. But these tobacco-spitting men from the mountains, they knew all about them. How do you suppose that was, then?'

'I've no idea. But I've got a horrible suspicion you're going to relieve me of my ignorance.'

Harry grew still, like a cat preparing to pounce, making sure of his foothold. 'Someone else organised this, Mike.'

'You're losing it, my friend.'

'No, Mike, it's the only way. These guys could never have pulled this off without help. Couldn't have found their way to the airport by themselves, let alone burrowed into the hidden depths of the English Establishment. They're just the choirboys. Somewhere out there is – let's call him a cardinal, someone who knows where all the priest holes are, and how to really piss off the congregation.'

'Fascinating. And of course you have a name, perhaps an inside leg measurement.'

'Not yet.'

'Thank God. I think we've got our hands full enough with the bastards we already know about, let alone those who seem to be swimming around in the bottom of your bin.'

'Yes, you're probably right.' He finished off the last of his coffee in one draught. 'But there is one thing you might be able to help me with, Mike.'

'What's that?'

'That inside leg measurement. Do cardinals wear trousers underneath the rest of their clobber?'

7.00 p.m.

'We've got him, Home Secretary!' the man from MI5 enthused as they gathered once more at the Cabinet table in Downing Street. 'Masood. From Waziristan, as we previously thought – the High Commissioner, too. All of them. From the Mehsud tribe.'

'So when you say we've *got* him, you mean it in the sense that . . . ?'

The question hovered above the table.

'In the sense that we know who he is,' MI5 responded, deflated, searching surreptitiously through his pockets for his nicotine stick. She was good at that, deflating men.

'Ah, I see,' Willcocks said. She had made her point, no need to push the matter any further, least of all to remind him that it was not he but that wretched man Jones who raised their identities as Mehsuds. She smoothed an imaginary wrinkle from the tablecloth with the flat of her hand. Why did she dislike Harry Jones so? His attitude? His arrogance? His wealth that made him impervious to the pressures that can be applied to most others? Or was it simply that he was one of the few men who might, just might, be better than she was?

'What other progress can we report? It's nearly seven hours since the start of the siege, how much nearer are we to resolving it?' She glanced along the table at the representatives of the security services, but they all kept their heads down, except Tibbetts. In spite of his promise to stay out of her hair, he couldn't ignore her completely. She smiled gently at him, deceptively, as if old slights were forgotten.

'It seems to me there are three options,' he began. 'First, we try to negotiate, do a deal with them, as distasteful as that may sound. Offer to let them go in return for safe conduct to another country. Something of that sort. We declare a draw and hope we can find some honour in it. But I have to tell you frankly, Home Secretary, that since the telephone link was installed we've made every effort to engage with them in some sort of dialogue, and got nowhere. They're not interested in any form of compromise. These men are for real.'

Outside the windows the light had gone, and taken with it the beauty of the day.

'The second option is that the Metropolitan Police hands over control of the situation to the SAS and we bring an end to the siege by extreme measures. I'd like to introduce Brigadier Neal Hastie, Director Special Forces.' A man in his mid-forties with an eruption of red hair nodded from his seat at the far end of the table. His fresh-faced complexion made him look younger than his years and it would have been easy to mistake him for a country vicar who was up in town on holiday. Indeed, that is what he might have been, following his time as a theology student at St Andrew's, but sadly for his career in the cloth he had discovered the attraction of young women all too intense. One of them, heartbroken, had tried to take a melodramatic overdose in his rooms. It had put an end to theology and St Andrew's, and had brought him eventually to Hereford. He was still a devout believer in his God, yet, as Hastie had found, there were many ways to serve.

'Welcome, brigadier,' the Home Secretary said. 'Are you yet in a position to give us any sense of the options?'

'Home Secretary, my squadron arrived at Wellington Barracks less than two hours ago. It's taken a little time for the plans of the House of Lords to be located. I can't yet give you a recommendation, but if you were to insist that we try to storm the building I believe we could be ready in . . .' – he glanced at his wristwatch – 'thirty-seven minutes.'

His mood was calm, matter-of-fact, the blue eyes alert and his voice soft. Willcocks nodded in approval. 'Can you release the hostages?'

'Oh, most of them, certainly, if we have the advantage of surprise. The doors are booby-trapped – not a problem in blasting through them, but we don't want to give the enemy any warning. That's why we needed the plans, to identify any recesses or ducts – ventilation chambers, access tunnels, that sort of thing – that we might be able to use. If you feel able to give me more time to prepare our positions, we should be able to place snipers in these vantage points, and I would estimate a good ninety-per-cent survival rate.'

'Forgive me for interrupting, but couldn't you use smoke? Blind them?' a minister asked.

'No. Smoke on its own isn't going to stop them firing and hitting a large number of hostages. You see, they're all bunched together. Easy hits.' He went over to the television monitor pumping out its pictures.

'Then what about gas?' the minister persisted.

'Hold on a minute. Sounds like a rerun of the Moscow theatre siege,' Willcocks interrupted. She'd been doing her homework. 'Hundreds died, didn't they?'

The brigadier nodded. 'That was in 2002. I'm sure you'll remember the broad details, gentlemen, just as the Home Secretary has. Chechen rebels took an entire theatre audience hostage. Three days later special forces of the FSB raided the theatre using gas, some weaponised form of fentanyl. In its basic form it's an anaesthetic for cows and horses. The plan didn't work. The terrorists had respirators, and instead the gas killed innocent theatregoers, 129 of them. The FSB ended up having to hunt down and shoot the rebels.'

'Scarcely encouraging,' Willcocks muttered.

'There is nothing about this situation that I find encouraging, Home Secretary. But the SAS is not the FSB, and we have something rather better than fentanyl. *But . . .*' He let the word hang for just long enough to make sure they were all listening. 'The problem, I'm sorry to say, is Her Majesty the Queen. They have an explosive jacket that is positioned beside her at all times. They change the guard with the jacket every two hours, so they're alert. The only time she's allowed to move is when she uses the toilet, and when she does the jacket goes with her. It's probably not a huge amount of explosives in there, and we have no way of knowing precisely what they're using – I understand the wheelchairs they used to smuggle in the material are being analysed for chemical traces – but my guess is they've used something like TATP. Triacetonetriperoxide, to give it the full name. It's similar to the sort of stuff that was used in the 7/7 attacks on London, it's relatively easy to produce from materials you can buy on any high street – acetone, hydrogen peroxide, mineral acid, the sort of ingredients you find in nail varnish remover and hair bleach. In its pure state it can be about eighty per cent as effective as TNT, but it's extremely unstable so they've probably calmed it down with some desensitising agent. Fat or oil, that sort of thing.'

'How likely is it that it will work?' Willcocks asked. 'We all know of cases where some of these home-made bombs have failed.'

The brigadier steepled his hands, as though in prayer. 'That's a very good question.' He meant that it was an almost impossible question. 'So far these terrorists have proved themselves to be extremely well prepared. I think we have to assume that they know what they're up to. I've no idea what they are using as a triggering device – if it were detonated by remote control we might have a chance of jamming the signal, but this . . . well, this sort of thing could be detonated by something as simple as a flashbulb – a party popper, even.'

'A party popper? We're being held to ransom by a party popper?' Willcocks exclaimed in horror.

'I'm afraid the device is simple, but its potential consequences are exceptionally complex. One terrorist is always attached to the device, and it will be extraordinarily difficult to take him out without running a very high risk of setting off the bomb and taking out Her Majesty, too. Even if we were able to push in enough gas to knock everyone out – which frankly I doubt in a room the size of the House of Lords – the terrorist's falling body could trigger the explosion and it would be likely to account for not only the Queen but also the Prince of Wales.' He looked around the room at the ashen faces of his audience. 'Of course, there would be an excellent chance of stopping the other terrorists before they do too much harm. We should be able to save the Prime Minister, if that's any consolation . . .'

The ensuing silence declared that it was not.

'One thing in particular we can't calculate or measure. That's the degree to which the terrorists want to survive. One of the reasons we were so successful with the Iranian embassy siege was that, fundamentally, the terrorists wanted to stay alive. Only one of them did, of course, and that was only because he managed to disguise himself as a hostage. By the time we rumbled him he was facedown on the pavement outside in front of a thousand television cameras; too late to deal with him then. If these terrorists are hoping to get out in one piece, then it gives us a chance to use that weakness against them. If we confront them with overwhelming force and present them with the choice of surrendering or dying, they might just throw in the towel. But that's a judgement call – and someone else's judgement other than mine. I'm behind on developments. If we are managing to identify the individuals, is there anything in their backgrounds that gives us cause for hope? A glimmer of flexibility? Family members or loved ones who might be brought in to make an appeal?' He looked around the table.

'I think it's the loss of their family members that has brought them here in the first place,' MI5 muttered gloomily.

'Ah, I see. Well, unless we can find some form of leverage with them, I've got to advise you that this operation is unlikely to be clean. There will be casualties.'

'That is unacceptable, of course. Not the Queen,' the Home Secretary replied. There was general nodding from around the table. She turned once more to Tibbetts. 'You said there was a third option.'

'The simplest one of all. We let them have what they want. Give them Daud Gul.'

'Give in? Is that what you are suggesting?'

'It's an option, Home Secretary.'

'Not on my watch it isn't.'

'Then, I think we must decide what we *are* going to do, and when.'

Instinctively, as she did when she was faced with a dilemma, she began ironing the brown baize tablecloth with her hands once more, this time using both palms. She was interrupted by the entrance of an official. He looked harassed, and announced that the White House was on the phone asking for an update.

'Tell them I'll call the President as soon as I've finished this briefing,' Willcocks instructed.

'It's the President herself on the phone,' the official said, clearly agitated. 'I gather she's not in a mood to wait.'

Her own briefing wasn't finished yet and Tricia Willcocks's instincts screamed that she should refuse to take the call. She wasn't ready, hadn't thought this one through, and it wouldn't do to end up in a catfight with the most powerful woman in the world. Yet to refuse her call would be to turn possibility into certainty and ensure the claws came out, and there were just so many battles she could fight at one time. 'Put her through. On the speakerphone. I might need your help with this one, gentlemen.'

The voice with the stretched vowels soon filled the room. 'Tricia, this is Blythe. How are you doing? I feel so very much for you right now.' Ah, the personal, woman-to-woman approach, so much warmer than the last time they had spoken. A gesture of goodwill.

'As I do for you, Blythe.'

'I hope you'll forgive me, but it's now six hours and more into this awful situation and I really need to share with you.' What she meant, of course, was that the other woman should share with her. 'How are things progressing? What's going on behind the scenes? My poor husband's at his wits end.' So, she was playing the family card.

'I am sitting here with my advisers, Blythe, what is effectively my War Cabinet.' It was meant to sound impressive, but to those around the table it seemed a touch pompous. 'We are reviewing all the options; I assure you that we're doing everything possible. We've secured the area, we've already opened channels of communication with the terrorists' – well, a telephone link, at least – 'and we'll do everything humanely possible to resolve the situation peacefully.'

'I am so reassured by what you're telling me, Tricia.'

'Thank you.'

'But they almost shot your Prime Minister, didn't they? It doesn't seem like they're hot on conciliation.'

'We did resolve that situation.'

'I think it was my ambassador who did that. It's just that . . . well, can I speak to you, mother to mother?'

Willcocks had no children, but this wasn't the time to get sidetracked by detail.

'Go ahead.'

A pause while the President collected herself. Her voice, when it returned, had lost its soft edges. 'The next on their list is my son, Tricia. We can't simply sit back and wait for them to decide who they're going to kill and how many. Surely, we have to take the initiative, don't we?'

'Initiative? How do you mean?'

'Tricia, my ancestor, the first President Harrison, was an old Indian hand. Fought hard, drank hard. A decisive, no-nonsense sort of fellow. Fact is, he was something of a military hero. He didn't go looking for trouble but when it started knocking on his door with tomahawks, he took them on at their own game. Gave 'em a taste of their own medicine. Pushed back the Indian raiders, then took on Tecumseh's entire Indian confederacy and whipped them. That's what won him the presidency.'

'What are you trying to say, Blythe?'

'How many Indians you got there, Tricia? Eight? That's scarcely a game of craps. Just take them out.'

'I think that's premature, Blythe. We want to minimise the chances of bloodshed.'

There was no mistaking the change that came over the President's tone, even through the tinny distortions of a speakerphone. 'There has already been bloodshed. From what I can see, there's going to be more – until we can stop it.'

The Home Secretary stared at the telephone, then with increasing urgency, at those around her, looking for support.

'What's the problem, Tricia?' the President came back again. 'Eight men. They haven't got a nuclear warhead in there, have they?'

'They have our Queen.'

'And?'

'I don't understand.'

'They have all sorts of people in there, Tricia. Monarchs, statesmen, ambassadors, politicians. Young boys, even. You telling me you're putting one life above any other?'

'She is the Queen.'

'And she's eighty-how much? One dear lady, for sure. But there are other lives at stake here, just as important. And surely the point about monarchs is that the system goes on, no matter what. I hate to put it so bluntly, but what is it you say? The Queen is dead, long live the King – words like that? I don't want to sound harsh and uncaring

133

here, Tricia, but you're not going to risk the lives of nearly a hundred people for the sake of one elderly woman.'

'She's not just an elderly woman, she's a national symbol.'

'And so is a President's son. He represents the youth of all America.'

A cold gale had begun blowing through Downing Street. Willcocks was growing tense, leaning forward in her seat.

'We have to try all means other than force first.'

'Sure. And if jaw-jaw doesn't work, you just make sure you're ready to make war on those bastards.'

'As I have said,' Willcocks insisted, struggling not to raise her voice, 'we are reviewing all the options.'

'Excellent. I'm not sure what deadline you're working to, but I think the terrorists gave us . . .' – a slight pause for consultation – 'sixteen hours and thirty-five minutes.' Another pause, this time to allow the settling of ruffled feathers. 'Look, Tricia, we're in this together, you and me. Side by side. It's going to be fine. You talk them out, or we blow them out of business. Either way, we'll show the world that we'll never allow terrorism to win. They're going to be grateful, Tricia, I'll make sure of it. I can see a Nobel Peace Prize in this for you. So let's hope these Indians crawl back to the reservation, but just in case they don't, I've got a Delta force unit on a joint NATO training exercise in Germany. They're like your SAS. I've mobilised them, they should be in the air very soon.'

'What on earth for?'

'To come and give you a little support. Like I said, you and me, side by side.' She was pushing, hard.

'We don't need Delta—'

'Of course you don't, Tricia. But it's vital at a time like this that America be seen to support you with more than words. And what message could be more powerful to the terrorists than to be facing British fire and American steel?'

'This is a British operation, Madam President.'

'And American, too, Tricia, never forget that. They have our ambassador. And my son. We're in this with you. Why, they'll be talking about you as the next Winston Churchill, sure they will. And we will talk again, Tricia. Very soon.'

Then the phone connection was cut.

'Oh, Christ,' whispered the Home Secretary, 'they're going to invade.'

Six

IT WAS LESS THAN AN hour since Hastie and his SAS had arrived, and already things were changing. The surveillance helicopter that had been banging through the air above the parliament buildings was brought lower, and gradually, over the ensuing hours, it would be brought lower still. Light tanks began to parade imperiously around Parliament Square and also along the road that passed directly outside the House of Lords. They were mostly Scimitars, nearly eight tonnes of metal, and their six-litre diesel engines and segmented tracks kicked up a hell of a racket. From this point on they would manoeuvre on a frequent basis. It wasn't that they were likely to need their machine guns or smoke grenades, let alone the armour-piercing shells, but all the to-ing and fro-ing combined with the pounding of the helicopter created a thick jungle of noise that would provide cover for the SAS when they went in, if they went in.

Yet already it was clear to Hastie that the House of Lords posed formidable problems. Under cover of the noise they might attempt to put around a few snipers, in fox-holes carved out behind the wood panelling or stonework, but the galleries that ran all the way round the chamber obstructed the line of sight, and if they tried to creep up on the doors they were likely to be spotted. In any event, the SAS preferred to blast their way in through the windows, pouring down on the enemy from above, throwing flash-bangs and confusing the

Michael Dobbs

crap out of them, but the windows here were a daunting forty feet high, built not just of ornate glass but solid bone-crunching stone and entangling lead – nothing that a frame charge couldn't take care of, but that would still only get them down to the galleries, not on to the floor where the hostages were being held. Actions like these depend crucially on the element of surprise and in these circumstances, with so little time to plan, the surprises might well lash out in both directions.

All this they had to consider, and somehow to overcome, yet still they were no nearer resolving the problem of how to save the Queen.

7.52 p.m.

Robert Paine crossed the room and greeted the Home Secretary, holding her hand longer than was decreed by formality.

'I appreciate you coming in, Robert. What you have been through is terrible.'

'Not easy for any of us, Home Secretary.'

They were standing in the White Drawing Room in Downing Street that looked out over the park. Spotlights played on the branches of the trees and a fountain gushed into the lake. All seemed so deceptively peaceful.

It had been a bruising hour for Willcocks. The Queen's private secretary had been on the phone, demanding an audience, growing increasingly irritated and unpleasant when he was put off, while Frances Eaton was upstairs under sedation after breaking into their briefing meeting in the Cabinet Room close to hysteria. If that weren't enough, Tricia's husband couldn't be found; he wasn't answering his phone, and as she thought about it, it suddenly struck her that he often went missing on a Wednesday evening. It was becoming a little too regular for comfort. She wondered if he was taking care of more than simply his law practice. Then that intellectually challenged dwarf who had recently been elected as Mayor of London had appeared at the front door of Number Ten, demanding to be included in the strategy sessions. They had only let him in to avoid a public fuss in front of the cameras, and to throw him rather more quietly out of the back. And, inevitably, the media were feral.

She had nothing to say, not yet. It was too early. Perhaps she might offer them a photo opportunity later. Walk down to Trafalgar Square for a few minutes. She'd heard that a prayer meeting had started in the church of St Martin's in the Fields and had grown to such a size that it had spilled out into the square. They were gathering beneath the feet of Nelson, their ancient saviour, and had started a candle-lit vigil, thousands of little pinpricks of hope that danced in the night as they knelt and gazed in apprehension down Whitehall towards the parliament buildings illuminated in the distance. These people represented the conscience of the nation, and Tricia thought she might join them, not to say anything, she wasn't much of a religious person, but simply to reassure them with her presence and through them, perhaps, give comfort to the country at large. A simple act of faith and national unity, carried out before the cameras of the world.

The siege had become a global sport. Prime Ministers from every corner had been calling, offering their support while gently but persistently enquiring about the fate of their ambassadors; Japanese, German, French, and so many others. But she had to deal with the Americans first. She gazed out of the windows as she spoke; no eye contact, not yet.

'Robert, neither of us have time for the diplomatic pleasantries, so I'll be blunt. Your President seems to have the bizarre idea that she should send American troops to assist us. Let me assure you – and through you, your President – that we need no such assistance. We can deal with the matter ourselves.' She turned, her face set hard. 'This is British turf. Your troops are not invited to tread on it tonight.'

'Home Secretary . . .' He spread his hands wide, as though clutching for something that might bring them together. 'My

President sees a most valued ally under attack, its government shorn of most of its leaders, its decision-making processes under extreme duress.'

'They are working perfectly well, thank you.'

'And we are under attack, too. If an American stands threatened anywhere in the world, we have a duty to protect him. International law grants us that right of self-defence, and the many mutual defence treaties between our countries give us a duty to respond in these extreme circumstances.'

She gave a dismissive snort. 'That's a barrel of bullshit, Robert, and we don't have the time to waltz our way delicately around it. This is about your President and her son and I will not allow personal entanglements to run roughshod over the facts.'

His face clouded. 'I see. President Edwards was hoping that you and she might see this through together – yes, woman to woman, if you like. I must admit to you, Home Secretary, that she had come to the conclusion you would need her support.'

'And how is that?'

'If we are to talk of personal entanglements, your own involvement in the matter scarcely makes you impartial.'

'What?' she snapped, startled.

'I'd like to find a delicate way of putting this, but given the circumstances . . .' He scratched awkwardly at the back of his hand. 'It's not simply that the British allowed these terrorists to walk in, when you are the minister responsible for security—'

'Even for a diplomat that's a bloody disgraceful thing to say!' Her words flew like pellets from a shotgun.

'It's also the fact that Masood, their leader, was trained by you, the British.'

She was about to give him the second barrel when she caught the weight of what he had said. There was no explosion. Instead, when the voice reappeared, it seemed to be stumbling in the dark. 'Explain yourself.'

'Masood is one of your boys. Didn't they tell you?' A frown of sympathy burrowed across Paine's brow. 'A few years ago the British government began a programme to educate some of the elite members of the mountain tribes in that part of the world – to bring them here, befriend them, educate them, and pack them off back home as leaders you could trust. Agents of Western influence, opponents of al-Qaeda and all the other Islamic rabble. What you'd been unable to gain by force of arms over several centuries, you sought to gain by flattery and education. A perfectly sensible idea. Except it didn't work. All you've done is create a better breed of mountain warrior. And Masood is one of the best.'

She let forth a most undiplomatic curse.

'He was here in Britain for two years. Under a different name, of course. Got himself an accent, then went back to the tribe.'

'It isn't on our computers,' she whispered lamely.

'Oh, it probably is. It's just that the CIA has bigger computers than your security services, got to it quicker. Or perhaps . . .' His voice softened as it trailed away, tantalising, like an angler's fly. 'Perhaps they decided it was better not to tell you, just yet. Keep it quiet. Locked away from the public eye.'

She looked at him, bemused and suddenly deeply anxious.

'Maybe they were never going to get around to letting you know – letting anyone know – that Masood is Daud Gul's son.'

She was speechless.

'You're right, Tricia. This is about personal entanglements. That's why the President thought you'd understand, and agree to meet this thing together. You see, you were the Education Secretary when these things happened. Masood, the terrorist's son, was trained on your budget and during your watch.'

The room was filled with the sound of her career shattering into a million irretrievable fragments.

'I guess you'd like to reflect on this a while,' he continued. 'We've all got a lot to ponder. I think I'd like to go to my church, pray a little.'

He gave her a respectful nod. 'With your permission, I'll come back later this evening for your answer.'

8.25 p.m.

The will to survive is extraordinary and at times overwhelming, capable of fashioning some form of normality even out of the darkest hour. Inside the House of Lords the hostages were beginning to prepare for the long night that lay ahead. They were confined to a small part of the chamber so there was little room, but they found comfort on each other's shoulders and in each other's arms. It wasn't the first time many of them had fallen asleep on these benches.

Harry had made another food run – not just sandwiches this time but salads and hot soup. The captors frisked him once more, not only on the way in but again on his way out, even though he was still dressed only in his underwear. They, at least, weren't relaxing. They knew that it was in the night, during the small hours when a man has to fight to keep his wits, that any attempt to snatch back the hostages was most likely to occur. They would be prepared.

As Harry walked back towards the small post office, pushing his trolley before him, he found the adrenalin that had been sustaining him draining away with every step. His legs were heavy, the cold tiles were now attacking his feet, he felt exhausted, and he knew he was afraid. Sometimes people assumed that brave men feel no fear; it is only because they are afraid that they are brave.

It was as he was climbing wearily into his clothes that his phone fell from the pocket of his trousers. It had been switched off these past hours and only now, out of habit, did he switch it back on. It was an unthinking gesture for immediately it started whining in protest; dozens of unanswered voicemails and texts had been left over the preceding nine hours. With a low sigh he stabbed a finger in the direction of the power button, intending to switch it off, but before he could do so it rang yet again.

'Harry, old chum, where the fuck have you been?'

He recognised the crisp voice immediately. Jimmy Sopwith-Dane – known as 'Sloppy' to everyone who served with him – had been a fellow officer from the Life Guards before being invalided out and heading for fresh pastures in the City. Sloppy had become a public relations adviser, a damnably successful one in a career that was carried along on a combination of upper-class charm, personal loyalty and exceptional, if usually hidden, dedication. Eventually, it had brought him the post of Director of Communications at the Financial Services Authority, the body that acted as the financial policeman within the City of London. The job was serious, which only served to enhance his eccentricities, but the Edwardian accent and studied foppishness hid a selflessness that had once taken a bullet for Harry in the bandit country of Armagh. That bullet, in his knee, had ended his military career; in Harry's view, that allowed Sloppy the right to limp his way around Harry's world with total freedom.

'Forgive me, Sloppy, got a bucketful to take care of.'

'Too busy crying in your Cristal, I suppose.' Harry could hear Sloppy was in a bar, and he sounded as if he'd been there some time. 'Just wondering how much you got hit for this afternoon.'

'Hit for what? I don't understand.'

'Where you been hiding? Don't you know? Stock Exchange forced to close early. Brokers practically throwing themselves from windows. Squillions knocked off the value of everything, including Harry Jones, I assume. That's why I've been trying to call you. It's been horrible out there, old chum. Slaughter of the innocents.'

'Been a bit tied up,' Harry mumbled, thinking he could hear a champagne cork popping in the background. That would be Sloppy, going down with masts at full sail.

'This bloody siege's turned the world on its head. Been worried about you. Thank God you didn't get caught up in it.'

'This bloody siege's turned the whole world on its head. Been worried about you. Thank God you didn't gat caught up in it.'

'I rather have. I'm the man in the white suit.'

'Christ, was that you? Didn't recognise you in long shot. Or in your underwear.'

'Yes, perhaps I should sack my tailor.'

'Please, old chum, take care of yourself. Don't go playing the hero.'

'In for a penny, in for a pound.'

'Too bloody right. Talking of which—'

'Look, Sloppy. I'll have to go.' Harry tried to interrupt, but his old friend was not to be so easily deflected.

'It's going to take a while before the old ship rights herself at this end, Harry. 'Twixt you and me, this afternoon wiped out three years of carefully regulated larceny amongst my little hoard of stocks and shares. Crying shame. But you, you lucky bugger, with all those inside connections of yours, if you happen to know how and when this little skirmish is going to end, you'll make a tidy bloody fortune.'

'Run that one by me again, Sloppy.'

'Intelligence and surprise, my old mucker, same old game. Forewarned and forearmed. Just like the night we raided that IRA council meeting – you remember? Caught those Fenian buggers in bed with each other's daughters. Remember how we laughed afterwards? So there were those this afternoon who got caught with their pants down waving their willies, while some other lucky sod's had it away with the daughters and by now is probably in the Cayman Islands.'

'Er, who, Sloppy?' Harry asked, fighting his confusion.

'Who? I dunno. I don't mean anyone in particular. Talking figuratively, old chap.' The sound of a woman's laughter came down the phone.

'But if someone had known about it, Sloppy . . . Look, put that bloody glass down and concentrate. Could you find out if anyone did make a killing? A real stinker of one? And if so, who?'

'Don't worry yourself, dear boy, these capers usually come out in the wash somewhere. That's what we do at the FSA. Run it all through our little computers and see if anyone's had more luck than they really deserve. Then we pursue them all the way back to whichever little sand castle they're using as a hidey-hole. Bloody Lone Ranger, that's me.'

'How long does that all take?'

'What?'

'How long before you pick up the patterns?'

'Weeks. Months, even. Depends.'

'But we don't have time for that, Sloppy!' Suddenly, the adrenalin was pumping again, making Harry's head hurt. 'Look, it's chaos at this end, but we need to know if anyone's got his hand in the pot and we need it now.'

'No way, the shop's all shut up.'

'Listen, and listen good, old chum. We need to know if anybody has been betting on this siege – if they knew about it in advance. And every hour, every minute longer that takes, puts lives at risk.'

'It's not the way we do things, Harry,' he complained.

'Sloppy, this may be the most important thing I've ever asked you to do.'

The other man said nothing for a moment. He rubbed his mangled knee; Jones was always a pain in some part of his anatomy, but it meant that life was never dull and that's what made him such a damned fine friend. When Sloppy came back on the line, his voice was entirely sober. 'Can't promise. Can only try. Put a few ferrets down. Do my best.'

'That's always been good enough for me.'

'You're a total shit, Harry Jones. Always spoiling my fun. I was looking forward to drowning my sorrows this evening, others were depending on me.' A burble of feminine disappointment gushed down the phone. 'Be back in touch. Soonest. But you'll owe me for this one. Dinner, my call, somewhere disgracefully expensive with a magnum of Yquem thrown in. The 2001.'

'It's yours. Thanks, Sloppy.'

It was a long shot, but so was everything at this stage. Harry stabbed at his phone, about to turn the thing off before it started its protests once more, when his eye caught the call list and he froze. 'Oh, Christ – please, no,' he swore. 'No!' Then he fled from the room.

Despite the road blocks and the chaos around Trafalgar Square, he made it to the Ivy in the back of a commandeered police car by 8.47 p.m. There was no sign of Melanie anywhere in the panelled dining room. His heart was thumping and, despite all his years of training, he was hyperventilating.

Melanie, he was told, had arrived a statutory twelve minutes late. She'd been in a health spa all afternoon to prepare herself for this meeting and had somehow contrived to miss most of the chaos that had spread across London during the afternoon. Reluctantly she had ordered a glass of Chablis to keep herself amused and had made it stretch for twenty-one minutes before she had got up and left. And, no, there wasn't a message for him.

Her phone was switched off. Harry tried it twice, then borrowed the restaurant phone in case she was blocking his number, but wherever she was, she wasn't answering.

Harry stumbled from the restaurant into the night. The police car was waiting. It had been put at his disposal by Tibbetts, who had insisted he needed to know where Harry was and be able to get him back within five minutes, but Harry didn't want to go back. He instructed the driver to take him to his old home, in a mews tucked away behind Berkeley Square. When they arrived he pounded on the door, but she wasn't there, either.

He had little problem with the concepts of duty and sacrifice, that's what his life had been bent around all these years, serving others, fighting for them, with so much that was personal and private pushed to one side, sometimes almost forgotten. And yet . . . duty wasn't enough, of course it wasn't. The concept was inspiring, for decades Hollywood had made films about it, but the reality . . . well, right this moment the reality was about as inspiring as a bit of old celluloid left too close to the fire. He sat on the doorstep of his old home, his arms hugging his knees, leaning against the railings, knowing that something inside was curling up and dying.

Yet in the midst of all his misery, Harry knew there was more dying to be done, and he also knew that how much of it, and who, might just be down to him. Some would die, of that he was sure, yet some lives might be saved, important lives. What could be more important than that? But who would save his unborn child? Sure, Queen and country needed him, and so did that tiny, unnamed being growing inside his wife. Harry had so much experience of life, yet so little knowledge of family, and perhaps that was why he'd made such a mess of things. Being a novice didn't stop him wanting to try.

9.03 p.m.

Delta Force. The winged avengers. America's equivalent of the SAS. And from its temporary base in Ramstein in Germany where it was training with elite troops of other NATO nations, the A squadron of Delta Force was on the move.

Its pedigree didn't stretch back as far as the SAS. Too short on experience, too long on hair and too big on balls, that's what their British counterparts said. Delta men suited themselves – quite literally, dressing in whatever took their fancy. They also chose what weapons to carry and which tactics to employ. You were as likely to meet a Delta man with a week's growth of beard kitted out in hockey helmet and hiking boots as you were to discover a politician offering an excuse. Delta was different, unorthodox, and had often made a name for itself for all the wrong reasons. Their first major engagement had been in 1980 when they had attempted to spring the American embassy hostages being held in Teheran. Operation Eagle Claw, it was called, and it turned into a fiasco. Eight US servicemen were killed without Delta Force ever engaging the enemy. They also left behind a long list of CIA contacts operating in the country. Total fuck-ups didn't come any bigger than that. For an organisation that was supposed to operate in the shadows it was a humiliation almost beyond redemption, its failure illuminated for the entire world by the burning wreckage of US helicopters scattered across the Iranian desert. The reputation of Delta Force never fully recovered. After that, its successes would be recounted in whispers while its failures were turned into disaster movies. That was the price of leading with an unshaven chin.

And now they were heading for Britain.

Tricia was still at the Cabinet table. The room was dressed in shadows; she sat in a pool of light cast by a solitary table lamp, with Robert Paine's words still ringing in her ears, drowning out her attempts to concentrate. It wasn't that she had personally approved the financial and educational support given to Masood, any more than she'd overseen the security arrangements for the State Opening, but it was her backside on the seat and her signature at the bottom of the paper. About the only certainty she could find in this onrushing disaster was that afterwards there would be a hunt for scapegoats which would show no mercy. The media would dress in robes that would do credit to the Inquisition and demand that someone be hauled to the scaffold as an example of public retribution so terrifying that it would ensure such negligence would never again be tolerated. And there was no denying it, her neck fitted neatly into the noose.

She shivered. It was cold in here, in Downing Street – or was it merely her hormones playing up again? She remembered Margaret Thatcher once saying that she didn't have time for the menopause, she just got on with things. Tricia Willcocks insisted she was built of similarly stern stuff but, dammit, she was freezing. And so alone. It amazed her she could be sitting here at the very centre of power and yet feel so isolated. They were shunning her, the civil servants, the advisers, the lackeys, the short-dicks who were so eager to share in the spoils and so adept at distancing themselves from disaster. She was left with nothing but the mute insolence of the television screen flickering in the corner. These bloody men – oh, she'd played them all her life, taking advantage of their insensitivity, their inflexibility, their insatiable egos, even their lusts, ridden them like horses to the whip, and now they were waiting to exact their revenge. Even Colin. She couldn't prove it, not yet, but her instinct told her he was having an affair, in some tart's arms right now, this evening, even while she faced disaster. She didn't mind so terribly about his infidelity; after all, she'd scarcely been a spectacular example of devotion herself, but these things always had a habit of ending in a fight and she wasn't in much of a position to take him on right now, not as she had with her previous husbands. Colin was a lawyer, a particularly successful one, with friends in all sorts of low places, and she was a public figure with so much to lose. Once they had hanged her for incompetence he would take delight in burning what was left of the carcass if it reached a fight in the divorce courts. And she wasn't as young or as attractive as she once was. It wasn't just the circulation, it was the moods and the fading hair and the sense that her life was changing. She might not be able to rebuild it. Suddenly the ghosts of all forsaken women were whispering in her ear, insinuating, mocking, like witches on the heath.

She stared at the phone, hoping it would ring. She wanted to pick it up and issue some far-reaching instruction that would save the day. Instead she asked for a whisky. It had been Maggie Thatcher's favourite drink and had seen her through many a long evening, so if it was good enough for her . . . Had Maggie found it lonely, too, Tricia wondered? Sitting in this chair, with its leather padded arms, waiting for reports from the distant Falklands to find their way back? Tricia had been in her last year at uni at the time, remembered the sense of apprehension that had overwhelmed the country – what was this bloody woman doing, sending out a task force and even the QE2 to pile disaster upon defeat? Yet she had taken her courage and a Union Jack in her hands and paraded them before all those doubting men, and stuffed it right up them, not just the Argentinians but many back home, too.

The Americans had been pathetic, even then. Wobbled all the way round the United Nations. Wasn't it always like that, America First, the rest left to cough and splutter in the dust? A nation founded on the loathing of kings yet which had placed itself in harness to a few families who acted with a sense of divine right that would have felt entirely at home in the court of Caligula. Kennedys, Bushes, Clintons, now the Harrisons, all taking their turn to grab the reins of history.

As she sat there, she knew they were coming. Even as she finished her whisky, a C-130 transport of the USAF's 435th Air Base Wing was lining up on a night-lit runway, its four turbo-props whining, turning its nose into the wind. On board were nearly fifty men, along with all the equipment they deemed necessary. Soon they were lifting above the dense forests and the surrounding hills which stretched out towards the nearby town of Kaiserlautern. The plane levelled out at 18,000 feet. It didn't set course directly for its destination since that would require entering French airspace and the French had long, inquisitive noses, so instead they headed for the Netherlands, following a flight plan that claimed they were on a training mission. It was while they were in Dutch airspace that they were joined, briefly, by a second C-130, and for several minutes until they were over the North Sea they danced a careful minuet in the night sky before parting. Only one of them set course for Heathrow.

For the while, Tricia Willcocks could only guess at much of this. What would Maggie have done, she wondered? Ordered a second whisky, just as she had? It was having its effect, warming her up. She kicked off her shoes, stretched her toes, wishing they were buried in warm sand somewhere far away, and not having to share a beach towel with Blythe Harrison Edwards. She'd been looking into the American's background, getting to know her enemy, curious about the hokum that the ancestor had been a great Indian fighter, but it turned out to be true. William Henry had destroyed not just the Shawnee chief Tecumseh and his entire army but also crushed the European allies who fought with him. It came as no surprise to discover that those allies just happened to be the British. The war of 1812. Falling out with prime ministers seemed to be something of a family habit with the Harrisons. The bitch.

Tricia rinsed the whisky round her mouth and let it trickle slowly down the back of her throat, wishing she could rid herself of her troubles as easily. But they would grow worse, of that she was certain. She couldn't confront both terrorists and Americans at the same time, and even to try would surely mean disaster. It wouldn't be much of an epitaph, would it, the woman who single-handedly smashed the Special Relationship, who turned the trans-Atlantic alliance on its head and left Britain outcast and utterly alone? And maybe even got her Queen killed. Suddenly, sitting alone in the dark, she felt very frightened.

She wanted to order another whisky but daren't; they'd use that against her, too, the woman who drank herself dotty while the world around her burned. She stamped her foot in anger but succeeded only in barking her stockinged foot against an unforgiving chair leg. She yelped in pain, but as the fire spread from her leg and towards her brain, it began to burn off the befuddling blanket of alcohol and despondency that had settled upon her. Tricia Willcocks was a fighter, as good as any bloody Harrison, so to hell with defeat – and with the Americans! It wasn't all over yet. She had no intention of going with grace, that wasn't her nature, and there was still something she could try. Call the Americans' bluff. Stop them. Stand in their way. Defy them! And when it was all over, if there was any retribution ricocheting around, she could try to make sure it landed on the President's desk. Already she was feeling warmer. Anyway, what had she got to lose? If they were to drag her away, she'd go down fighting, just like Maggie, like a roaring lion, leave her nails embedded in the carpet. Or better still, buried in their throats!

9.43 p.m.

Sloppy's efforts hadn't met with overwhelming success. He had worked hard to gather in as many members of the FSA's market monitoring staff as he could, but his pickings were sparse. Only ten of them, and none were of any great seniority. Their head of department was abroad, others were on leave, and those he had been able to gather in had been wrenched from the arms of assorted friends, family and restaurateurs. Now they had gathered in their open-plan office in one of the more modest buildings in Canary Wharf, which, like all offices after working hours, had a cold, funereal atmosphere that entirely matched their own mood. It was clear they weren't brimming with enthusiasm, and some were almost rebellious. Several hadn't even taken off their coats.

'So what's this all about, Sloppy?'

'Simple. The country's in a total fucking mess and we might just be able to do something about that. We've got to find out if anyone's making money from this siege nonsense. Need to see if there are any trails, then discover where they lead.'

'A wild-goose chase.'

'I don't chase wild geese, I shoot them. Saves all the trouble.'

'It can't be done, not just like that. There are procedures, protocols for this sort of thing, and you know that we of all people have to work by the rules.'

'Rules? There are no rules for this one. It's not just money, there are people's lives on the line here, so bend the bloody rules, break them, if necessary, whatever it takes, so long as we get the answers we need.'

'This isn't just one of your PR stunts, it comes from the top, right?'

'Look,' Sloppy insisted, directing their attention to the hostages huddled together on the television screen, 'right now there is no top. No one to cuddle us or cover our arses. And I can't promise there'll be invitations to tea and biscuits at the palace next week, because right now we can't be sure there'll even be a bloody palace. We can only do what we think is right. It's called using our initiative.'

The doors of the lift sighed as they opened, spilling another couple of colleagues into the room. They were carrying large insulated satchels over their shoulders.

'I can't help you in this,' Sloppy said. 'You are the people who know what to look for and which buttons to press on your shiny screens. Do what you have to do, call up friends and call in favours, get them out of bed or away from whichever bar they're propping up, but whatever we do, it has to be done now. Tonight.'

'And if there are any repercussions, you'll get us out of jail, will you?'

'I can only promise you two things,' Sloppy replied. 'That if any of you lands in the shit, you won't be alone. I'll be right there along with you. The only other thing I'll promise is an endless supply of what I consider to be the finest curry in town.'

The two recent arrivals opened the satchels and the aroma of Indian cooking began to attack them all.

'So how about it?' Sloppy asked

For a moment there was silence. These were men and women, mostly young, whose professional lives ran by clearly set rules; they were the police force of the City who worked by means of methodical, painstaking inquiry. No one paid them to rush about taking initiatives. Outside the windows of their office, the world was dark, the City skyscrapers left abandoned to the cleaners and the night owls. It seemed almost surreal. Most of them were desperately undecided, waiting to see in which direction the wind would blow.

Eventually, a grumbling voice broke the silence. 'Whatever. Anyway, my ruddy mother-in-law's visiting,' it complained.

'You wouldn't have a veggie biryani in there by any chance, would you?' one of the younger women asked.

'What time is it in the Caymans anyway?' another demanded.

'I just want to make sure no one gets curry on my keyboard,' insisted another as he threw his coat over the back of his chair. The others began to move and, like an old steam locomotive, puffing and complaining, the enterprise got underway.

10.36 p.m.

There are many pieces that go together to make up a disaster. Some of these pieces may be small but, nevertheless, can be of crucial significance. One such piece was Levrenti Valentin Bulgakov. He was in his late sixties, a swollen blot of a man with a decidedly delicate heart condition who lived in exile in Islington. That, apparently, was where former KGB officers went to die when they ran out of secrets and grew perilously short of friends.

Bulgakov was an old hand, with a track record stretching across much of Central Asia and the Middle East, but he'd made his reputation in Afghanistan. He'd arrived there in the late Seventies when the Russians were interfering and creating such a godless mess in the hope that when it was all over they would be the only big beasts left in town. The recipe had been simple. Find conflicting loyalties and stir vigorously. Play one faction off against the other, one tribe against the next. Bulgakov had been at the heart of it, working out of the Residency and sowing disorder everywhere he stepped. In the end the chaos the Soviets created grew so intense that it surprised even themselves, and they had been forced to send in their own troops. The 108th Motorised Rifle Division arrived in Kabul on Christmas Day 1979, where they found Bulgakov waiting to welcome them. He'd even done his own bit for the invasion by shooting the Afghan head of counter-intelligence, putting a bullet through his back while the man poured him tea. After that, things had got really untidy. The Soviet Army stayed for a decade, during which time thousands of villages were destroyed, a million Afghans killed, four million made refugees, and somewhere along the way they even managed to kill the US ambassador. As Bulgakov was fond of saying, you couldn't break heads without cracking a few skulls. Confusion reigned throughout the country, and Bulgakov was in his element.

Then that treacherous impostor Gorbachov had arrived and hijacked the Soviet system, and called the invasion of Afghanistan a mistake. Just that. And he made them withdraw, the job only half done, tails between legs. At that point the blame game had begun, and all those who had been associated with the invasion became non-persons. Overnight Levrenti Valentin had gone from being folk-hero to fall guy.

Some of his class had made the transition with little difficulty, transferring effortlessly from the KGB to its young sister, the FSB, or moving into banking or oil or mineral exploitation and cleaning up in the post-Soviet privatisation jamboree. They became oligarchs and hideously rich in the process. But although Bulgakov had garnered huge experience he had found few friends, and not just because he was a paedophile. He wanted to remain loyal to a system that no longer existed, and was too slow to accept the changes going on around him, let alone profit from them. Eventually, in despair, he had packed his bags along with a caseload of sensitive papers and followed the exodus to London where several of his old colleagues had already made the journey. But the stupid English! Although they were polite and professed gratitude for his offer when he opened his case of intelligence files, Mitrokhin had got there first, his trunks stuffed to the lid with some of the finest secrets the West had ever seen. They had no need for Bulgakov, so they had thanked him for his kindness and shown him the door. They'd offered no appointment, no pension, grew embarrassed when he was forced to raise the matter himself. The only thing they let him have was a residency permit, rather like a dog licence; no one had the heart to kick him out. So he had stayed, and been forced to find another route to salvation.

Although he had few friends, he was a man of many contacts and he had hung around the margins of the tsarist courts set up in exile by youngsters like Ambramovich and Berezovsky and Gusinsky. He'd used his knowledge to gain a little leverage and make a few millions here and there in those early days, but he had never been accepted as one of the band and when, inevitably, the information he had grew stale and lost its force, they had no qualms about discarding him. As the years passed, Bulgakov had grown old and sick. He had also grown implacably envious. His looks deserted him, his sexual prowess let him down, his breath turned sour, he found himself down to his last few millions and that, in his mind, seemed like punishment. He found the injustice of it all rubbed in over breakfast every morning as he scoured his newspaper, and after dinner every evening when he scanned the Internet, reading about the rich kids, the new guys on the block, none of whom had done half of what he had. He couldn't even read the football results without feeling pain. Bulgakov believed he deserved more than these upstarts could ever dream of and, as he fretted, he developed an old man's sense of unquenchable rage.

Yet the means of his retribution was at hand. During these last hours he had switched his attentions between television screen and Internet link, watching both the siege and the markets. And as he saw the chaos, his hopes soared. Never again would they turn their backs on Levrenti Valentin Bulgakov! He was about to show them, visit his revenge upon the richest men in Europe, humiliate them, and make sure they would remember him. The prospect made him even more breathless than usual.

He hurried to his appointment that night by the bridge over the Regent's Canal, popping peppermints for his breath, chuckling to himself. He was sweating when he arrived, his eyes glassy bright with a mixture of celebration and expectation. He knew he wouldn't live for ever, but what time was left to him would put right all the many wrongs that had been done to him. He could settle scores, buy friends and afford the prettiest boys in the business; even if he was no longer able to join in himself, he could still watch the show.

It was with such happy thoughts as these that he met his contact at the shadow-dimmed steps that led down to the canal, and it was with these thoughts that Levrenti Valentin Bulgakov died. His body came to rest at the bottom of the steps. It didn't really matter that his heart couldn't stand the shock; the fall alone would have killed him.

10.38 p.m.

Harry was still sitting on his doorstep, hugging his knees to his chest like some homeless vagrant trying to keep himself warm. The cold had long since travelled up through his body but he ignored it; there was too much else to occupy him, for the longer he sat on his own doorstep, the more he realised he didn't belong here. He didn't know if he belonged anywhere any more. His father had once joked that the reason Harry was an only child was because he was an experiment that had failed, yet as much as Harry had tried to slough off the banter, it had struck home and struck deep. Perhaps that's what had driven him all these years, an unconscious attempt to win the approval of his dead father, a desire that he should belong somewhere. People assumed he was entirely self-contained, a man who lived off his many successes, yet they had no idea how much he had always needed others.

Bloody Mel. She wasn't home, and wasn't coming home, no matter how much he tried to persuade himself otherwise. The light hanging above the door was off, and it was a habit of hers to leave it blazing to greet her when she was coming back late. The only light came from lamps inside the house that were part of the security system, someone pretending to be home. He sat in darkness, and punished himself for being a fool.

There was a pub further down the mews. It was a place of too much *kitsch* and too little change for Harry's liking yet it was always busy, crowded with estate agents and advertising wannabes, and as he sat on his darkened doorstep, two customers tumbled out and on to the cobbles. They were clearly the worse for wear, laughing, clinging to each other for support. The mews had never been the best-lit stretch of town and the occasional old-fashioned street lamps cast long and forbidding shadows, yet there was enough light for Harry to see them, a young woman and an older man, and judging by the way they fell upon each other they were unlikely to be father and daughter. An embrace upon the cobbles quickly turned into desperate fumbling in a doorway where they thought they could remain unobserved; they didn't see Harry almost opposite. The woman was complaining in a whisper that he was ruining her blouse, but soon there was nothing more than giggles that turned to urgent moans, and lumps of pale flesh peering out of the shadows.

As Harry observed their struggle, he found himself feeling nothing, neither titillation nor contempt, just an emptiness inside. It was far from being the first time he had watched people having sex; trips to the seedier basements of Soho had been a rite of passage at Sandhurst while his intelligence work in Northern Ireland had required him to witness far more than this, yet as he watched this ageless act taking place in the doorway of an art gallery, he had only one thought throbbing insistently inside his head. Where the hell are you, Mel? Where are you with my child?

He couldn't see – and didn't want to see – everything that was going on in the shadows, but he couldn't miss the girl stretching out her fingers until they curled around a plant that was growing in one of the gallery's luxuriant window boxes, grasping it ever tighter until, with one final involuntary spasm and a strangled cry that caught in her throat, the stem was wrenched out by its roots. It made a hell of a mess.

For a moment there was silence, nothing but panting, but then Harry could hear complaints. About the damp earth and bits of twig that had got everywhere, the fact that he hadn't even bothered taking off his bloody raincoat, and the tear in her blouse. Soon the pair grew sullen, wrestling with zips and buttons and buckles once more, and he was muttering about finding her a taxi.

'And twenty quid,' Harry called softly.

The couple froze; only now did they see him on his doorstep.

'Twenty quid,' Harry repeated, 'that should cover it, for the plant.'

'Fuck you,' the man snarled, until Harry rose slowly but purposefully to his feet. The man caught the sense of menace. 'Oh, what the hell,' he grunted, struggling as he dug into a pocket while at the same time trying to fasten his belt. Eventually he emerged with a note that he stuffed through the letterbox. 'Bloody do-gooders,' he muttered as he made a final adjustment to his clothing.

'But cheap at the price, wouldn't you say, darling?' the girl declared in a refined accent that tinkled like a chandelier in Knightsbridge. 'Buck up, the poor fellow's only jealous. Probably hasn't had a good shag in months.'

Which had been true, until last night . . .

'Anyway, time for me to be away,' she announced. She linked her arm through his and dragged him away, her hips swinging provocatively as they left Harry behind in the shadows. He watched them disappear. She would soon be home, unlike Melanie. Where the hell was she? And what had their marriage been about? Perhaps their life together amounted to little more than what he had just seen, something that was animalistic, essentially mindless, and over. This morning he had been in love with her, and now . . . all that was left was an empty light. This was pointless, she wasn't coming back, not this evening, not ever. Three wasted years. And he wondered how many notes the lawyers would make him pour through her letterbox as a mark of his gratitude. Considerably more than twenty quid a pop, he suspected, but none of that would matter if only – if, please God – he could save the child.

He was standing in front of his house taking one final look at his old life when a car swung into the mews, its headlights white, blinding. For a moment his spirits rose in hope . . . But, no, not Mel; it was his police driver.

'They need you, sir,' the driver called through the window. 'The commander implied it was rather urgent.'

He shouldn't be here, he had to get back. Leave all this behind. He climbed in, and the driver put his foot down.

11.00 p.m.

It wasn't until that moment that Celia Blessing realised you could hear the tolling of Big Ben from inside the chamber. Up to this point she had always been distracted, but now everything was so quiet, with people talking in nothing but whispers, that she could hear the bell as a dull, distant thudding, like the closing of a castle door.

'I do so love this place,' she said distractedly, 'but you never have, have you, Archie?'

He grunted. 'Always struck me that the Lords is the last desperate resort of people who've got no future nor even much of an interesting past. We only get the second-class crooks in here. The top class all go off and live somewhere warm.'

'You're such a smelly old cynic,' she said, but without malice.

'Cynicism's been a good friend to me. Rarely let me down.'

'Oh, why are we here?' she sighed.

'I reckon, lass, because neither of us have much else better to do.'

Sadly, Celia realised he was right. She had come to that lonely stage in life when she spent too much time looking back. It was all very well growing old disgracefully and running your umbrella along life's railings, but when you'd annoyed as many people as possible and told yourself you'd thoroughly enjoyed it, you still had to return home to a cold hearth and deal with it on your own. That's why you spent your evenings looking back, surrounded by memories, not because you were eaten up by the warming comforts of nostalgia but because you were becoming afraid to look too far forward. Old age was a little like being confronted by a rebellion in the colonies. You simply closed your eyes and refused to recognise it, until you were forced to. Then you declared that you would give in gracefully, and hated every joint-aching minute of it.

'What's wrong with you, Archie?'

He sniffed. Typical of a bloody woman to be so direct. No man would ever come out with something so blunt. 'I hate bloody sandwiches,' he muttered.

'No, really. What's wrong with you?'

He paused before he spoke again. He'd had no practice in doing this, there had been no one else to tell. 'Got cancer. Inoperable. Maybe six months.'

'I'm sorry.'

'Made my will. Cats' home included. No children, you see. Damned body never was any good. That's why the wife left me all those years ago.'

'Hang on, what about . . . ?'

'Sonya? How desperate do you think a man has to be to try it on with a money-grubbing little tart like her? The open arms of aspiration and the parted legs of desperation, that's what one of the press buggers wrote, and I fell into both. Truth be told, I actually enjoyed the headlines. Did my street cred no end of good. Stood me a whole month's worth of free drinks in my local.' His face brightened. 'You see, lass, there's always some good to be found even in the stickiest situation.'

'Evidently your wife didn't think so.'

'Oh, but I got my own back on the bastard she ran off with.'

'How was that?'

'I let him keep her.' There was an engaging twinkle in his eye, but the smile took courage.

'So that's why you've stayed behind.'

'You ever seen anyone die of cancer? Not pretty, is it? Got no stomach for it myself. Won't be long now, can already feel it. Makes me sick with disgust. I loathe myself, what my life has become. So . . . well, I thought these boys here might even be doing me something of a favour. I'm bored and I'm dying, Celia, and they are two of the worst companions I've ever had. Who knows, these little foreign chappies might bring me just the sort of excitement I need.'

'You don't mean you *want* to—'

'No, no, I'm not the type to go looking for it, but these guys have done me a favour. Brightened up my week no end. And let's face it, duchess, I've got so little to lose, so much less than almost anyone else in this room. And if, somehow, I can pass on that favour . . .'

'How?'

'Not entirely sure. Wait and see, I guess. So that's what I'm doing here. Waiting and seeing.'

'But what can you, a . . . a . . .' She was struggling to find the appropriate words.

'An old hulk with rotting timbers?'

'What can you of all people do, Archie?'

'But that's it, you see, duchess. I've been waiting, and while I've been waiting I've been watching. And I think I might just have found a use for these old timbers.'

'Surprise me.'

'I've got a plan, you see. Not much of a plan, maybe, but buggers can't be choosers, as they say. It's just that there's one little problem. Sounds silly, I know, but it involves the Queen's lavatory.'

'I've always said you were an utterly ridiculous man.'

'Oh, and perhaps a second, very tiny problem,' he muttered, suddenly a little shame-faced.

'I think I've already figured that one out, you old fool.'

'You have?'

'Of course. You're going to need my help.'

11.18 p.m.

Paine found Tricia Willcocks standing in the garden of Number Ten, wrapped up in a man's borrowed overcoat, her hands thrust deep inside the pockets, looking up at the stars that were splashed like tiny pebbles of light across a dark beach. The moon was almost full and the night unusually still and quiet; there was no rumble of traffic from the streets of London. It seemed as if the entire world was holding its breath.

'When I was a young man I wanted to be an astronaut,' he said, walking across the grass to join her.

'So why weren't you?'

'Too much to do down here, I suppose. But right now I'd find the prospect of being somewhere the other side of the galaxy rather appealing.'

'You have come for your answer, Robert.'

'I said I would. And there's not much time left. Delta Force is on its way.'

'I know.'

She cast around the sky as though looking for landing lights. Her breath sent up little clouds of smoke in the November sky.

'Home Secretary, the President will not back down. She feels as if she has the weight of history and, if I can put it like this, a thousand generations of Harrisons behind her.'

'Impressive. But I guess there've been quite a lot of Willcockses along the way, too. I'm not sure we've ever spilled as much blood as the Harrisons, but from what I know of them, they're as stubborn and as cussed as a haemorrhoidal mule.'

'I hate to be put in this position, to have this conversation with you, but—'

'It's your job, your duty, Robert.' She rather liked Paine, fancied him a little. He was good-looking and reeked of loneliness; it appealed to her feminine side.

'As you say, my duty.'

'I think there might be a frost,' she said, as if she hadn't a care in the world. 'What do you think?'

'Tonight I think even hell might freeze.'

'It will do before I let in your troops.'

'They're only here to help. And the President will not be dissuaded.'

'But she has no right. The law, every scrap of it, is on my side.'

'The law?' Slowly he shook his head. 'The law is written by those who win.'

'Ah, the Wild West.'

His voice flooded with emotion and urgency. 'Tricia, don't try to call her bluff, I beg you.'

'But it's folly for a President—'

'She's not thinking as a President. She's acting as a mother. That's why she will not back down.'

'Then I must think for her.'

He wrung his hands in despair, his pain evident. 'I fear for the consequences of what we're doing tonight. You know, tomorrow the stars will still be up in their places, but our world may never be the same.'

'That's the trouble with the Willcockses, we just don't know our place.'

11.32 p.m.

The slow American voice flooded into the ears of the air traffic controller. 'Heathrow Tower, this is Shadow Six Zero. We are fifteen, I say one-five, miles south for a straight-in approach to land on runway zero-nine. Request permission to land.'

The silence that greeted the message had a life span no longer than that of a mayfly, but it was enough to holler confusion. Then a crisp, bitten-off English voice: 'Shadow Six Zero, Heathrow Tower. Er, say again.'

The American repeated the message.

Another screaming silence before: 'Shadow Six Zero, Heathrow Tower. Confirm aircraft type, number of people on board and airfield of departure.'

'Well, Heathrow Tower, we're a big bird with two wings and a whole lot of hungry guys on board. Is the Ritz still serving dinner?'

'Shadow Six Zero, Heath—'

'OK, OK,' the American came back. 'We're a Charlie one-thirty, forty-eight souls on board and we're inbound from Ramstein.'

'Shadow Six Zero, Heathrow Tower. A moment, please.' That was the point when, with ever increasing velocity, it began to hit the fan. The controller turned to his assistant, who called downstairs to the supervisor, who was soon trying to contact the military air defence authorities, but by the time they'd reached agreement that none of them had the slightest idea what was going on and they should scramble RAF interceptors, it was too late.

'Heathrow Tower, Shadow Six Zero,' the American was calling. 'Now eight miles, finals on runway. Request permission to land.'

'Shadow Six Zero, Heathrow Tower. Negative. Negative! You are not, repeat *not*, cleared to land. Orbit in your present position.'

'Heathrow Tower, Shadow Six Zero. I'm getting interference on reception. Say again, say again.'

But the message, even when repeated, made no difference.

'Heathrow Tower, Shadow Six Zero,' the American came back. 'Continuing the approach. Now five miles finals. Gear down. Clear to land.'

By this time several layers of decision makers were trying to control the situation. They discussed whether to switch off the landing lights, or block the runway with fire trucks, but even as they did so the realisation dawned that it was already too late. The aircraft was four miles away, almost at the point of no return. The Americans had called their bluff. Thank God it was almost midnight and the airport winding down.

'Shadow Six Zero, this is Heathrow Tower. Clear to land. I repeat, clear to land. Surface wind 270. Fifteen knots, with the likelihood of severe local disturbances. I think you can expect a warm reception.'

'Heathrow Tower, Shadow Six Zero. Copy that. Could you get them to hold my reservation at the Ritz?'

11.48 p.m.

Harry made the last trip of the day with his trolley. Only bottles of water, there was little appetite for more sandwiches. He was feeling drained, his mind distracted with Mel, his spirit still squatting on his doorstep. He recognised this as a danger sign, it was getting towards the time of night when body and mind begin playing tricks, slowing down, blurring reactions, yet he could see that Masood and his men were up to the challenge. Two were lying down, resting for the night ahead, while the one behind the throne and guarding the Queen had also been changed. Staying alert.

Many of the hostages appeared drowsy, exhausted by their ordeal. Some managed to doze despite their difficult circumstances, a couple were bleary-eyed, dabbing distractedly at their cheeks with handkerchiefs, while the Prime Minister stared ahead, his eyes hollow and his mind seemingly elsewhere. Others watched Harry with ferocious intent, looking for a sign, but when none came they diverted their eyes as though he had betrayed them. Yet as Harry walked through the chamber delivering the water, he became aware that one of the peers was continuing to stare at him, his brow creased, his body tense. It was Archie Wakefield. Harry knew him only by sight, and as he returned the stare, the peer began tapping agitatedly at his forehead with his finger, as though trying to convey some important message by telepathy. Harry could sense the other man's anxiety and he looked cautiously around, trying to see what might be the cause, but he saw nothing out of the ordinary, or what had become ordinary on this most extraordinary of days. A stillness, even lethargy, had descended upon most of the captives as they waited.

Outside the House of Lords the tanks had begun to manoeuvre once again, their engines screaming, their tracks clattering on the pavement, the sound mingling with the throbbing of the helicopter from above. Harry knew this was when the armed police of CO-19 would be infiltrating further into the parliament building, creeping forward to take up positions, climbing into ventilation chambers and crawling into sewers, trying to make sure that however the gunmen had got in, they would never get out. Yet Tibbetts's men took care not to get too close to the chamber; they had to avoid at all costs arousing suspicion or raising the alarm.

But they failed, the plan didn't work. As Harry bent down over his trolley to retrieve another water bottle, he sensed a movement behind him and felt the muzzle of a gun, the prick of death, nestling against the nape of his neck.

11.50 p.m.

The captain who commanded the detachment of the Household Cavalry knew his task. He had deployed his men at the exit of the road tunnel that led from the airport to the complex of motorways beyond, just as, elsewhere around Heathrow, he knew that other units were doing much the same. They had been ordered to make sure the cork was pushed so tight into the bottle that the mischievous genie called Delta Force could never escape.

The Household Cavalry had a history that stretched back 350 years, the oldest and most senior regiment in the British army with battle honours that stretched back through Overlord, El Alamein, the blood-soaked fields of Flanders, the Boer War, and all the way to Waterloo, yet this day it had screwed up, monumentally. They'd been the only front-line military unit guarding the monarch and in this simple duty they had failed. So what if they had been armed with nothing more than ceremonial swords and horsehair plumes? The responsibility had been theirs and they had failed. Their shining breastplates were now smeared with humiliation, and it was the mark of Cain that would be passed down through generations of brother officers.

Yet now they were back where they belonged, in battle gear behind the machine guns and thirty-millimetre cannons of their Scimitars. A chance to put things right and redeem the history of an entire regiment, that's what the captain had been told.

His orders had been specific. Establish a checkpoint and a chicane at the end of the tunnel that would bring any American convoy to a halt. Prevent them from progressing any further. Hold them, persuade the men of Delta Force to accompany them to a holding point inside the airport perimeter where an SAS officer would be happy to brief them on what the British were up to. Just like any other training exercise. It couldn't be long now, he had been advised that the C-130 carrying the American troops had landed more than ten minutes ago, but as he waited, the captain knew that this was not to be the Household Cavalry's day. His orders had seemed specific in the briefing room; intercept and interdict. But what did that mean here on the ground? Stop them, sure, but what if they chose not to co-operate and kept coming? The men of Delta Force were well-known Neanderthals who had got themselves into any number of scrapes. What if they refused to co-operate, what if he were forced to offer them something more persuasive than a cheerful wave, what if he had not only to stop but also to seize? He would have to judge the situation, use his initiative, but this wasn't like hunting down the Sadr militia or the Taliban. These were Americans, for God's sake. He'd trained with them, got himself drunk with them; why, his brother the investment banker had even married a couple of them, not very successfully, it had to be admitted, but that was no reason to start a shooting war against them. Could he really do that, if that's what it would take?

As he gazed at the mouth of the tunnel, he knew there could be no honour for him here. The Americans were faced with devastating firepower – but only if he gave the order to fire. And he really didn't want to do that. What the hell was all this about, putting up against the Americans – allies, friends – when there were so many other bad guys out there?

This wasn't any fun, and was growing ever less fulfilling with every minute that passed. It was only as he stood and began to grow cold with the waiting that he realised it wasn't going to happen. They should have been here long ago. The Americans weren't coming, not this way, at least. He wouldn't have to shoot them after all. As he realised this, the young captain was overcome with relief.

11.53 p.m.

Duncan had been the awkward one in the FSA's market monitoring unit, the one who'd raised most resistance and heaped most gloom upon Sloppy's proposal. Even a double helping of curry hadn't lightened his mood, but he was from the Western Isles and about as much fun as a bootful of seaweed when he was without a drink, and his had been left in the lounge of some pub hours ago along with a seat in front of a televised football game. Duncan was not a happy man. Now he sidled over to Sloppy. 'Thought you'd like to know.'

'Remember that I'm no economic Einstein so make it clear and concise, otherwise you'll lose me.'

The Scot gave his colleague a look of disdain; he'd never quite figured out whether Sloppy was always taking the piss or genuinely congenitally backward. He perched cautiously on the end of Sloppy's desk. 'OK. This is it. You get a disaster, but it's still all swings and roundabouts. Even when the market's crashing there are always some winners, people who have made money by selling something short, but what we're looking for is a pattern, right?'

'Right.'

'So, what have we got? A siege. A catastrophe. A situation in which you can pretty much guarantee that equities will head south and sterling will get butchered while the price of gold goes up. Those are the areas we've been looking at most closely. Now, because of the swings and roundabouts, literally thousands of punters have made a paper profit, but that's not enough. What we've been trying to figure out is what you would do if you had planned all this.'

Sloppy was nodding his head in approval.

'If you were behind it,' Duncan continued, 'you'd know when the chaos was about to start, of course, but the thing you couldn't guarantee is when it would finish. That's not up to you. So you'd be in and out as quickly as you could, right? We've been sniffing out those who've been closing their positions and running off with the cash – and all within that tight window between the time the siege began around noon and when the Stock Exchange closed early.'

'Makes sense, even to me.'

'So we think we've found a pattern. An unusual number of relatively small placings in derivatives but which in the circumstances have reaped huge returns.'

'Errr . . .' Sloppy interrupted, waving his hands in confusion.

'OK. You don't buy individual shares outright but you place a bet on the Stock Market Index. And if you gamble on it going down, you've just made a killing. Now, there have been a number of investments – bets – that in normal circumstances wouldn't have come up on our computer scans because they'd be regarded as too small, but in today's conditions, they've been about the only lifeboats around. And quite a number of lifeboats were hauled out of the water before the Stock Exchange closed this afternoon.'

'You mean—'

'It looks like someone took the money and ran. Now either they were smiled on by the good luck fairy – and that's possible – or they had a direct line to God.'

'Or those guys with the guns.'

'Anyway, thought you might be interested.' He glanced at his wristwatch and rose from the end of the desk. 'Can I go now? I'm still in time to catch the highlights.'

'So who's been sailing in these lifeboats?'

'Impossible to say, of course. We could only find that out through the brokers and they're away with the fairies until opening hours tomorrow morning.'

Duncan looked hard at Sloppy, but found the other man returning the stare with even more resolve.

'No, you're kidding me,' Duncan protested. 'You expect us to kick down the doors of the brokers and drag them into their offices at this hour? It's almost midnight!'

'England expects.'

'I'm a Scot!'

'Which therefore makes you determined, irrepressible and extraordinarily resourceful.'

'You bag of English wind.'

'I'll get the coffee, then, shall I?' Sloppy suggested, reaching for his mug.

11.53 p.m.

The scene inside the chamber was displayed on the video wall in the Ops Room in terrifying high definition. Harry was on his knees, his chin on his chest, with his head being forced down by the barrel of the gun that was at his neck. A little way off, Masood was shouting into the mouthpiece of the phone.

'What is going on? What are you trying to do?' he demanded. 'Get rid of the noise or he dies!' He made a violent chopping motion with his hand. It was the first time since the siege had begun that he had appeared stressed.

In the Ops Room a police negotiator was attempting to calm him with words of reassurance, but Masood was having none of it. 'What are tanks doing out there? Why do you need tanks? You are fools to think you can mess with me, so it is entirely your fault that another one dies!'

On the screen they could see him waving instructions to the gunman standing over Harry. Harry's head was twisted; he was trying to look at Masood, his face cruelly twisted, even as he was being forced lower and lower. His head had almost touched the floor when Tibbetts snatched the phone from the negotiator's hand.

'This is Commander Michael Tibbetts,' he said, trying to keep his voice measured. 'I am the police officer in charge of this operation. The tanks and the helicopter are there at my instruction.'

'Get rid of them, commander.'

'I can't.'

'Then he dies!'

'No! Listen to me. Do you have any idea what's going on outside the parliament buildings?'

There was a slight hesitation before Masood came back: 'Suppose you tell me.'

'Can I suggest your colleague lowers his gun. It would make it much easier to talk.'

'I'm making the decisions around here right now, commander, and frankly I have no intention of making things at all easy for you. He dies in five seconds, so I suggest you get on with what you have to say.'

'You have to know that thousands – literally thousands of people – are trying to get as close to the siege as possible. You know what people are like. We've pushed them back but they're still on the streets, on the bridges, on the tops of buildings, anywhere they can find a place to gawk. They want to see what we're up to – and what you are up to.'

At last there was silence on the other end of the phone as the other man listened.

'This is the only story in the country and it seems everybody wants a piece of it. Even as you and I are speaking the pictures from inside the chamber are being seen around the globe. The whole world's tuning into this. Millions. Watching you. I'm told it's the biggest television audience in history.' It was a lie, he had been told no such thing, but he suspected it might be true and he reckoned that was what the other man wanted to hear.

'So why the tanks and helicopters?' Masood demanded.

'The last thing I want is some idiotic journalist or drunken vigilante trying to get in on the act. You are serious men and I need to be able to treat with you in a serious manner; we can both do without a circus right on the doorstep.'

'I see. It seems that at last you are being serious. Excellent. So when will you release Daud Gul?'

'I'm not here to offer any deals, Masood, that's for my political masters, but so long as I'm in charge you have my word that this situation is going to be handled properly. That's why I need a helicopter watching from above and, yes, a couple of light tanks on Parliament Square to show those outside we're not going to put up with any nonsense. Look at it this way, they're here to allow you and me to get on with what we have to do.'

Tibbetts waited for a response but none came. He looked up at the screen; Harry was now bent completely double, under great pressure, his head pressing on the floor.

'Come on, Masood, the show is for those outside, not for you. What do you think I'm going to do, break down the door of the House of Lords with a tank and start shelling you?'

The phone connection went dead. Tibbetts turned to the screen, filled with apprehension. For a few seconds the scene was frozen, then Masood slowly lowered his hand and the gun was removed from the back of Harry's head. Tibbetts slumped into a chair, exhausted but at the same time exhilarated. What could never have been achieved by threats, he had gained instead by a little flattery. These men were human, after all. It meant they were fallible. For the first time since the siege had begun twelve hours earlier, Tibbetts felt a flicker of hope. He wiped his palms; they left a trail of sweat across the front of his shirt.

Seven

FROM SOMEWHERE NEARBY A CHURCH clock struck the hour.

'I really should go home,' Melanie said.

'Why?'

She didn't answer.

'The husband?'

She considered the question before shaking her head. 'I gave him one last chance – a chance he'd asked for. And he blew it.' She shivered, even though the room was warm. 'Left me like a gooseberry. At the Ivy, of all places. I felt such a fool.'

'Where did he get to?'

'Who knows?' Almost as an afterthought she'd scanned the list of names in the *Standard* of those caught up in the siege, but he wasn't there. It left her both relieved and intensely irritated. 'He's always off doing things for other people and I seem to come way down his list. I'm just an afterthought.'

'Sounds serious.'

'Sounds over.' There, she'd said it, not just to herself but to someone else. Somehow it made it more real.

'You mean that?'

Once more she considered the question, before whispering: 'Yes. Yes, I do.'

'In which case . . .'

'What?'

'There's not a lot of reason for you to go home.'

Suddenly he was laying siege to her nipple once more.

'What, again?' she laughed.

'Oh, yes, please. Again . . .'

12.32 a.m.

If Melanie hadn't been on her back but instead standing by the window of the hotel overlooking Hyde Park, she might have noticed the arrival of two USAF MH53Js. These helicopters, the largest and most powerful in the world, had twin turbo-shaft engines which kicked out more than four thousand shaft horsepower each and drove rotor blades that were seventy-two-foot long. The downdraft these monsters created was immense, hurling leaves, twigs and all sorts of ungathered rubbish high into the night air across the park. Long before the rotors had stopped turning, the men of Delta Force's A Squadron were fanning out across the low grass, establishing a perimeter while others began unloading their vehicles and heavier equipment. They'd brought a variety of weapons with them, an assortment of Armalites with Heckler & Kochs, and even a few grenade launchers – they hadn't known what to expect, but neither had the British. There was no opposition, no one to contest their right to use the banks of the Serpentine as a marshalling area. The nearby park police station had long since closed for the evening, and the troops in the Wellington Barracks overlooking the southern aspect of the park were mostly engaged elsewhere. After all, the attention of the British was still focused on Heathrow; they were only slowly beginning to realise that the military plane, obstinately stuck at the far side of the airfield and refusing to respond to instructions, was a decoy, a little game played almost for the sake of it, to distract attention from the other C-130 that had flown on what was listed as a training exercise to the USAF base at Mildenhall in Suffolk. That was where Delta

Force had switched to the helicopters before heading straight to Hyde Park.

Inevitably there was a no-fly zone in force above the capital but for the last ten miles they had flown very low and very slow, below the radar horizon, and with so much other military movement on the streets and in the air, two further helicopters succeeded in raising no alarms, despite the noise along their flight path. Their coming had been witnessed by little more than a couple of stray dogs, who watched in bemusement before turning tail and running.

12.58 a.m. (7.58 p.m. Eastern Standard Time)

President Edwards gazed out of the window of the Oval Office as if she were trying to get a full view of the action, even though it was taking place more than three and a half thousand miles away. She stood for some time, imagining, calculating, listening, trying to recreate in her mind the laughter of William-Henry and his friends as they had taken over a corridor for football practice or tried out their barber-shop harmonies in the Cross Hall. Wonderful echo, the Cross Hall. And suddenly she feared that an echo of her son was all she might be left with.

She was brought back from her private terrors by her cat, Psycho, winding his tail around her legs. Come to think of it even the cat reminded her of her son; William-Henry had given it to her as a gift on her first day in the White House and had insisted on naming it in his usual playful manner – 'after the Vice President,' he had said. And he hadn't been far wrong there.

She turned to face those in the room, not the Vice President but her Defense Secretary, the Secretary of State, and her National Security Adviser. They, too, were standing, uneasy, not feeling comfortable enough to sit.

'You know, gentlemen, even this desk is British,' she said, leaning on the large partner's desk that stood before the windows. 'A present from Queen Victoria, apparently, made from the timbers of one of their ships. It got stuck in the Arctic ice and we had to rescue it for them.'

'Seems to have become something of a habit over the years', her diminutive National Security Adviser suggested, his tone typically brash and a little mean.

'They've been on the ground more than five minutes now, Madam President,' the Defense Secretary said. 'And all's quiet so far.'

'What did you expect, cheerleaders?'

'I expect the British to cave in,' he replied. 'The most they might do is send one of their marching bands to try and blow Delta Force off the park with a chorus of bugles.'

'Don't underestimate them. Their military is formidable.'

'But not this fifth-round draft choice they've got squatting in Downing Street right now.'

'She's a woman. You never know what to expect from them.' She said it without a hint of a smile. 'What are we going to tell the world?'

'We've got no problem justifying it, Madam President,' the security adviser assured her. 'We can drag in any number of treaty obligations, the right of self-defense, cite whole volumes of law.'

'We're permitted to gatecrash their party by law?'

'We'll find one. We own the law.'

'No, I think you're wrong there. That attitude led us into the swamps of Iraq and Afghanistan. Law doesn't grow out of the barrel of a gun.'

'It did in the first President Harrison's time.'

'The world's moved on a little since then, I hope.'

'Are you . . . having doubts, Madam President?' the Secretary of State asked tentatively, his long face more doleful than usual.

'Of course.' She ran her finger along the rich imperial carving of the desk. 'This is the most difficult day I've had.'

The Secretary of State, his hands in his pocket, squeezed his balls. He was sixty-eight years old and was feeling dog-tired, yet needed all his wits about him for what he had to say. 'I would be failing in my duty if I didn't warn you, Madam President, of the price of failure. Whatever the grey nature of international law, this is one of those enterprises that in political terms has to be successful. Without that, the consequences would be dire. You'd be left fighting for your political life.'

'I understand. But I think fighting for my son's life is more important.'

'If you have doubts, Madam President, then please voice them now. We're very close to the point of no return.'

She looked up, her face drawn. 'Oh, I think we're well past that, don't you?'

1.07 a.m.

Tricia Willcocks decided that the time had come to join those who had gathered in Trafalgar Square. Her mind was made up when she heard that Frances Eaton, still distraught but dealing rather better with her plight, had suggested she might do much the same thing. In such circumstances two is not company and Tricia felt it only right that she should get there first.

They tried to stop her, of course. Her protection officers were against it on security grounds, but she told them that this was an hour of national peril shared by all the people and she felt it appropriate to spend a little while empathising. That was the word she used. The protection officer wasn't entirely sure he understood the implications of it, but in the face of her unwavering insistence he had little choice but to back down.

Officials at Number Ten were also opposed. Having been reluctant to allow her to sit in the Prime Minister's chair, they now seemed keen to keep her there. What if something happened, if she were needed urgently, they argued? But there was little to do at this hour except to wait, and Trafalgar Square was only one minute away by car. If she were needed, it would take her no longer to be with them than if she were in the ladies' room.

Her car brought her to the crowd barriers at the top of Whitehall where it entered the Square, and as she stepped out she caught her breath. At the dullest of times the square has a peculiar imperial magnificence with its column and lions and fountains, yet this evening it was as she had never seen it. On every ledge, in every corner, on steps, on plinths, around fountains and across every foot of pavement, people had come together in fear and in hope. Many prayed, some sang – not the jingoistic songs of Victorian times but softer songs of the Sixties, the quiet but insistent tones of the civil rights movement. 'We shall overcome,' they sang, and there was John Lennon to follow. Candles flickered defiantly in the cold night air. There was no traffic, the roads were impassable, flooded with people, and those who had squeezed into the square would long remember the stillness and simplicity of the moment.

She joined in, chatting quietly, stooping to console, helping to light a few more candles, even providing a shoulder for a young girl to weep on. She didn't stay long, only a few minutes, but long enough to symbolise a nation come together in its hour of need, and for the photographers to capture the images that she knew would make the morning news.

1.23 a.m.

A tramp found the body. It was lying face down beneath bushes along the towpath. It was a large man, not tall but stocky and overweight, almost bloated; that fact, and the cheap cider he'd been drinking, made it difficult for the tramp to roll the body out from beneath the spiky branches of the bush. It soon became clear that someone had got there first; there was no wallet to be found in any of the pockets, no mobile phone, and the only reason they seemed to have left the wristwatch was because its face was smashed. Yet that appeared to have been a mistake, for some tattered memory dredged up from his former life suggested to the tramp that the watch was one of the fashionable and hugely expensive kinds. The shoes were well crafted, too, and about the right size. Since the body had no further use for them, for a moment the tramp thought about an exchange deal. He took another swig from his bottle of cider and asked the body outright: 'You don't mind, do yer?', and since the body raised no objection he set about organising a swap. The overcoat would come in useful, too, and the soft cashmere scarf, although he drew the line at the trousers. After all, he had no idea who this man was. The tramp was drunk and old, and his calloused fingers didn't work as well as they might, but it wasn't long before the deal had been consummated and he had become one of the most exotically tailored tramps in the whole of London. He had another drink to celebrate.

It was these clothes that drew him to the attention of the local constabulary a few streets away and a little while later, and it was the stench of cheap drink that got him arrested. He was toothless and foul-mouthed, so no one took the slightest notice of his protestations about how he could help them solve a major crime. They just threw him in a cell to wait while he sobered up.

And that was why Bulgakov, the cardinal of the conspiracy, lay in the shadows with his secrets for a little while longer.

1.43 a.m.
'I can't let you go back in there again,' Tibbetts said.

For the past hour Harry had been sitting in the corner of the operations area in New Scotland Yard, sipping coffee, keeping his own counsel. Now he looked up with a cold, concentrated look in his eye. 'Mike, you can't stop me.'

'But—'

'He was a whisker away from pulling that trigger, Mike – I could feel it. You know what that's like?'

'Glad to say I never got quite that close.'

'Like falling off a horse. You get right back on and give the bastard a bloody good kicking.'

'You've done enough.'

'You saved my life in there, Mike.'

'And you still have sympathy with them?'

'I *understand* them – and even better now. They will kill again, of that I'm sure. So we know our enemy just a little better.'

'And fear him even more. All the greater reason for not sending you back in there.'

Harry toyed with his Styrofoam cup, breaking little pieces off the rim and flicking them towards a wastebasket. He missed consistently. 'There's something important in all this, Mike. It's not simply that you can't order some other poor sod to take my place and risk getting his balls blown off, not if he's got wife, family, the works – and Masood will be supremely suspicious of any new faces. It's . . .' He hesitated. 'It's about us as a country, a culture. Our self-respect. I've got to go back in there to show that we won't be cowed, that we're not running for cover simply because someone waves a gun at us. Hell, if I run, everyone in there will know it. What message will that send to them? That we've abandoned them, put our own safety before theirs, left them – quite literally – for dead?' He waved his finger at the screen. 'It could all fall apart in there, Mike, you know that. Those hostages aren't battle-trained troops but frightened men and women who came out today to do nothing but celebrate what this country stands for. And right now we have to remind them what that is, and what they might be dying for.' He crushed what remained of his plastic cup in a fist and hurled it towards the bin. It hit dead centre. 'I know patriotism is an old-fashioned concept, but it's part of what helps make us who we are. British. Men and women who believe in freedom and fair play – and silly things like crowns and Christmas and even a little cricket if it's not raining too hard. We may not do any of it very well any longer but we are still Britons who come from a long line of bloody-minded men who laid down their lives so that we could close our front door and tell the rest of the world to go fuck themselves when we've a mind to. Now, our friend Masood just kicked down that door. I can understand him as much as I want, but if we let him get away with it we lose not only what made this country great but also what makes it British. We have to get those hostages out, not just for who they are but for what they represent. They die – and we'll look back on this as the day our country died with them.'

Tibbetts was looking at Harry with a steady eye, trying to assess this exceptional man who somehow managed to carry a sword and burnished shield even when he was wearing nothing more than underwear. The policeman's job had marched him through most of the meaner streets of life where he hadn't met many men like Harry Jones, and he was sorry for it. 'So do I take that as a Doubtful or a Definitely Not?' Tibbetts said.

'Always sitting on the fence, that's me,' Harry responded, cracking a smile. 'Only one thing I'm sure of right now,' he added, rubbing the sore spot on the back of his neck. 'I've a little unfinished and very personal business with those gentlemen in the Lords.'

1.57 a.m.

The early hours are when minds begin to wander into places they have never been. Magnus sipped slowly from a bottle of water. Nearby, his father feigned sleep, doing battle with the devils within.

'Dad?'

With reluctance, John Eaton opened his eyes. 'Try to get some sleep, son.'

'No, Dad, I need to ask.'

Deep inside the father gave a cry of anguish. He knew what was coming; it was what he had tried so hard to avoid. He couldn't look into his son's eyes.

'What do I . . . ? How do I . . . ? What should I do? If it comes to it?'

'It won't, Magnus, I promise.'

At last he looked into the face of his son and saw that he was not believed.

'Dad, it's important. These men mean what they say. So if I have to die, I want to know how to do it properly.'

'There is no proper way for a man of twenty to die, for God's sake!'

'We don't choose our way, Dad. We just have to deal with it, as best we can. I . . . I want you and Mum to be proud of me.'

Tears were falling into the father's lap, splashing over his clenched hands. 'Magnus, there is nothing you could do that would ever stop your mother and I being proud of you.'

'But . . . I'm afraid.'

'We all are.'

'No, not that. I'm afraid I won't be able to do the right thing – you know? I don't want to piss in my pants or anything childish. Haven't done that since I was five. You remember? At Auntie Lucy's when she tickled me that Christmas?' He was trying to make light of it, his fears tumbling out in silliness, while the father writhed in misery. He brushed the tears from his face but he was sweating now, too, prickles of fear erupting on his brow. He tried to bury his wretchedness in a handkerchief.

'Make sure you tell Mum how much I love her.'

'Tell her yourself!' The words were spat out between clenched teeth. Eaton refused to accept any of this, wouldn't discuss it, was angered that his son insisted on continuing down this road.

'I love you too, Dad. Very much. I know as a family we don't do the emotion thing very well, but I think it's important to say. Now, most of all.'

The father grabbed his son's hand and held it very firmly. 'Magnus, it will not come to that. They'll storm the place before they allow anything like that to happen. They do drills in this sort of thing all the time. Remember the Iranian embassy – no, of course you won't, you weren't even born then, but the SAS are the best in the business. Just remain alert, be ready to take cover, when the time comes.'

'Dad, I need your help, this is important. It may be the last thing—'

'Don't you dare talk like that! It won't happen. I've given you my word.'

'That the SAS will come.'

'Yes!'

'Just like you said they'd release Daud Gul.'

'Don't taunt me!'

'I'm not taunting you, I'm playing for my life and asking for your help in what to do if it all goes wrong, Dad.'

'You cannot ask a father such things,' he moaned, writhing in his seat.

'OK. Fine. I'll go and ask Genghis Khan or whatever his bloody name is.' There was a framework of steel within the young man that had totally eluded his father. They were so very different; there was no way his father could help, except to resort to words and, if necessary, lies, as was his custom.

'I promise you, Magnus. I give you my word, as your father. I will do anything.'

'But you can do nothing.'

'Trust me!'

And with that, the politician sat back on the bench, using that as an excuse to turn a fraction from his son, hiding his shaking hands beneath his armpits while he prayed for the drink that would stop him trembling and drive him into the depths of absolute oblivion.

2.10 a.m.

Sopwith-Dane phoned while Harry was toying with a plate of full English that had been brought up from the Scotland Yard canteen. He didn't know when he would next get to eat and he needed to restore his energy levels, but it had been a mistake; the plate was cold and greasy by the time it reached him, and to make matters worse he'd just smeared ketchup on the sleeve of his shirt. Hand-tailored, Turnbull & Asser, Jermyn Street, bloody expensive, but now it looked like a rag. It had been taken off and slung over so many chairs while he stripped to his underwear that it had lost any remnant of its dignity, and it had also lost one of its cufflinks, a chip of turquoise set in silver that had been a birthday present from Mel. She said they matched the colour of his eyes. Not any more they didn't. His eyes were raw and bloodshot. The colour of ketchup. He replaced the cufflink with a bent paper clip.

'Three hundred years ago they'd have burned you as a witch, Harry, my boy. And bloody good riddance, too, I say. You know, I was on to a very hot date when you turned my world upside down.'

'You're always on to a hot date, Sloppy, which is why you're already three wives and several small fortunes behind the pace. Still, who am I to shout.'

'Ah, I sense trouble at the homestead.'

'Yes. I lost a cufflink.'

The revelation stunned the voluble PR man into momentary silence.

'You were telling me I should've been burned,' Harry encouraged.

'Seems your powers of astrological insight were spot on. Someone's been a clever little shit.'

Harry pushed the grease-covered plate away from him. 'Tell.'

'It's like those bastards in wine bars who always serve you short measures. No one will notice if they're not too greedy, if they do it little by little, but over time it makes one hell of a difference. So it seems that someone set up a very substantial number of companies in every imaginable tax haven across the Caribbean and even a couple of companies set up in Shanghai – ever been there? Wonderful place. You go to sleep, and next morning you find a skyscraper's been built overnight right outside your window, complete with bicycle racks and thousands of tiny yellow people running mail order businesses.'

'Sloppy!' Harry growled in warning.

'Ah, yes. Well, seems these companies have been set up for no other purposes than to lay a few bets on just such a day as this. Selling everything short. Betting that the Stock Exchange would take a dive but never placing such sizeable bets as would normally raise the interest of the regulators. Half a mill here, three-quarters there;

relatively small change to some of the big boys. But you place enough small bets and by the time you've finished you can stare George Soros in the eye without having to count your buttons. We're talking tens, perhaps even a hundred million here, Harry, that's how much some lucky tart's made from this little caper. The boys at the FSA are still checking, got a few more brokers' legs to break, but the fog is lifting and the battlefield grows clearer.'

'Well done, Sloppy.'

'Thank you, dear boy. I feel it's my lucky night. Why, my hot date might still be waiting for me.'

'And the name?'

'Christ, Harry, you'll be wanting her telephone number next!'

'Not the girl, you fool, the bloody punter. Mr Little and Large. What's his name?'

'Haven't the slightest. Far too soon to tell.'

'Then I fear, my dear Sloppy, that the young lady will have to wait. You've got a long night ahead.'

'We've already got rather a long night behind us.'

'I'm sorry, but—'

'It must be the witch in me, too. I'd rather guessed that's what you'd say.'

'Predictable, am I?'

'Predictable enough for me to have already sent out for doughnuts.'

2.33 a.m.

COBRA. The name conjured up many mysteries for those who had heard it whispered around the corridors of Westminster, like the inner sanctum of the temple whose secrets are known only to a select few. In fact, the name was a rather dull acronym for the Cabinet Office Briefing Room, a facility located near Henry VIII's tennis courts at the back of the Privy Council Office in Whitehall. It had the most modern communications facilities and was supposed to be secure from all types of eavesdropping. If anyone wanted to find out what had gone on, they would have to wait for the Sunday newspapers like everyone else. If it might loosely be called a war room, it was unlike anything seen in most Hollywood films – no vast screen of the world indicating where missiles were flying, no rows of military personnel seated behind computer consoles waiting to push buttons. COBRA seemed almost dull by comparison, not much more than a central table around which ministers and others sat, with advisers and support staff seated behind or in one of the subsidiary rooms. It wasn't so much a facility for waging war as dealing with national emergencies like bird flu and fuel strikes. It was more convenient than the Cabinet Room at Number Ten, which had little more than a telephone and an imported television, and it was to COBRA that Tricia Willcocks had moved her centre of operations. Sitting in the Cabinet Room and waiting on her own had grown oppressive. Anyway, she wanted another whisky and needed a fresh glass.

COBRA wasn't typically the place where foreign ambassadors were greeted; it was entirely against convention to allow outsiders access, but convention had been buried at around noon the previous day. When Robert Paine arrived he looked drawn, as though he had aged considerably in the last few hours. He elected not to sit. The informality they had shared in the garden of Downing Street was gone, and he sensed the meeting would be short. In any event, he found it easier to recite scripted lines while he was on his feet. 'Home Secretary, I asked for this meeting because matters are coming to a head. I have just spoken with the White House. It seems that Delta Force is now in a position to provide you with active assistance in this emergency. Conscious of the need to do everything we can to support such a valuable ally, our troops are ready to proceed directly to Westminster in order to support your own forces. The President is sure this offer of international assistance will be accepted in the spirit in which it is offered, between two of the oldest allies in the world.'

Tricia Willcocks stared at him, keeping him guessing. She had the palest of green-grey eyes. When she was younger they could rip a man's clothes off, but now, with age and with anxiety, they had turned to ice. Her reply, when it came, was offered slowly and with deliberation. 'You tell your President that she'll get her bra straps caught in a mangle over this one. If her flying hoodlums so much as make a move or even sneeze loudly, they'll be detained.'

She said no more, she simply sat and stared at him. She was trying to do a Maggie, browbeat him, but he had been told that Thatcher had always been immaculate even at times of extreme stress, while at this time of the morning the Willcocks hair was clearly in need of a few moments in front of a mirror. He also thought he could detect a whiff of whisky in the air. This wasn't going to be the moment to talk her round with bullshit about astronomy. He took a deep breath. 'That might be difficult, Home Secretary. They have orders to assist where possible – and to insist when necessary. The United States cannot be party to any deal with terrorists—'

'We're not offering one.'

'And since it seems unlikely they will offer to surrender, there can be only one outcome to this siege. We both know that.'

That was possible, even probable, but not yet certain. She didn't reply. She wasn't going to negotiate with him, either.

'The siege will have to be ended by force,' he insisted once more, 'and perhaps it is better that way. It will stand as an example to anyone who might consider resorting to terrorism in the future. If we can stand up to them now, together, we'll show them that all such acts are futile, doomed to end in failure.' He made a chopping gesture with his hand. 'The way we see it, there is no logic for the siege being allowed to continue.'

Ah, but the Englishwoman could, although she couldn't share her own logic with the American. She hadn't shared it with anyone yet. It still sat inside her, burning like acid.

'And so, Home Secretary, my government formally requests that this situation be brought to an end before any further deaths are incurred,' he said, finishing off his script.

'I can't do that. Such things need to be discussed. With colleagues.' She had no very high opinion of them, but they might yet provide a little cover.

'I repeat, Delta Force stands ready to assist you.'

'And I repeat, they will be intercepted.'

'They will not come quietly.'

She smiled, one of her cold gestures, but the words were pregnant with menace. 'Then they can come kicking and squealing, but come they will. Be sure to tell your president that. She can't go building her Alamos on my lawn.'

'They are already here.'

'And so is half the British Army!' It was a gross exaggeration, they both knew that military commitments around the world had left the British desperately overstretched, even at home, but the defiance matched her mood.

'You surely wouldn't fire on friendly troops.'

'You would if I sent a task force up the Potomac!'

'But we are allies . . .'

'Allies. Not lap dogs!'

'But that has never been the case.' And it was his turn to exaggerate wildly.

'I've bent over backwards to give your president the chance to change her mind, I've even left Delta Force squatting in Hyde Park when they should all be sitting in cells, every one of them, but this cannot go on. It must be brought to an end. So you hear this, Ambassador, and you hear this good. She has about twenty minutes to turn those troops around or suffer the consequences.' She slapped the table with the palm of her hand. 'And that is my last offer.'

The rims of her eyes were sore. Anger? Exhaustion? Perhaps the alcohol? Did it matter much which? Paine wiped his lips with the back of his hand. 'I fear she will not accept it.'

'Then we shall see who's got the sharpest claws.'

There was nothing more to be gained from talking to her. Another couple of whiskies and she might simply crumble and fall asleep. On the other hand, she could be like the Boston Irish who started a fight just for the fun of it. Only time would tell. The dogs of war had been let loose and it might take the rest of eternity before they were brought to heel. 'I think there's little more I can do here.'

'On that we are agreed,' she said primly.

'I will take my leave, Home Secretary.' He bowed his head. The audience was over. He was about to turn when she spoke again, her voice far softer now that the formalities were done.

'What will you do now, Robert?'

He pursed his lips in thought; they seemed tight, dry. 'I have to report your views back to my superiors.'

'Yes, do that. Do your duty.'

'Sometimes it feels like a curse. We bury our souls in duty.' For a brief moment it seemed as if he wanted to say more on the matter, to unburden himself of a great weight, but it passed. 'I shall be available for a few hours, in case of developments. I have some letters to write. After that . . .' He offered a thin smile. 'I must rejoin my friends.'

'I hadn't forgotten. And I hope that none of this is personal between the two of us. We both have our duty, Robert. I think you understand.'

Without a further word he turned and disappeared into the darkness.

2.53 a.m.

The police cells should have been quiet at this time of night. There was a routine that normally kept things running smoothly; every twenty minutes the prisoners were inspected for signs of attempted suicide, or sickness, or arson, or any of the other unpleasantries that go with being forced to stare your fate firmly in the eye, even smearing the walls with excrement. That happened; sometimes in the morning they had to hose the place down. But tonight all had been peaceful, up to now. Then, in an instant, the place flooded with commotion. There were shouts, protests, doors were being kicked, all to the accompaniment of an unholy animal-like wailing that was coming from behind one of the doors.

The duty sergeant rushed to the cell. He was a man of many years' experience who thought he had seen everything in his time, yet no sooner had he peered through the spy-hole than he stepped back in astonishment.

The tramp was sitting on the padded cement platform that made up his bed. The overcoat he had been wearing was now spread out beside him, ripped to pieces, its lining completely separated from the cloth. His mouth hung open, exposing all his blackened teeth, tears were streaming down his face, and he was laughing. Hysterically. The sergeant had never heard such a sound, nor seen such a sight, for around the tramp were strewn dozens and dozens of crisp fifty-pound notes, like cherry blossom in May. It was more money than the tramp had ever seen at one time in his life. And scattered amongst it all were three shiny new passports.

3.15 a.m.

The alleged irresistible force met the self-proclaimed immovable object at the bottom of Constitution Hill, beside the wall that ran around the gardens of Buckingham Palace and less than a mile from Delta Force's landing point beside the lake. Two British Spartan armoured personnel carriers were enough to block the road. The Americans could easily have found a way round them, through the park, even on the pavement, but the confrontation had to take place somewhere and this was as good a spot as any.

The leading Delta 4 by 4 braked sharply to a halt, its tyres skidding on the surface of the road. Those coming up behind spread out to give cover. From all sides came the insidious sounds of weapons being made ready. It was several seconds before a British Army officer marched out from the shadows and, as he reached the first Delta vehicle, saluted smartly, his right arm as tight as a spring.

'Captain Merrick Braithewaite, First Battalion, the Scots Guards,' he declared before standing at ease.

The American in the passenger seat of the lead vehicle gave a gentle wave back and spat out a large wad of gum. 'Colonel Nathan Topolski. The American Automobile Association, Phi Beta Kappa and the Sons of Cincinnati. At your service.'

The British officer cleared his throat. 'Colonel, under other circumstances it would be my pleasure, but I have orders to hold you here. You are not needed and, I regret, not very much welcome, either.'

The American took some time in lighting a small cigarillo. 'Don't remember you guys saying that in 1941.'

'Yes, you were late for that one, too.'

'So,' the American muttered, sucking deep on his cigarillo and exhaling a cloud of dense blue smoke, 'what's the punishment for trespass in these parts, captain?'

'We normally let people off with a mild caution. If they behave and leave the property immediately.'

'Funny thing, seems to me, you calling it trespass when the fire brigade's come to put out your fire.'

'Danger of getting wires crossed and hoses tangled, I'm afraid.'

'Horse shit.'

'I beg your pardon?'

'There's a danger of slipping in horse shit, too. Surprised you didn't mention it.'

'You could be stepping in a whole pile of it, colonel,' the captain responded, his voice lower, less gentle.

'But that's what we do, captain. Delta gets all the mucky jobs.'

'Colonel Topolski,' the young captain sighed, 'I don't get a lot of pleasure out of this. Indeed I find it rather awkward. The fact is, I rather like Americans.'

'Oh, really?'

'I saw action alongside your colleagues in Afghanistan. I also watch *The Sopranos* and I never say no to a bowl of Baskin-Robbins. And I lost a brother in 9/11. So, yes – really. But I have my orders which are unambiguous. You may return to your Starship Enterprise and transport yourselves back to your own galaxy, or, if you would prefer, I would be more than happy to entertain you to an early breakfast in the officers' mess. But you will not proceed any further.'

Slowly, the American flicked away his cigar butt, which performed a slow arc of death in the darkness. 'Now ain't that a bitch. You see, I've got my orders, too, which are to head on and help you out with your little situation. And since I'm a colonel and you're only a captain, I guess my orders beat yours. And I don't have time for breakfast. Nothing personal.'

'No offence taken. But we have a situation and you will not be permitted to proceed.'

'Delta don't turn tail.'

'Then we shall have to provide whatever degree of persuasion is required for you to change your mind.' He turned and shouted over his shoulder. 'Sergeant Major, tell the lads to make ready!'

The American glanced out into the night. Two APCs . . . 'I figure we outnumber you eight to one.'

The captain stiffened, rose on to the toes of his boots. 'Nevertheless.'

'What, you gonna light up this place like Disneyland?'

'Like Old Trafford.'

'Who?'

'Those are my orders.' It was said in a manner that allowed for no doubt.

'Hell, captain, then you're right. We have a situation.'

'It is one I very much regret, colonel.'

'Me, too. Saw myself what you guys did to the Taliban. Fought with you – fucked with you, too, when we got the chance of a little R&R.

I'm part English myself, on account of my grandpa marrying one of your girls when he was over here in '45. I'm on your side, captain – we all are. That's why we're here. But I guess you and me walked into one mother of a cat fight.' He began rummaging through the pockets of his blouson in search of another smoke, but came up empty-handed. He sighed. 'So you gonna shoot me?'

'I might ask the same.'

They stared at each other, as best they could in the darkness, neither of them willing to take the next step in a dance that had been choreographed by others. When at last the British officer spoke once more, his voice was low, as though he wished to be heard by no one other than Topolski.

'Know what, colonel? I think it would do no harm for us both to take a little guidance on the matter. Wouldn't do for you and me to start an international incident all on our own, now, would it? It seems that your President and my Home Secretary are calling each other's bluff and using us as bait – that's fine, goes with the job, but perhaps we should both report back on the operational difficulties we have encountered. Yes, *operational difficulties*, that's the thing. Give them a little longer to consider the consequences, perhaps find an alternative to you and me blowing each other's balls off. No need to rush things.'

While the American considered the proposal, instinctively he began scrabbling in his pockets once more, but no sooner had he started than the captain had taken a couple of brisk steps forward and with the skill of a magician was proffering a cigar case. 'Havana,' he explained, snapping the case open.

It took a while before the American stretched out a hand and accepted one, passing it beneath his nose, sniffing it with approval. 'We don't get these Cuban cigars. Embargoed.'

'All condemned men deserve one last smoke.'

'Specially one like this.'

'I suggest we enjoy it – while we both report back?'

Already the American was striking a match.

3.38 a.m.

Harry's phone buzzed.

'Wouldn't take a holiday to the Caribbean in the near future if I were you, old boy.'

'Why do you always talk in riddles, Sloppy?'

'In case someone realises how thick I am.'

'But you went to Harrow.'

'You can stuff the boy into education, but you can't always stuff the education into the boy, old chum. Nevertheless, I seem to have my uses. Been busy. Cayman Islands. British Virgin Islands. Dutch Antilles. We've been flapping our towels around them all. You won't believe the number of people we've had to bribe, browbeat or otherwise grotesquely threaten to get to the bottom of this. I've promised at least four of my contacts that the Home Secretary will sleep with them.'

'Was that the bribe or the browbeating?'

'She's seen as something of a sex symbol in the Caribbean, apparently. Must be a power thing.'

'I'd rather have my toenails pulled.'

'Anyway, these companies that have been placing bets on the Stock Exchange indices. All shells, of course. About thirty of the little blighters.'

'Who runs them?'

'With these sort of shell companies you'll find nothing but names on a brass plate. By law all the directors have to be local residents, but that's only for the sake of the paperwork. The beneficial ownership is always elsewhere.'

'Such as?'

'Mmmm, can't be sure, not yet. The local boys have still got a few doors to kick down and files to ransack. But they say it's got a very powerful whiff of Russia.'

'What?'

'It's all a bit coincidental at this stage, but you can usually smell the elephant long before he treads on your toes. Now, this might not have passed by your periscope, but later today the Russians were planning to float off another huge chunk of their metal mining industry on the London Exchange – you know, copper, magnesium, aluminium. This is really big business. They were hoping to raise more than a couple of billion pounds, but they can't now, of course, with the market falling apart. So, in a word, they've been stuffed, as tight as a Christmas turkey. The value of their existing shares has taken a huge hammering, while those investors who were lucky enough to sell them short are sitting on a killing.'

'And?'

'Now here's that magical coincidence, old boy. The companies who have been selling the Russians short—'

'Are the same shell companies in the Caribbean who have been betting on the siege.'

'Precisely. Hell of a coincidence, isn't it?'

'If you believe in fairies.'

'So it's back to the gulag for Boris and Yuri. Come a real cropper, they have; it'll cost them several vast fortunes. Bears with a very sore head.'

'But who, Sloppy, who's behind it? There are several hundred million Russians, we need to get a bit closer than that.'

'One slice of salami at a time, old chum.'

'Not good enough. We need the whole sausage, Sloppy. Get that, and maybe we can finish all this without a bloodbath. We need a name.'

'It's just not possible. The world out there sleeps, they won't jump out of bed just because we ask them. The shell companies in the Caribbean are owned, inevitably, by other shell companies. It's like the dance of the seven veils, goes on for ever. It'll take days, maybe weeks before we get to the bottom of it.'

Harry banged the table with his fist. 'Those poor bastards in the Lords only have a few hours!'

'Yes, I know. I feel wretched. I can only do my best.'

Harry hauled back hard on the anger that was threatening to overtake him. It wasn't his friend's fault. 'Thanks, Sloppy.'

'I'm so bloody sorry, Harry.'

As he closed his phone connection, Harry felt overwhelmed by exhaustion and hopelessness. His shoulders hunched and he seemed physically to shrink in his chair.

'You still chasing shadows?' Tibbetts asked, sipping at yet another mug of coffee.

'Yes. But we think they're Russian shadows.'

'Sounds like progress.' He looked up sharply from his steaming coffee. 'But it has to be a Russian with a British connection.'

'Narrows it down from a few hundred million to a few hundred thousand, I suppose. More progress.' Harry sighed sardonically.

'But what are the bloody Russians doing wrapped up in all this? Doesn't make a bit of sense that I can see.' The policeman bit his thumb and winced, hoping the pain might help bring some order to his thoughts. When he opened his eyes once more, he found a young detective constable standing in front of him. The young officer was hesitant, shifting awkwardly from one foot to the other.

'Sorry, sir, for interrupting. Couldn't help overhearing. Something about the Russians.'

'DC Witherstock, isn't it?' Tibbetts enquired.

'Yessir.'

'Well, Witherstock, what about the Russians?'

'It's just that . . . something strange has been going on up in Highgate. There's a tramp in the local nick who's walked in with a coat stuffed with fifty-pound notes. Several thousand pounds sewn into the lining, apparently. Clearly not his.'

'So?'

'Also inside the lining were three passports. They were in different names but evidently of the same man. A chap they think is actually Russian. Called Bulgakov.'

'Lavrenti Bulgakov?' Harry snapped. 'He's one of the Russian exiles we let squander their money around London.'

'Seems so, sir. I just thought there might be, you know, some connection.'

'Yes, but what?'

'Dunno, sir.'

'Then we'd better find out. And sharp. Get Bulgakov brought in,' Tibbetts ordered, 'wherever he is.'

'Oh, we can't do that, sir.'

'And why the bloody hell not?'

'Seems he's dead. They just found a body. Matches the passports.'

'Bugger!' Tibbetts snapped in frustration.

'But that's wonderful!' Harry interjected, leaping to his feet, his energies suddenly restored.

'That the man you've been searching for all evening is dead?'

'I don't believe in coincidences, Mike. Like one of those Russian *matryuoshka* dolls – you know, you take the lid off and there's always something hidden inside it. I'll bet what's left of my pension fund after this miserable day that Bulgakov is mixed up in the siege. A man of many passports could surely find a few fake IDs for Masood and his chums and—' Suddenly the outburst of enthusiasm drained into the sand and he froze. Reluctantly, he let slip a curse. 'It only leaves us with one question, Mike.'

'Which is?'

'Who the hell killed Bulgakov?'

'A mystery that must wait, my friend,' Tibbetts replied, reading from the pager that had begun vibrating on his belt. '*La Tricia* calls. The royal summons.'

'I don't think there's a vacancy for Queen, yet.'

'No. But I suspect she thinks there may soon be one for Prime Minister.'

3.53 a.m.

The war council had gathered in the COBRA briefing room. It included the intelligence services, defence chiefs, junior ministers from several ministries, a handful of the most senior civil servants, including one from the Attorney General's office to ensure fair play while they figured out how they would kill the terrorists. Every one of them looked drained and most were in various stages of dishevelment, even Tibbetts, as he searched for a second wind. Harry still had ketchup on his shirtsleeves, and no tie. The police commander had smuggled him in; Willcocks pretended not to notice, at least for the moment. She had other battles to fight.

'We have eight hours left before the deadline,' she announced, rapping the table with a pen to gather their attention. 'We have to decide on our course of action. I've asked Brigadier Hastie to give us another briefing.'

The Commander of Special Forces stood up and walked to the screen on the wall at one end of the room with its picture from inside the chamber. His red hair stood out incongruously against the claret of the leather benches. 'This is an interesting situation, Home Secretary,' he began in typically understated military fashion. 'As I told you earlier, we have difficulties with the exceptionally high windows, the overhangs of the balconies and the fact that the doors are all booby-trapped. But we can get round those. The camera feeding the television pictures is mounted in a specially constructed platform set high in the public gallery, which is at the opposite end of the chamber to the throne. It's inevitably compact, only room for one man, but in the last couple of hours we've managed to get a sniper inside who has a full view of everything. Took a risk getting him there, but it's paid off. And the Victorians were wonderful craftsmen; Barrie designed this building with all sorts of shafts for ventilation and heating. We've managed to get another couple of snipers inside these, which gives them visual over different parts of the chamber through access panels. It's a problem that much of the rest of the chamber is extremely stoutly built, so we'll have to go in through the doors, blow them. Follow up with grenades – we call them flash-bangs – designed to create maximum confusion. There is, of course, also a royal protection officer still inside, but it's possible he might be as disorientated as we hope the enemy will be, so we can't rely on him. We estimate the entire operation will be accomplished in no more than forty seconds.'

'And casualties?' Willcocks asked.

Hastie sucked his lips. 'Earlier you will recall I estimated a ninety per cent survival rate.'

'But that will have improved now you have your men in position.' She made it sound like an instruction.

'Indeed, Home Secretary. However, there's still a problem. The enemy appears to be not only well armed but also well trained. Established excellent firing positions here, here, here and here,' he said, pointing to the screen. 'We can't assume they're amateurs. If we also assume that they are dedicated, willing to give their lives and ready to act with maximum prejudice . . . well, it makes it much more difficult.'

'How many will die, brigadier?' she pressed.

'There are too many imponderables to be specific. If we could use the windows, or have more men in position, or knew we could rely on the protection officer . . .'

She leaned forward, waiting to pounce. Everyone else in the room shifted uncomfortably, coming to the edge of their seats.

'Brigadier, I haven't asked you here for a description of how to dance a waltz. I want to know your best estimate, and I want to know it now.'

He returned her fierce stare, but his voice had dropped. 'I believe the survival rate might be slightly higher than ninety per cent, Home Secretary. But that is unlikely to include Her Majesty.'

'That is unacceptable!' She banged the table in irritation. 'Have none of you found a way of saving the Queen?'

'There is still no way around the problem of the explosive jacket.

If the terrorist holding it is willing to die, then so will the Queen. It's as simple as that. If she could manage to escape, even for a few seconds . . '

'She's eighty-four years old, for pity's sake.'

'We can take the terrorist out, but that action in itself will in all probability trigger the device. We have to assume it's likely to work.'

'Then find another way.'

'I cannot, Home Secretary.' He stood in front of the screen, defiant. 'And because of the unique circumstances, and particularly the risk that any action will pose to the safety of the Sovereign, I'm sure you will understand that I will require a written order before I proceed.'

Along the table, the Chief of Defence Staff was indicating his agreement.

They all turned their eyes on Tricia. She had known it would come to this, the blame game, the parcelling out of responsibility, allocating guilt for what was to happen. Someone would have to pay for the killing of the Queen, and if they had their way, they would leave her to swing on her own. The sacrificial lamb.

But they underestimated Tricia Willcocks. She was a survivor, and even if she couldn't save her Sovereign, there was a chance she might yet save herself. She was one step ahead of them all. Slowly she began shaking her head. 'No. You cannot.'

'Home Secretary?'

'You cannot proceed.'

'But what are the alternatives?' someone asked.

'You cannot proceed – yet. If we order an attack that results in the death of the head of state, without it being clear even to the most jaundiced eye that there was no other option, then each and every one of us will be as culpable as those who signed the execution warrant of Charles I. Go in too soon and it would be a disaster. We are staring history in the face, gentlemen, we must hold our nerve.'

'We should go now, while they're sleepy, catch them off guard,' Hastie said. 'If we delay, it will only get worse.'

'I disagree. It might make our position very much easier, brigadier. Justify everything you may be forced to do, no matter what the outcome. If we wait, we test the terrorists, and they will give us the absolute proof that we had no other choice.'

'What more proof do you need, Home Secretary?'

Suddenly they had all caught up with her, and as they came to understanding, they felt sick. All eyes went to the screen, and to the spot where Magnus and William-Henry, the two youngest hostages, were sitting. The gunmen had said these boys would be the next to die, and if that came to pass, their innocent blood would wash away all guilt for what happened thereafter.

Eight

'Are you asleep, Mama?'

She said nothing, but pursed her lips in a withering expression of denial.

'Some seem to have managed it,' the son protested in his own defence. Charles Philip Arthur George, the Prince of Wales and, alongside that, the Earl of Chester, Duke of Cornwall, Duke of Rothesay, Earl of Carrick, Lord of the Isles and Butt of Much Criticism, stretched out his stiffening legs and surveyed the scene in front of them.

'Then they have a better conscience than I,' his mother replied.

'You've no reason for reproach.'

'They might die, these people, all because of me. And they know it. If I weren't here, then none of this would have happened.'

'These thugs would have found some other excuse.'

'Perhaps, but today I bear the responsibility.'

'As every day.'

They were speaking in whispers, leaning towards each other, conscious of the gunman immediately behind them and trying not to attract attention, looking out at the others rather than at each other, as they had done for so much of their lives.

'I am afraid, Charles.'

He shifted in his seat. 'You – afraid?'

'Not for myself, of course, not that, but for what this day might do to us. The Family. The monarchy. I fear it might bring about the end of it all. The people might say that if this is the price we have to pay, then we no longer wish it.'

'I've often thought precisely that myself,' he responded wistfully.

She shot a caustic look at him from the corner of her eye.

'But it's true, Mama. I sometimes wonder if any life is worth the indignities that are inflicted on us.'

'We have a choice?'

'It's too late for you and me, of course. But the boys . . . They should be able to make up their own minds.'

'And if you'd been given a choice?'

'In another world, another life, who knows?' he replied, his voice filled with unfulfilled dreams. Then, as so often, the other side of his nature kicked in. 'Things grow so contrary, Mama. You never know, this nonsense might just as easily make us more popular.'

'Perhaps. But public opinion is like one of those heavy cannon they used in the Great War, so desperately unreliable, so fearfully inaccurate, yet hurled at one target after another until nothing is left but wasteland.'

'Democracy is often heavy pounding.'

'Particularly in the hands of Mr Eaton.'

'You don't approve?'

'Of that?' She bent her head in the direction of the crumpled figure that was her Prime Minister.

'I thought – I had read – that you got on well.' His mother's views were often a mystery to him, communicated through formal notes, blazoned across front pages or occasionally thrust across the breakfast table at Balmoral. Their minds rarely followed the same track.

'Mr Eaton would like people to think that he and I have a warm and glowing relationship, which is why he spreads the story. Anything for a headline. A man of mirrors, not of substance.'

'You don't normally express such strong opinions.'

'I'm not normally allowed, but for one day in my life, Charles, I think I shall grant myself a little dispensation. A queen is allowed a few of her own judgements, particularly on a day like this. I'm just so desperately sorry you have been forced to share it with me.'

'Kismet.'

'No. I'm sorry, Charles, you are here because I insisted you should be. Dragged you here against your will, we both know that.'

'I suppose I'm used to it.'

'I thought I was doing right, showing you off as my son, the heir, the next in line. You've waited so long.'

'You're tired, Mama. Don't torment yourself.'

'I am also old, Charles. I'm beginning to think I've lived perhaps longer than was wise.'

'Nonsense!'

'But it's true. Over these last years I've seen so much of what I cherish, those things that truly matter to me, demeaned and under-mined. The Church, our Family, our gentle way of doing things in this country. Everything nowadays is taken to extremes. What happened to us, where did all that respect for each other go?'

They sat staring at their attackers, weapons in their hands, watching over their captives, before she returned to her theme.

'In some ways it would have been better had I died young, like my father.'

'You talk of death as though it were simply another part of duty,' he protested.

'In some ways it is. The death of a monarch is also a time of renewal.'

'Not for the chap involved.'

'We have to separate self from it all, Charles.'

He wrung his hands in agitation. 'One can't simply be a mere cipher, a monarch without one's own identity.'

'You cannot, perhaps.'

He bristled. 'Meaning?'

'This is a day when we must all do our duty, quite irrespective of self.'

'Are you implying that I don't always know my duty?' he demanded, growing heated. It was a raw point. So many others had said as much, accused him of being selfish, interfering, a prince who didn't act up – or down – to his station, but he was damned if he would hear it from his mother.

'I imply, Charles – oh, I imply that my shoes are killing me,' she said, rubbing one ankle against the other and adeptly changing the subject.

'If I were you I'd kick them off. To hell with what others think.'

She sighed. 'I think you've rather made my point for me.'

4.02 a.m.

COBRA was in turmoil. They sat stunned at what she was proposing, and struggling to find the weakness in it.

'So we are to sacrifice our firstborn,' whispered a civil servant.

'No one will die, unless the terrorists insist on it,' Willcocks retorted.

'Is it not time to consider, in these dire and unique circumstances, letting their leader go?' he pleaded.

'Think it through, man,' she replied waspishly. 'They are assassins, cold-blooded killers. And you would let them go – why, because you are afraid to stand up to their threats? Leave this country open to every blackmailing bastard? Who do you think we are,' she spat, 'Belgium?'

'We might at least propose the outline of some deal – a trial of Daud Gul by an international panel, perhaps, or release in return for a promise of his future abstinence.'

'Trust the word of a terrorist? Are you mad?'

'Something, we must try something!' the civil servant responded, quite in despair. 'We cannot allow them to kill the Queen.'

'You think giving in to terrorism would save her? Surrender – never! Every drop of blood shed in future by these swine would be on your hands – and her hands, too. We'd be throwing away the rules of justice on which we have built all our freedoms – for what? For *whom*? Is there any other person in the country we would do that for?' She glanced around her; her eyes were exhausted but behind them still burned a peculiar passion. 'Imagine the headlines – oh, not tomorrow or the next day, perhaps, but soon, and for ever after. She would no longer be the symbol that brings us all together but a target of envy. We'd be right back to the days of divine right, them and us, the haves and have nots, one rule for them and to hell with the rest of us. Can't you hear Rupert Murdoch already sharpening the axe? And once the media started, they'd do just as effective a job of murdering her as those terrorists, except it would be done more cruelly. No, you wouldn't have saved her, you'd have dragged her to the block!' Her nostrils flared with defiance. 'So if you value your Queen, as I do, this is the only chance she's got.'

'It's a deal with the Devil,' the civil servant persisted.

'No!' she retorted, her pale eyes blazing with anger. 'What *you* propose – giving in to terrorists – is that!'

The civil servant pushed himself back in his seat as though trying to force himself away from the table, appalled at the ferocity of her attack, and struggling with its logic. Others around the table rustled in discomfort, until Tibbetts spoke. 'There might be an angle we haven't considered – that I hadn't considered until a few minutes ago. I'll ask Harry Jones to explain, it's his baby.'

Harry looked at Tibbetts; the policeman raised an eyebrow in a gesture of apology and despair. He was pushing his friend into an arena full of lions, but what alternative did they have?

'We lack solid evidence, it's all rather circumstantial,' Harry began, 'but there appears to be a strong Russian connection here.'

There was a marked change in the atmosphere around the room.

Most around the table sat up attentively; they liked the sound of that, having the Russians to carry the blame. Even Tricia, for once, looked interested in what he had to say.

'Bulgakov. Levrenti Bulgakov,' Harry began.

'Levrenti *Valentin* Bulgakov?' the man from MI5 interjected, as though he had been offered the finest of clarets and delighted at last that matters might be moving back on to his patch.

'He's one of the Russian playboys we allow to squat in this country while they conduct ancient vendettas against each other and squander their ill-gotten billions. Bit like Danegeld; they pay their taxes and we let them get on with it, until it breaks out into open warfare on the streets.'

'Or on our soccer pitches,' Five added smugly.

'Bulgakov's relatively low-profile, so far as I know . . . ?' He looked for reassurance at Five, who shrugged and nodded in acquiescence. 'Certainly not one of the usual suspects,' he agreed.

'But he seems to have known enough about the siege to have made several considerable fortunes from it.'

'Has he? *Has he?*' Five exclaimed, suddenly taken in excitement. 'My giddy aunt, yes! Don't you see . . .' He glanced around him. 'Bulgakov was old KGB. Sharp-end stuff. Stirring up discontent in one quarter and ruthlessly squashing it in another. If memory serves me correctly, his last operational posting was in Afghanistan – up to his armpits in Uzbeks and Pashtus and Wazirs and Mehsuds and all their delightful little blood feuds.'

'You're saying he might know Masood?' Willcocks pressed.

'Quite possibly. Might even have slept with his granny.'

'Russians!' she exclaimed, with enthusiasm.

'It may not be quite that simple,' Harry continued. 'He may also have been playing a game against his fellow Russians. One of the casualties of this siege is the Russian attempt to float off a huge chunk of their metals industry. It was supposed to come to the market later today but that's been ruined, and in the process could well come close to ruining several of the Russian oligarchs he's fallen out with. This isn't just about money, it also seems like a complicated game of settling old scores.'

'So he had motive, ability and opportunity,' Willcocks declared, counting the tally on her painted fingers, her mangled nail forgotten.

'And it's far from being the first government he's held hostage,' Five added, as others began to talk with relief and growing excitement about the connection. They were all willing to clutch at an opportunity to absolve themselves of responsibility for infanticide, and even Willcocks joined in the new spirit. The Russians might prove an ideal ally to help muddy the waters.

'Before we get ahead of ourselves, there's something else,' Harry said, interrupting the flow of enthusiasm. 'Bulgakov's dead.'

The announcement threw the room once more back into silence.

'His body was discovered an hour or so ago,' Tibbetts added.

'Nothing too peaceful, I hope,' someone muttered.

'Too early to say,' the policeman replied. 'Found at the bottom of some steps by Regent's Canal. An autopsy's underway.'

'But unless we believe in divine intervention, I think we can assume it was probably foul play,' Harry continued.

'Pity,' Hastie said. 'We might have been able to use him to negotiate.'

'Perhaps we still can,' Willcocks said, her voice lower, having lost its sharp, combative edge. 'Let them know that their little plot has been rumbled. Tell them we've frozen their money, or that their paymaster's run off without them, that they're on their own. Surely it gives us some sort of psychological advantage, something we can use.'

And they were off again, talking animatedly across each other, suggesting ways in which the Bulgakov connection might bring them out from beneath the shadow. Their cell door had been opened, even if only a fraction, and they were desperate to hurl themselves through it.

'Hang on, if he was murdered, don't we need to find out who killed him?' Harry tried to intervene, but in their relief and their haste, no one seemed very interested.

4.13 a.m.

Inside the chamber they had come to the bleakest hour of the night, when hope and resilience fade into a greyness of the soul. The prince stirred, unable to sleep.

'You don't suppose there's a chance these men are undercover reporters from the *News of the World*, do you?' he asked, feigning levity.

'I fear not,' his mother replied.

'You can never tell nowadays.'

'Just this once I wish they were. I wish so many things – that we might wake up and discover we were merely players in one of your dreams.'

The prince stiffened. His fondness for analysing his own dreams had been the cause of much ridicule over the years. 'Why do you mock me?'

'I don't, Charles. At least, I don't intend to. If I've been clumsy, I apologise.' Silently, she scolded herself for being clumsy, but he had always been a sensitive soul. 'You're a man who is so easily bruised.'

'There you go again,' he said sorrowfully. It wasn't the time to revive old squabbles, but they were exhausted, tense, too tired to resist themselves.

'That isn't criticism, Charles, it's a fact of life – of *your* life, at least. You have something of your grandfather in you.'

'He was never attacked in the way I have been.'

'True, but he took advice to protect himself. And you've never taken kindly to advice.'

'Not from your advisers.'

And they were off, cantering round a course that had seen so many headlong races in its time.

'You have never allowed me to help, Charles. You lecture the entire world about their problems, yet you never come to me with your own. You treat me like a public audience.'

'You never knew – never wanted to know – what was going on in my life.'

'Not true!' A close observer might have imagined that she raised her hand, just fractionally, and slapped it down again in frustration. 'Sometimes I have known too much, more than any mother ever should. But I have turned more blind eyes to my family than there are jewels in a crown.'

'Blind eyes and closed doors,' he muttered resentfully.

'I don't follow.'

'One of my earliest childhood memories, Mama. I was five – possibly six. I had no playmates, no friends. I seem to remember that my favourite game was walking past the guardsmen on duty. It forced them so they had to come to attention and stamp their feet in salute. I even started throwing snowballs at them one winter, until Papa ordered the sentries to start throwing them back.'

'A royal life is often a lonely one, you know that.' It was a comment meant to convey sympathy, but he mistook it for complacency.

'So then I came one day to the door of your office – do you remember? No, of course you wouldn't. I asked you if you would come and play with me. Like other mothers.'

This time she offered no comment of any kind.

'You said you were busy, and you closed the door on me.'

'A royal life is often a busy one, too . . .'

'Too busy for your children? It's a mistake I've always been careful to avoid.'

She bridled at the implied insult, yet in the same moment her heart was shredding. The confusion drained all the colour and tenderness from her reply. 'You have been a magnificent father.'

'But as a prince?' he demanded. He seemed determined to provoke her, to find the least intended of slights and to punish himself. It was a habit that had grown old with him, and been with him too long to avoid.

She considered his question carefully – too carefully; she had never been one to take royal duties lightly. 'As a prince,' she replied softly, 'you have strayed from the path too often.'

'The path?' He was colouring as words of anger rose in his throat. 'Do you mean the path set out by my father? Or your sister? Or your uncle? Or your great-grandfather? Or—'

'I am not talking about personal morality,' she interrupted. 'I'm talking about public duty, and I make no apology for complaining when I find myself seated beside the Chinese head of state, trying to engage him in diplomatic small talk over dinner, while your condemnation of him and his entire regime is still ringing in his ears. "Appalling old waxworks", is that what you called them?'

'That's unfair. You know those comments came from private diaries.'

'Oh, Charles,' she sighed, 'nothing we do can ever be truly private, haven't you learned that yet?'

'And why not? Are we supposed simply to sit back and watch our lives, our loyalties, our way of life, ripped apart by those who spend their days scribbling in sewers? Should we raise no hand in protest when we see them doing the same to those we love – our children, even? That might have been good enough for you, but for me – never!'

'Charles, you wrote a book about it all – or had your friend write it for you. About the most private things in your life, your family, your marriage, your . . .' Now her hand did move, only slightly, but in a dismissive gesture. She had no desire to mention her son's adultery, even if he had written about it and discussed it in agonising detail on television. But she didn't need to mention it; he knew exactly what she meant.

'Still you blame me – for the marriage!'

4.26 a.m.

Tricia Willcocks had moved to one of the private COBRA suites to take the call. She'd been avoiding it, even though she knew it must come as inevitably as weeds follow the spring sun. Whatever its outcome, she knew matters could never be the same; you didn't cross the President of the United States and call her bluff yet manage to walk away with no scars. 'Madam Home Secretary,' she heard the voice say. 'Madam President,' she replied. They were like two fencers presenting their blades.

'I think we need to speak,' the President began.

'I thought we had spoken.' It was a blunt, instinctive and undeniably harsh rejoinder by Willcocks, which left her wondering whether she had done it intentionally, as a deliberate tactic designed to unsettle the other woman, or whether she had been unsympathetic simply because it was her nature. Perhaps it was the whisky egging her on – but, no, she hadn't finished that, the glass was still half full.

President Edwards pretended to ignore the slight. 'It's less than eight hours to their deadline. I need to know what your intentions are.'

'My intentions', she replied, 'are to ensure the security of my Queen and my country. From all comers.'

A long pause. Then, slowly: 'Please understand. We want to help.'

It was an olive branch; Tricia Willcocks grabbed it, only to snap it in two. 'One of my earliest political memories was of another American President saying much the same thing. About a place called Vietnam.'

'Don't fight me, Tricia.'

'Then back off, Madam President.'

But neither of them knew how. They hadn't risen so high by seeing the other man's point of view.

Edwards sighed. 'I see this in one of two ways. Let's move ahead – say, a couple of months. You and I are together at the White House, and America is throwing the biggest street parade you've ever seen, in your honour. The whole world sees us standing side by side, just as we did throughout this crisis. How does that sound?'

'I have this thing about invitations delivered on the point of a bayonet.'

'I offer nothing but the hand of friendship.'

'So why is it at my throat?'

'For pity's sake, Tricia, what's with all this hostility? America has rights, too, under mutual defence treaties and any number of tenets of international law.'

'Which would those be, precisely?' Willcocks demanded in a voice marinated in scepticism.

'I'll get the State Department to send you over a list.'

'And that's your second option, is it? America just takes over once again?'

'I think the world would understand why we were so keen to help. Look, I didn't want to have to make this point, but others will so I'm just going to go ahead and do it for you . . . This is a crisis of your making as much as anyone's. You're under pressure, an untested minister thrown into a position way beyond her swimming depth – one who, sadly, had screwed up big time and who gave assistance to the leader of the terrorist group in the first place. I could see some *very* unpleasant headlines coming out of that.'

'You wrap your threat up so skilfully, Madam President,' the Englishwoman said, leaning forward as she spat into the phone. It brought her closer to the whisky.

'I don't threaten. I simply point out to you the likely outcome. Instead of a tickertape parade and marching bands, they'll be lining up to throw trash at you. Your career ruined. That's not what I want, believe me. I admire the way you fight your corner, stand up for yourself. I'd like to think that if we got to know each other better, we'd be friends.' Hell, it was another olive branch. It would probably be used for kindling, but what had she got to lose? 'But know this. If you end up being responsible for the death of my son, there is nothing I can or would do to stop them bombing your reputation back into the Stone Age. I hope I make myself clear.'

'Perfectly. But I think there's something you may have overlooked.'

'I'd like to hear it.'

'Scenario One. We go in, release the hostages. I'm a superstar. In which case, what need do I have of invitations to the White House?'

'And if you fail . . .'

'Ah, Scenario Two. Well, that's the point where I get round to blaming it all on you.'

'On me?' President Edwards sounded astonished.

'Not just sending Delta to get in our way, yet another example of American imperialism at its most inept. I think the media would insist on knowing about your personal interference. Of your hyper-emotional state. The mother of all muck ups.'

'Jesus H Christ, you play it rough.'

'It's a rough situation,' Tricia retorted, noticing that her nervous tapping of the table had brought her hand to a point directly beside the glass.

'Don't you understand that I don't give a rat's ass what happens to me. All I want is my son.'

'And that's your weakness, just as it has been John Eaton's. Two parents whose judgement was consumed by a guilty conscience.'

'Guilt? What the—'

'And if those kids die, don't blame me. It should be on your conscience for as long as you live.' And now she drank.

There was a sound that may have denoted a breathless gasp – or was it a half-muffled cry of agony? – from the other end of the phone. 'I feel sorry for you, Tricia, a woman who seems unable to distinguish between love and guilt. Who simply doesn't know the difference. What a sad, sad life you must have led.'

'Don't patronise me!' she bit back, immediately wishing she hadn't. The personal note had got to her. For the first time she was rattled, it had burrowed under her skin, and they both knew it.

'I didn't mean to patronise. I apologise. There are some things in this life we simply can't control.'

Tricia bit her thumb in the forlorn attempt to ward off the sudden onrush of pain. Did this bloody woman know? Had someone told her – about all those husbands, about the waiting rooms and medical treatments, the excruciating examinations and the catastrophic disappointments she had been forced to endure as she had tried to become the mother she so desperately wanted to be? As each fresh round of doctors and sour-faced technicians had dug their way into her, each more urgent than the last, they seemed to have scraped away a little more of what had been left of the lining of Tricia's soul. Nothing had worked, and she had withered inside. She was barren. Now every hormonal flush seemed to mock her, and she wondered if the other woman was mocking her, too.

'One last thing I'd like to know, Home Secretary, if I may? Do you intend to mount an assault? And if so, when? I think I, of all people, have a right to know.'

'It's not decided. Perhaps not even necessary.'

'Not necessary? But how . . . ?'

'We have a Russian card to play.'

'A Russian card? I don't understand. Please – *please*, Tricia. Save my child . . .'

Her child? *Her child?* Tricia's life had been filled with other people's snivelling children, smiling at them, pretending she was happy for them, and suddenly she could take it no longer. She cut the connection. As the room fell silent she reached for the comfort of her glass, only to find it empty, like so much in her life. Slowly, she refilled it with tears.

4.47 a.m.

'I wasn't the only one to write a book,' the prince muttered bitterly. 'She wrote one, too. Everyone writes books, so why not me? Why shouldn't I? Why should I always be the one on the receiving end? The whole wretched world seems to be filled with authors who know more about me than even I do.'

'But you are the heir to the throne. And books can have such a bitter aftertaste,' his mother replied. 'I had a governess when I was a child. Crawfie – you've heard me talk of her. A most wonderful, loving woman. Sixteen years she was with us. Helped make me who I am, and much better than I was. Then she blabbed. Wrote a book. We could never speak to her again.'

'But I had to speak out,' he persisted. 'I felt so dreadfully let down.'

'You have always looked at the dark side of the moon, Charles.'

'And you?'

'For myself, I have always tried to see the best in a situation. I have to. How else can one deal with such odious creatures as Mr Eaton?'

'You couldn't deal with Diana, any more than could I.'

'True enough. Do you remember, she once upstaged me at the State Opening? Used it to launch her new hairstyle. I seem to remember having a few harsh words about it at the time – but in private. Always in private, Charles. And, yes, I always knew she would be impossible.'

'You didn't tell me.'

'Oh, but I think I did. I believe you failed to listen.'

'I had to marry her. What choice did I have? All the sensible girls had turned me down.' He bit his lip. 'I feel – I *felt*,' he said, correcting himself as though to give himself a little distance from what he was about to say, 'that you gave me no support.'

'I was there for you, whenever you wanted me. I didn't interfere, that's true, because I know how difficult these things can be. Being married to your father could scarcely be described as a relentless song of joy, but we've made it work. And there seemed to be enough people already interfering in your marriage – no, not Camilla, I mean your friends, the entire world's press, even the Government. But I was always there for you. And I always will be.'

'Didn't seem that way. What did the poet Larkin say? They mess you up, your mum and dad.'

'I believe his language was a little more brutal.'

'Wives, too.'

'And children.'

'Not my children!'

'Not them, thank the Lord.'

'They fuck you up, your mum and dad . . .' He shook his head in sorrow.

For once she didn't admonish him, and, for the first time, turned towards him. 'Yes, there's a lot of your grandfather in you, Charles. I loved him so.'

'And your Uncle David?'

'Him? No. He was a romantic, too, like you, in some ways. But he never had a fraction of your commitment to any cause other than his own, and that awful Mrs Simpson. You have always been a man of enthusiasms, and if they have sometimes seemed to me to be perhaps sometimes misplaced, I've always thought it better to be a slave to enthusiasm than to indulgence.'

'I'll take that as praise.'

'And I meant it as such. You dream of a world as you would want it to be, Charles. Sadly, I have to deal with the world as it is.'

'It seems we're both going to have to do that today.'

5.13 a.m.

They were still waiting for her, gathered in the main conference room of COBRA. She had refreshed her lipstick but beneath the make-up she was pale and the eyes were rimmed with a red frost. She was dabbing at her nose, which appeared damp, and she stumbled slightly as she sat down in her seat. Exhaustion was biting at them all. These were the most dangerous moments, the greyest watches of the night as it stretched out towards dawn, the hour when colours fade, resolution wanes and judgement fails. Such hours are often left to those with the most to prove, those who are driven, obsessed by some inner sense of failure that requires redemption. Perhaps that is why so many politicians are night birds, and amongst them, Tricia Willcocks was a hawk.

'So, we play a little Russian roulette, I think, gentlemen,' she declared. 'Yes, the Russian factor, use that to confuse the hell out of them.' And if that didn't work, she could blame the Americans, or the incompetence of the British military. Whatever it took, Tricia Willcocks would survive. Yet, the earlier enthusiasm that some had found for the Russian connection had faded; her announcement was greeted with silence and distracted doodling on the margins of notepads.

'They're pirates,' she continued, trying to rouse them. 'Up to their old tricks. They haven't changed. Ambushing us in our own port, and it all under false colours that had us looking elsewhere.' The analogy was exhausted, almost too much at this time of the morning. 'Time to blow the bastards out of the water!'

She was trying too hard, being too masculine and, although they didn't know it, she was also a little drunk, but her alcohol-fuelled energy failed to find much reflection within the room, not even with Harry, who felt as though some wild animal had clamped its claws deep into his shoulders, leaving him numb and useless. Exhaustion. It got to them all, in their different ways.

'So this is what we do, gentlemen,' she continued, intent on grabbing her moment. 'We use the Russian link against the terrorists. Try to undermine their confidence, make them realise they've no chance with this one. At the same time' – she turned in the direction of Hastie – 'we make sure we're ready for an assault, if it's needed. The moment they give us cause.'

Eyes flickered guiltily towards the screen and its two young hostages.

'And we deal with the Americans,' she added, making it sound like an afterthought. 'Disarm them.'

At last someone spoke up. It was the Chief of the Defence Staff, the head of the armed forces. 'Home Secretary, I really don't believe that's necessary. I understand the situation is contained and—'

'They're heading home?'

'Not quite.'

'Then they must be disarmed,' she repeated, quietly, but with force.

'Consider the repercussions, Home Secretary. An armed altercation between the two greatest allies on the earth. Surely it gives the Russians – if that's who's behind this plot – exactly what they want.'

But her confrontation with the President had convinced Willcocks that such an outcome might be very much to her advantage. 'Hold on a minute, you just think of the repercussion if we don't! Goodness' sake, it was bad enough being spat at for being Washington's poodle all the way through the war in Iraq. If we give in now, you might as well rip up the rules of cricket and start whistling Dixie through your rear ends. But that's not going to happen. It stops. Here.' She was jabbing the table with her bitten finger.

'It can assist only our enemies,' the Chief implored.

'You'd play the spaniel?'

'I would do anything to preserve the Western alliance, Home Secretary. It's what I've dedicated my professional career to.'

'No, general, your career's been dedicated to serving your Queen and your country, not the Americans. That's what you're about – what all of us in this room are about. The Americans – they can go hang. They're over played, over stretched and over here!' she exclaimed. She rather liked that, not bad for this time of the morning. 'They've got – what, forty or fifty men? And you're sitting there quaking? Time to call their bluff, general. Take them!'

'Home Secretary, that is not an order I feel comfortable with.'

'Shouldn't we simply play for time?' another voice added. 'It's worked pretty well so far.'

'Are these the sons of Nelson?' Her feminine scorn filled the room. 'The successors to Wellington and Churchill? You could take those men with a catapult.'

'I don't wish to take them at all,' the Chief responded doggedly. 'They are our allies.'

'So what are they doing here?'

'As I understand it, the Americans have offered to help. In our fight against terrorism.'

'I'd take that more seriously if American money hadn't funded every IRA bomb that did murder on the streets of London. They want to take control. It's the American disease, got to show they're in charge. Well, not here, gentlemen, not while I'm in this seat.'

She was laying down her claim to pre-eminence, *primus inter pares*, while the Prime Minister was otherwise engaged, and several around the table began to rustle in discomfort. A manufactured cough interrupted the tension. It was the man from the Attorney General's office, a mild-looking fellow with sparse hair and a desperately unfashionable thin moustache that he was wiping nervously. 'It does raise the point, Home Secretary, that lines of authority are a little confused at present. Here we are, no Prime Minister, no Cabinet, proposing to attack a royal palace. Why, technically I don't think that's legal without the permission of the monarch herself and she . . . well, she can't give it, can she?'

'If we succeed in releasing Her Majesty, do you doubt for one moment that she will approve?'

'Well, no . . .'

'And if we are not successful in that . . .' She paused while they considered what she was implying. 'Well, sadly the problem will have resolved itself.'

'But—'

'Am I not the most senior Cabinet Minister in a position to issue instructions?'

'Well, yes, I suppose—'

'Then what is the basis for your confusion?'

The civil servant could take no more. He was not a fighting man, so he retreated into the safety of renewed silence, and with him seemed to shrink the hopes of many in the room.

She glared around the table, determined to capitalise on her victory. 'Be assured that I wish to handle this situation in the proper manner, so . . . Does anyone here deny that the ultimate civil authority in the country at this moment is me?'

No one moved.

'And that it is the civilian authorities from whom the military take their orders?'

As she defied them, one by one, no one would take up her challenge or even return her intimidating stare, until she came to Harry.

'For what it's worth,' he said, sounding almost casual, 'I don't contest your right, merely your judgement. This Russian link – the more I think about it, the more it seems likely to be a distraction. Sure, somebody's making a small fortune out of this, but do we really think that money is the motive? It's a diversion, a red herring, if you will.' He tipped his head in apology at the unintended pun. 'I think—'

'Harry, dear Harry,' she smiled poisonously, cutting right across him. 'I can't thank you enough for stumbling upon the Russian connection and bringing it to our attention. But, you see, you have no official role here, no standing. Drenched in our gratitude as you are, I think it's time for you to leave.'

An embarrassed shuffling and clearing of throats began to ripple round the table, yet when they raised their heads, it was not Harry but the Chief of the Defence Staff who was on his feet. His head was bowed, chin on his chest, in sorrow rather than submission. As he looked up he gazed directly into her eyes, and chose his words with care.

'Home Secretary, I believe your instructions to use force against the Americans are misguided. If it were up to me I would not issue such orders. But, as you say, I am a military man, not a politician, and I believe in the proper order of things. I find myself in an impossible position. I cannot deny your authority, yet neither can I accept your judgement.'

'Then perhaps we should find someone else to do your job.'

'Home Secretary, my grandfather lost his life in the service of this country, and my great-grandfather both his legs. And you threaten me with losing my job?' His contempt was like a slap across her face. Her cheeks coloured. 'I place no great value on the pursuit of office, I see others start on that race who discard every principle and friendship along the way, and I thank the fates that as a military officer it is my duty to serve others and not myself.' Authority is held together not simply with legalisms but also with the mortar of respect, and with every one of his words, her authority was being chipped away. 'I have breakfasted in the company of brave men,' he continued, 'and watched at nightfall as they have returned in body bags. So give me no lectures. This is to be a time of violence and there are those alive this morning who will die this day, perhaps captors and hostages alike, who will never see their families or embrace their loved ones again. That is as it must be, for this is not a battle of our choosing. But if you order me to use force against the Americans, that will be your choice, and I cannot support it. If I were free to do so, I would lay down my office and allow you to instruct others to take up the task, but it goes against every bone in my body to walk out on a matter that still hangs in the balance, to quit while duty is left undone. So I will do your bidding, to the best of my ability, and afterwards you may have my career, if you still have one yourself. But I will not sit here and listen to you browbeat and cajole like some playground bully. So if you will excuse me . . .' He pushed back his chair.

She could sense the change of atmosphere in the room and the fever of insubordination that was spreading. Others were about to follow the general, even the man from the Attorney's office. She had tried to play them at their own game, and lost. It was time to move on. She scrabbled at the papers in front of her, gathering them together. 'Thank you, gentlemen, we all know what to do and I suggest we get on with it.' Already they were flooding away from her.

Harry passed nearby; she looked up, caught him. Her frown spoke more of curiosity than anger. 'Why do you always oppose me, Harry?'

He stared at her, said nothing, but took in the bloodshot eyes and the subtle perfume of whisky.

She shook her head in puzzlement. 'You know, there was a time when I thought we'd make a great team, me as Home Secretary, you as my Minister. Thought we had real prospects, you and me.' But slowly any trace of wistfulness was fading; the frown was gathering ragged edges. 'Dammit, you're always so uppity. You can never do as you're told. That's why you'll never succeed, Harry, because you've no respect for anyone. And always so bloody rude!'

He bent close to her ear. 'Never unintentionally, I hope,' he whispered, before following the others out the door.

Nine

S HE CREPT OUT OF the bed as quietly as she could, but still he
stirred. He turned, stretched for her, found nothing, forcing
open his eyes.

'I've got to go,' she whispered.

'Wh-at?' he croaked.

'I have got to go,' she repeated, more firmly.

'Why? What's the rush?'

'Got a busy day.' She was dressing, covering up the body that had
afforded him so many delights, and he felt cheated.

'Will I see you again?'

'Would you like to?'

'You kidding?' He stretched beneath the duvet. He was sore; it
would take him days to recover from this one. Of course he wanted
more.

'Then . . . perhaps,' she said.

'Give me your number.'

'No. I'll call you.'

'Playing hard to get.'

'No, just playing married.'

He scribbled down a number on his bedside pad. 'For future
reference – if there is a future – you always get up this early?'

'No. It's a special day.' Already she was brushing her hair.

'I'd like to buy you breakfast next time.'

'Wow, you eat breakfast, too?'

'Look . . . I'm sorry, but I don't think I even know your name.'

'That's because I didn't tell you.' She stared at him, his body laid out across the bed. 'It's Melanie.'

And she was gone.

5.52 a.m.

Topolski eyed the young British soldier. 'It's been a pleasure, captain, but I'm afraid I've got fresh instructions. I'm ordered to proceed.'

'It does seem as if we've run out of cigars. Such a pity.' Captain Braithewaite blew a final, reluctant smoke ring.

'You bet.'

'So what do we do next, colonel?'

'I guess it goes something like this. We get *on* our way, you get *in* our way and' – he waved the stub of his cigar – 'things get messy.'

'I think not. I have a much simpler idea.'

Suddenly Braithewaite was standing at attention and as the American looked around him, from out of the shadows in the park emerged a large number of British troops, all bearing arms, every one of which was pointed at his men. He threw away the remnants of his cigar in disgust. He watched it splutter and die, much like this mission. This was getting to be as bad as the fiasco in the Iranian desert, and his name would be all over it.

'So you want to shoot this out,' he said wearily.

'Not at all, colonel.'

'Then why the pointed guns?'

The British captain shook his head, slowly and seemingly in sorrow. 'I can imagine what's going through your mind, colonel. Let's just say that this is an invitation for you and your men to breakfast. In Wellington Barracks, just the other side of the palace. We can be there in less than five minutes.'

'At the point of a gun?'

'There are bad men abroad, colonel. I wouldn't want you and your men to lose your way.'

6.00 a.m.

It wasn't yet light, but those fortunate souls who had managed to snatch some sleep were now beginning to stir and wake to a world that was turning to mayhem. The media were in a frenzy, desperate to find a new angle, pouncing on anyone who had been at the State Opening and who was willing to share their story. The backgrounds of William-Henry and Magnus were examined in excruciating detail; their friends, their love lives, even their astrological signs. A BBC Breakfast presenter who had turned up for work in a multicoloured blouse was instructed to change it for something more demure. She chose black. They told her to change that, too.

The mayhem spread. Transport systems ground to a halt. At Heathrow and other airports, the inevitable additional security measures were already throwing flight schedules into chaos, made worse by the no-fly zone above Central London. The London Underground system was in tatters with Westminster and St James's stations closed and lines suspended, and many central roads blocked. There were predictions of shortages in Central London shops. Panic buying broke out, supermarket shelves were emptied and many cash machines dried up. It was traditional on such occasions for the British to embrace what they described as the spirit of the Blitz and to take all adversity in their stride, but on this day that spirit seemed to slip. Perhaps the British weren't what they once were.

The Chairman of the London Stock Exchange hadn't slept, besieged by uncertainty as he watched the chaos spread and infect overseas markets, where British-connected stocks were collapsing like victims of an ancient plague. So jumpy were investors that even a Florida-based company named Sovereign Enterprises Inc., whose interests extended no further than the manufacture of stair lifts for elderly people, had been hammered. And it was about to get worse.

The London Exchange hadn't been closed for business for more than sixty years, not since the day of monumental socialist upset when at a stroke Prime Minister Attlee had devalued the pound by forty per cent. It hadn't shut for 9/11, 7/7, nor any other emergency; it had battled on through bomb, bullet and every kind of banditry. But not today. The rules had changed. The chairman consulted his colleagues on the board and they were of one reluctant mind. The Exchange, which had closed early yesterday, wouldn't open today. Russian metals wouldn't be the only victim.

And the Bank of England let it be known that in order to protect the value of sterling they would be doubling overnight interest rates from ten o'clock and would double them again if necessary. Homeowners everywhere wept as they watched.

It was estimated that more than eighty per cent of the entire adult population of the country tuned in that morning to what was going on in the House of Lords, and it wasn't far short of that in many other countries, particularly the United States. In living rooms, at their places of work, on portable radios, on mobile phones, on podcasts, in high streets, pubs, clubs, on screens that seemed to have sprouted from nowhere, they watched, and they waited. Britain ground to a halt.

6.12 a.m.

As the approach of dawn began to flush colour through the night sky, a change began to occur inside the House of Lords itself. It was astonishing how many hostages had managed to snatch a little sleep, yet as the bells of the clock tower struck six and the air about them began to vibrate, they opened their eyes and tried to prepare themselves for the most difficult day of their lives. It was also the time when Masood was roused from his two hours off watch. He had slept soundly, but with his hand on his gun. He began to stretch the life back into his limbs, walking in front of the throne, and as he did so the Archbishop of Canterbury watched him carefully, attempting to peer inside his soul. He found nothing but darkness. Awkwardly, for he, too, had grown stiff through the night, the archbishop fell to his knees upon the claret carpet and began to pray, silently, his hands clasped in front of his face. He hadn't asked permission for his act of faith, he knew it might spark outrage amongst his captors and even lead to his death. He didn't think he was a brave man, and certainly he had no wish to die, not here, not in this sordid manner. He'd always rather hoped to pass on rather late in life, on a couple of soft pillows, surrounded by his family and with a game of cricket somewhere in the background, England thrashing the Aussies. Yes, he was willing to wait that long. But he would die, sometime, and if this were to be his moment then he wanted to be in direct contact with his Saviour and show no fear in it. So he eased himself on to his knees, his hands gripped in prayer, and waited. Masood strode by, hesitated for a moment, wondering. Then he moved on. He wasn't a fundamentalist, he could live with other people's faith, if they were willing to die with it. And soon others were on their knees, even the Chancellor, who was a well-known atheist.

The Queen did not kneel. She remained seated in her throne, as she had done all through the night, but she bowed her head, joining with them. And when she had finished praying, she nodded to one of her captors, who nodded back, and she rose to attend to her morning toilet, accompanied as ever by the gunman with the explosive jacket. And even as Archie Wakefield remained on his knees, he watched her every step, chewing at the inside of his cheek, making his calculations.

'Didn't realise you were God-fearing,' Celia Blessing whispered to him.

'Try anything the once, excepting your party, of course,' he muttered back. 'Now help me up, woman. Me knees are so stiff I can scarcely move.'

'And you so keen to play Robin Hood.'

'You make a pretty ridiculous Maid Marian yourself. Just shut up and haul away, will you?'

She held out her hand and tugged, and tugged some more, and between them they managed to hoist him back into his seat. But still they held hands, neither wanting to let the other go.

6.18 a.m.

The only view of the chamber given to the outside world was provided by the camera set high at the far end of the chamber, the one that had been hastily abandoned by its operator. He had jumped down his ladder so fast that he'd sprained his ankle rather badly; he would, in time, apply for extensive sick leave from the BBC, but only after he had milked his sudden notoriety for a fistful of fifties in appearance fees on rival channels. The other remote cameras were still operating and controllable from Daniel's den within Black Rod's Garden, but there was no basis for switching the television coverage from one angle to another. This wasn't a game of football, and any sudden changes so beloved of directors ran the risk of arousing the suspicions of the gunmen. Anyway, Daniel was too tired to make decisions; he, like so many, had been at his post all night and the police wouldn't let anyone else in to relieve him. So the one view stayed. It was only by chance that the abandoned camera had been left on a shot that was a little like looking out of a bedroom window on to the street below, giving a reasonable view of what was going on, although individual figures in the picture were indistinct. The Queen could be seen clearly, but at a distance, and viewers couldn't see the expressions of her face, which after a night of misery on her throne was a blessing to all concerned.

It was as the hostages took their turns to set about the slow process of their morning toilet that two important changes occurred to the picture. The first was when the SAS sniper, cocooned inside the tiny television tower, decided he needed to take his own leak. Normally he would have been rotated every two hours but they daren't run the risk of being spotted as they clambered up and down the ladder that gave them access to the tower. They'd been lucky once but they couldn't stretch the elastic of fortune any further. So he had stayed. He had brought with him water containers and a little high-energy food, mostly Mars bars, and one of the water bottles now did service in the other direction. It was as he was peeing, very cautiously, in the confined space, that his cramped muscles momentarily seized and he lost his balance. He knocked into the camera; it shuddered, and for a moment the picture wobbled for the entire world to see, a telltale sign that something was going on in the television tower. It might have been the end of it all, but no one in the chamber was watching. By some chance or delightful miracle the moment passed unnoticed. Perhaps someone had been listening to the archbishop's prayers.

The other change was taking place on the floor rather than up in the rafters. As William-Henry and Magnus walked back from their turns in the closets towards their seats, they were stopped by a gunman. They were prevented from taking their place amongst the other hostages, instead they were forced towards a place on the benches set away from the others. They were being taken to their dying place. Prayers only reached so far, it seemed.

There had been those who, after a snatched sleep, had hoped that the world had turned and yesterday was simply another piece of the planet's bleak history, a nightmare that would dissolve with the fresh breezes of day, but the nightmare was still amongst them. The gunmen were declaring their intent. Death still called.

6.23 a.m.

Harry didn't want to go back in. He had no choice, of course, but he was filled with a sense of foreboding, aware of what he was likely to find. There was no Stockholm Syndrome here, that condition where hostages wrapped up in sieges begin to identify with their captors. There hadn't been time for that, and the separation of Magnus and William-Henry from the other hostages had changed things, drawn the life out of the rest of them like the gutting of a chicken. He

233

pushed his cart into the chamber but they had little appetite for food or drink; instead they sat, the men unshaven, the women untidy, the pallor grey, the spirit sagging, all of them in their turn casting furtive glances towards the boys. In every corner, on every bench, expressions told the same story, of how fear had eaten through their hopes and left nothing but dust. These were faces Harry had seen before, in war zones around the world, where Moslems had found themselves surrounded by Serbs, or Tutsis by Hutus, inside African villages stripped by AIDS where the oldest surviving inhabitant had been a twelve-year-old girl, and amongst the rubble in Iraq and Afghanistan. The previous day some of the hostages had caught his eye with a look that spoke of continued defiance; now most seemed lost within an inner world that shut Harry out. There was, however, a few who left an impression. That madman Archie Wakefield was still tapping his forehead and gaping at Harry with a ferocious glint, as though demanding the keys that would let him out of the asylum. On another bench, the archbishop behind his beard seemed to have found his peace, as if he had battled with private fears and found the means to overcome them. Behind the archbishop sat the Japanese ambassador, and for a second Harry thought he had winked mischievously at him, but it turned out to be no more than a nervous tic. The ambassador glanced away, embarrassed.

When he looked towards the throne, Harry found the Queen wearing an expression that at first he didn't recognise. As both a soldier and a politician he had seen her in contrasting moods, sometimes looking stern on parade, sad and sombre at the Cenotaph, or gritting her teeth as she read out yet another prepared speech. There were occasions when the real woman burst forth, as when she accepted flowers from a young child on her birthday, or watched her mother's coffin pass by. He'd even watched her burst into laughter in the Royal Enclosure at Ascot, dancing a gentle jig like a young girl as her horse came home. He thought he was rather good at reading what was going on behind the royal mask, but on this occasion he couldn't read her at all. She seemed far away, staring at some distant star, her mouth cast down, her expression betraying a little fear, he thought. It took him a moment to realise she was looking at the boys, unable for once to hide her heart. Her fear was for them. She caught him staring, knew he understood, and for a single heartbeat she allowed him to share her emotion before she looked away and hid once more behind the mask.

Of all the hostages it was John Eaton who appeared to be faring worst. Ever since their captors had separated him from his son, he seemed to have shrunk, as though the core of him had been hollowed out like an old tree. His shoulders hunched, his hands were clasped round his knees, his head bowed in a manner that had his normally carefully groomed hair falling about his face. It made him look not only unkempt but strangely old. His body rocked stiffly, back and forth, as though trying to force out the dread that had infested it.

They were all suffering. Most were over sixty years old and some older still, even older than the Queen. And there were those who were sick, chronically so, with weak hearts, or Parkinson's, or MS, or some other malady for which they required daily medication. In the cart, along with the food and drink, Harry had a bag of medicines that had been supplied by worried loved-ones and doctors. Somehow it seemed a futile gesture – what, after all, were they trying to save them for? – but he had promised to try to hand them over. Attempting the delivery would also be a test of the captors; what mood were they in, how would they react? He trundled his cart towards one of the gunmen – the one who had been ready to shoot him in the back of the head. 'I have these,' he said, holding out the bag.

'What are they?'

'Medication. Pills. For some of the people here who are sick.'

'But why do they need pills?'

'To keep them alive.'

'And what is the point of that?'

Before Harry had a chance to reply, the stock of the gunman's weapon came down across the back of Harry's hand, very sharply, causing it to explode in pain. He knew it was broken. As the pills dropped they scattered like rats across the floor.

'I'm going to kill you!' Harry screamed, but only to himself, yet he couldn't control the look of hate that flushed into his face, and that, like the pills, was also wiped away by the stock of the weapon, sending Harry reeling to the floor with a gash that went down to the bone at the top of his cheek. He could taste blood inside his mouth. The gunmen were growing impatient.

He looked up, staring into the barrel – that bloody barrel – for what seemed to Harry to be a good chunk of eternity. Then it was waving him on. He could go, get up and leave, bind his wounds, live a little longer. But still he knew he would have to come back.

6.34 a.m.

The sight of Harry, bloodied and beaten, dragging himself from the chamber, had a profound effect on the hostages, throwing them into a still deeper state of gloom. The mood had infected the prince. For a while he seemed lost in a world of his own, his face creased in concern, twisting his signet ring in a manner that betrayed inner turmoil. To those who knew him best, it was a sign of an impending outburst. Finally, he turned to his mother. 'I can't do this any longer,' he declared.

'What is that?'

'Sit here and be utterly useless.'

She sighed. 'I fear we are all rather redundant at the moment. Anyway, no one could ever accuse you of being useless.'

'That's not always as I remember things.'

'Don't rake up the past, Charles. Not today.'

He sat silently for a while, wearing away at his ring with its three-flowered crest. He felt a deep sense of futility, not just today but for most of his life, a life that had been without use or clear purpose. 'I hope it doesn't sound cruel, Mama, but I so envy you and what you've had.'

'What have I had, Charles?'

'Love. Respect. From the people.' His tone was wistful. 'For sixty years I have watched you enchant them as their beloved monarch—'

'Oh, your memory plays tricks. It has rarely been like that. Some wonderful times, yes, but more than the occasional *annus horribilis*.'

'No, Mama, the failings were never yours. They have always adored you, and when the rest of us let you down and they couldn't perhaps adore you, still they admired you. For almost sixty years you have sat on the throne and found fulfilment while I . . . I may not get sixty minutes.'

'The role of heir, it's always a troubled chalice, Charles. If I could make it otherwise. . . .' For a moment she paused, trying to understand his confusion. 'There are no auditions. It's a duty imposed upon us, regardless of our talents or personal interest. The only common factor is that it must be done with dignity.'

'There's no dignity in being butchered like a sheep in the field.'

'Please, Charles, it will not come to that.'

'Oh, but it already has for me, every time I open a newspaper! There's not a single part of my life that hasn't been stripped from me and laid out to bleach in the sun. Even Christ was only nailed to his cross once.'

'Charles!' she rebuked, but he had no intention of being deterred. He stirred restlessly in his seat.

'All I have to do is look over a hedge and I'm accused of interfering.'

'You shouldn't mind the rabble.'

'But I do, I mind so very much. Being made into a public spectacle by those whose only interest is to find some piece of malice to fill their newspapers, when every crumb of nonsense is grabbed by them as eagerly as they lay their hands on a passing waitress. They are bastards.' He spoke slowly, whispering his scorn, the words born not from a momentary anger but a lifetime of pain.

'They do seem to have adopted their own divine right to rule,' she conceded.

'How I would love to get our own back, eh? Just this once.'

'We should pass a law. This Christmas, around the table at Sandringham. How about that?' Her tone was light, trying to lift his humour.

'The Royal Retribution Act.'

'We can take turns at writing a clause each.'

'Would you let me start?'

'No, I think that honour should go to your father.'

'You strike a hard bargain.'

'Not too hard, I trust.'

He offered a wan smile, and for the moment the dark curtain was drawn aside, but soon he was back tormenting his signet ring once more. When he spoke again, his words came slowly, set deep in earnest.

'In the next life, I want to be something simple. Not a prince, just something very ordinary. A gamekeeper, perhaps.'

'You believe in that, don't you, in reincarnation?'

'Yes.'

'You know—'

'Yes, I know, Mama. I'm also next in line to be head of the Church of England and I shouldn't hold with such mystical nonsense.'

'Just don't go preaching it from any pulpit.'

'I won't. You know, it's never been easy, walking that tightrope between my conscience and the constitution, but even a prince should be allowed to sit at the same table as his conscience occasionally. Above all a man has to be true to himself.'

'And to his duty,' she said, returning to her favourite theme.

'Ah, yes. *Ich Dien.*' He sighed. 'But what is duty unless it's built on conscience?'

She was wondering where all his metaphysics was leading when suddenly he stiffened and grimaced in pain.

'Charles, what is it?'

'My bloody back. Killing me. Forgive me, bad joke. But I can't sit here any longer.'

'I fear we must.'

He closed his eyes in momentary contemplation, struggling with his pain, before continuing. 'No, Mama. What I mean is I can't sit here and watch those boys being murdered. My conscience – or is it my duty? I really can't tell which – whatever it is, I won't sit here *uselessly* and watch them suffer.'

'What are you talking about?' An edge of alarm had crept into her voice.

'They remind me so much of our boys, with their whole lives ahead of them. I can't allow that to be wasted, not if I can stop it.'

'But . . . how can you stop this?' From the sorrowful, defiant look in his eyes she thought she knew. 'No, Charles, I will not allow it.'

'As my Queen?'

'As your mother,' she pleaded.

'And yet, Mama, you are my Queen and I owe you duty. But I owe those boys duty, too.'

'Please, Charles!' Tears were gathering in her eyes.

'Don't cry, Mama,' he said softly. 'You are the Queen. You are not allowed to show weakness, remember.' He was gently teasing her, while she was struggling to control herself.

'I am your mother, Charles. Sometimes such things must come before simply being royal.'

He smiled, full of affection. 'At last, I have found someone who understands me.'

'You cannot do this, Charles. I am your mother,' she repeated.

'And I your dutiful and most loving son.'

He sat quietly for a moment, composing his thoughts. 'Ironic, isn't it? She always said I would never be King.'

'Who?'

But he said no more.

He reached over, and for a brief moment touched his mother's hand. With that, he stood up.

6.38 a.m.

It was the rule set by the gunmen that the hostages didn't move around without permission, so when the prince stood and stepped from his throne it attracted immediate attention. He walked slowly, with heavy, reluctant feet. It seemed to take for ever for him to reach the bottom of the steps. Masood was waiting for him.

'And you want?'

The prince stood erect, as dignified in his uniform as the uncomfortable night had allowed, tugging at the cuffs of his shirt. 'I wish to take the place of the boys,' he said softly.

'Forgive me, I'm not sure I understand.'

The prince ran a tongue across his dry lips. 'If you must shoot anyone, then let it be me, not them. I offer myself in their place.'

Masood eyed him with curiosity. 'You want to be die? That is most noble of you.'

'Noble?' The prince raised his chin and attempted a sardonic laugh. 'Not really. I just want to be a gamekeeper.'

'What?'

'It doesn't matter. Just do the sensible bloody thing and let me replace them.'

'But what sense is there in that?'

'Sense? You ask about sense?' Suddenly his voice rose in resentment and the veins on his neck began to stand out above his collar. 'I have just watched you club a man half-senseless for trying to help the sick! Where's the sense in that?'

'Mukhtar's mother was sick, too. She had a fever, with no medicine, and could not run when the air raid began. Your planes blew her small house apart. When Mukhtar found her, he needed help to make sure it was his mother and not one of the other women of the village. Perhaps now you understand.'

'Then I grieve for him. But of all the people in this place, those boys are the youngest, the least guilty, the most blameless of any of us. In the name of whatever God you worship, you must surely realise that it cannot be right for them to die. So spare them.'

'And take you.'

'You want a trophy, I'm a much bigger one.'

'Mr Wales – do you mind if I call you Mr Wales? My people never got into the habit of bending their knee to your family, no matter how hard your soldiers tried to teach us.'

'Names can't hurt. Call me what the devil you like.'

'Then, Mr Wales, and with respect' – and, for the first time, Masood's voice showed neither mockery nor anger but a tinge of admiration – 'I decline your offer.'

'But why? Do you have no mercy?'

'Mercy? Is that what you have shown my people? You still don't understand, do you? We never wanted this war with you, we didn't start it, but it has been forced on us year after year until our villages are destroyed and those we love murdered before our eyes.' Despite the words, his voice was remarkably controlled. 'And now you talk to me about mercy. We are way beyond that, I'm afraid. It is no longer the quality of mercy that matters but the quality of death, and its quantity, and the fuss it will cause. That, I think, has been your strategy in my country for many years, so now we follow it.'

'Spare the sons. Let me stand in their place – please!'

'We are all the sons of our fathers, and like all creatures there will come a time for you and for me to die. But their time must come first.'

The prince examined the man in front of him, searching for some spark of clemency, but as he stared he found only cold Himalayan stone. 'You believe in God?'

'Of course. We are all God's children.'

'Then I would like to meet this God of yours, to see if I can understand his quality of mercy.'

'You seem in such a hurry to meet your Maker, but you must wait a little longer, I fear.'

The prince knew there was little purpose in arguing. This battle was lost. And with that understanding, the courage and resilience he had spent so many hours assembling began to flood away. He could feel his legs growing unsteady; it must be a twinge from his aching back, he told himself. He was shaking as he climbed back up the steps to his throne. He prayed no one would notice.

6.43 a.m.

They had delayed their game of Russian roulette because they had thought it best to wait until the gunmen were fully awake, but the beating up of Harry showed there was no point in hesitating any longer. As Tricia had sat and waited for the moment, she had begun to feel increasingly powerless and insecure. It was all very well putting on a tough front, but she knew that the penalties for failure at a time like this would be overwhelming, not just for her, but for many of the hostages, too. Her fate was linked inextricably with theirs, and her self-confidence had been worn down by exhaustion and her bruising encounter with COBRA. She had loaded the gun, but was relieved that someone else would have to use it for her.

The task fell to a detective inspector with SCD7, the Met Police Hostage and Crisis Negotiation Unit. His name was Parry. He had an excellent record but this situation was way beyond his usual orbit – most of his work involved preventing someone committing suicide, not killing dozens of others. In any event, negotiation requires dialogue, yet Masood had shown himself totally unwilling to play ball. He had demanded almost nothing from the authorities except for the release of his leader and the supply of two chemical toilets, and Parry had little to offer him in return apart from a choice of filling in his sandwiches. It had been a barren exercise, about as useful as testing a concrete parachute, as Parry had put it. Yet now, perhaps, he had a chance.

He made the call from the Ops Room, routed through the parliamentary post office. Tibbetts was listening on an extension, and everyone had eyes fixed on the screen. It seemed to take an age before they saw Masood walk across to answer the buzzing phone.

'Good morning, Masood, I've got something interesting for you,' Parry began, concentrating hard on the briefing notes spread out in front of him.

Masood gave no answer. He needed more bait.

'We know about your Russian contact,' Parry said.

At last he bit. 'And which Russian would that be?'

'Bulgakov.'

Again a silence, but this time it seemed to have a more significant quality. Then: 'I wish to talk with your superior, Mr Tibbetts.'

'I'm afraid that's not possible at the moment,' Parry responded, trying to retain control of the conversation, 'he's tied up in a meeting.'

'Don't treat me like a fool, of course he's there. He wouldn't let you talk to me like this on your own.'

Damn the man. He knew this game, too. Parry's heartbeat quickened, trying to force oxygen and inspiration into his brain, but it was hopeless. Across the room Tibbetts knew he had to make an instant decision. He wasn't a trained negotiator and this was all too important to be left to an amateur, but what choice did he have? Reluctantly, he shrugged his shoulders and nodded.

'I'll see if I can get him out of his meeting,' Parry said forlornly.

Tibbetts waited a few seconds, trying to give his colleague a little cover, before he spoke. 'Commander Michael Tibbetts,' he declared into his extension, as Parry scrabbled to lay his briefing notes out on the table before his boss. 'How are you this morning?' Tibbetts enquired, trying to give himself a little breathing space. Not too well, and about to get very much worse, he hoped quietly.

'You can see for yourself,' Masood replied. 'Shall we get on with it?'

'We know about Levrenti Bulgakov.' He waited, giving Masood the opportunity to dispute the connection or profess ignorance, but he didn't. 'And about the money,' Tibbetts added.

'Money?'

'Many, many millions of pounds and still counting,' Tibbetts retorted, shuffling through Parry's notes to try to find the latest estimate.

'Treat me as a slow learner, commander. Explain it to me.'

'The millions you've tried to make on the markets because of the siege. You know, Masood, for a moment the world thought this was all about releasing your leader. I wonder what they're going to think when they realise that it was really just another grubby exercise in extortion.'

Parry began waggling his hands, trying to indicate that Tibbetts shouldn't get too aggressive.

'And you know what, Masood? Bulgakov double-crossed you. He was trying to run off with it all. Every penny for himself.' It was a lie, of course, but one they had agreed in order to put pressure on Masood.

'Tell me, commander, may I assume that you have been doing your homework during the long night, perhaps finding out about Waziristan?'

'Yes,' the policeman replied cautiously.

'So what makes you think that anyone in Waziristan wants your money? What on earth would we do with millions of your British pounds? We don't need cars – we have almost no proper roads – and there are only so many goats to go round.' He was mocking.

'But—'

'What Mr Bulkagov has been up to I neither know nor care. If he has run off with all that money, it's only what Russians do. Careless of you to give him the chance.'

244

Tibbetts took a deep breath; this wasn't going well, the revolver was firing on spectacularly empty chambers. He only had one shot left.

'Bulgakov's dead.'

'Commander, I think I understand your game, but it hasn't worked. Bulgakov's dead? May rabid dogs pursue him to the gates of Hell. I congratulate you on your discovery but it changes nothing. I killed my first Russian when I was eight, so do you really think I'm going to worry about one more? You see, they were a little like you, wouldn't leave us alone, not until we had killed so many of them that they couldn't wait to run back to their homeland. But you are not Russians, of course. It won't take thousands of bodies to change your mind, just the handful of people in this room. All in all, you will get away very cheaply by comparison.'

Tibbetts swallowed back the bile that was rising in his throat. They'd played the game, and he had lost. It was time to move on. 'Masood, we want no deaths, not yours, not anyone's. Now I'm a policeman, I've no authority to negotiate, but I'd like to see if there are any avenues we could explore. We might be willing to consider placing your father in the hands of some international tribunal so that justice can be seen to be done, totally impartially, and—'

'You mean in the way justice has been done to the families of the Mehsuds?' he bit back, his voice grown sharper.

'We have no argument with your people.'

'You have an argument with my family . . .' Masood's voice faded. Tibbetts could see him hanging his head, could sense the pain eating him inside. 'With my own bare hands I dug them from the ruins, and with these hands I buried them. Oh, I'm sure they weren't the intended targets, the bombs were meant for some militant Islamist group you hated and had forced into our lands, but what did it matter to my wife and my son – what does it matter to me – who the bombs were intended for? But now the gun is in the other hand, Commander Tibbetts, and I shall use it to pursue you to damnation.'

'But what good will shedding more innocent blood do?'

'I shall tell you. It won't bring back my wife or son, of course. But it will make me, Masood, feel so very much better!' He was pounding his chest with his fist, so hard it seemed as if his bones might crack. 'And when your sons die, perhaps then you will think very carefully before you return to my country.'

'There must be some other way . . .'

'Commander.'

'Yes?'

'It doesn't matter to me if you have no authority to negotiate, because I have no intention of negotiating. What I want is very simple. Black and white, no little areas of grey or pink or blue to confuse you. It is an entirely colourless proposition. Release my father, that is all I want, and what I insist upon. I have lost enough members of my family to your Western justice. I thought I had made that clear.'

'But—'

'It seems you may be colour-blind, commander. I'm afraid you have been wasting time and time is not on your side. I gave you until twelve o'clock to release him but you have been trying to make a fool of me with your games.'

'No—'

'And my patience is worn down. It will not last until twelve. Not eleven, nor even ten. Nine – nine o'clock. That is all the time you have. After that, the hostages will start to die!'

'But you said—'

'Nine o'clock, commander!'

'You can't! That's barely two hours . . .'

But already it was too late. Masood had slammed the telephone back into its holder as though he was pushing a detonator.

6.58 a.m.

COBRA. Suddenly it seemed a ridiculous name for such a toothless body. Its members reconvened immediately, but what was there to be

246

done? It had all gone wrong. They gathered silently, sullenly, without the wounded Harry, as Brigadier Hastie once more rehearsed the scenario of what he called the Deliberate Action Plan. It was much as before. 'But I must revise my figure of survivability,' he added. The more he talked about death, the softer his voice seemed to grow, as if he were saying goodnight to children. 'As I made clear, my earlier estimate was based on an attack executed during the night while the terrorists were in a state of distraction. But as we can all see, that is no longer the case.' His blue eyes settled on the Home Secretary, chiding her. 'They are alert and we have lost whatever element of surprise we might have enjoyed. Consequently, I have to advise you that the casualty rate will be higher.'

'How much higher?' Willcocks demanded, but her voice had lost its edge of bravado.

'Difficult to assess.'

'*How much higher*, brigadier?'

'Up to another ten per cent.'

Yet even as his words swept through them like a winter gale, the scene on the floor of the House was changing once more. John Eaton had spent the last hour hunched over, lost in his despair, ignoring all efforts of those around him to offer comfort. He appeared as a man whose spirit had been broken beyond repair, but now in a flash he sprang to his feet and confronted Masood, face to face.

'Let me go,' he said, the words fraying at the edges.

'And why should I do that?' Masood responded, stepping back to place a little more room between himself and this unexpected adversary.

'I will sort this out for you. I will get your leader released.'

'But you have already tried. You failed.'

'That's as much your fault as mine. Inside here I am nothing more than a hostage but outside – outside I am the Prime Minister. Release me and I will give you what you want. You know I will. You have my son.'

'But you are the same man inside as out.'

'I will be a different man, believe me,' the Prime Minister replied in a state of extreme agitation. He moved forward, as though wanting to shake belief into Masood. In reply, the other man raised his rifle. Eaton ignored it.

'You have made me think harder in the last few hours than perhaps I have done in my entire life. About what we have done – and what we have failed to do. In all honesty – and I tell you this on pain of my son's life,' he said as he waved in the direction of Magnus, '– I have never had any intention of doing your people harm. And if I have done so, inadvertently, then I beg your forgiveness. What was done was done out of ignorance, not malice, it was a policy aimed at others, not you. Your people were caught up in a tide of history that seemed to sweep beyond the control of anyone. But I vow to you – that will change. It *will* change, yes, it will! Because *we* will change!' He threw up his arms, like a preacher. 'Show that you are merciful and I make you this vow. I will devote myself to your cause. Become your ambassador. Be your advocate. Take your case to Washington, to the United Nations, to the people of the world. Give me my son's life and I will give your people a future and make sure that what goes on in the mountains of your homeland is never again forgotten.'

Masood began slapping the stock of his weapon in mock applause. 'Hah! What a splendid performance. Truly memorable. But you forget one thing, Prime Minister. What *I* am doing will make sure that we are never again forgotten, and so much more effectively than any words you can offer. I will make the whole world listen.'

But Washington listens to no one, while the United Nations listens to everyone and can decide nothing. The people of the world are far too weary with their own troubles to have time for little Waziristan. As you have admitted, you knew nothing of my country, and didn't care.' Masood patted his weapon once more. 'I will change all that.'

'But you have made your point.'

'I have scarcely started.'

'Please – let me go.'

'You would run away.'

'I want to save you. And my son.'

'As I wish to save my father. But the only way they will let Daud Gul go is if your son dies. Nothing less will persuade them. And even then I suspect they will still say no.'

'Please . . .' Eaton lowered his head, and his voice. 'I beg you. I will do anything for my son.'

'Yet you did not lift a finger for mine!' Masood was now struggling to control his emotions; his lips moved but he could not speak, as though pain had made him dumb. It was some time before he spoke again. 'My people have been raised in a hard world, Mr Eaton. For hundreds of years we have been persecuted, when we had asked for nothing more than the right to sit round our campfires and grow old. Now the time has come for the smoke to blow in a different direction.'

'You quote me ancient history? You will die for what is already dead?'

'The past isn't dead. And It isn't even the past. Look, the evidence is all around you, here, in your House of Lords!'

'I would do *anything* to save my son.' The words came forth individually, washed in torment. 'If the entire world were an ocean I would turn my back on it all for this one drop. Let me give up my office, my reputation, my life, but leave me this. He is my only child . . .'

'As little Sardar was mine. There, you didn't even know his name, did you, Mr Eaton?'

The Prime Minister dropped to his knees, the last of his resistance gone. 'Then I beg you, kill me first. I will not watch my own son die!'

'That, of all punishments inflicted on a man, is the most cruel. To watch your son die. That I know.'

Eaton was sobbing, his shoulders heaving.

'Don't worry, Mr Eaton, you will not suffer long, and certainly not as long as I. Hours, I promise, that is all. For I intend to take your life, too. After your son, you will be the next.'

The shoulders stopped heaving, and simply fell.

'But you will not be alone, I promise you,' Masood continued. 'I think you shall die alongside your Queen.'

Ten

'**D**oes he mean it? *Does he mean it?*' the Home Secretary demanded. Her world was spinning off its orbit. Whichever way she turned, she saw nothing but chaos.

Tibbetts was the first to respond. 'He's already shot one Cabinet minister, beaten up Harry Jones and the US ambassador. We've precious little basis for disbelieving him.'

She sat with her head in her hands, her battered red nails standing out against skin bleached pale by exhaustion.

'We need to decide, Home Secretary,' Five pressed.

When, at last, she raised her head, her eyes were rimmed with anguish. 'Then I believe we go in as soon as they start shooting the boys.'

'That won't be in time to save them,' Hastie reminded her.

Her nostrils flared in frustration. 'No, not the Queen, either, so you keep telling me.'

'So why wait. Why not let us go now?'

'Because!' she snapped, frustrated that she should be forced to repeat the argument once more, knowing they doubted her. 'Because any attack would *guarantee* that the Queen will die. The only hope she has is if they're bluffing, and as slim as that hope might be, we have to cling to it.'

As she finished, one of the phones on the table in front of her began to ring. 'What?' she snapped, punching the speaker button in impatience. She had no great desire to share the conversation with everyone in the room, but she was afraid that if she picked up the receiver her trembling hands would betray her.

'It's the Queen's private secretary,' a voice informed her. 'From the palace.'

'And he wants?'

'Just a word.'

A voice filled the room. It was refined, gentle, draped with sorrow. 'I have just been watching, Home Secretary. I thought I might be of some assistance.'

She could do without fresh hands trying to push her around, but politeness required her to listen. 'Thank you, Sir Peter. And precisely how do you think you can help?'

'I have just been speaking with Prince Philip. Both he and I are of the same opinion, which is that Her Majesty would understand. Whatever it is you felt you had to do, and *whatever* its consequences' – he hit the word just sufficiently – 'she would support you. And so will the family.'

She glanced around the table, trying to judge the reaction of the others. Her voice had lost her stridency when at last she responded. 'You realise the implications of what you're saying – for the personal security of Her Majesty?'

'I believe I do.'

She paused while the words sank in. 'Then I'm grateful to you for your call, Sir Peter. We will let you know.' Slowly, she reached out to push the button that cut him off. 'He's telling us to go now. Not to wait.'

'Excellent!' Hastie declared.

She couldn't resist the volcano of suspicion that welled inside her. Had Hastie put the private secretary up to this? But what difference did that make now? She had been outmanoeuvred, by men, and by events. As she struggled to consider the implications of what had been said, a host of fresh opinions from around the table began to hem her in as voices dressed in various shades of courage and caution tried to outdo each other. Or were they merely voices inside her head? She was about to bang the table for silence when the phone interrupted them once more. 'For God's sake!' she snapped.

'It's President Edwards.'

She bit through another nail. Something inside told her she wasn't going to like this. She sighed. 'Put her through.'

'Home Secretary,' the American began. There was no fanfare, no niceties, no attempt to reach out and do that woman-to-woman stuff. 'I have instructed Ambassador Paine to go back into the Chamber with a message for the terrorists.'

'You have no right!' Oh, the wretched woman! The arrogance! But there was no time for empty protest. 'Message? What message?' She put on her most haughty of voices. 'Might I remind you, Madam President, that all communications must go through me? This is an operation under British control.'

'But if only it were under control, then none of this would be necessary.'

'I don't understand. What – what is necessary? You can do nothing without discussing it with us first.'

The sigh of exasperation from the other end of the phone was clearly audible. 'Tricia,' the President said, 'this isn't up for discussion. I'm calling to let you know that as of now the United States is taking over command of this operation.'

7.18 a.m. (12.18 p.m. BIOT time)

It wasn't much of a prison cell, so far as those things went. There wasn't a call for such things on the British Indian Ocean Territory of Diego Garcia. Sure, they occasionally had a problem with rapes and a little GBH, and a few years earlier there had been a case of murder, but there was a limit to how much trouble you could get up to on a coral atoll, and if anyone did get out of hand they were quickly shipped out to Hong Kong or home to the States. The cellblock was supposed to deal only with the minor stuff like drunkenness, smuggling pornography or being found peeing on the Queen's Birthday Palm Tree. Normally they wouldn't have kept an important prisoner here so long, but these weren't normal times. Daud Gul had been lodged in a cell at the end of a grey corridor within the BIOT police building from the moment they'd flown him in, in the middle of the night. They told him he was on Diego Garcia but that meant nothing to him; more important to him on a daily basis was that the place was damp from the humidity and smelt of puke and pee from the drunks who were left to sober up on the benches in the corridor outside his door. As much as they scrubbed the place the following morning, the sour smell never went.

He had expected worse. Sure, they'd pushed him around a little, and on a couple of occasions beat him up badly, but he had blocked his mind to it all, even the occasional pain. They seemed to think he was of far greater significance than he was, a man with links to every liberation group he had heard of, and quite a few he hadn't, and he saw no reason to lift the veil on their delusions. For some reason they thought he wanted to rule the world when all he sought was the comfort of his homeland, so he had locked himself away inside his imagination, up in his mountain eyrie, beyond their reach, in a battle of wills. And when he opened his eyes, through the window of his cell, he would see these self-styled defenders of freedom throwing up and fouling themselves in the corridor, and he felt not only better but superior. No, they wouldn't break him.

Once again there was commotion outside in the corridor. More drunks. Raised voices. Anger. More drunks, he supposed. But, as he listened, he decided they were not drunks, after all. This was something different. It was his British guards who were protesting, raising their voices in alarm. Moments later the lock of his cell was being turned, the door opening, and the men who crowded through weren't British policemen in their tan uniforms and short trousers but Americans in brown and green camouflage fatigues with bulletproof vests. They were also armed.

Daud Gul knew what this meant. The end. Summary execution. No more of this British softness with their pink-faced embarrassment when they hit him. These American thugs meant business. Gul stood up; he wanted to die like a man, on his feet, facing his enemy.

'You're coming with us,' one of the Americans growled.

Of course. This was it. 'May your sister die beneath a hundred men,' he spat in Pashto.

Then they said something that almost made the Mehsud fall back upon his chair with surprise.

'Hurry up,' they told him. 'You're going home.'

7.23 a.m.

Robert Paine was back inside the chamber before there was anything Tricia Willcocks could do to stop him. He had changed his clothes, looked fresher than anyone else in the room, and stood for a moment at the doorway, taking in the rows of greying faces as they turned towards him. His nostrils puckered. Despite the air-conditioning the atmosphere inside the chamber had grown heavy with hopelessness and the insistent, acrid smell of latrines.

'So you have returned, ambassador,' Masood greeted cautiously.

'I promised I would.'

'With good news, I hope.'

'I think so. The rules of the game have changed. We are in the process of releasing Daud Gul. We will fly him to any airport you care to nominate.'

And suddenly it was spring. From the benches around him faces began to revive, voices were raised in joy and relief, and even John Eaton seemed to stage a recovery, his body unfurling like young bracken, his eyes silently weeping. Someone cheered, others began to applaud, to laugh, and the tumult grew on all sides until Masood waved his gun and brought them back to a quivering silence.

'How do I know I can trust you?' he scowled at the American.

'Because I am here. I'm a guarantee of Daud Gul's safe conduct. And if the British will allow it, you can speak to him.'

'But if he is to be released, why would the British not allow me to speak to him?'

'Ah!' Paine steepled his hands and touched his fingers to the tip of his nose. His voice grew lower, more intimate, as if there were things he wanted to share with the other man and no one else. 'It's a matter of sorting out a few crossed wires. You see, Daud Gul is held in Diego Garcia, which legally is a British protectorate, but effectively under American control. And we – the United States – are releasing him even as we stand here. It might just take the British a little while to catch up with things. So you see, the game's over. You've won. The guns can be put aside. There's no reason for anyone else to die.'

But still Masood was not smiling.

7.25 a.m.

There was no echo of joy to be found inside COBRA, either. The news came like a grenade rolling through the door, and it sent Tricia Willcocks into a state of shock. She didn't know how to respond. Somewhere, deep inside, she was relieved that the siege might soon be over, that there would be no more killing. There was still the matter of what to do with Masood and his men, of course, but in the circumstances that seemed a mere trifle. Yet whatever the outcome now, it would undermine her. She had failed, lost control. This wasn't like marriage, screw up and move on; she wouldn't get a second chance. The others were sitting, watching, waiting for her to say something, but in vain. Rats were scratching away inside her skull, she couldn't see, everything was going dark and the pain was coming back. Another migraine.

'Game, set and match, I think, gentlemen,' Five said, gathering his papers.

'If you'll excuse me, I must go and give some fresh instructions,' Tibbetts said, rising.

'Me, too,' Hastie added.

'I need to lie down,' Tricia whispered.

And soon the room was empty, save for her.

7.26 a.m.

Masood waved his weapon once more for silence. Like young grouse on the moor, they froze.

'You say Daud Gul is released?'

'He's in the process of being released,' Paine responded. 'As I understand it, he should by now be on his way to the air base on the island.'

'He is still in your hands?'

'We need to know where to take him. You name it, we'll fly him there.'

Masood stepped around the ambassador, like a fox, wary, one paw at a time, his eyes cautious, alert. 'So, he is not yet free.'

'Diego Garcia's a mighty long way from anywhere you might want him to be, so just tell us where, and we'll work out the best way to get him there.'

'I don't trust you, ambassador.'

'No reason why you should. That's why I'm here. I'm insurance.'

Masood continued to stare suspiciously at the ambassador. Paine stared back. Eventually the gunman tired of the game.

'Peshawar,' he said. 'You know it?'

'Of course. In the North-West Frontier province of Pakistan.'

'You can see the mountains from the airport. It will be appropriate to release Daud Gul there.'

Paine knew that it wasn't simply the view that made Peshawar an ideal choice. The town stood at one end of the Khyber Pass. Within an hour of landing, Daud Gul would be lost to the world once more.

'You fly him there,' Masood continued, his eyes still fired with mistrust. 'But I wish to speak with him first.'

'I believe that might be arranged.'

'And ambassador, understand that my deadline still exists.'

'What?'

'If he is not free – free of you, out of US and British custody – by nine, then the hostages start to die.'

'You cannot be serious.' For the first time since the siege began, it was Paine's turn to offer a thin, mocking smile.

The gun was up once more, prodding at Paine's stomach. 'I think you will remember how serious I am.'

'Diego Garcia is a thousand miles or more from anywhere and, God knows, it must be two or three times that far from Peshawar. We fly pretty damned fast but we don't do time travel. God knows, he won't be in the air for an hour. So I tell you this, and you have the word of the United States government on it: he will be in the air just as soon as is humanly possible, and he will be flown direct to Peshawar as quickly as a jet can fly. But if you harm one more hostage in that time, whenever that happens, wherever his plane is, we'll drop your friend overboard. I understand those things fly at about forty thousand feet. Should be one hell of a homecoming for Mr Gul.'

The two men stood toe to toe, locked in their battle of wills. No one else in the chamber moved, dared breathe, and from around the world millions watched as the fate of the hostages hung once more in the balance. For many moments Masood's face was frozen in thought. Then it cracked. He smiled, an expression that conveyed no warmth, not even a passing shadow of goodwill. 'You are a very good negotiator, ambassador. We shall do as you suggest,' he declared. 'I hope your word can be trusted. Your life depends upon it.'

7.43 a.m. (12.43 p.m. BIOT time)

Daud Gul walked slowly, as is the habit of mountain men, from his cell, into the sunlight outside the blue-painted police headquarters, and climbed into the back of a 4 by 4. A guard held the door open for him. A British civilian who appeared to have dressed hurriedly was arguing with an American major, but however much the Briton threw his arms about or raised his voice, it made no difference to the American. At one stage the Briton banged his hand on the bonnet of the vehicle, and Gul smiled. Never beyond his wildest dreams had he thought he could bring these two Satans to each other's throats. Perhaps he had already gone to Heaven.

He was curious; this would be his first view of the island – and last, he hoped. He'd arrived several months earlier in the middle of the night and had no idea where he was in the world, except for the smell of the air and the cloying heat that told him he was a long way from his beloved mountains. Now they were driving along a clean, white-kerbed road with neatly clipped ribbons of coarse grass on either side, beyond which lay a tangle of lush tropical vegetation with tall palms that bent in the breeze. No mountains, no hills, but through the gaps in the vegetation he suddenly saw the sea, a lagoon filled with molten lapis. Then a roadside sign that said he was welcome in Diego Garcia. Wherever it was, this was a strange land, like nothing he had ever seen before.

He still didn't believe them, that he was going home. They'd offered no word of explanation, and he'd given them nothing in return. Perhaps it was another of their tricks, raising his hopes, only to dash them again and hope to break him down. There had been no preparations – but what was there to prepare? He had no possessions, even the clothes he stood in weren't his; there were no books he wanted to take with him and he had written nothing down in all those months, knowing that his jailers would read every word. He hadn't even many memories to take with him, just periods of blankness, particularly when they had beaten him. They hadn't even done a good job of that. Back home, in the mountains, they knew how to do these things, but these British and Americans had come from the far side of the world yet had learned nothing.

They were still as ignorant as goats. And, he prayed, they would share the same fate.

7.45 a.m.

When Tibbetts arrived back in the Op Room he found Harry waiting for him. 'Christ, Jones, you look a mess.' Two of the middle fingers on Harry's left hand were in splints and a police surgeon was sewing stitches into the puffy wound beneath his right eye.

'Never felt better,' Harry muttered, in a manner that indicated there might be a tooth or two missing.

The commander reached for a mug of coffee, filling it with sugar and cosseting it as though it were a rare champagne. 'At least we can begin to relax now. All we have to worry about is the public inquiry and getting measured for our own funerals.' He looked more closely at Harry, whose single open eye returned no hint that he shared the other man's sense of relief. 'Oh, for God's sake, Harry, it's over.'

'Is it?'

'And what the hell do you mean by that?' demanded the policeman, irritated that his sense of wellbeing was already being rocked.

Harry waited until the police surgeon had finished his embroidery. 'It's simply this, Mike. We still have almost eighty of the most important people in the country locked up in one room together with a load of fanatical gunmen.'

'Come on, look on the bright side, it's only a matter of time before they're all walking out and heading for a psychiatrist's couch.'

'Perhaps. But one thing still bothers me.'

'Just one?'

'Why hasn't Masood demanded any means to make his own escape? Strange, don't you think?'

'You just don't like him.'

'Let's say I owe him one,' he reflected, holding up his battered hand. 'But that still doesn't answer my question.'

'Which is what, precisely?'

'They've arranged transportation for their leader, so why have they arranged nothing for themselves? How do they propose to escape?'

'I dunno,' Tibbetts blustered.

'Perhaps it's because they don't mean to escape.'

The thought took a little time to worm its way between the folds of Tibbetts's rumpled mind. 'You're suggesting . . . ' But the words faded away. He didn't like the taste of them.

'I'm suggesting that if this were like any normal grubby siege they'd be talking twenty million dollars and a getaway plane. Yet they've demanded nothing for themselves.'

'And your conclusion?'

Harry got up and began pacing the floor; he seemed to have picked up a limp somewhere, too. 'Just give me a moment and follow this thing through. They pack up and go home, and what have they got?'

'Their leader.'

'A respite. Nothing more. People will say they got lucky, and that the British got sloppy, but in a couple of years' time no one will remember them and what they did. Nothing will change out there in the mountains, they'll still have the whole world breathing down their necks, using them as a doormat for their own ambitions. Is that going to satisfy Masood after watching his entire family being butchered?'

Tibbetts scooped an extra spoonful of sugar into his coffee. 'He's got Daud Gul out of his hole, and that shows Masood's a serious player.'

'Precisely. Not one to waste an opportunity, and as opportunities go this is the best anyone's had since Guy Fawkes got his matches wet. Masood and his chums aren't going to go back home with nothing more than a tourist T-shirt.'

'Then what do they want to go back home with?' Tibbetts put the question slowly, in the manner of a schoolmaster examining a recalcitrant pupil and not expecting to get back the answer he wanted.

Harry began prodding at the side of his jaw, searching for the tooth. 'That's just it, Mike. I don't think they're intending to go back home at all.'

'You mean this is . . .'

'A one-way trip.'

'No, Harry, no!' the policeman insisted. 'That's preposterous.'

Harry had grown still, leaving his hurts to themselves. 'They're not leaving that place,' he said. 'And they're going to take as many of those people with them as possible. Their day in the House of Lords isn't over yet, and by the time it's finished, I believe a very large number of those hostages are going to be dead.'

'You sure that knock on the head didn't affect you? Why would they as good as commit suicide when they could walk out of there? We'd have to let them go, you know that.'

'And why did those guys on the 9/11 planes fly them into the Twin Towers when they could have gone to Miami? Why did the Underground bombers on 7/7 fill their rucksacks with explosives rather than Big Macs? Why do men and women walk into coffee houses all around the Middle East and blow themselves up rather than ordering a cappuccino? We have to get into the mindset of these people. If they walk out of there, they'll be nothing but a footnote and the Mehsuds will be shoved back into the same pit they've been in for hundreds of years. But if they decide to stay and finish the job . . . think about it.'

'Tell me you're not serious,' whispered the policeman.

'It would be like 9/11 and the Battle for Berlin all rolled up in one glorious, bloody day of revenge that will never be forgotten.'

'It would be self-defeating,' Tibbetts protested, 'We'd send an army in after them and root out every single Meshud leader, surely.'

'We've been trying that ever since we stumbled across them,' Harry replied. 'Oh, they'd be the mother of all fusses about bringing those responsible to justice – but what if those responsible are all dead, apart from Daud Gul? We'd go looking for him, sure, maybe get lucky again, but much more likely is that everyone will quietly agree to give Waziristan a very wide berth in future and find some other spot on the globe to conduct their mutual bloodletting.'

Tibbetts moaned, deeply and violently. 'Harry, you really mean this, don't you?'

'I'm rather afraid I do.'

'So if you were Masood . . .'

'As soon as Daud Gul's out of harm's way, I'd set about slaughtering everyone in there.'

'Everyone?'

'Starting with the Queen.'

8.12 a.m.

When COBRA reconvened, it did so at the request of Mike Tibbetts. Tricia Willcocks was content for him to take the chair, pleading a migraine, and it was apparent to everyone present that a change had come over her. She seemed to have shrunk, both physically and emotionally, content to let others have their head. Not everyone believed it was a migraine; some of the more uncharitable members put it down to the effects of whisky, while others assumed it was an ego dragged to repentance. For a few hours she had straddled the world, but her footing had slipped and no one could tell how far she might fall. She had overplayed her hand and been made to look utterly foolish. For once she didn't know what to say, so wisely she said nothing.

Tibbetts was ill at ease. 'I've asked you back because there's something I think you ought to consider,' he began, casting a dark glance at Harry, still desperately hoping this was a huge error of judgement. 'There is a view' – his tone made it clear that he would love to distance himself from it by the length of several mountain ranges – 'that the siege isn't yet over. That irrespective of what happens to Daud Gul, they intend to start killing the hostages.'

His words froze every heart in the room.

'We need to consider it,' he sighed in apology. 'Harry, this is your idea. You run it up the flagpole.'

All eyes turned. By this stage Harry looked a most pitiful specimen, his clothes tattered, his hand smashed and his swollen face beginning to bruise like a mouldering pumpkin. He appeared an unlikely source of inspiration as he began outlining his theory. He raised his flag, yet no one seemed keen to salute.

'An interesting theory,' mused Five, when Harry had finished, 'but only a theory.'

It was a point Harry was forced to concede.

'And what probability do you give to the chances of your being right?' Hastie asked, glad that for once someone else was under the cosh.

'Brigadier, you know as well as I do that the estimates that get traded round this table aren't worth a bucket of spit, yours included. No one can know these things, not for sure. We're not infallible, yet nevertheless we are forced to play God. It's possible I'm deluded and I've got this completely wrong, but if you insist on a figure—'

'I'm in no position to demand, but I would be most interested, Mr Jones.'

'Then my experience says my scenario's better than fifty-fifty, and my instinct – for what it's worth – goes even further.'

'You're not being just a little oversensitive, are you?' a junior minister pressed. 'After all, you've taken a bit of a battering; it would be understandable if you – how can I put it? – wanted to get your own back? You wouldn't be happy watching them walk away.'

'A fair point,' a civil servant added, then hesitated, realising the implied offence. 'We can't be too careful.'

'Yes, it's a fair point,' Harry accepted. 'But not an accurate one.' He stood up. 'I hope you'll forgive this little show of histrionics, but it's important.' Rather clumsily with his one good hand he hitched up his shirt and the vest underneath to reveal the lurid red weals of the scars left by his years of military service.

The civil servant winced.

'Yes, I've taken a bit of a battering,' Harry continued, 'but the point is I'm used to it. So shall we get rid of the personal motivation stuff and get back to the point at hand?'

'You'll allow us all a little personal animus, I hope,' Five intervened. 'It would give me no end of pleasure to find some way of making the Americans grovel. It's their turn, I think. But even if you're right, Mr Jones, we still face exactly the same problem as before,' he said, wagging his nicotine stick. 'How the hell do we go in without losing the most valuable prize of all – the Queen?'

'If I'm right, we lose her anyway,' Harry replied softly.

'But our chances of success have increased,' Hastie said. 'They won't be expecting an attack now, not with Gul in the air. That gives us back the element of surprise.'

'Even so,' Five countered, shaking his head, 'who is there amongst this merry band who would take his courage – and Mr Jones's analysis – and screw it to the sticking-place?'

'You, commander?' It was Tricia, her first contribution. Her voice was weak, as though it came from a distance, but she wasn't going to miss the opportunity of making someone else squirm under the pressure.

And Tibbetts had feared this point. It was one of the reasons he'd been happy to take the chair, enabling him to move the pieces around the board, putting off the moment when they stopped on his square. 'I simply don't know. I wish to God I could be certain that Harry was wrong, but I can't.' His shoulders heaved in resignation. 'I'm afraid I'm no Inspector Morse.'

Harry jerked upright as though something had struck him. 'What did you say?'

'That I don't know . . .'

'Morse. You said Morse,' Harry muttered. 'Of course!' He slapped his hand down hard on the table; it was his good hand, but even so the effort made him wince. Others looked on in alarm. Tibbetts was staring very pointedly at the face wound and trying to remember what he knew about secondary concussion.

'That old bugger Archie Wakefield,' Harry continued, suddenly brimming with enthusiasm. 'I thought he was cracking up, couldn't take the strain – he's been tapping his head like a lunatic. But he hasn't lost it, he's been trying to use Morse code. To talk to us from inside the chamber.'

'And what was he trying to say?' Five asked.

'I thought signals interception was your baby.'

'Morse code, Mr Jones?' Five wrinkled his nose. 'Went out with the dinosaurs.'

'Then give me twenty minutes.' Already he was heading for the door.

'Where are you going?' Tibbetts cried.

'To dig up a few fossils,' Harry said, leaving them in a state of bewilderment.

8.22 a.m. (1.22 p.m. BIOT time)

It took only minutes to drive from the gaol to the airfield. It was barely four miles, with little other traffic, apart from Filipino workers on their bicycles. No one spoke to Daud Gul. At times he was forced to squint as the sun scorched off the surface of the road, but he caught glimpses of many low brightly painted buildings. They also passed a huge satellite dish, and what appeared to be a fuel dump. Often the sea was hidden by the thick scrub that bordered the shore, but occasionally he saw raked beaches and, far beyond in the lagoon, the hulking presence of grey transport ships. The hated symbols of the Stars and Stripes and the British flag were everywhere.

As they pulled up alongside the airport terminal building, the American major turned to him and spoke for the first time. 'We need you to talk to your friends.'

Friends? He had no friends here. But they showed him to an office where a US soldier was talking into a telephone. When he saw Daud

Gul, he muttered into the phone: 'He's here,' and rose from his seat, indicating that Daud Gul should sit. A voice was coming from the earpiece.

'Daud *Khan* – are you there? Can you hear me, Daud *Khan*? This is Masood.'

But could this be, that Masood was in the next room, because that was how it sounded?

'I am here, Masood *Jan*, my son.'

'Are you all right? What have they done to you?'

'They tell me they are about to put me on a plane. To release me. I'm not sure I understand—'

'I have some people with me here who have been very persuasive on your behalf.'

'Then may God bless them.'

'In His own way. Daud *Khan*, it is so good to hear your voice. Soon you will be back home. *Azadi!* You will soon be free!'

'Then may God be doubly blessed. And I owe you much, Masood *Jan*. I wait to embrace you.'

'*Inshallah.*'

'May He give us both strength.'

8.32 a.m.

Harry arrived more than a little breathless at the OB van in Black Rod's Garden. He was bordering on exhaustion and only stubbornness forced him on. Two armed policemen stood guard at the door, their mood relaxed, like actors at that point in the play when the lines are done, the curtain is about to descend and there is nothing else to do but pray for applause. They stood catching the light of a bright morning sun that was bouncing off the burnished aluminium walls of Daniel's den.

Yet inside the van Harry encountered a picture of darkness and squalor. People had been sleeping in a pile of blankets that had been thrown into one corner of the floor – in fact, it was moving even as

Harry watched – and littered on every surface apart from the control desk were the remains and packaging of every type of takeaway food that could be obtained within half a mile of the place. It was crowded, more than a dozen men and women, all still at their stations, unambiguously unwashed and over-ripe; they'd been here more than twenty-four hours and although Daniel had tried to cut down on the numbers, they had refused. This was history, they were making it, and no one was going to be told to miss out. Anyway, most of them were on extended overtime. It wasn't the moment to cut and run. Sleep-fogged eyes turned to greet Harry as he stood in the doorway.

'Can I help you, Mr Jones?' Daniel asked from his desk.

'We know each other?'

'I'm Daniel. I've been watching you.' He indicated the wall of screens in front of him. Harry's heart leapt. While several carried the wide-angle view that had been spread across the airwaves ever since the siege began, others came from the remote cameras around the chamber that were used for the everyday broadcasting of the Lords. Daniel had adjusted them so that every aspect of the siege was covered. Much to Harry's joy, in the middle of one of the screens sat the portly form of Archie Wakefield.

'That man.' Harry cried, jabbing his finger at the peer, 'can you get closer?'

'But of course,' Daniel said. 'Suzie, would you oblige?'

And further down the van, one of his colleagues made adjustments and an image of Archie came zooming into view that showed every individual eyelash.

'And do you – please tell me you can do this – do you have recordings from that camera of what's been happening since the siege began?'

'We've been recording everything.'

'I need to see what that man was doing at the times when I was in the chamber. Can you do that?'

Daniel sucked the end of his pen thoughtfully. 'It might take a couple of minutes,' he warned.

'Daniel, whatever it takes. Show me those pictures and you can name your price. They'll put up statues to you at Television Centre for this.'

'A parking space would be sufficient.'

'Done!'

'Ah, a politician's promise,' Daniel muttered. 'The day is clearly returning to normal.'

And as Harry watched, screens started flickering as the images of the previous day flew past at eye-baffling speed. While this was going on, another shadow loomed in the doorway.

'Tinker at your service, Mr Jones.' A man with a thick Brummy accent, around sixty years of age and not far off the same number of inches in girth, stepped inside, sniffing the air and wrinkling his nose. Paddy Bell – 'Tinker' to all who knew him from his early days – was a doorkeeper in the Palace of Westminster. Like most of the doorkeepers he was ex-military, a former 'scaly back' or radio telegraphist in the Royal Signals with a twenty-two-year army career that had taken him through the Falklands and up to the first Gulf War. He was a slow, solid man who now ran an informal investment club that operated amongst some of the palace staff. It was through the club that Harry had got to know him well. It wasn't that Harry had ever been asked for insider information, particularly not as a Minister, but Tinker kept his ear to the ground and was masterful at interpreting the significance of a raised eyebrow or chewed ministerial cheek. Since he'd been helping run it, the club had been returning close on twenty per cent a year. It was one of Westminster's most closely guarded secrets.

'Tinker, thank God you could get here,' Harry replied in relief. He didn't bother with introductions.

'Sorry it took so long, boss. I was expecting the day off.'

'You may just be about to perform the most valuable day's service of your life – look!' Harry waved his finger as the pictures of Wakefield pounding at his head flashed into life.

'That's Lord Wakefield, ain't it?' Tinker observed. 'Decent sort of fella, he is. For a hairy-arsed *matelot*.'

'A sailor, was he?'

'A merchant marine sparks. A wireless wally.'

'Which would explain it!' Harry declared in triumph.

'What's that, boss?'

'That,' Harry said, pointing, 'unless I'm a pig's arse, is Morse code.'

Tinker leaned over the control desk, breathing heavily and squinting hard. 'You know, I think you're bloomin' right.'

'So what is it? What's he saying?'

For a few minutes that seemed to stretch to half of Harry's lifetime, there was silence, punctuated only by Tinker's heavy breathing. Then he straightened his back. 'Well, blow me down,' he muttered, shaking his head.

'Report, Yeoman Bell!'

'Sorry, boss. He's sending the same thing. Over and over again: "*Attention. Believe can deal with bomb. God save the Queen.*" '

Eleven

THE PRINCE OPENED HIS EYES. Much to his dismay, nothing had changed. The wretched world was still out there, waiting to humiliate him. He felt pitiful, almost shamed. He had believed he could have made a proper end of it, like the other Charles, but it had proved to be nothing more than yet another wasted gesture in a worn-out life. He had been humiliated, and not even a stinking terrorist would take him seriously.

He had struggled so hard, yet 'they' – those whose respect he so longed for   seemed determined never to accept him. There was never a moment when they didn't accuse him of arrogance or indulging in double standards. He had devoted himself to the environment, yet they mocked every time he flew. When he wrote to Ministers, entirely privately, to encourage or gently to cajole, they ran to the media to accuse him of meddling. He had spent years building up the estates of the Duchy of Cornwall, transforming them, modernising them, providing jobs, improving the countryside, yet all they could do was sneer that he charged a pound for every slice of ham.

And then there had been the marriage. They'd always sided with her, killed any chance of it ever working, and as good as killed her, too, in the end. Shouldn't have been like that, any of it. He'd done some bloody stupid things, to be sure, but hadn't any couple whose marriage was falling apart? Only difference was that other people didn't get their phones tapped and their servants bribed or have microphones thrust between the sheets. God, it had hurt. And the boys – all that got him through the mess of those years had been his sons, he owed them everything, and perhaps that was why he'd become so emotional about saving the two out there. Pity's sake, he didn't want to die, but finding something to die for seemed to be such a whole lot better than having nothing to live for and yet he couldn't even do that properly. Buggered that up, too. Everything he did ended up being thrown back in his face, just like the guardsman and that snowball. So he closed his eyes and pretended to sleep, crying in his bones and hiding his humiliation.

He was still struggling inside when he felt something touch his wrist. He opened his eyes on to the same wretched, deceitful world and wondered for a moment what had distracted him, until he looked down and saw his mother's hand resting on his. She was gazing at him in an odd, unfamiliar manner. He didn't understand it at first but it reminded him of – what? Something, some occasion, a time long ago in their lives that he could no longer fully recall. He closed his eyes, trying to capture the brief-lived images, using the techniques of dream therapy he had mastered to snatch at these fleeting glimpses from the corners of his mind. And slowly they came back to him. Of course! It was perhaps his first memory. Of the coronation. That day when she stopped being his mother and started being his Queen – at least, that's how he remembered it. She had been so serious, that day, so stern even, until the time when they had gone out on to the palace balcony for the last fly-past and taken the final, impassioned roar from the crowd. He had stood on tiptoe to wave and watch it all. He had been four.

She had put him to bed that evening, had come to tuck him in and say goodnight. Not something she often did. And she had looked down upon him – in just the same way she was looking at him now. She had seemed so serious, hadn't smiled, but had held his hand and brushed his forehead until his eyes had begun to droop.

'Remember, Charles, that you and I are like no other mother and son in the whole country.'

'Because I'm going to be King one day?'

'Yes, because of that. I fear it will come between us.'

'Why?'

'Because it always does. There will always be people getting between us, telling us what to do, even though they have no idea in the world what it is like to be you and me. You and I will always look at the world differently from other people, and only you and I will know it. So remember, my little one, that we may not always be together, but we will always be as one.' She bent to kiss him. 'And I will always love you in a very special way.'

He hadn't remembered her ever coming to tuck him in bed that way again. Yet now her eyes were those of that young woman once more, unguarded, unquestioning, loving without reservation.

She smiled. 'What you did was the noblest act I have ever seen. But it's over now, Charles.'

He looked out once more over their troubled world and frowned that most famous frown. 'For us, it's never over, Mama.'

8.35 a.m.

'But how? How the hell's he going to knock out the bomb?' Harry exclaimed in exasperation.

'He doesn't say,' Tinker replied.

'If only we could ask him.'

The silence that consumed them was broken only by the sound of Daniel gulping messily at a slice of cold pizza, muttering an apology as he did so. He picked up a paper napkin to wipe the grease from his chin.

'You know, we might be able to,' he said, still sucking at something stuck between his teeth.

'Might what?'

'We might be able to ask him. Perhaps we can transmit a bit of Morse back to him, over the screens.'

'How?' Harry demanded.

'Well, sort of . . . digitally block off a small section of the screen. Nothing too big or conspicuous, the sort of thing that a viewer sees when reception gets screwed up. Nothing that the attackers would think was unusual, even if they saw it. Look . . .' He moved to a seat in front of one of the sets of controls. 'Give me a moment, it's been a while since I've touched these things, but . . . something like this?' He punched a button and a black square suddenly appeared over a small section of the scene from the House of Lords. 'We just take out the digital signal so the picture in that part of the screen goes to nothing – black. Don't worry, they can't see anything in the chamber, this is only for our pleasure at the moment but . . .' He manipulated a small joystick and the square began to move around the screen. 'And we can even change the size.' He grabbed a control like a gear stick and the digital square first waxed, then waned, until it had all but disappeared.

'But how does that help us?' Harry enquired cautiously.

'Oh, sorry. Yes. You see, you can cut it in and out. Like this.' And the producer began tapping a button that made the square disappear, then reappear. 'Could even change the shape, if you wanted, make it into a star or snowflake. Whatever you want, actually. But I suspect straight old boring squares is what you need.'

'You mean, by tapping that button there, it's like a Morse key. We could make that square talk? And just on those screens in the chamber, not to the outside world?'

'Exactly.'

'Danny Boy.'

'Yes, Mr Jones?'

'How many parking spaces do you want?'

8.52 a.m. (1.52 p.m. BIOT time).

The ground crew at the airstrip on Diego Garcia had been told to expect a package for onward handling, but the rest of their instructions had convinced them that those issuing the orders couldn't as usual tell the difference between their elbows and an afterburner. Strip the plane down, they'd been told, junk all the stores and ordinance except for three bags – additional fuel pods – under the wings. What the hell for, they had wondered? Even with the extra fuel it couldn't go anywhere. The F-18F Super Hornet was a twin-engine fighter-attack aircraft, a forty-million-dollar bundle of the most sophisticated fly-by-wire avionics that the US Navy possessed. It had a normal combat radius of 150 nautical miles; no way was it a delivery wagon.

They'd been given less than an hour to work on the plane. All they knew was that a package was to be strapped into the rear cockpit seat. Perhaps the base commander's Martinis needed a good shaking. They were astonished when they realised that the package was a passenger, and doubly so when that passenger turned out to be Daud Gul. 'Gonna shove him out at thirty thousand feet,' the armourer suggested. 'Turn her over and just flip the lid.'

For a while, Daud Gul thought much the same. 'It is one of their angels of death,' he whispered to himself. They dressed him. A flight suit, gloves, leather boots, ear plugs, a pair of over-trousers they called a G-suit. He felt extraordinarily uncomfortable, claustrophobic, far more so than in any cell he had ever known, as though they were binding him in, making him totally defenceless. They were talking to him, giving him instructions about barf bags and piddle packs and what to do if he had to eject. They were losing him, he didn't understand all their jargon. 'Don't matter a damn in any case,' drawled one, 'if he ejects he'll probably break his friggin' neck.' Then the helmet, as though they wanted to crush his skull. He felt sick. The smell of jet fuel and exhaust fumes was overwhelming. He had to struggle not to vomit.

They strapped him in. For a moment he considered refusing, but if he was going to die he wanted to show no fear. There were voices in his head, instructing him not to touch anything, and strange dancing screens in front of him with switches and flickering lights. A second plane stood alongside them on the runway, its pilot signalling with his thumb; suddenly the engines began to roar and someone was shouting in his ear: 'Macko flight, you are cleared for take-off. Climb pilot's discretion, runway heading, to flight level three-one-zero, contact departure when airborne.' Without warning and from nowhere, a terrifying roar attacked Daud Gul and his head was thrown back into his seat. Out of the corner of an alarmed eye he saw the runway moving beneath them at an extraordinary rate, and ever faster.

Then he was flying.

9.01 *a.m.*

The COBRA suite contained one of the most sophisticated communications systems in the world, intended for every type of emergency. Patching through to Harry in the BBC's OB unit was not even a challenge.

'Harry, what's going on? You said twenty minutes.' Tibbetts didn't attempt to hide his impatience.

'Got a little caught up, Mike, but we may be on to something very hot. Archie Wakefield's been trying to communicate with us.'

'To say what?'

'That he can deal with the bomb.'

Harry could hear the stirrings of excitement at the other end.

'How, for God's sake?'

'Don't know yet. We're just trying to communicate back with him, flashing a message in Morse code through the screen.'

'But won't that alert the terrorists?'

'Don't think so. It'll look like nothing more than a pretty poor picture, a bit of atmospheric interference or something.'

'You know what the terrorists have said about us screwing around with the picture.'

'I remember. But I don't think that's our biggest problem.'

'Then what is?'

'Archie isn't looking at the bloody screen.'

'What do you propose to do?'

'Give him another ten minutes.'

But ten minutes creaked by, with Harry hovering impatiently over Tinker's shoulder. Then they waited another five, and still Archie Wakefield hadn't seen.

9.16 a.m.

Sometimes, no matter how hard you try, it's not enough. No amount of willpower could draw Archie's attention to the screen.

'I don't think this is going to work,' Daniel muttered, crystallising the thoughts of everyone in the OB unit.

'Then make it work, Danny!' Harry snapped. 'Find some way of attracting his attention. Don't sit on your arse wringing your hands in despair!' It took him a few deep breaths before he had calmed. 'Sorry,' he muttered. 'It's just that I don't understand what you're doing. This is your kingdom and I can't help. It makes me edgy.'

'Think nothing of it,' Danny replied. 'You want to hear my editor.'

Harry placed his hand in gratitude on Danny's shoulder. 'I'll owe you a drink after this.'

'Grand. And since I can leave my car in the car park it'll be a very large one.'

'So, my friend – find me a solution.'

'I suppose we could take the whole picture out. You know, massive interference. Make sure everyone sees it and pray that Archie's the only one who understands Morse.'

Before Harry had a chance even to consider the proposition, the speaker crackled into life. 'Harry, speak to me. What's happening?' Tibbetts demanded. He, too, was growing edgy.

Harry hesitated only for a second. 'We're going to try to attract his attention by taking out the whole picture. Just for a moment.'

Several voices began talking across each other in COBRA, their words tangling, but all joined in warning.

'What if the terrorists understand it?' a tired voice broke in. 'Isn't that a huge risk?'

'I think we own the risk business right now,' Harry replied.

More voices broke across each other. 'Do nothing, Harry,' Tibbetts instructed. 'We're going to have to consider this very carefully.'

And Harry knew they would consider it to the death. 'Too late,' he heard himself saying, stumbling into a maze of subterfuge from which he knew he might never escape. 'It's already underway.'

As Tibbetts's voice came over in alarm, Harry looked inquisitively at Daniel, who frowned, then shrugged, then nodded, and once again began to manipulate the controls. Immediately the screen began to flash and jerk as pixels tumbled in and out until, with a grand fanfare, they disappeared completely, only to reappear and start the whole performance over again. It went on for several seconds. On the other screens they could see everyone in the Lords beginning to turn in their seats to look up at the show. Then, at last, Archie Wakefield joined them.

'Right!' instructed Harry. 'Back to the full screen. Tinker, get to work.'

And the complete picture was back, except for a small black square that was pulsing inoffensively in one corner, giving out its message in a series of bursts, some short, others a little longer, that repeatedly spelled out the letters 'C' and 'Q' in Morse. It was an instruction to make contact.

Almost in slow motion, they saw a tight smile etch its way across Archie's face, and he began tapping away once more, marking on his forehead the letter 'K'. Roger. I understand.

A sense of excitement gripped everyone in the OB unit; Archie's face was now held in close-up, cameras catching him from two different angles. Daniel's face lit up as he shook Harry's hand; others applauded silently.

Archie had repeated the tapping sequence for the third time when the sound of gunfire sliced through their joy. Splinters of old ceiling oak came cascading to the floor. Masood was standing before the throne, his face contorted with rage.

9.23 a.m.
'Harry. *Harry* . . .' Tibbetts was calling. 'What the hell do we do now?'

Masood was shouting down the phone to the police negotiator, demanding answers.

Harry's mind was swimming, not so much with confusion as with exhaustion. Four hours' sleep in the last forty-eight, being beaten, broken, almost killed, had been enough to wear down the sharpest mind, *but* – and there was always a condition – he knew Masood would be in scarcely better shape. His reactions would be slowing, his mind numb and that made him vulnerable. And impatient. Harry knew he had to move rapidly, to push Masood's anger in a different direction before it became irretrievably set.

'What do we do?' Tibbetts repeated over the speaker, his tone a mixture of anxiety and reproach.

'Say it's a signal problem to the screens,' Harry suggested.

'I think we need to consider . . .' another voice broke in, but Harry cut him off.

'We don't have time for this!' he snapped. 'Masood needs an answer now. So tell him . . .' His words trailed away as Harry searched frantically for inspiration.

'What, Harry? Tell him what?'

Then it came tumbling out. 'That the cables run outside the building and must have got damp during the night. It's only temporary cabling, wasn't set up for overnight use. Yes, tell him we can fix it, but that'll require us sending engineers inside the building.'

'But he'll never agree to that.'

'Doesn't matter. All he has to do is to believe it. So go on, ask him!'

Masood wouldn't permit engineers into the building, of course, but as he spoke to the negotiator and the rest of the world watched, they saw Masood slowly lowering his weapon as the surprise and suspicion seeped from his body. Yes, he was vulnerable, too. And on another of the screens Harry saw Archie resuming his tap-tap-tapping.

9.32 a.m.

Harry had led them deeper into the maze of deception and he knew he had lost several of the COBRA committee along the way. Even Tibbetts was beginning to express his doubts. It wasn't surprising; Harry was having ferocious doubts himself.

'So what do we do now, Harry?' the policeman asked.

'We need to test them. See what frame of mind they are in.'

'Somehow I suspect we're about to hear another of your inspired suggestions,' a fresh voice interrupted. It was Tricia. She was back, quietly relishing Harry's discomfort.

She had felt abandoned. The American President had abused her, her own colleagues had turned from her, and she had panicked until she had grown so giddy she had almost passed out. Yet the moment had moved on from her humiliation. Others were coming under pressure, starting to stumble, and in this she sensed opportunity. They weren't doing so well on their own, without her. Her mind was still swamped, her thinking processes drained of clarity, but she had found what she wanted – someone to blame if it all went pear-shaped. Harry had stepped forward so willingly, so brashly, and the blame when it was spread around would reach at least as far as Tibbetts, too. The prospect was enough to revive her. Her personal authority had dried up within COBRA and wouldn't return just for the claiming of it, so she stepped out carefully. 'Have I got it right, Harry, you want to get into their minds? I'm intrigued, tell us more,' she suggested, her tone implying that nothing he said was likely to be taken too seriously.

'I suggest we get Archie to fake a serious medical situation. Call for a doctor. See how they react.'

'And what is that supposed to tell us?' she pressed.

'If they agree, it would be a sign that they're relaxing, looking ahead.'

'And if not?'

'It'll show nothing has changed. That they still mean us harm.'

'So far as theories go it sounds about as tenable as wet tissue,' she reflected.

'But we have to reach a decision,' Tibbetts countered, reasserting his own authority over the discussion. 'Daud Gul's in the air, and getting further from our reach with every minute. We don't have time for certainties.'

'That doesn't mean we should take leave of our senses, too,' she muttered, not as an official contribution but loud enough for everyone to hear.

Tibbetts refused to be deflected. 'In my view this is about as good as we're going to get. Worth a try. Unless you have a better idea, Home Secretary,' he challenged.

But she had done what she wanted, tested the ground to ensure that it would once more take her weight. It wasn't the time to go charging ahead, not yet. She put up no further opposition.

Across the speaker in the OB Unit, Harry could hear other voices, all cutting across each other as they discussed his proposal. He could make little sense of the electronic gabble until Tibbetts's voice came through again.

'The gods have smiled on you, Harry. You can go ahead. But if they let a doctor in,' he warned, 'the consensus here is that we should trust them. Frankly, we're praying they will.'

In the OB Unit, Tinker wiped his brow and waited, his finger poised.

'Time to sound the advance, old friend,' Harry instructed.

Slowly, doggedly, the message was tapped out: '*Fake medical emergency. Demand doctor. Over.*' And Archie's forehead was glowing in reply. He understood.

The arrangements took little more than a minute. As they watched their screens, they saw Celia Blessing half rise in her place, then collapse with a wild groan of pain, clutching her chest. It was like a stone cast into a pond, disturbing everything around; people began leaning forward, offering advice and help, all of which Archie waved away to give Celia a little breathing room. With obvious tenderness he laid her light frame out on the leather bench, stroking her forehead, checking her pulse, releasing the button at her neck. He looked up in distress towards his captors.

'She needs a doctor.'

Masood offered no expression.

'A doctor, for pity's sake!' Archie cried.

'No one comes in.'

'Then let me take her out.'

'No one leaves.'

'Please, I beg you. Let her get help!' pleaded Archie, and although he couldn't be aware of it, in COBRA they were biting their thumbs and nicotine sticks in agreement. 'You want her death on your hands?' Archie demanded.

Masood shrugged. 'I don't even know who she is,' he replied, and turned his back.

9.50 a.m.

An hour gone, and six hundred miles closer. The Super Hornet had used almost sixteen thousand pounds of fuel cruising at 38,000 feet, trying to catch the following winds, yet if it were to make it to a landfall of any sort it would need much, much more. Above his head, Daud Gul saw the sky looming dark while below him the earth was lost in a milky haze, much as it had been ever since they had left Diego Garcia. Yet something was changing. The other Super Hornet that had been flying with them ever since they took off, holding tight in formation on the right-hand side, had vanished, disappearing from view only to reappear seconds later and a matter of feet in front of them. It was getting closer – too close! Daud Gul almost cried out as the twin engines of the other jet seemed about to smash into the cockpit, but as his eyes filled with disbelief, he saw a hose line extending from beneath the other plane with what looked like a basket of some sort attached to its end, and his own pilot was moving in to meet it, the two planes engaging in an agile dance that made Daud Gul forget his fear and for a moment of weakness admire the skill of these enemies. Then drogue met probe, they were locked, and for many minutes the two planes matched each other, thousands of feet above the earth, like two angels frozen together on the doorstep of heaven. As they embraced, Gul could see one of the gauges in front of him changing colour and steadily climbing.

Then it was done. The two planes parted gently. Once more Daud Gul's body was being forced back into his seat as his plane climbed steeply, as steep as any mountainside. He closed his eyes, fighting the nausea. When he opened them again, the other craft had gone. They were on their own.

9.58 a.m.

She was lying with her head cradled in Archie's lap. He ran his fingertips across her hair, casting around in apparent anguish, and keeping his eye on the screen.

'*What next?*' he tapped, and once again when at first he received no answer. It required fifty separate fragments of the Morse code.

'*What plan for bomb?*' the reply came back.

'*Recommend wait until Queen—*'

But suddenly Archie was looking directly into Masood's eyes, knowing he was undone.

'What do you think you're doing?' the terrorist demanded, his lip curled in suspicion.

'What – this?' Archie began fumbling theatrically and ridiculously at his forehead. 'Why, just a nervous habit, I suppose.' He tried to smile, but that only inflamed the other man's mistrust.

'If you want to keep your fingers, and your head, then if I were you I would keep them well apart,' Masood said, his eyes burning into Archie. 'I shall be watching you.'

Reluctantly, Archie's hand returned to stroking his patient's hair.

Those watching howled in silent despair. With his good fist, Harry made a substantial dent in the OB van's aluminium wall, sending instant and merciless spasms of regret shooting through his broken fingers. Somewhere inside the van, someone swore luridly. Then Tibbetts's voice, reeking of despondency, came over the speaker link. 'Harry, I think we need you back here. Right now.'

10.24 a.m.
'What is it to be?'

Tibbetts's question failed to raise any spark of enthusiasm or fresh insight. They had waited for Harry to arrive, but the additional time had done nothing to clarify their thoughts. Disaster was still spelled the same way.

'Let's begin with an update from Brigadier Hastie, please,' Tibbetts said.

The Scot cleared his throat. 'Little has changed, I'm afraid. We still have three snipers in place, but one of them has been on station for nearly eight hours. He'll be tired, not capable of operating at a hundred per cent. I give him one good shot, but no more, which leaves seven gunmen. Our objective is to get to them before they can do damage to the hostages. The other two snipers are hidden in the ventilation shafts and they should be able to account for two targets each, assuming that the targets don't suddenly shift their positions. So we're down to three. It's those three that will do the damage – assuming that we are pro-active. If we wait for them to move first, I still have to stick to my twenty-per-cent casualty rate amongst the hostages. And there is still, of course, the matter of the bomb.'

The bomb, the bloody bomb, everything kept coming back to that.

'Have you – has anyone – any idea about how Lord Wakefield might deal with it?' Tibbetts gazed around the room; he found faces coloured with the ashes of an empty hearth, and no answer.

'What about the royal protection officer?' someone eventually asked.

'Potentially very useful,' Hastie responded, 'but only if he knows what to expect. Otherwise he'll be taken as much by surprise as anyone.'

'Can't we alert him?'

'He won't read Morse. And he's sitting in a different part of the chamber to Lord Wakefield. I think the only way to alert him would be to get someone inside. If we could do that, we could also organise some sort of distraction. It might shift the odds sharply in our favour.'

They all turned to Harry. He now seemed a pitiful sight. The eye was still closed, the lip swollen, with a bruise on his cheek that was beginning to scream. 'I think I just got volunteered,' he mumbled. He was finding it increasingly difficult to talk through his damaged mouth; two of his teeth were swaying like young trees in the wind; some orthodontist in Wimpole Street was going to get rich out of this.

'No, Harry, you've done enough. We can't ask you to go back in there,' Tibbetts said.

'So who else did you have in mind, Mike?'

The policeman pursed his lips as though he had a mouthful of lemon.

'You send a stranger in there right now and they're going to *know*,' Harry protested. 'You can't do it. Anyway, I expect that the latrines will need cleaning by now, and I'm just the man for that. Isn't that right, Tricia?'

She smiled, all sweetness.

'Look, we can still talk to Wakefield through the screens, even if he can't respond. So we tell him that whatever he's going to do, he must do it when I'm next inside. While I'm there I find some way – eye contact, that's probably all that's required – to bring the protection officer up to alert. And we wait on old Archie to . . . well, do whatever he's going to do.'

'You'd be placing yourself back in the firing line, Harry,' Tibbetts reminded him.

But Tricia was waving her hands. 'Let's slow down here a little. We're rushing this.'

'No one's rushing – except for Daud Gul,' the commander replied. 'We have to review our options.'

'And one of those options is to assume that they'll release the hostages once Daud Gul arrives back in his homeland in' – she glanced at a screen on the wall that was showing the progress of the Super Hornet – 'around two hours.'

'And if they don't?'

'*Then* we go in.'

'We will have lost the element of surprise.'

'But gained the element of justification, remember. And the only justification for going in beforehand is a theory based on Harry's spectacularly wayward instinct.' The claws were coming out, but very slowly.

'Are you afraid of making a decision, Tricia, is that it?' Harry asked.

'The only thing I'm afraid of is discovering we've made the biggest mistake of our lives. We're playing for huge stakes here.'

'I've got something, that might be relevant,' Tibbetts said tentatively. 'Not sure what it means, but for what it's worth, I've just had the autopsy report on Bulgakov. Seems he was suffering from a clapped-out heart. Cardiomyopathy. Had months to live, maybe only weeks. He was killed by a heart attack caused by the fall.'

'So – death by natural causes,' Tricia added doggedly.

'That depends on why he fell. Whether he was pushed. Whether he tripped.'

'He was pushed,' Harry insisted.

Tricia sighed, like a patient mother. 'But how can you know?'

'Because his death stretches coincidence to the breaking point.'

'Why are you always looking for conspiracy, Harry? Building up a case to call in the *kamikazes* – and for what? For no better reason than some sick old man had a heart attack!'

'Some sick old man who had helped organise the greatest crime of the century.'

'Look, I hate to make this personal,' she said, turning to the others, 'but so much of this comes down to the matter of Harry's judgement. It's an issue here, and I'm afraid the record shows that his judgement has been seriously flawed, not just in politics but even in the Army.'

'What on earth do you know of my military career?'

'I know a great deal about it, about you. You were vetted by our friends in MI5 here.'

Five wriggled in embarrassment. This really wasn't the way the game should be played.

'When you became a Home Office minister,' she continued, 'I got a nice thick file. All about your run-ins with your senior officers, your bending of the rules . . .'

'I think that's called initiative.'

'Always taking risks.'

'That's what you do in the military.'

'But too many risks in the opinion of your senior officers. Didn't you take your airborne brigade on a para drop in conditions that were considered reckless? I seem to remember the official report said that broken bodies were left scattered across Sardinia. Some crippled for life. Sometimes you seem to place a very low value on other people's lives, Harry.'

'I'm not sure any of this is relevant,' Tibbetts intervened.

'I'm afraid it's entirely relevant,' she retorted. 'We are proposing to take a course of action that, if it goes wrong, could result in one of the most mind-blowing catastrophes in our country's history. That decision should be based on something more solid than the views of a man whose judgement has been shown to let others down time after time.' Even when she was trying to be restrained, it seemed there was no mercy.

They looked towards Harry, but he would say nothing. He wouldn't climb down into the gutter with her.

'After all, Harry's not part of COBRA,' she continued. 'Not a minister, not an official. He's really nothing but a passer-by. I believe he's been allowed to take too much on himself.' There it was, Harry the scapegoat, along with a reminder that it was their fault, not hers.

During this exchange Five had begun squirming in his seat. He didn't like the game she was playing and he didn't like her – it wasn't that he didn't care to take orders from women, it was this woman he found distasteful. No small talk, just fangs. As his sense of irritation grew, he began gripping his nicotine stick ever tighter, so tightly that with a loud snap it broke in two, interrupting Tricia Willcocks in mid flow. Eyes turned to him.

'You wish to confirm what I've been saying, Five?' she asked, smiling.

Five cleared his throat. 'A passer-by,' he repeated, washing it around his mouth, 'that's one way of putting it. But with quite a track record. It's coming back to me now – from that file you mentioned, Home Secretary. Active service in Northern Ireland, the first Gulf war, and some rather hush-hush operations we get rather twitchy about discussing which took place in western Africa.'

She tried to interrupt but he rode through her.

'We're not talking about pushing paper clips here, but putting one's life on the line – and getting various chunks of it shot away. Can't remember how many medals and commendations he's got for all that' – he drew circles in the air with one part of his nicotine stick – 'but I think there was a Military Cross and a bar, with a GSM thrown in there somewhere, too. Desperately unfashionable stuff nowadays, in some circles, at least. But I think it entitles him to have an opinion.' A general rustle of approval crept round the table.

'Not in COBRA,' she persisted.

Tibbetts intervened. 'I'd like to remind you, Home Secretary, that I'm the official charged with the responsibility for this situation. It's my decision what we do next.'

'I don't deny that.'

'Thank you.'

'But I am Home Secretary.' She intended it to sound like a threat.

'A fact of which I am eternally conscious.'

'And I would like to ensure you stick by the rules.'

'This is COBRA. There are no rules,' Tibbetts replied, growing exasperated.

'Then I would like the proceedings minuted,' she continued. 'It would be helpful afterwards if we could have a written record to see who was responsible for what,' she said.

'Oh, I'm sure your friends in the press will see to that!' he snapped.

And with that, their game had changed. His defiance and contempt for her had now been pushed into the open. He shouldn't have allowed that, but he was exhausted and she was impossible. The battle lines had been drawn.

'I suspect you may be seeking early retirement after this, commander.'

'But not in the next twenty minutes. I propose we move on.'

'Yes I think we should,' Five intervened. 'Daud Gul's almost halfway there. We're running out of time.'

'We have to resolve this,' Tibbetts said, trying to regain control of his temper. 'Since this is such an important issue, I'm going to ask each of you for an opinion. I know it's not the way we usually work within COBRA, when we try to use more subtle means to reach a consensus, but I fear this is too important to allow for any misunderstanding. I'll go round the table one by one. I'd like to start with you, Colonel Hastie. After all, you and your men will be in the firing line on this one. Do we wait for Masood and his men to walk out – or do we go in and kick them out?'

Hastie drew breath, not wanting to hurry this. 'I've been studying them very carefully. I see no sign of them lightening up, let alone letting up, as I would expect if they intended to release the hostages. I believe we should accept the risks and go in.'

'Thank you. And you, Chief?' Tibbetts turned to the Chief of the General Staff.

'Ditto,' he said with military abruptness.

And so it began. A civil servant insisted he had no opinion, couldn't decide and wouldn't decide, even when Tibbetts pushed; the Minister from the Foreign & Commonwealth Office leaned towards delay, as did the one from Health, while their counterpart from Defence refused to disagree with his senior military officers and sided with the Chief. As Tibbetts went round the table, pressing them all, the matter showed as many phases as the moon.

'Thank you, everyone. I think that's about it,' Tibbetts concluded.

'But what about me?' Willcocks demanded, glaring.

'I beg your pardon, Home Secretary,' Tibbetts offered in genuine apology, 'I thought you had already stated your view with unimpeachable clarity.'

But Tricia was never as simple as that. 'I have raised questions, that's all, none of which have been satisfactorily answered. But as you say, we must move on and it's your neck on the line. My conclusion, for what it's worth, is that I will support you in whatever you decide, commander.' It was a most skilful side step. Her views were as clear as a lighthouse on a calm night, but no one was going to be able to accuse her of undermining any operation, if that's what he decided. Yet history is written by the winners, and by those friends she had scattered around the media, and she was determined to leave herself sufficient wriggle room to line up on the winner's side, whichever that turned out to be.

Tibbetts saw through her, but what could he say? He offered her his gratitude, which she accepted with a nod of her head and a tight smile. It disappeared rapidly when she discovered that he wasn't quite finished.

'And you remind me, Home Secretary, that perhaps there is someone else whose view I have taken for granted.' The policeman turned in his seat. 'Harry?'

It took a few seconds for Harry to compose himself. His lips were exceptionally painful; he still had the salt taste of blood in his mouth. The words came slowly.

'We vowed we would tread gently in their land.'

It was a vow that every one of them knew had been broken. He had their attention.

'The Mehsuds were warriors, as they were brothers, long before we came into their land, and as they will be long after we have left. They are strangers from a distant place about which we know too little, and yet we have made them our enemies. That is a tragedy, and one day, perhaps, we might give as much attention to their troubles as we do to their threats, and remember that in the eyes of their families and those they have left behind, each of the men in that chamber is their Black Prince, their Nelson. So I suggest, whatever it is we decide to do today, that we do it with humility and not from hatred.' His tongue probed the swollen part of his mouth while he sought his words, still finding raw wounds. He would need stitching inside, too, after this.

'It's a big step to take a human life. We should not do it lightly. I hope I have never done it without asking myself a thousand times if what I was doing, and had done, was right. And today we must decide again, yet we have no way of knowing for certain what is in the minds of these men. It's possible the Home Secretary is right, that they might leave without inflicting further harm. But we must go beyond that, for what we do matters not just for today, but even more for the days yet to come. If we do nothing in the hope that they will simply walk away, I suppose it might save the Queen. But it will do irreparable damage to our freedom. From this day forward we will live in fear of when they will return – and they *will* return. There is no limit to the ambitions or the imagination of those who play the game of terror, those who know they can take advantage of us – they will return like jackals to the prey, time and again, in the sure knowledge they will get fed. If we allow them to walk away, we open the doors to disaster – not today, maybe, but tomorrow and for as long as anyone remembers this day and the weakness that we showed. We wouldn't be saving the Queen; instead, we would be condemning her realm. Yet if we look disaster in the eye and face it down, they will not come here again. Then, whatever the outcome, we will have won the day.'

The room had grown still. Slowly, after a long pause, the eyes that had been fixed on Harry turned to the police commander. He seemed not to move, apart from the methodical rising and falling of his chest. His attention was focused on a thin manila folder that lay on the desk in front of him. Reluctantly he opened it.

'I have here a letter that hands legal authority for dealing with this situation over to Brigadier Hastie and his men. We all understand what that means; it effectively amounts to a warrant of execution. No one has signed such a thing in this country for nearly thirty years.'

He looked round the table, waiting for objections, but none came. He picked up a pen and, with a slow hand, put his name to it.

'And God help you,' Tricia Willcocks said as she pushed back her chair and walked from the room.

Twelve

11.18 a.m.

THE USS *ABRAHAM LINCOLN* had been on station south of the Straits of Hormuz, several hundred miles off the Pakistan coast. It was one of two carriers in a task force stationed permanently in the region in support of Operation Enduring Freedom, that ongoing and seemingly ever-lasting campaign constructed of chewing gum that had been designed to kick the Taliban out of Afghanistan and put a blast of cold air up the collective arse of the Iranians – a campaign that, like gum, had stretched much further than expected and had proved impossible to get rid of. The *Abraham Lincoln* had history; it was the carrier on which, a lifetime earlier, an American President had looked over the smouldering battlefield of Iraq and declared 'Mission Accomplished'. Many more missions had been flown from the carrier since then, and precisely how much had been accomplished was still a matter of mystery to the skipper.

Several hours earlier he had been ordered to head his ship south-southeast at all due speed and await further orders. Now those orders had arrived. His was not to be a glamorous role on this day, but it would be vital nonetheless. Instinctively, the skipper searched the late afternoon sky. Even though the carrier had been making 36 knots they were still 300 nautical miles from their target. Half an hour's fly time for a Super Hornet. Then another mission would have been accomplished.

11.30 a.m.

Archie Wakefield could feel sweat beginning to trickle down his temples. He'd read the message that was being flashed up on the screens three times, and still it didn't change. He grew short of breath and was struggling to control a rising sense of trepidation. From her position beside him, still prostrate, Celia Blessing sensed his confusion and opened one eye to find out what was happening.

'*Urgent*,' the message read. '*Believe terrorists still intend attack. Require you deal with bomb.*'

Archie knew what that implied, but did they? Did they realise what they were asking him – *requiring* of him? He had little to lose, but even so, this needed him to find resources within himself that in truth he didn't know if he possessed. It was all very well bragging to Celia, impressing her, and he'd meant every word – then. But now?

'*Chamber to be stormed*,' the message continued. '*Pull ear if understood.*'

But when? How? He wanted to ask all sorts of questions, but his captors were still keeping a wary eye on him. Yet the more he thought about it, the more he realised that everything depended on him, and he sweated all the more. They would have to build an attack around him, for without him, the day was lost. 'Bollocks,' he declared quietly. If he screwed this up in front of Celia he'd never live it down. That was right, he'd never live it down. Celia was still staring at him, her solitary eye open wide in concern.

He bent down, close, as though to inspect her, and whispered. 'Know something, duchess? It's time for you to stage a remarkable recovery.'

11.33 a.m.

Harry began slipping off his shirt for the last time as he prepared to go back into the chamber. He struggled with the buttons, one-handed; they were awkward and he couldn't get the wretched thing off. Not the best of omens.

Strange, he pondered, how almost Jacobean this situation had become, the high game of politics reduced to the most basic of struggles, a matter of bloodlines. Fathers, mothers, sons, all players, and all potential victims in one way or another. A President whose entire sense of purpose had become focused on her son, while the Prime Minister's had been cruelly undermined by the presence of his. There was Daud Gul's son, too, who had come halfway round the world to save his father and turn all their lives on their heads. And the Queen and Charles. She had been sitting there for almost twenty-four hours now, seeming impassive to it all, but how could she be? No one else was. Strange, this parent thing.

Harry, too. Not for a moment had he forgotten about his own son – yes, it would be a son, that's what his instincts were telling him. Yet he had become so wrapped up in other people's lives. Perhaps he'd got his priorities wrong, he should be sorting himself and Melanie out first, let others deal with this nonsense, but it was too late now, his decision had been made, although whether by him or for him he wasn't entirely sure. So, go in, get it over and done with. If he walked out in one piece he'd still have time to sort things out with Melanie and if he didn't – well, it wouldn't matter then, would it?

Bloody Mel. Where was she? With a girlfriend, he assumed, or was that merely what he hoped because he couldn't deal with his fear of the alternative? *Come on, Harry, relax!* Yes, she would have been deeply hacked off by his no-show at the restaurant and in turmoil over her predicament with the baby, so for sure she would have sought comfort on the shoulder of a girlfriend, and that's where he'd find her, later this afternoon, after . . .

Fuck it, there was no point in pretending. This was his fault, too; he'd neglected her, given more time to other people than he had to Mel. Little wonder she had grown so distracted. He should put aside all the harsh words and do a little grovelling, tell her he was sorry, give themselves at least a chance of putting things back together again. And he should do that right now, this minute, before he went back inside, just in case. He stopped fumbling with the shirt and reached for his phone. He dialled; still no answer. Voicemail. He hesitated. With a pang of anguish he realised this might be the last message he ever left her. What should he say? *Where the hell was she?* Yet the more he tried to put aside his suspicions, the more insistent and hurtful they became. He ended up punching the red button.

He scolded himself, he was distracted, confused. He had to concentrate, focus on the task that lay ahead, clear himself of the clutter. He was about to walk back into the chamber on the most important mission of his life and he knew he might not be walking out again. The danger would only deepen if his mind were caught on thorns, yet the more he struggled to set his thoughts free the more they became hopelessly entangled. He wasn't ready for this, none of it. In frustration he snatched at his shirt; there was a tearing sound, a dozen sharp-toothed weasels seemed to rip at his left hand and the buttons raced mockingly away across the tiled floor of the parliamentary post office. Suddenly, Harry realised he was afraid, not just of the danger that lay ahead but about many things. No, he really wasn't ready for this.

11.35 a.m.

Other people, too, were lost in their private thoughts. John Eaton kept glancing at his son, trying to make eye contact, but Magnus seemed determined not to oblige. Even if Eaton hadn't known it before, he did now; there was nothing he wouldn't do to save his son. Years of guilt and fatherly pride – and, yes, *love* – weighed heavily on him and had forced him into humiliating capitulation in front of the terrorists. That would cost him dear, no doubt. He had probably lost the respect of his son and certainly that of others, and he would lose his job, too, after this, but that seemed of little consequence so long as Magnus survived. He would prefer to live with his son in torment than not to live with him at all.

Robert Paine was another who knew that the world around him

had changed for ever. Whatever the outcome of this siege, it would leave all sorts of wreckage in its wake. Leaders would be called to account and found wanting. Oh, they would spin themselves to dizzy heights and vow that such appalling failures would never be repeated, but it would take more than the head of that poor, broken fool Eaton to appease the cries for retribution. Windows would be broken not just in Downing Street but in the White House, too. Yet at least the Prime Minister and President might have the privilege of watching their sons grow to manhood; it was far, far more than they deserved.

By contrast, Tricia Willcocks was in less pessimistic mood. She had showered and undertaken running repairs in order to prepare for the outcome, and whatever that might be, she believed she could embrace it. If it were all to end in bloody disaster, she knew she'd left enough of her misgivings littered around the floor of COBRA to be able to wash her hands of those medding Boy Scouts. Yet – and she had been so careful about this – she had not vetoed the operation, as she might have tried to do, and if through some process of divine intervention their efforts succeeded in saving the day, she would be the first to applaud, and be sure to do so very publicly. Why, she'd been in charge, had counselled them, cautioned them where necessary, and wished them God's guidance even as the decision to attack had been made. She'd be suitably modest, of course, but the truth was she was responsible for the entire thing. Rejoice! Rejoice! Anyway, so great would be the outbreak of public rejoicing that no one would have patience for any cockroaches and critics who might crawl out with complaints after the event. She'd shown she could take the pressure, handle the responsibility, and even though her name had been marked as the first victim she had been lucky enough to survive. The media liked lucky leaders. All in all, she thought she'd done rather well.

Nothing more was required of her, except to wait.

11.48 a.m.

Daud Gul had never known such terror. The Americans had promised that he was going home, but they had surely lied. Instead they were trying to terrify him to death. It was a tactic he knew they used, like waterboarding, when they strapped you to a plank of wood with your head below your feet and your mouth and nose covered while they poured water over your face, so you thought you were drowning. Sometimes you did, choked to death, or broke bones in the desperate struggle to free yourself from the restraints. Yet now he didn't even have time to prepare himself. He'd been thinking of his mountains, lost in a world of dreams, when without warning his inner calm had been shattered by a loud female voice. 'Bingo Fuel!' it shouted at him. 'Bingo Fuel!' it repeated. He opened his eyes in time to see the indicators in front of him changing from green to yellow and beginning to flash. 'Bitching Betty', as the voice was known, was announcing that they were running short of fuel. He glanced anxiously out of the window but could see nothing except a haze where sky and sea seemed to melt into each other, and he couldn't even be sure which way was up or down. He knew he was far, far from his home still; outside the cockpit there were no mountains, no land of any kind, and now the plane was dropping from the sky, falling lower and lower, the instrumentation changing all the time. He had been prepared to meet his death ever since they had captured him, but he had hoped for a warrior's death, a bullet or a blade; he hadn't counted on this.

Only at the last moment, as he knew they were about to crash, did he see the carrier beneath them, a tail of tortured water stretching out behind. And no sooner had he seen it than they were upon it, hitting it hard, his entire being shaken like a lamb in the jaws of a lion. It took him some time to realise that he was unhurt; now he understood why they had strapped him in so tight. And as they opened the cockpit he was assailed by noise, men shouting, machines pounding, everything around him was moving, his head was spinning. That was when he threw up. All over their bright and shining airplane. No time for the barf bag. The American engineers cursed, and he might have been proud of himself had he not taken it for a sign of his own weakness.

They dragged him from his seat, shouting in his ear, but he understood little of it, his attention focused on the mayhem of machinery that whizzed past and around him, all seemingly intent on killing him. But then he was inside the ship, they were stripping his soiled flight suit from him and telling him to use the head. Then they began hauling him back into another set of their tight, chest-crushing flight clothing. Oh, God, he cried, they were going to start with torture all over again.

11.50 a.m.

The mess at Wellington Barracks, in the lee of Buckingham Palace, was an unusual sight. The forty-odd men of Colonel Topolski's Delta Force detachment appeared to be relaxing in whatever way they wished; some ate, drank water, coffee, nothing hard, while others played cards or sat propped against walls and dozed. Some even smoked, although that was against the law, but no one seemed interested in interfering. They even had their weapons at their sides. Only the presence of armed guards standing on the other side of the mess doors gave any hint that they were not entirely at their ease.

When the door opened to admit two men, Topolski was relieved to see that one of them was Braithewaite. He liked and respected the man, and the fact that they had ended up at opposite ends of the barrel could only be explained by the outbreak of some virulent form of swamp fever. The man accompanying the British captain was considerably older and more senior, but the American was fighting the fog of fatigue and was too disorientated to recognise him or immediately identify the salad bowl of ribbons that hung from his chest. Topolski stubbed out the remnants of his cigar – one of a fresh supply provided by his British captor – and stood. The older man saluted and extended a hand.

'Colonel Topolski,' he said, 'I hope we've been taking care of you. But I'm afraid I must ask you and your men to move out. Right now.'

'You're just in time,' Topolski muttered. 'We were about to tunnel our way under the wire.'

'We need you at Westminster,' the other man continued, undeterred by the American's flippancy. 'You see, we're just about to go in, colonel. And you're part of this operation. We very much want you to be flying the flag beside us, as usual.'

'I don't—'

'What? You didn't think for one moment we'd try to keep you away from the fun, did you? Not after you've come all this way.' The older man offered a clipped smile. 'I can't promise that we'll need your men for the operation itself, but I wanted to come down here personally to say how extremely grateful we are for your support – as always, eh? So if you and your men are ready, I'll leave it to Captain Braithewaite to take care of the arrangements. You'll forgive me, but I have to be elsewhere. I hope we'll meet again later, colonel, after this little dance has been done. In the meantime . . .' And with the crispest of salutes, he was gone.

'Who . . . ?'

'That,' Braithewaite responded. 'was the Chief of the Defence Staff.'

'So why . . . ?'

'I think he wanted to ensure there had been no misunderstanding.'

'And this . . . ?' The American cast around him at his men in their informal but unambiguous confinement.

'Never happened.'

12 noon.

They made their final preparations under cover of Big Ben as it tolled the hour. The clatter of the helicopter overhead had become so much part of the scene that those inside the chamber had long ago discounted it, blocking out the pounding on their ears, and they failed to notice as it dropped just a little lower still. It was much the same with the clatter of the light tanks outside as they shifted positions yet again. Like a flood tide that laps around the unsuspecting, spaces that only moments beforehand had been empty were occupied by whispering men, waiting to strike.

Most of the members of COBRA were still around the table, watching screens, waiting. Tibbetts, however, had retreated to his Ops Room. He wanted to be with his men. He sat in the corner, reading once more his copy of the letter he had signed handing responsibility to the SAS. *By this letter I formally pass over responsibility for the siege taking place within the House of Lords to military authorities* . . . It made Tibbetts redundant, for the while, but he knew that it would not absolve him from what was to come. The letter was a prescription for legal murder, and his signature was on it. He ran his forefinger over it, time and again, mechanically trying to smooth away the folds in the paper, and drank more coffee.

Brigadier Hastie also wished to be with his men. The SAS had set up their headquarters on the committee corridor in the Palace of Westminster, a floor above the entrance to the Lords. The final briefing had already been delivered. On the wall, pinned across sumptuous Pugin wallpaper, were photographs taken from television cameras of each one of the gunmen, and across a table was spread a large hand-crafted diagram of the chamber and its entrances. On it was marked the location of every single person, both captives and captors, all numbered or named. Hastie said little as his squadron commander set about the task, occupying his time by listening intently as the various SAS sticks reported in, counting them off as they verified their locations and states of readiness.

A million miles away in Washington DC, President Blythe Edwards had just received news of the impending attack was going through moments of torment that there was no chapel in the White House. A hundred and thirty-two rooms, but not a single place to get down on her knees and pray. She knew she needed God to help her face the coming trial; she had interfered, meddled in the affairs of others, been arrogant, and it had all gone wrong. The American sin. She sat on the edge of her bed, looking out across the dawn that was emerging feebly above the Potomac and watching grey skies weep. Slowly, like the raindrops that were tricking down the windowpane, she fell to her knees. She clasped her hands together and prayed to her Lord that she would find the strength to get through this day, and that her son would find protection. And when she had finished with that, she asked for forgiveness, not just for herself but for those who were about to commit this ludicrous, insane act of carnage at the moment when Daud Gul was almost home. They would need God's forgiveness, those people, for they'd never receive a crumb of forgiveness from anyone else.

Meanwhile, back in London, Tricia Willcocks climbed into a fresh set of clothes and began toying with the phrases she would use to mark the end of the siege. Unrestrained joy or the most sombre sadness. Whatever the outcome, she would be prepared.

12.15 p.m.

When they strapped him in for the second time, Daud Gul simply closed his eyes, ready for whatever might come. He had gone limp, couldn't obstruct them but wouldn't co-operate, so they had treated him like a sack of rice and dumped him in the rear hard seat, tightening his restraints more fiercely than ever. This was a new plane, no vomit, just the stench of fuel once more, and a different pilot, more talkative, not filled with sullen hatred like the last American. Daud Gul looked out from the cockpit and saw nothing but water. Despite himself, he felt panic rising once more in his throat.

When the steam catapult of the *Abraham Lincoln* threw the plane into the air he was thrown back against his headrest and he hit nearly 4 Gs, but it didn't last. Soon they were climbing once more up the side of a sky mountain, heading for the stars. He couldn't see properly, grey patches had formed at the edges of his vision, and he shook his head trying to regain his senses.

'If you're gonna throw up again, don't do it in your helmet,' the voice of the pilot interrupted. 'You do that and you'll choke.'

But even as he spoke, the plane was easing back, levelling out, no longer pointing vertically. And as they flew on, one of the screens embedded in the instrument board in front of him began to change. Instead of showing nothing but emptiness, it began to give way to something that appeared harder, more substantial.

For the first time, Daud Gul spoke. 'What is that?'

'That?' the pilot responded. 'Why, that's land, Mr Gul. The coastline of Pakistan. You're practically home.'

12.25 p.m.

At a signal that was relayed to him from Hastie's squadron commander, Harry re-entered the chamber, pushing his trolley. He was needed; the hostages were growing impatient in expectation of imminent release, and with their impatience had come appetite. Masood's men stared at the battered figure, his bloodied face, his broken hand, his now badly stained shirt, but he had become familiar and they paid him no special attention. Around the chamber hung an air of quiet anticipation that had raised the humour and resilience of most of those there, but the mood hadn't infected everyone. Elizabeth sat, impassive as always, inspecting Harry as though seeking some sign, as if doubting the face value of what she saw; did she know, or sense, that all was not as it seemed? The American ambassador was dark-eyed and sombre, the Prime Minister carried a haunted expression as if he was searching for something that lay a thousand miles in the distance, while nearby the two sons had faces bathed white in pain.

Yet Archie Wakefield's eyes were bright, searching. Harry nodded. Slowly, cautiously so that the gunmen could read nothing into the gesture, Archie pulled his ear.

And as Harry pushed his pile of food and drink still further into the chamber, he snagged the attention of the royal protection officer by staring at him with an intensity that screamed in warning. The officer didn't understand but he wasn't required to understand; he needed only to be alert. He sat up, braced his shoulders, stretched his arms, more in curiosity than expectation, but that was enough. He was back in the picture.

Harry went about his task of distributing the supplies with woeful slowness but he had a ready excuse in his physical condition and the fatigue that was running through them all, yet he couldn't stretch it out for ever. He couldn't afford to raise suspicions. He grew anxious. He looked once more across at Archie, willing him on, begging him to make his move – everything was hanging on him, surely he knew that? The bomb must be dealt with first. But Archie sat there, impassive, and when Harry's despairing eyes hit him he did nothing but tug at his bloody ear once more.

Oh, God, it wasn't going to happen. Archie had frozen, wasn't up for it. The attack would have to start with the bomb still in place. And one of the terrorists was now eyeing Harry with more than idle mistrust, waving him on with the muzzle of his gun. This wasn't going to work.

12.42 p.m.

As Harry began to feel despair biting at his heels, half a world away and for the first time, Daud Gul was sensing that surge of excitement that told him he had won. His plane grew lighter as it burned up its fuel, flying ever faster towards its destination, at almost twelve miles a minute, and although Daud Gul knew none of this he could see far below him the shapes and shadows of land, and knew it was Pakistan.

'How much longer?' he asked.

'If we maintain this tail wind, thirty-six minutes,' came the reply.

Thirty-six minutes. And in little more than that he would be back in his mountains, where the last few months would seem as a passing, feverish dream.

Hastie knew as much, too. Time was running out. His attention kept switching from the chamber to his watch, and back again, knowing that they must soon, very soon, wash their hands of Archie Wakefield and go it alone, knowing that the consequences of doing so would be some shade of disaster. As his eyes flicked back once more to the screen, he saw the Queen seeking approval from Masood to use the facilities of their makeshift toilet. She rose in her seat, dignified, slowly, as befitted an elderly lady who had spent a night in extreme discomfort.

And as she made her way to the closet at the side of the throne, shadowed as always by the gunman in the explosive jacket, in another part of the chamber Hastie saw Archie Wakefield assist the struggling Celia Blessing to her feet and follow.

12.45 a.m.

The field telephone in the chamber rang. Masood picked up the receiver and nestled it to his ear. It was Mike Tibbetts. The policeman had considered it only right that he should volunteer for this unpleasant duty.

'Masood, I thought you'd like to know. The aircraft with your passenger on board will be landing in Peshawar in approximately thirty minutes.'

'Excellent.' For the first time through the siege the young tribesman appeared to show excitement.

'I think we need to discuss the arrangements when he gets there.'

'They will be very simple,' Masood responded, and began to bark animated instructions into the phone.

12.47 p.m.

The closets behind the throne had no internal lighting. As a result, it was necessary to leave the door ajar in order to allow those inside sufficient light to find their way around. Many of those in the chamber found this situation embarrassing and lacking in dignity, but none had to withstand the humiliation that was inflicted upon Elizabeth. Where she went, the gunman and his jacket followed, not just up to the door but even inside the closet itself. She tolerated it without complaint; she had no choice in the matter and in any event it was no worse than the conditions many people of her age had to withstand. With so many people in the chamber the closets were kept busy, and occasionally a small queue developed, waiting, although that somehow never applied to the Queen herself. Masood would permit no more than one or two people to linger, but on this occasion the next in line was Archie and the clearly distressed and frail Baroness Blessing, whom he supported with an arm around her shoulder. They seemed an incongruous pairing, he so swollen, almost bloated, and she with a frame so like that of a sparrow that she all but disappeared within the folds of his arm. They glanced around them, seemed to exchange a whisper, almost a smile.

As the door to the closet opened wider to allow Elizabeth and her escort to emerge, Archie and Celia Blessing were no more than four feet away. Archie straightened, and seemed to grow several inches in stature. The gunman hovered in the doorway, immediately behind the Queen, almost touching her. It was time.

In a scene that would be replayed for as long as anyone wished to define the meaning of sacrifice, Archie's body seemed to shake and he hurled his entire seventeen-stone bulk at the much smaller man. Archie was neither well nor fit but it was an unequal contest. They both tumbled into the closet. As they did so the Baroness, now remarkably recovered, grabbed the Queen by the arm and threw her to one side. Elizabeth fell heavily, dragging Celia Blessing behind her, while Archie and his victim disappeared from view.

12.47 p.m.

TATP is an explosive that can come close to matching the power of TNT, but it doesn't react in the same manner. TNT creates its power by breaking up its molecules so that the fragments then recombine to release a large amount of energy, while TATP explodes in a very different way, breaking each of its solid molecules down into separate molecules of gas. These gas molecules of ozone and acetone don't react or combine with each other but in the first instant of their creation they occupy the same volume as was originally occupied by the solid explosive. Yet they are gas, and can take the place of the solid only at a far, far higher pressure. The gases expand outwards, forcing air and any other surrounding materials away at vast velocities.

The first surrounding materials that the explosion encountered were the two bodies. The gunman was beneath, on his back, flattened by Archie, whose huge frame lay like a smothering blanket on top. Death for both of them was instantaneous, but not in Archie's case purposeless. His body absorbed some of the blast wave of the bomb, reducing its impact, but what remained looked for the route of least resistance, which was through the open door, blasting it off its hinges and sending it cartwheeling into the chamber. The next weakest link was the roof of the closet, little more than timber and not load bearing, and this was fractured into splinters that flew into the air, some of which became embedded in the roof of the chamber itself. But the walls, the walls, it was the walls that did it! The walls of the closet were generously thick, particularly that one which stood against the throne, for it was this wall that supported the vast golden edifice of the canopy behind the throne. It cracked and crumbled and large amounts of debris were blown from it, but its heavy Victorian carcass proved wonderfully resilient. And it was this tough, resistant wall that stood between the bomb and those in the chamber. The main force of the explosion went to the side, and up in the air, not out across the red leather benches.

Yet, even so, the damage it caused was substantial. As the bomb gave up its life it created a huge amount of noise and dust. Debris flew everywhere, causing many injuries in the chamber. Most of those on their feet were knocked over, and while the hostages found some protection behind the leather benches they were all thrown into a state of deep confusion. What most of them hadn't realised was that the bomb was not the first explosion to take place. In the fragment of time that passed between Archie's assault on the gunman and the detonation of the jacket, explosions were taking place at many points around them, but so close together in time that for most they melted into one. The SAS had placed frame charges against all the side doors that led into the chamber, both on the ground floor and also the doors that gave access into the galleries. The charges exploded simultaneously, triggering the booby traps in the Coca-Cola cans. These later proved also to have been made of TATP with detonators fashioned, as Hastie had predicted, from nothing more complicated than toyshop party poppers.

There were other explosions. In the same breath as their colleagues were setting off the frame charges, the three SAS snipers hidden in the ventilation shafts and the television tower received their authority to fire. Two of them immediately claimed their victims, including the sniper in the tower who had been holed up for almost twelve hours, but the third couldn't get his shot away. Sod's law. At the crucial moment a hostage had stood up to ask permission for a toilet break, covering his line of fire. Only three down.

The fourth was Masood. He, of all people, proved too trusting. Even as he was talking enthusiastically about arrangements in faraway Peshawar, he had no means of knowing that the telephone receiver he was using had a remotely activated explosive device concealed in the ear piece. It was only small, of necessity, but it blew a four-inch hole in the side of his skull. As Tibbetts later said, the only pity was that he never knew what hit him.

Now the chamber was full of smoke and bewilderment, with the cries of the wounded hostages mingling with the explosion of flashbangs hurled by the SAS as they stormed the doors. These flashbangs were stun grenades, designed to create a blinding light and enormous noise that incapacitated rather than killed, and it was in the midst of this maelstrom of confusion that the royal protection officer, forewarned and well trained, got in his kill. The Pakistani high commissioner was standing right behind him and had been disorientated by the grenades. He was still rubbing his eyes, trying to recover his senses, when the protection officer stretched across the leather bench and from a distance of less than a foot put a bullet in his brain.

Yet there were still three gunmen alive and armed. Even if they were temporarily blinded, with little idea of where they were, they could still release ninety rounds from their Kalashnikovs in three seconds. In such crowded conditions, surrounded by hostages, the death toll could still be huge. Harry had known what to expect. Even unarmed and with a broken hand, that gave him a huge advantage. As soon as Archie had disappeared inside the closet, Harry had dropped to the ground to shield himself from as much of the ensuing blast as possible. He also knew that he shouldn't look towards the doors when they were blown or he'd be blinded by the flashbangs, but the gunman nearest him, the one who had beaten him so badly, was not so wise. When Harry reached his side, he was only just beginning to recover his sight, yet his weapon was being raised and readied to fire. Harry was behind him. He hooked his left arm under the other man's throat, crying with the pain as he hauled the gunman off his feet, twisting him round as he did so. With his good right arm, Harry knocked the weapon from his grasp. Now he was on top of him, the other man face down, yet still stretching for his weapon that lay only inches beyond his fingers. Harry's left arm was still round his throat. He put his knee in the back of the other man's neck and pulled back, savagely, as hard as his screaming hand would allow, until he heard a click. The body shook, then went limp.

Elsewhere in the chamber, matters did not go so smoothly. One of the two remaining gunmen had been momentarily lost within the fog of confusion and smoke. He managed to discharge half his magazine before he was killed. One of his victims was the royal protection officer, standing over the body of the Pakistani high commissioner.

The final gunman was found crouching behind one of the red leather benches. As he saw the approaching SAS, he pushed his weapon away and cowered in submission. He was the last man to die, with eleven bullets in his head.

Yet success exacts its price. Seven hostages died. Two were shot by the same gun that caught the protection officer, while the Italian ambassador was killed when he was struck by the flying door of the closet, blown from its hinges. One elderly peer succumbed to a heart attack and another was hit by a splinter of wood that turned to shrapnel. There was Archie, too, of course. And Celia. She and the Queen had been closest to the source of the main explosion, and while the Queen's body had been protected from much of the blast by the steps that led to the throne, Celia had no such cover. She shielded her monarch from the cascading debris, but her own body was completely exposed. The sparrow would fly no more. Celia Blessing and Archie Wakefield died together.

Thirteen

ELIZABETH WAS MOTIONLESS WHEN the medical team reached her, yet she stirred as soon as they had removed the body of Baroness Blessing that was lying against her. She had been too embarrassed to move while her friend could not, and even a little ashamed that she had survived. The helpers brushed the dust and debris from her face and checked her vital signs, then sat her up and brought to her side both a wheelchair and a medical trolley.

'Don't be silly,' she said, rebuking them and rising with as much dignity as possible to her feet, allowing them to provide no more assistance than a supporting hand.

'We must get you straight out, Ma'am,' they insisted. 'There might be another bomb. We need to secure the area.'

'A little late for that, aren't you?' she suggested, dismissing them.

It was Charles who had taken the heavier knock. He had been thrown from his throne and tumbled down the steps, striking his head and badly twisting his ankle, yet it might have been far worse. A chunk of wooden shrapnel had pierced the heart of his mother's throne, which sagged wretchedly to one side. Elizabeth stared at it, reflecting on what might have been. They implored her once more to clear the scene but she continued to ignore them, insisting on walking through the chamber with her son, calming the other hostages and giving what comfort she could to the injured. When, at last, they came back to the spot where the body of Celia Blessing lay, they stood awhile in silent prayer, alongside the archbishop. Only then did they prepare to leave, yet still they insisted on doing things in their own manner. They would not go quietly, through some rear door – sneaking out like thieves, as Charles put it.

'Are there cameras outside?' he asked.

'I'm afraid so, yes, sir,' one of the armed officers replied.

'Good,' he muttered. 'Let the buggers see us walking out. Let the whole bloody world see us!'

And even though he was limping he offered his mother the support of his arm. 'Go out as we came in, eh, Mama?'

But she wouldn't depart. 'Not until I am properly dressed.'

He bowed his head in understanding. With as much dignity as his crooked leg would allow, he hobbled back up the steps to the foot of the throne. The imperial crown was there, covered in filth and with one of the supports looking decidedly sickly after a direct hit from a piece of flying rubble, but otherwise it appeared intact. He knelt and with a handkerchief brushed away as much of the dirt as he could. Then, stiffly and with extreme care, he carried the crown down the steps to where his mother was now sitting.

'I fear it's not looking its best,' he said.

'It looks rather special to me,' she replied. She inclined her head gently, and he fixed the crown back on. Only then would she agree to leave.

Waiting for them at the Sovereign's Entrance was one of the State cars, a specially constructed Bentley that carried no registration plates. With considerable tenderness the prince helped his mother into the rear seat, ensuring that her crown remained firmly in place and came to no further harm, before claiming his own seat at her side.

'We'll have to return to the palace along Birdcage Walk, Ma'am,' the accompanying protection officer explained. 'Can't get anywhere near Trafalgar Square. There's a huge crowd gathered; half the country seems to be there.'

'But I think we should let them see us,' she said.

'Security, I'm afraid, Ma'am.'

'Security? From our own people? As long as we've paid the Congestion Charge, I rather think we can risk it, don't you?' The sweetness of her tone implied the swiftest lash. Abashed, the projection officer began muttering into his radio.

They pulled slowly away from the Sovereign's Entrance. As they did so they passed a troop of American soldiers. They were a motley collection with a variety of uniforms, some even had moustaches and straggly hair, but no American troops had ever stood more rigidly to attention or presented their arms with more pride. Above their heads, the Stars and Stripes caught the breeze and gently unfurled. Topolski was still saluting long after the car had passed from view.

1.14 p.m.

As rapidly as their condition allowed, others were being led from the Lords. Once they had recovered their wits they began to congratulate each other and to express thanks for the support they had found in each other's company

'I think we should all leave together,' one member of the Cabinet suggested.

'I will leave with my son,' John Eaton replied awkwardly.

No one argued with him; indeed, he had noticed that the expressions of relief and joy they had been sharing had not extended to him. A wall had risen between them. He knew why.

He said nothing to Magnus, couldn't find the words, simply placed a hand on his son's shoulder, squeezing as though to reassure himself that it was real and not a trick of his imagination. William-Henry walked alongside. Neither of the boys would take his eye.

As they made slow passage out through Pugin's vast doors, their footsteps echoed forlorn and hollow from the tiled floor. 'We got out, Dad. That's the main thing, isn't it?' Magnus said.

'Of course.'

'The *only* thing.'

'Not quite,' his father whispered. 'I died in there, too.'

'No!'

'My colleagues will already be planning the details of my burial, editors polishing the casket. Everyone will be so wise after the battle is over.'

Magnus stopped and at last turned to face him. He found tears of sorrow gathered around his father's eyes, but also tears of relief. 'What you did in there, Dad . . . you did it for me. I know that. I appreciate that,' he said, struggling to find the words they had never used. 'I will never stop loving you for it.'

'Then I have found the happiest of epitaphs.'

1.20 p.m.

The Super Hornet prepared for touchdown. At last Daud Gul could set aside the fear that had dogged him ever since he had climbed into this machine. He'd been blasted off ships, been thrown about, flown thousands of miles, been refuelled in mid air high above the Indian Ocean, so high that he felt he could touch the stars, but now he would be landing on solid ground – his ground. He had seen the mountains rushing beneath the wings. Almost there.

There was a jolt as the plane hit the concrete surface; it was a mild sensation compared to the shakings and battering he had received earlier in the flight. The tyres beat their path across the seams in the runway, striking up a steady and hypnotic 'kerthump, kerthump'. He closed his eyes, his lips forming a silent prayer of gratitude to those brothers and tribesmen who had won him his freedom, and to his son most of all. He knew the risks they must have taken; he vowed they would not be in vain.

The plane came to a halt. Daud Gul opened his eyes, yet what he saw when he looked out from the cockpit surprised him. There was none of the expected bustle, no sign offering him welcome to

Peshawar, merely a line of military vehicles on either side that were swarming with American troops.

'This is not Peshawar,' he said, almost to himself.

The pilot's voice crackled in his ears, as polite as ever. 'No, Mr Gul, and it's not even Pakistan. Peshawar's a little under a hundred-and-fifty miles to your right. On the other side of those mountains.'

'So . . . where are we?'

'Bagram. The main American airbase in Afghanistan.'

'But . . .'

'A little change of plan, Mr Gul. I'll let those gentlemen with the rifles explain it all to you.'

1.25 p.m.

It took a little time for Harry to emerge from the chamber. He wasn't in his best shape. He'd made a mess of his elbow during the fight and the face wound had opened up once more. It took a while before the medics could staunch the bleeding. They'd wanted to take him off to hospital but Harry had refused, so they'd taken him back to the little post office where his clothes were waiting and tried to clean him up. It wasn't an easy job. It was while they were fussing over him that he saw Tibbetts hovering in the background.

'Think you could do with some time off,' the policeman said. 'You look bloody awful.'

'I won't ask you to look at the other guy.'

'You did good, Harry.'

'We both did.'

'If you're up to it, I'd like to take you back for a short debrief. While everything's fresh. I know it's a lot to ask but—'

'Later, Mike. Got a call to make first.'

'Where, may I ask?'

'Mel.'

'Ah. Of course. I'm sorry. Should've realised. I'll organise a car. And you'll need some new clothes. I've got a fresh set waiting for you back at the office. You'll forgive a little official larceny on your wardrobe, I trust.'

'There's something I want in return, Mike.'

'Name it.'

'I want you to look into the family connections of everyone involved in the siege.'

'What are you looking for?'

'I'm not sure,' Harry said, wincing as the medic probed his swollen cheek. 'It's just that this whole affair's been like a game of Happy Families. Something's nagging at me, at the back of my mind, and if ever I get rid of this headache . . .'

'Harry, relax. It's over.'

'Is it?'

'For you, yes.'

'Please, Mike, just do it, will you?'

Harry gave him an obstinate, one-eyed stare and the policeman sighed. 'You're a stubborn sod. But, I suppose, just this once . . .'

'Thanks.'

A few minutes later they were being driven back to New Scotland Yard.

'Now there's a sight to behold,' the policeman muttered.

'Where?' asked Harry. His left eye was completely shut and much of the world was passing him by. He stretched his neck, causing him to wince with pain, and what he saw made him grimace even more. Tricia Willcocks was on College Green, a strip of grass adjacent to the House of Lords much used by the media. She was standing before a vast array of cameras, television lights and microphones, giving interviews. She was animated, gesticulating, pointing in the direction of the Lords then throwing her arms about as if embracing everyone who had been in it.

'Normal service has resumed, I see,' Harry said. He started laughing, shaking with uncontrollable mirth, and he carried on laughing, no matter how much it hurt.

*

It was late in the afternoon before Mel returned to her home, carrying a small overnight bag. She stood on the doorstep in a shaft of pale early winter sunlight and looked beautiful, he thought. Harry watched from the back seat of the car as she scrabbled for her door keys; she could never remember the difference between the front door and back door key, let alone the key for the cupboard under the stairs. She was still fumbling when Harry climbed out from the car.

She started in alarm, dropping the keys. Not even his fresh set of clothes could hide the damage. The bruising, the swelling, the wound trying to burst from behind the stitches. His left arm was in a sling, with broken fingers sticking out from the open end. And he was limping.

'What the hell happened to you?'

'Busy day at the Lords.'

'What?'

'The Lords,' he repeated, standing on the pavement below the doorstep. He bent to retrieve her keys. He noticed she had a new fob.

'You were there?' she gasped.

'In my underwear.'

'That was you?' As realisation dawned, her manner changed, beginning to soften. 'I didn't know, I couldn't tell, not from the television pictures.' She stepped forward, instinctively, protectively. 'Are you OK, darling?'

'I guess what you see it pretty much what you get.' He tried to smile, but it hurt. 'That's why I was a little late last night. I did come. But you'd already left.'

She took it as accusation and protested. 'I didn't know,' she cried. 'I was sitting there feeling like Little Orphan Annie and . . . I'm so sorry.'

'But not sorry enough to call and find out.'

'I've been busy.' Her cheeks lit briefly with embarrassment and she hid her face, turning once more to the door and to fumble with her keys.

'We need to talk, Mel.'

'About what?'

'You know what. The baby.'

She faced him, looking down on him from the doorstep, taking a deep breath. 'Harry, there is no baby.'

'What are you saying?'

'I've just come back from the clinic. It's over.'

So that was where she had been, since this morning, at least.

'But you said tomorrow . . .' he protested.

'And you said you wanted to talk about it last night!' she spat back.

'How could you?'

'There was a cancellation,' she muttered distractedly as though they were discussing diaries.

'It was our child, Mel, our decision. You had no right!'

'I had every right!'

'And what about my rights? As a father?' He was pounding his chest with his good hand as his hopes melted into thin, unsustaining air.

'Oh, Harry!' Suddenly she was wailing, crying herself, her eyes shut tight in shame. 'How can I tell you? You know how it's been between us, but . . . please believe me. I never meant to hurt you.'

'What are you talking about?'

She was trembling, having to force the words from her. 'The pregnancy. It wasn't yours. Sorry.'

He stood on the pavement, unable to speak as at last he was overwhelmed by pain.

'It wasn't yours,' she repeated, more firmly. 'Now do you understand?'

Oh, yes, now he understood, many things, but far too late.

Like an animal drags himself off to a cave to nurse his wounds, Harry found himself in his favourite French bistro. L'Artiste Muscle occupied a corner of the secluded Victorian enclave of Shepherd

Market. It had few pretensions, was minuscule, and in warm weather spilled out on to the pavement, yet no matter how crowded it was, they could always find a place for Harry.

He arrived late, almost the last, eating on his own, the Toulouse sausage and flageolet beans, easy enough to manage one-handed and a sensible foundation on which to build the monumental bender that was about to follow. The chef, Marcel, wiped his hands and sat to share his second bottle.

'You have been in the wars, Harry,' the Frenchman said, raising his glass in salute.

'Almost got me this time.'

'Your lover's husband catch you out?'

'No. My wife.' It was said in a tone that stripped the humour from the night.

'I argue with my wife all the time,' Marcel said, 'but not like this.'

They drank.

'So what do you argue with her about?' Harry asked.

'Oh, only unimportant things. Money. My mistress.'

'You have kids?'

'We argue about them all the time, too, but that is different.'

'In what way?'

'We have three of them. We argue not because we disagree about them, but because we want so much for them. Too much, I'm sure, but somehow kids take over your lives. And then there is not enough room left for ourselves.'

'We are that sad generation, Marcel. Screwed up by our parents, screwed up by our kids.'

'You got kids?'

'No.'

'Then perhaps you can manage another bottle?'

'With a little help.'

'It is yours, my friend.' Marcel reached for the third bottle, driving home the corkscrew until its arms were lifted up in surrender.

Harry's head was beginning to pound, not just from the alcohol but the effects of everything he had been through. He was also still a little deaf from the explosions and the battering he had taken; he leaned forward to catch what Marcel was saying.

'Without my kids, I think my life would be impossible,' Marcel said. 'All I would have left is my wife and little Claire over there' – he nodded in the direction of a waitress, far too young and nubile for Marcel's good, who was washing glasses. 'I would go mad.'

'Now, if she were my daughter . . .' He shook his head in uncertainty.

'If she were your daughter, I believe I would be the one looking like you right now,' Marcel chuckled. 'Our children become our guiding stars, our reason for being, our sanity, and without them – *pouff!*' He made a gesture at his head with his fingers. 'Take my children from me, and you rip away the meaning of my life.'

'I've seen that myself, these last few hours.'

'Yes, it is a great difficulty. With your kids you lose all your money, without them you would lose your mind. Fatherhood is a form of madness. Why else would we even try to commit ourselves to just one woman?'

They laughed until they were halfway through Harry's third bottle, and his mind was slowly draining. Marcel had moved on to more important matters, something to do with the prospects of his football team, but Harry paid little attention. His brain was slipping gear, going into reverse – it was something the Frenchman had said, it was important, perhaps fiendishly so, but Harry couldn't understand why, or remember what it was. Thoughts moved around his head like tectonic plates, crashing into each other and causing earthquakes in his mind. Or was it just the rehearsal for the hangover to come?

Marcel was still holding forth, leaving Harry stranded somewhere between Stamford Bridge and the Champions League. He knew now that there was something he had seen, or sensed, that was the key to unravelling the plot, but every time he tried to concentrate and hold on to a passing thought he realised he was too far gone. It was like trying to catch clouds. He needed his wits, but if he sobered up he was terrified that in the morning he would remember nothing. So he stretched for the bottle and refilled his empty glass.

It was late the following afternoon when Tibbetts and Harry called upon the ambassador in his residence. US marines stood at the gates as they were swung open to admit the visitors to the vast grounds set in the heart of Regent's Park. O'Malley the butler opened the door. 'He's in the garden, sirs, taking a breath of the air.'

The setting was magnificent, the trees dressed in their full autumnal glory, but Paine seemed to have aged, withered a little since the previous day but, in their own way, each of them was older. The ambassador was throwing a stick for his red setter to retrieve, the dog chasing through a thick carpet of chestnut leaves like a train through fresh snow, setting the stick down at his master's feet before repeating the whole process time and again. 'Much like a diplomat,' Paine reflected as they approached. 'Always fetching and carrying, doing your master's will.'

'I think you do a whole lot more than that, ambassador,' Tibbetts said.

'Perhaps. I try, at least. So what can I do for you, Commander Tibbetts, Mr Jones?' he asked as with a slow, deliberate tread he followed his dog though the slush of leaves.

'In the first place I want to thank you for everything you did for us,' the policeman began.

'I appreciate that, commander, but really I did no more than many others – and far less than Mr Jones here. We all owe him more than I suspect we can properly express.' He turned to Harry. 'I hope I'm not speaking out of turn, but even as we speak, Washington is scratching its collective head to find a suitable means of expressing its gratitude.'

'I have a friend who wants a parking space at the BBC. Anything you can do to drop a good word in . . .'

The ambassador laughed. 'You British!' He threw the stick once more for his dog. 'A parking space? Now, if you were American, you'd be demanding at least a helicopter pad. And something suitably large to put on it.'

He led them back inside, the red setter tracking dutifully behind. The animal was both well groomed and well trained, the sign of a clear-minded master. Tea and coffee were waiting on a side table but he passed them by. 'It's a little early, I know, but after yesterday . . .' He poured three large whiskies, then handed the glasses round. 'You're not on duty, are you, commander? Anyway, your colleagues can't arrest you here, this is United States territory,' he laughed.

'It was really quite a day, ambassador,' the policeman replied, taking the glass but not drinking.

'And not yet finished,' Paine responded. The dog settled dutifully at his feet. 'I hear rumours – wild speculation, no doubt – that the Prime Minister has made up his mind to resign his office. He intends to take responsibility for the whole ungodly mess and fall upon his sword.'

'A politician accepting responsibility,' Harry mused. 'Unusual, but in this instance entirely appropriate. Almost noble.'

'It won't have escaped you, Mr Jones, that there's an element of classic tragedy in all this. Not just the personal but the political. Who'd have thought it possible that in one afternoon the foundation stone on which our Western world has been built could be ripped from its place? Britain and America, torn apart, the Special Relationship consigned to the garbage heap of history. It's terrifying to think how close the terrorists came to destroying everything.'

'It gets even more curious,' Harry added. 'You'll have heard by now of the Bulgakov connection?'

The American nodded, rolling his crystal glass between the palms of his hands.

'There's something else we've learned,' Harry continued, reaching for the last and most brilliant of Sloppy's many nuggets that had been dug out from the mines of Canary Wharf. 'All the dummy companies he set up to exploit the markets and make monkeys out of his Russian colleagues led back ultimately to just one account. It was set up recently in Switzerland, under the name of *Boyarny Deny Zavodi*. Roughly translated from the Russian, it means Lords' Day Enterprises.'

'Extraordinary. Quite extraordinary.'

The policeman picked up the story. 'We've come to the conclusion that Bulgakov never had any intention of getting away with the scam; in fact, strange as it may seem, he all but insisted on being caught. We got there much quicker than he might have expected: it would normally take weeks rather than a few hours to unravel the threads, but he must have known we'd get there sooner or later. He didn't hide his activities well, not nearly as well as he might. And that's the point. He wanted us to know.'

'He wanted to get caught? But why?'

'He was sick. Had very little time left. Couldn't possibly have used the money he already had, let alone a new fortune. Do you know it amounted to almost a hundred million pounds in one afternoon? We'll freeze the accounts, of course, get most of it back, but some of the Russian oligarchs took a real pounding. They won't recover so easily.'

It was Harry's turn once more. 'The oligarchs were his enemies, they'd turned against him, squeezed him out of the action, and he was out for revenge. So he not only wanted to rob them, he had to be sure they'd know it was Levrenti Bulgakov who did it. He intended to die laughing at them and continue laughing from beyond the grave.'

'What sort of man would do that?'

'Someone who was eaten up by frustration, a lonely man who was burning away inside with a sense of injustice,' Harry suggested. 'There's almost no knowing what people like that might do.'

'Did you ever know Levrenti Bulgakov, ambassador?' Tibbetts asked casually.

Paine frowned, his forehead split in concentration. 'No, I don't believe I ever did. Although you meet a lot of strange people in London, of course.'

'We were thinking you might have met him elsewhere,' the policeman continued, 'when you were an assistant director of the CIA some years back. You had responsibilities for central Asia, didn't you? We wondered if that's where your paths might have crossed.'

Slowly Paine rose to his feet; his glass was empty, he refilled it. 'I see you're not drinking, commander. On duty after all?'

'Bulgakov,' the policeman pressed.

Paine leaned against the mantel of the fireplace. 'I can't remember meeting him,' he said, his voice a shade less convivial, his features more alert. 'Anyway, the whole business is done with.'

'Not quite,' Tibbetts said.

'He's dead.'

'But it doesn't explain who murdered him.'

'Or how he managed to break the security system at the State Opening so comprehensively,' Harry added.

'But he was KGB. Surely . . .'

Harry was shaking his head. 'He couldn't possibly have done it on his own. He needed help, from the inside. Someone who knew how things worked.'

'Foxhunters and feminists break into Parliament to stage their demonstrations; I don't see why it should be so different for trained terrorists.' Paine's fingers were drumming in impatience. 'And as we were discussing, it brought our two countries to the point of total rupture. That's a Russian plot if ever I saw one. Lenin would be proud of him.'

'But it was more than that, and yet not quite that at all,' Harry persisted. 'This seemed to be as much about the sons of Britain and

America as much as the countries themselves – as if they needed to be punished, too. Magnus and William-Henry.'

'For what?'

'For being the sons of important and powerful people.'

'But who would do something like that? What could possibly be their motivation?'

'A sense of overwhelming injustice, of a great wrong that needed to be put right. That's what we were talking about, weren't we? Perhaps a sense that these people had no right to their sons.'

'You have lost me utterly,' Paine remarked, in a tone that indicated he was beginning to find the conversation tedious.

'This plot wasn't really political. The terrorists in the chamber wanted the release of their leader, of course, and the wobbling of the Western Alliance was an added extra, a bonus. But at its heart, this was something desperately personal, about two boys, and two sets of parents.'

'It was about the Queen.'

'Yes, I wondered about that for a while, but if it was about her then why wouldn't they take Charles when he had offered himself in exchange for the two boys? It was because he was the *wrong* son. This was about taking revenge on the President and the Prime Minister.'

Paine's fingers had stopped dancing, his body grown still and tense; the dog, sensing the change, slunk away, its tail curled between its legs. The ambassador's gaze wandered back and forth between the two Englishmen, wondering who would strike next. It was Tibbetts.

'How long ago did your own son die, ambassador?'

'I beg your pardon?'

'Your son. He was a Robert T, too, wasn't he? When did he die?'

The American took his time before he replied. His features had frozen into a rigid mask but behind the eyes they could sense that some extreme and unremitting form of emotional warfare was taking place, a civil war, a war within that involved no one but himself, and different parts of himself, one that had been going on for a very long time. When at last he spoke, the voice came like a creeping frost. 'Do you mean, how long ago was my son's life wasted? Thrown away? That was almost two years ago.'

'Is that what you think – that his life was wasted?'

'He died for his country, fighting for a cause. Then his country forgot about him – your country, too. Their leaders washed their hands of the cause for which he had given his life and wandered off to other things, while their own sons were pampered, sent off to the glittering spires of Oxford where the greatest challenge they ever faced was a deadline for the weekly essay.'

'I suspect they must know what it feels like now, the agony of watching their child suffer.'

'They didn't do too well, did they?'

'You sound almost pleased.'

'Pleased? What the hell have I got to be pleased about? Our governments begin these half-brained wars from the comfort of their armchairs, sending the best and the brightest of our young men to die, while the rest of the population reach for their remote controls to wipe away the last trace of any embarrassment.' He all but spat in disgust. 'They don't suffer, they make no sacrifice, they never come down from their pulpits to mourn their dead. They simply wash their hands and look the other way. That should not be.'

'But you are an ambassador, Mr Paine, committed to defending your government's policy,' Harry prodded, sensing the inconsistency.

'And you, Mr Jones, are a politician who, like all of your kind, are committed to the highest standards of public integrity. So perhaps you can explain to me why politicians everywhere are despised and always seem to end up in the shit.'

'Ambassador, we have this little difficulty, you see. Bulgakov needed help, and he was also murdered. And you are the only one we can find with anything that looks like a motive,' Tibbetts said.

'Motive?'

'I think you have just set out a motivation very clearly.'

'Being an ambassador with a private conscience is not yet a crime.' Paine offered a smile of ill-disguised contempt. 'You try to peer into a man's soul, commander, and you will lose your way. This is nothing but idle speculation.'

'Then let me speculate a little more. I'm pretty sure we'll discover that you knew Bulgakov of old. That we can establish as fact. And what we believe is that you formed the idea and gathered all the insider information, while he found the resources in Masood and his merry men. A pretty lethal combination – not just for the gunmen in the chamber but also for Bulgakov. And you were the only one to leave the chamber, the only one with the time to kill him. You had both motive – and opportunity.'

'I can see why you need to cover your own incompetence, commander, but this is all not only desperately circumstantial but also utterly implausible. I'm the United States ambassador, for God's sake.'

'You changed your clothes,' Harry intervened. 'After you left the chamber.'

'Yes, I plead guilty to that and throw myself upon your mercy, gentlemen.'

'Might we be allowed to see the clothes?' Tibbetts asked. 'Let forensics take a look.'

'I would be more than happy,' Paine replied, 'but . . . I see a problem with diplomatic immunity. It would set an unfortunate precedent.'

'No matter. I expect CCTV cameras will put some meat on the bones of our hypothesis. And forensics have found footprints by the bridge. Size ten.'

'I'm size twelve.'

'That's size ten UK, ambassador – size twelve American.' Tibbetts was staring at Paine's feet.

The ambassador shifted uncomfortably. 'Me and around five million others,' he suggested.

'But only one with both motive and opportunity. And size ten feet.'

Paine rose to his feet, letting forth a sigh of impatience. 'Then I look forward to my day in court, gentlemen. In the meantime, I think it's time you took your fantasies elsewhere.'

Tibbetts rose reluctantly, but Harry stayed stubbornly seated. 'Oh, it'll never come to that, ambassador,' he said. 'They'll never give you your day in court.'

'They must. If they share your fantasies.'

'You present the authorities with a formidable quandary, Mr Paine. Look, may I talk to you man-to-man? I have no official position in this, I'm little more than . . . I think the Home Secretary called me a passer-by.'

'An astonishing woman,' Paine said. But Harry had intrigued him; he sat down once more. Tibbetts stood quietly by the door.

'There will be no public platform for you, ambassador, either in court or outside. They won't charge you, that would simply be too humiliating. It would give Daud Gul and all the enemies of the West too much gratification, do their job for them. And they won't let you go, either, because that would cause just as much embarrassment. Yet the truth will come out eventually, no matter how deep they try to bury it.'

'I will insist!' Paine barked.

'Of course. And when the truth does emerge, they will simply say that these were the acts of a madman.' He hit the last word softly, like the burying of a blade.

'Ridiculous!' the American snapped in exasperation.

Harry twisted the knife. 'They'll say it, nonetheless. They will cast you down as delusional, put you away quietly, secretly. Your own very personal form of extreme rendition. You will disappear, no one will know. A padded cell made of silk. That's what they'll do, they've done far worse.'

'I shall speak out!'

'The screams of the lunatic asylum,' Harry mocked. 'Who will listen?'

'Even they can't cover up an act such as this.'

'So you admit it.'

'I admit nothing!' the ambassador shouted, banging the arms of his chair.

The two men were locked together like gladiators in an arena, eyes held fast, watching each other's every move, oblivious of the outside world and bound within their own very private battle as they pushed each other to extremes.

'So, you are the God,' Harry said quietly.

The American cocked his head slowly in puzzlement, thrown off balance. 'What?'

'It's how I knew you were responsible. It was never just about Masood and the others – couldn't be, they were just the choirboys, as I called them, singing to a score set for them by the cardinal. Bulgakov. But behind a cardinal stands God – God the Father, whose son died for others. That's the role you've been playing, isn't it?'

'If I were guilty, why wouldn't I admit it? I have nothing to hide, nothing more to lose.'

'I wonder what your son would be thinking now, if he were here. He was a brave man, one who was willing to lay down his life for his country. How do you think he would feel about the father who betrayed it, and him?'

'I would never betray my son!'

Harry shook his head dismissively. 'You said you had nothing more to lose, ambassador, but you do. You have your good name, which is also your son's good name.'

'He was the last of the line . . .'

'Don't you understand what you have done? You've destroyed the only thing that was left of him – his memory. Because of you, the name of Robert T Paine will stand for nothing but treachery, and because of you, his death will truly have been in vain.'

Harry put the suggestion with force, and it seemed to shake the ambassador. The war taking place inside was slowly twisting out of control, tearing him to pieces. 'I keep his photograph by my bed. I have his medals in my drawer. His sword and service pistol on my bookcase. I have the flag from his coffin. I talk to him every night. His memory means everything to me . . .' Then he sobbed, a hoarse, dry sound, like the sputtering of a damp fuse before it dies. For the first time, doubt crept into his eyes. 'Is it possible to love a son too much, Mr Jones?'

'A friend of mine, last night, told me that fatherhood is a form of madness.'

'I think perhaps he was right,' the ambassador gasped. Then he fell to silence, retreating to a place deep within himself, his haunted expression suggesting he was finding nothing but ghosts. He stayed there some while. 'What will happen?' he asked eventually.

'We can't touch you,' Tibbetts replied from the doorway. 'You have diplomatic immunity. You will be recalled home. I suspect all that Harry has said is right. You will disappear for a while. If ever you are heard of again, it will only be to drag you out through Traitor's Gate.'

'What have I done?' he gasped.

'Done?' Harry replied. 'Why, you have lost, ambassador. Lost everything.'

'I wanted nothing for myself, not like the others. I wanted nothing but—'

'But to see those who had wronged you suffer, like you have suffered.'

'I longed for my own death, not that of the others. Do you understand that? An end to it all.'

'I think so,' Harry said. 'That was why you went back into the chamber. A stray bullet. A simple conclusion. It would've been seen as an heroic sacrifice, one fit for the long tradition of the Paines. And with you dead, none of this would have come out.'

'A neat solution.'

'For you. And your son. I would hate to see his name dragged down. He was a brave young man. He deserves none of this.'

Paine moistened his lips as he tried to fashion the words. 'If only I could turn the clock back, just a day. Finish things off properly.'

'It's never too late, ambassador.'

Tibbetts flashed a look of alarm, but Harry's own eyes lashed him into silence.

'A soldier's death, Robert. No shame in such things. So much better than what is to come.'

'I have a choice?' the American asked quietly.

'I think so.'

'Thank you.' The American stood from his chair, stiff, like a puppet. 'If you'll excuse me.' Awkwardly, as though his joints needed oil, he turned and walked from the room. The red setter refused to follow.

The policeman did not speak – there were many things best left unspoken at a moment such as this – but there was agitation in his eyes.

'It's better this way, Mike, believe me. For everyone,' Harry whispered as he busied himself making a fuss of the dog.

It was a few minutes later when, from somewhere upstairs in the great house, there came a sharp sound they both recognised. The dog lay down and whimpered.

'I'll take a guess he used his son's service pistol,' Harry said.

'You pushed him into it.'

'I gave him a choice, Mike, which is more than he gave others. Believe me, it was the only way.'

'For who? The politicians?'

'For his family, his son. But mostly for himself.'

'I'm a policeman, Harry, this isn't the way I work.'

'Tell you what, Mike, if it happens again next year, we do it your way. In the meantime, I need a drink.'

'And I've got a million forms to fill out.'

'That's fine, then. Business as usual.'

Afterword

I T WAS REMARKABLE HOW QUICKLY the British Establishment regrouped and repaired the hole that had been blown in it. A Royal Commission was set up to inquire into the siege and came up with two main conclusions. The first was that the security surrounding the State Opening was woefully lax and based on assumptions that were at least a decade out of date. The second conclusion was that no one individual was to blame for this state of affairs.

The man who shouldered most of the responsibility was, inevitably, John Eaton. The following weekend he declared that he was resigning as Prime Minister and retiring from the House of Commons with immediate effect. It seemed ironic, after all that had happened, that after a period of grace no longer than six months he should be offered a peerage and became a member of the House of Lords.

When the contest to succeed him began, Tricia Willcocks threw her hat into the ring. However, within days of her announcement a Sunday newspaper revealed that her husband, Colin, had been leading a double life and had fathered a daughter with one of the younger partners in his law firm. It seemed not only deceitful of Colin but also very clumsy of Tricia not to have known. Privately she blamed the leak on what she referred to as 'that stick-sucking bastard at Five', while publicly withdrawing her candidacy with as much grace as she could muster, declaring that she would fight another day.

The Royal Family went through one of their occasional bursts of popularity. The Queen was raised almost to sainthood, while Charles's offer to take the place of the other two sons was seen as being the dotty act of an ever-more eccentric man, but one who was now admired for his peculiarities rather than reviled. The period of royal popularity proved to be prolonged.

President Edwards ran for re-election and won. Robert T. Paine was buried with full honours, his suicide the result, it was claimed, of the unbearable stress brought on by his heroic defiance of the terrorists.

Harry got himself both a George Cross, the highest civilian award for gallantry, and a divorce. The new Prime Minister offered him a Cabinet post, but he declined. The speculation was that he was too busy spending time with outrageously unsuitable women.

Hastie and Tibbetts also got medals and promotions, but despite a whole paragraph in the Royal Commission's report praising his dedication, Daniel never got his parking space. They might change the world but, it seemed, never the BBC.

Statues to Archie and Celia were placed either side of Pugin's entrance to the House of Lords, just as statues of Churchill and Lloyd George guarded the entrance to the chamber of the House of Commons. The day after the siege, a national newspaper began a campaign suggesting that the two of them should be buried together. Celia's family gave their enthusiastic approval, but despite several days of searching for relatives, no one could be found to speak for Archie. So they were interred side by side in Westminster Abbey. The Queen, President Edwards, and several hundred thousand ordinary people attended. They closed down the centre of London for that, too.

Acknowledgements

THE INSPIRATION FOR THIS book began many years ago when I was being given a private tour through the House of Lords. I had been promised that one day I would be a member of the place – one of those many failed promises that litter the carpets of Westminster – and I was getting acquainted with what I had supposed might become my new home. I remember standing in the chamber in a state of considerable awe, my eyes travelling from one corner to the next, overwhelmed with its richness and breathtaking craftsmanship. That was when I noticed a well-hidden door, one of two set into the gilded canopy behind the throne. 'What's behind there?' I asked, in some excitement, assuming I'd stumbled upon one of the deeper secrets of the place. Indeed, I had, but, as you now know, it wasn't quite the sort of secret I had imagined. Yet the truth tickled my sense of humour. I decided that one day I would write a story set around those two cupboard doors. *The Lords' Day*.

Yet, there is another reason for this story. The security surrounding the State Opening is, I believe, seriously and even outrageously flawed – just as I have described in the book. The planning apparatus is set in days of old, an era sandwiched between Guy Fawkes and al-Qaeda. I don't want to slip into pomposity, any more than I care to put ideas into the heads of those who wish us harm, but the laws of terrorism aren't suspended simply because the British are having a bit of a royal jamboree. Even while I wrote the book, a political protester walked unchallenged to within a few feet of the Queen during a ceremony at Westminster Abbey. To paraphrase Lenin, something must be done.

As a result, there are many who have helped me with this book who are still serving in and around Westminster and who may not wish to be counted publicly. They know who they are; I am deeply in their debt. However, one man I can include is Major Peter Horsfall. After his retirement from an illustrious career in the Coldstream Guards spanning thirty-four years, Peter became the Staff Superintendent in the House of Lords, where he assumed the awesome responsibility for keeping the place running smoothly. This he did with huge success and humour. He and his delightful wife, Mary, were my hosts that evening many years ago when I first discovered those two doors. Mary is no longer with us, but Peter remains a staunch friend. He has known nothing about the writing of this book – I suspect he might be horrified that anyone would want to do harm to an institution he loved and served so loyally – but I hope he will accept my thanks for a friendship that I have found inspiring in many ways.

I have also leaned on other former members of the British armed forces. The character of Harry Jones was largely stirred by my old friend, Ian Patterson, who has helped with many books, but none more than this. His friend (and mine), David Forster, has also been extremely supportive, and I owe a considerable debt to Julian Priestley, who was introduced to me by my cousin, Peter Dobbs. If on the military side I have got any of the technical bits wrong, is it simply because I am not bright enough to follow the sharp minds of these extraordinarily resourceful, retired officers.

Another former Army officer who has unwittingly helped is Colonel Tim Collins. I have plundered the glorious yet perceptive words he gave to his men on the eve of their action in Iraq to inspire one of Harry's own speeches.

Fellow graduates from the Fletcher School of Law & Diplomacy have shown their friendship and support in all sorts of ways. The name of Andrei Vandoros appears frequently in my roll calls of thanks, and once again he has been the best of supporters, introducing me to Andrew Popper who guided me through many of the financial bits. Mian Zaheen is another Fletcher classmate who has been splendid in trying to make me understand the extra-ordinarily complex nature of the Afghan-Pakistan frontier region, as has been his exceptionally graceful wife, Adi, and her mother, Mamoona Taskinud-Din. Rear Admiral Jim Stark, a retired senior US Navy officer and yet another Fletcher friend and graduate, also threw himself into the ring on my behalf, and brought with him other former senior colleagues from the US military, Captain Bill Cameron, Rear Admiral Phil Anselmo and Major Ed Dogwillo. With their help I hope I have been able to describe the flight from Diego Garcia to Afghanistan with reasonable accuracy.

As for information about Diego Garcia itself, I am deeply indebted to another former US military man, Ted A. Morris Jr., a self-styled Yankee Air Pirate (retired) and President of the People's Provisional Democratic Republic of Diego Garcia. He now lives in New Mexico (a state governed by yet another Fletcher graduate, Bill Richardson). New Mexico is a long way to go to take up Ted's offer of a cold beer, but at some stage in my life, I intend to make the trip.

Daniel Brittain-Catlin helped me to speculate about what might happen to the BBC's parliamentary affairs producer throughout such a crisis, and he should know, for he has been the man himself. I am indebted to his enthusiasm and sense of mischief.

Many others deserve my thanks for their unstinting enthusiasm, such as Jane Chalmers, Dilwyn Griffiths and Colonel Cliff Walters of the Royal Signals. I hope I have been able to do justice to their expertise.

Despite my protestations that the events outlined in this book could happen, inevitably I have taken many dramatic liberties – for instance, the role taken by Mike Tibbetts would almost certainly be split between two officers. Moreover, the State Opening is *never* held on the 5th of November. The ghost of Guy Fawkes is still at large. There are many other such instances for which I hope my friends and informants will forgive me. Yet matters never go quite as innocently as planned. In order to avoid clichés or unintended comparisons, I also deliberately gave the wretched Tricia Willcocks the job of Home Secretary, because no woman had ever filled that post – until, the week after I penned the final words of the story, Jacqui Smith was appointed. I congratulate her on her historic appointment, and apologise in advance for any inadvertent confusion.

Michael Dobbs,
Wylye, July 2007.
www.michaeldobbs.com